PATRICK M KANE

A DOUGLAS!
A DOUGLAS!

"Always before me brave heart"

A novel based on the life and adventures of
The Good Sir James Douglas

Printed in Victoria, Canada

Note for Librarians: a cataloguing record for this book that includes Dewey Classification and US Library of Congress numbers is available from the National Library of Canada. The complete cataloguing record can be obtained from the National Library's online database at:
www.nlc-bnc.ca/amicus/index-e.html
ISBN 1-4120-2412-9

TRAFFORD

This book was published on-demand in cooperation with Trafford Publishing.
On-demand publishing is a unique process and service of making a book available for retail sale to the public taking advantage of on-demand manufacturing and Internet marketing. On-demand publishing includes promotions, retail sales, manufacturing, order fulfilment, accounting and collecting royalties on behalf of the author.

Suite 6E, 2333 Government St., Victoria, B.C. V8T 4P4, CANADA
Phone 250-383-6864   Toll-free 1-888-232-4444 (Canada & US)
Fax 250-383-6804   E-mail sales@trafford.com   Web site www.trafford.com
TRAFFORD PUBLISHING IS A DIVISION OF TRAFFORD HOLDINGS LTD.
Trafford Catalogue #04-0240   www.trafford.com/robots/04-0240.html

10   9   8   7   6   5   4   3   2

INTRODUCTION

THE HISTORY OF SCOTLAND is abundantly rich in heroes. Their efforts and good deeds are etched with pride in the hearts and souls of the Scottish nation, and names such as William Wallace, Robert the Bruce, Rob Roy MacGregor and many others have fired the imaginations of and provided inspiration to Scotland's sons and daughters.

This is a tale based on the true life and adventures of a perhaps less well known, but equally inspirational, Scottish hero of medieval times, whose contribution to his country was second to none. It is the story of a gallant and brave man, Sir James Douglas, who devoted his entire life to the freedom and liberty of his nation. He became known as 'the good' to his own people; others called him 'the most feared Scotsman'.

Sir James's father, the first noble to take up arms alongside William Wallace, was imprisoned and died in the Tower of London. Edward I of England confiscated his estates. Sir James's destiny was pre-determined, he had no choice. He took up arms with King Robert the Bruce, fought alongside Bruce as his first lieutenant and most devoted friend and follower, and finally gave up his life while fulfilling the dying wish of his beloved King.

Douglas's life was one of constant warfare, a life where brother fought with brother, neighbour with neighbour and nation with nation. He sought out the one common enemy and became obsessed with its destruction. Sir James Douglas lived and died for his cause, perishing on his final mission, to carry the Brave Heart of Robert the Bruce into battle. Known to his enemies as 'The Black Douglas', his nation remembers him as:

THE GOOD SIR JAMES DOUGLAS.

'Whoever should undertake with skill enough to tell
his deeds of valour one by one would find many to tell.'

John Barbour, 14th century poet

ACKNOWLEDGEMENTS

A Douglas! A Douglas! is a work of fiction based on the life and times of the good Sir James Douglas. The story of Sir James would not have been recorded without the commitment, dedication, and skill of the chroniclers of those times who documented the inspirational life of this great Scottish knight and enabled future generations to appreciate and share the many amazing adventures of this often forgotten hero.

Many historians have researched and recorded their own interpretation of the life and times of Douglas, and have provided us with a truly magnificent and proud record of the history of arguably Scotland's most gallant Knight. It is difficult to single out those to whom we should owe thanks and appreciation for recording the factual version of this story. The ones that I have chosen to acknowledge are those whose contribution provided the inspiration for this story to be told.

The History of the Black Douglas. Chapbook. Francis Orr & Sons (1835)

A History of the House of Douglas. Sir Herbert Maxwell (1902)

The Bruce. John Barbour, edited & translated by G E Todd (1907)

Scalachonica. Sir Thomas Gray, edited & translated by Sir Herbert Maxwell (1907)

The Chronicle of Lanercost, edited & translated by Sir Herbert Maxwell (1913).

Froissart Chronicles. Jean Froissart, edited & translated by G Brenton (1968)

Robert the Bruce. Ronald McNair Scott (1982)

The History of the House of Douglas. David Hume of Godscroft, edited by D Reid (1996)

The Bruce. A. A. M. Duncan (1997)

The Black Douglases. M Brown (1998)

And finally to my dear wife Moira whose
constant patience, endless tolerance and
total support made it all possible.

PRINCIPLE CHARACTERS:
(IN CHRONOLOGICAL ORDER)

(Fictional characters in *italic* type)
Edward I, King of England
Lord William Douglas
Lady Eleanor Douglas
Bishop William Lamberton of St Andrews
James Douglas, 1st son of Lord William
Stuart Cuthbert, servant to Douglas family
Robert Fullerton, servant to Douglas family
Sir Robert Clifford, English Lord
Sir Henry de Percy, English Lord
Robert the Bruce (Earl of Carrick), King of Scotland
Bishop Wishart of Glasgow
Hugh Douglas, 2nd son of Lord William
Archibald Douglas, 3rd son of Lord William
David Davidson, follower of Bruce and Douglas
Sir Aymer de Valence, English Lord
Thomas Dickson of Douglasdale
Sophia, niece of Thomas Dickson
Thomas Randolph, Earl of Moray and nephew of Bruce
Edward II of England
Sir William Keith of Galston
Edward III of England
Sir William Sinclair of Rosslyn

1

BERWICK, SCOTLAND, MARCH 1296

ESCAPE FROM HELL

ON GOOD FRIDAY, at the start of this special day of holiness, the people of the borderlands awoke to a grey, misty and bitterly cold morning. It was a day intended for worship, set aside to remember the day the son of God gave his life for the salvation of their souls. Some had already started the customary preparation for celebrating the ultimate sacrifice. Others had forgotten, or had chosen to ignore, the significance of the day as they headed north across the border. Moving slowly and deliberately, they quietly emerged out of the early morning mist and approached the Scottish town of Berwick. The thick, hazy breath of the cavalry horses rose to join the mist and their loud snorting broke the eerie dawn silence as the cold, damp air passed through the beasts' powerful lungs.

A short distance away, the residents of the town slowly wakened. Some prepared themselves for worship, others made themselves ready for another busy day of commercial activity. The harbour traders, including many from foreign lands, had started early, anticipating another successful day of business at this busy port.

In the assembled army, instructions had been given. No words were needed as three thousand foot soldiers and almost twice as many on horseback slowly and quietly moved into position. All eyes were focused on one man, Edward I, King of England, also called Longshanks or the Hammer of the Scots. The soldiers waited, and watched for Edward's signal. He breathed deeply. Unable to hide either his nervousness or his hatred of his enemy Edward looked round, his face twitching with strong emotion. The soldiers signalled their readiness.

'They need to be taught a final lesson, and that lesson is fear – without fear there can be no obedience,' the King called out to those on either side of him. Slipping his left hand through the leather strap, he tightened the loop on his horse's reins and turned to look behind. The faces of his men as yet expressed no emotion; unquestioning loyalty and blind faith in their King were both demanded and given. The King's men were ready to commit, in his name, the sins of death and destruction.

Raising his arm, Edward slowly lifted the gleaming battle-axe above his head and steadied himself, as he prepared to dig his spurs into his horse's flesh. He pointed his chosen weapon towards his victim's place of residence and an almighty roar went up around him.

The charging cavalry swept through the first hundred yards without meeting any resistance, while those inside the town, shaken by the thunderous noise, braced themselves for the unexpected nightmare that was about to arrive at their doorstep. Inferior in numbers, the Scottish troops, who had been sitting half-asleep at various guarding locations inside the town boundary, were ill prepared for the abrupt charge of the screaming invaders. Those brave enough to stand in their way and offer resistance were immediately struck down by the crazed, blood-hungry execution squad, eager to seek revenge for past deeds.

As the cavalry charged towards the harbour, many of the merchants panicked, thinking that they were the targets for this invading army. Several immediately cast off their boats and retreated out to sea. Others, who were always on the alert for robbers intent on relieving them of their goods, quickly armed themselves, and attempted to present a feeble defence against the early morning slaughter. A few quick-thinking archers, located amongst the foreign merchants, managed to pick off several horsemen as they galloped through the community. A single deadly arrow struck one of the cavalry who rode close to Longshanks, killing him instantly and causing him to fall from his saddle and be pulled along the ground by his horse, his body quickly becoming mangled beyond recognition under the hooves of the other riders.

Longshanks, full of uncontrollable rage, charged into the first group of merchants. With mighty force he brought his razor-sharp axe down upon the heads and bodies of those unfortunate enough to be in his way. His cavalry followed behind, and diverted their attention to the destruction of these impertinent foreigners who dared present resistance. The charge towards the castle walls was temporarily suspended, while the remorseless execution of the brave but foolhardy foreign merchants proceeded.

Stalls were upturned and pulled into the deep waters of the harbour side, accommodation and stores of provisions were looted, set on fire or destroyed. Those who tried to escape only managed a few yards before they too were cut down by the swords and lances of Edward's cavalry which slashed and pierced their fleeing backs. Nor were the women and children spared. The lives of all the members of the merchant community, the humble and the innocent, the unarmed and the armed, were ended by the same merciless, destructive force.

Lord William of Douglasdale, the commander of the castle garrison, had awakened before it was light. He was immediately informed of the dawn attack. 'It's him, it's Longshanks, he's attacking us now,' called Fullerton, Lord William's loyal servant and personal guard, as he alerted his master. 'He's taking it out on the harbour side merchants. God only knows what those poor souls did to deserve this day.'

Douglas gestured for his family to be brought to him. A frightened Lady Eleanor, pregnant with her third child, with her youngest son, two-year-old Hugh, in her arms and accompanied by her eldest, ten-year-old James, quickly rushed to her husband's side.

To Douglas's terse 'It's Longshanks. He comes with his army,' Lady Eleanor replied 'We knew that it was only a matter of time before revenge would come.' She was alluding to the events that had occurred several weeks previously, when some locals had attacked a group of English merchants, many of whom were murdered and their goods looted.

'Well, revenge has come now,' said Douglas, 'and it looks like there is nothing we can do.'

'But you had no part in it, you did nothing wrong' said Eleanor, panic causing her voice to rise.

'I am afraid, my dear, that not having done anything wrong does not guarantee safety,' Douglas gently responded. 'Anyhow, he has other excuses to seek me out, for I have surely caused him great frustration.'

Longshanks and his men, meanwhile, continued with their destruction of all forms of life that impeded their progress towards the fortress. The English King's immediate plan was to get to the castle gates. Having completed the total annihilation of the harbour-side residents, he led his forces the short distance to the castle entrance where he turned and addressed his men. 'This place must be cleansed of these savages,' he called out. 'I am privileged to be King of England. This privilege has been given to me, not by man, but by God alone. In God's good name, I will cleanse this place of evil. The foul vermin will no longer attack our northern lands, nor kill our fellow countrymen. They will learn from today to pay homage to my Majesty.'

At the other side of the castle walls, unnoticed, a woman with two children, and accompanied by two armed men, was quickly making her way towards the protection of the forest edge. High up on the castle battlements Douglas made his first appearance. The exchange that followed was brief and to the point.

'What do you want?' Douglas called out. Longshanks immediately looked up, a nervous tic adding to the distortion on his already fierce face. 'Surrender!' shouted the King. To Douglas's terse 'Conditions?' Longshanks answered equally briefly, 'Your life!'. 'Or what?' asked Douglas. 'Death to everyone!' came the reply from Longshanks.

There was a pause. 'What of the garrison?' asked Douglas.

'Your garrison will be allowed to go, I give my word.'

'And of me?' Douglas asked.

'No harm will come to you, provided you lay down your arms and surrender yourself to my men,' shouted Longshanks.

'What of the people of Berwick?' called Douglas.

'One thing at a time,' replied Longshanks, adding 'I am no savage, unlike the animals that live here.'

'How much time do we have to decide?' asked Douglas.

'This time tomorrow,' replied Longshanks.

'We will speak then,' answered Douglas.

Longshanks's men retreated from the castle gates. However, as they did so, a section of the English cavalry was instructed to encircle the high stone walls and prevent any escape. The rest of the day was spent enjoying the riches that come from fear and domination, as the invading army feasted on the abundant provisions that this affluent town offered. The food was first, devoured as if never tasted before, then the wine and ale, mainly acquired from the foreign merchants.

As the day wore on, and the alcohol took effect, other more sinful bodily desires took hold. Men who were good and decent when at home became themselves victims of the horrors of war. Amongst many thousands of men, it started with one. Full of wine and bravado, one pathetic lonely soul, an individual who sought recognition and praise from his peers, grabbed hold of a young girl who happened by. She was the first to be violated. Other soldiers cheered, and then followed his example, committing the ultimate act of disrespect for a human being.

Throughout that day, and into the darkness of night, the normally peaceful and friendly town was subjected to relentless and unprovoked violence. The invading army took their pick of the pleasures that men at war seek. The obscene satisfaction of inflicting fear and humiliation on others was shared by many who took advantage of the power that strength in numbers presented.

As darkness descended, Douglas considered his options. The dilemma was pulling him in all directions: the safety of his garrison, the safety of the townsfolk, and above all else, the safety of his family. At this same moment his wife and children were being escorted to a safe place by two of the most trusted and loyal friends that any man could ever have. The experienced Fullerton and the young, gallant Cuthbert had served him well; he knew his family was protected. He thought of what Longshanks had presented to him. 'Could he be trusted?' he thought to himself. 'What if the choice is garrison or townspeople? What would I choose?' he pondered, as he looked out over the town that he had been given to command. He thought of Douglasdale, that peaceful place, abundant in beauty, his true and cherished home.

The following morning Douglas waited on the battlements, watching for the first movements. He was surprised that they were not prompt. However, he knew that the night of excess would no doubt have taken its toll. The invaders arrived at the gates some hours later than expected.

'Your answer?' Longshanks abruptly called out, as his horsemen surrounded the castle gates. Douglas, still undecided, looked at his own garrison, a few hundred loyal men, who, without hesitation, would follow any instruction that he might issue. 'Let me help you make up your mind,' called Longshanks as he signalled to his men. His cavalry allowed a gap to form, as men, women and children, taken as hostages during the night of ravage, were brought into full view. Swords and lances were pressed against the terrified hostages as they huddled in despair in front of the castle gates.

Three men were selected and pulled from the knot of townsfolk, violently pushed to the ground, and then forced to kneel. Screams of terror filled the air as the blood which spurted simultaneously from three deeply cut throats flowed along the ground and in amongst the petrified hostages. Hemmed in and unable to move, those at the front were forced to remain on hands and knees while the blood of the slaughtered men splattered over their bodies. Longshanks looked up and smiled. 'Do I have your answer?'

The sound of steel clattering on stone was the first sign of surrender, as a sword was thrown from the battlements and landed a few feet in front of Longshanks's horse. Several minutes later, the heavy castle gates slowly opened. Behind the gates Douglas stood at the front of his men. There was no humiliation in this surrender, which came not from cowardice, but from compassion and consideration for the townsfolk whose lives they thought they had just saved.

The men of the garrison were relieved of their arms and allowed to go free. Douglas, however, surrounded by several English guards, was taken prisoner and marched into the castle which had once been his home and was now his prison. The townsfolk began to gather in numbers and moved closer towards Longshanks's forces. Seeing the remaining hostages being freed and the garrison troops being released, it seemed to them that the terrifying nightmare was now over. In spite of the horrors of the previous day and night there was relief that so few locals had lost their precious lives.

Terror was replaced by increasing confidence, as more of the townsfolk gathered. The population of this town vastly outnumbered the invaders, and as the crowds continued to gather; those who had been the intimidators now became the intimidated. A few English soldiers, who were surrounded by the large crowd, suddenly found themselves face to face with the locals, and started to show signs of fear. A voice from deep within the crowd of townsfolk called out 'Scum!'

Others joined in. 'Murderers!' 'Rapists!' The crowd's feelings of safety grew each time someone shouted. Synchronised chants and loud venomous taunting replaced the individual shouts as the confidence of the crowd continued to grow and fear and apprehension diminished. Concerned at this reversal Longshanks called out 'Give me your obedience and I will give you safety and protection.' The crowd turned on the foreign King and gave him their reply. The air was stained with the roar of obscenities directed towards Longshanks. The crowd continued their verbal assault on the invading force, accompanying the hostile chants with crude gestures and the throwing of garbage.

Longshanks, now burning inside with rage, shouted once again, 'I am your King, give me your support and you will prosper.' The crowd replied with the same venomous answer. Longshanks immediately turned his horse and headed towards the castle. Briefly stopping at the entrance, and without turning, he gave the signal by raising his hand and quickly disappeared through the castle gates.

The most tragic and brutal slaughter of civilian lives in the history of Scotland then began. It took only seconds for the crowd's jeering to be silenced and replaced once more by screams of terror as Edward's cavalry charged at unarmed men, women and children, cutting them down with ease as farmers cut down an autumn harvest. Swords lunged, slashed and waved in all directions, axes swung viciously both left and right, cutting through flesh and crushing bones. Lances, aimed with deadly precision, brutally penetrated the bodies of the fleeing crowd. The only obstacle to the executioners' progress was the accumulation of the innocent dead that fell at their feet.

The townspeople continued to run in all directions, seeking cover, and desperate for somewhere to hide. The cavalry followed in pursuit. Young or old, weak or strong, man or woman, no one was spared, as the wave of relentless slaughter washed over the petrified souls. Some who had been fortunate enough to find cover felt safe until they were routed out by the foot soldiers who followed behind and continued the bloodthirsty assault.

Like the slaughter of the innocents by Herod thirteen hundred years earlier, this was no battle but extermination, its prime purpose to generate everlasting fear and achieve total dominance and obedience. As the evil demons that lie dormant deep inside some men were unleashed women and children suffered in ways that no decent mind can imagine or bring themselves to tell. The killing continued into the evening, through the night and on into the next day.

The silence grew as the screaming dwindled and the moans were extinguished. Thousands lay dead, their bodies remaining where they fell since none of those who had found shelter dared to come out to attend to them.

The slaughter was still in progress when the castle gates opened. Accompanied by a band of foot soldiers, Longshanks re-entered the town. His face was pale and expressionless as he walked out and in among the massive carnage, examining the piles of butchered innocents, the open wounds, the severed limbs and spilt guts. 'They should have listened to me. They only have themselves to blame, it was their choice,' he called out, as he continued to wander.

The King's religious beliefs, distorted or abandoned over these last few days, returned now to eat away at his conscience. He started to feel dizzy and light-headed, and waves of nausea rose inside him. Turning a corner, he stopped short at the sight of the body of a young woman. She had clearly been abused and hacked to death, and yet amid this orgy of savage butchery she had given birth to a child that still breathed. Longshanks was violently sick. On regaining his composure, he ordered the immediate cessation of all destruction and killing. He gestured for the newborn child to be cared for. With the miraculous birth of this child sanity had returned.

The aftermath of clearing the dead continued for several days. The body count would have been a matter of great pride had they been enemy soldiers. However, the slaughter of over sixteen thousand civilians was neither a victory to publicise nor one of which to be proud.

The imprisoned Douglas lay alone in his quarters inside the castle. No one came to see him, no one told him of what had happened, and yet he knew. The small south-facing window above his head told the story, not in words, but in the deadly silence of this once busy town and the unbearable stench of burning human flesh. He prayed for his family and for every man woman and child who had perished in these last few days

Over the next weeks of imprisonment Lord Douglas lost all sense of time and the recent events. His mind was solely focused on his family, on his beloved wife, Lady Eleanor, who had given him so much love, affection and comfort, the child she was carrying, his sons, little Hugh, who had yet to experience the hardship of living in a war-torn land, and James, his eldest son.

As he thought of James, Lord Douglas realised his eldest son was growing up much more quickly than he would have wished. He had spent very little time with this child, who, one day, would inherit his title. Politics, wars and countless other distractions had consumed valuable moments that should have been spent with his son. Yet, when he thought of James, he realised that the boy had not suffered. He knew that young James idolised him, and was constantly by his side during the occasions that they were together. 'I must get him off to a place of education, somewhere safe, where he can be schooled. I need to invest in James, for the future of my family,' he thought to himself.

Some months had passed in this way when Douglas, lying in his cell and thinking of his family, was brought abruptly back to the present by the sound of loud footsteps followed by the jingling of keys and the creak of the door, and found himself facing one of his guards.

'I have been told to let you go,' the guard announced. 'Leave now and say nothing.'

Douglas immediately walked towards the door and looked back at his jailer. 'Thank you for your hospitality,' said Douglas, prompting a grudging smile from the guard.

There were many who would welcome the opportunity to offer shelter to a Douglas in need, especially in these times. Good people like these had been looking after his family, in safe hiding, a few miles outside the town, since they had resolved to stay close to where Lord Douglas had been imprisoned. Lord Douglas hastened to rejoin his loved ones. His first act, however, was not to embrace Lady Eleanor or either of his two sons, but to offer his sincere thanks and appreciation to his two good men, Fullerton and Cuthbert, for what they had done. The family remained together for several more days, as the future was discussed and plans were made.

A few nights later a small boat was cast off in the evening darkness from Berwick harbour. 'We must go now, my dear,' said Lord Douglas. He put his arm around his weeping wife as she waved goodbye to the parting boat.

'Will he be all right?' she asked.

'Lamberton can be trusted. He has recommended the place. He will be safe,' replied Douglas.

On the boat, William Lamberton, Bishop of St Andrews, asked his young passenger, 'Are you not going to wave goodbye to your mother and father?' James, tears flowing down his white face and his hands firmly gripping the side of the boat, gently shook his head. 'You will be safe my son. Do not fret,' said Lamberton, as he tried to comfort and console his young companion.

The following morning, Douglas, along with Fullerton and Cuthbert, said farewell to Lady Eleanor. 'We must go now, my dear, our help is urgently needed.'

'Can those men you seek to join be trusted?' she nervously asked. At his reply, 'Wallace trusted? As much as I trust these two', Fullerton and Cuthbert nodded their heads in approval.

Douglas, seeking revenge against those who came to stake their claim to his lands, spent the rest of that year in bloody skirmishes. There were many Scottish nobles who had taken sides with Longshanks, who now made the outrageous claim of being the true King of this divided nation. However, in the man called Wallace, a commoner, there was a principle and there was a calling for all men of Scotland to join him as he took up the challenge with Longshanks. It was to this cause that Douglas offered his support and his good men.

2

SEAGATE CASTLE, IRVINE, SCOTLAND, 1297

SURRENDER THY SON

AS THE SUN gave off its last rays of light, the heavens were shot with streaks of glowing crimson and amber fanning out from the illuminated clouds just above the distant mountainous islands. The hell-like flames above were a visible reminder of the blood spilt on the lands below during recent times. At the gates of the dark-walled fortress of Seagate, Irvine, the sentry watched the spectacular display as, in the distance, three horsemen, silhouetted against the fiery sky, could be seen approaching. The urgency of their approach as they galloped nearer disturbed his peaceful evening reverie.

'Who goes there?' cried the sentry, his voice edged with fear and uncertainty, as he tried to identify the men making their way towards the entrance. The thundering hooves of the three exhausted horses drowned out the initial request. 'Identify yourselves,' commanded the vigilant watch in a firmer voice, but still there was no reply. The first rider was almost on top of the group of sentries before the answer was finally heard. 'Douglas,' shouted the leading horseman, in a manner that sent a cold shiver through the group of sentries and caused them to jump to attention and present arms.

'Let them enter,' cried an English voice from within. The three riders cautiously entered the shadowy courtyard. 'I must ask for your arms,' declared the leading sentry, as a circle of guards, with swords drawn, closed around the three threatened warriors.

'A Douglas does not hand over his arms without due cause,' declared the tall battle-scarred leader.

'If you want due cause,' replied the leading guard 'you have come to the right place,' as the large oak doors behind the three men were slammed shut and additional guards rushed into the courtyard with weapons drawn.

'You are expected,' declared the sentry, 'Lords Percy and Clifford request your presence'.'

Douglas declared that he would enter, but only if the safety of his men could be assured. 'Given,' replied the main sentry.

'Not so quick,' answered Douglas, in a manner that indicated he did not trust those who surrounded him. 'Release one of my men and provide him with a fresh horse and I will offer no resistance,' requested Douglas. The sentry agreed to this condition and a horse was brought over from the stable and offered in exchange.

'You know what to do,' said Douglas to the younger of his two companions.

'My lord, please let me stay and provide your protection,' requested the young man.

'There are those who have a greater need for your services, my dear Cuthbert,' whispered Douglas, as he embraced his loyal servant.

'My lord, you know I will devote my life to ensuring the safety and welfare of your good lady Eleanor and your young sons. I will not fail you,' responded Cuthbert in a low voice. As he looked into the concerned eyes of young Cuthbert, Douglas gave a smile that conveyed his thanks and appreciation for past, present and future loyalty.

'Let him leave now,' requested Douglas. The great doors were opened and the lone rider disappeared into the evening darkness. Douglas and his remaining companion then reluctantly handed over their weapons.

'Let us enter,' cried Douglas. The group made their way inside and proceeded along a poorly lit corridor. Loud voices could be heard from within the main hall; it seemed that an intense argument was taking place. The main hall door was pushed open, releasing an overpowering odour of roasted game. 'My lords! Lord Douglas!' announced the sentry. Douglas and his companion strode into the large hall, their sudden entry bringing a temporary halt to the noisy squabble taking place inside.

'Welcome, Lord Douglas,' said the leading English lord, Sir Robert de Clifford, as he made his way through the assembled group of Scottish commanders. 'Please take some refreshment,' he added, gesturing at the laden table.

'Sir, I will not,' replied Douglas firmly, 'not until I find out what this is all about,' and he glared at those around him.

'We have offered our surrender,' explained one of the Scottish commanders. Douglas approached Wishart, Bishop of Glasgow, for confirmation.

'We have,' replied Wishart, 'it's in the best interests of our people.' Wishart helped himself to the offered food and ale.

'We have no choice,' someone called. It was Robert Bruce, Earl of Carrick.

'No choice! More like no bloody agreement amongst ourselves,' disagreed Sir Richard Lundie, a Scottish noble who had become disillusioned by the constant treachery of his fellow nobles. 'Why don't you join the English, Lundie?' called one of the Scottish commanders. 'Perhaps I will,' replied Lundie. 'I am weary of serving with men who can't agree.'

'When did we ever agree to anything?' asked Douglas.

The English ambassador, Sir Henry de Percy, now made his announcement to the assembled Scottish nobles. 'My Lords, I have a message from Edward, King of England. Your surrender is acceptable to his Majesty. However, you will be held in captivity unless you offer up suitable hostages.'

Angered, Douglas instinctively attempted to draw his missing sword. 'Stop!' cried Clifford, 'We all want peace.'

'You will not be required to become hostages yourselves,' advised Percy. 'By offering up a close family member you will be free to go in peace.'

'And the hostages?' demanded Douglas, 'What of their safety?'

'They will remain unharmed as long as you submit to the wishes of King Edward,' Percy assured him, and turned towards the Earl of Carrick. 'Carrick, offer up a family member and you will be free to leave. No harm will come if you agree to submit.'

'No harm! Maybe, but what would be the consequences?' asked Carrick.

'Peace, wealth, your life, if you agree,' stated Clifford smoothly and confidently, sensing that a key Scottish commander was about to give way.

'And if I don't?' asked Carrick.

'Need I answer?' was Percy's reply, adding 'Send your daughter Marjorie. She would be well schooled and cared for.'

'So be it,' replied Carrick, after a few seconds' pause.

'You were very quick with your answer,' shouted Douglas, as he raised his clenched fists in disgust. 'There are many who would have expected more from you.' Carrick lowered his head and quietly muttered 'Not the right time,' then turned and moved away to the rear of the group of gathered nobles.

The room fell silent as the Scottish commanders, dejected and demoralised, realised they had been forced into surrendering the freedom and liberty of their nation. 'What can we do? We have been trapped,' declared one, and another 'The English know that if they take us, then our people will still fight!'

Douglas's firm tones rang out as he addressed the assembly. 'But if they take our families hostage we too will be imprisoned, in a prison without walls, unable to act for ourselves. At any attempt by anyone to continue the struggle for our freedom, the hostages we offer up will surely perish at the hands of Longshanks. I say no! I will not surrender my family to these heathens. The English may take me, but I will not submit to their request.'

A silence fell as Wishart approached Douglas. 'Lord Douglas, think of your family! You have a young son, do you not?' gently asked the compassionate Bishop.

'My family have been taken care of,' replied Douglas, glancing towards his loyal companion Fullerton.

'My Lord, I will give you a moment to consider the consequences of your decision' said Clifford.

'The consequences of my decision will be avenged,' replied Douglas without a pause, his steady gaze fixed on the wily Clifford.

'Guards! Take him!' instructed Percy. 'The rest of you have one week to surrender your hostages.'

As Douglas was taken from the crowded room, he cursed and swore vengeance against those who were about to betray their people. Bishop Wishart detached himself from the crowd and approached the solitary and silent figure who, throughout these heated conversations, had been standing beside Douglas.

'Sir, I don't have your name,' said Wishart. 'Fullerton, your Excellency,' answered Douglas's companion.

'Well, Fullerton, what of your Lord's family? Are they taken care of?' asked Wishart. 'I cannot say,' replied Fullerton. Wishart's voice was grave as he responded 'Then you must go now as swiftly as you can, and do everything possible to ensure their safety.'

3

REFUGE IN FRANCE

ON LEAVING THE CASTLE Fullerton rode hard so that by the following day he had caught up with Cuthbert. Together they made their way back to Douglasdale, approaching the town when the early morning mist hung over it like a great grey cloak, suspending the residents in sleep. 'What do you mean he surrendered?' asked Lady Eleanor indignantly, as Fullerton broke the news. 'Sir William would never surrender. Others yes, a Douglas no. Please, tell me what happened, has he been harmed, is he ...?' asked the now weeping wife, who appeared on the point of collapse.

'Do not distress yourself, my Lady, he is alive and unharmed,' Fullerton softly reassured her. 'But he was trapped into surrendering,' interrupted the angry young Cuthbert, as he supported his Lady's arm. 'It is true. My Lord Douglas was drawn into a trap,' Fullerton confirmed, as he and Cuthbert knelt in front of the now seated Lady Eleanor. 'He was offered a choice,' Fullerton explained, as he looked up into the tear-filled eyes of the distraught wife. ''Lady Eleanor began to wipe away her tears with her sleeve.

'My Lord Douglas was given the choice to offer up a family member as hostage, or be taken prisoner himself,' stated Fullerton.

'That is the explanation then,' said Lady Eleanor. 'My dear William was taken prisoner himself before and escaped. He always said that the time would surely come when they would take his family hostage in his stead.' Lady Eleanor began to regain her composure. 'My husband would never offer up his family in exchange for his own freedom,' she declared.

'It seems they only wanted the eldest child,' stated Fullerton.

'Then my dear William's prediction has been further confirmed,' said Lady Eleanor thoughtfully. 'He anticipated this. His arrangements for taking young James into hiding and care have prevented an even more tragic occurrence.'

'What of young James, my Lady? Will he still be safe?' asked Fullerton.

'Yes, for the moment anyway,' replied Lady Eleanor. 'Before my Lord Douglas went with you to join up with Wallace, he arranged for young James to be sent off to France, both for his safety and also to be schooled in a manner that was not possible in these war-torn lands.'

'But, are you sure that he is still safe my Lady?' asked Cuthbert.

'Yes, a very prominent and highly respected supporter of our cause looks over him and has ensured he will be in no danger.'

'My dear Lady Eleanor,' said Fullerton, in a gentle tone that belied his reputation as a fearsome warrior. 'We have both given Lord Douglas our pledge to ensure you and your children's safety.' He glanced at Cuthbert and received a nod of approval from him. 'We will protect you with our lives,' stated Cuthbert.

'I am most grateful,' answered Lady Eleanor. 'For the moment, I do not believe our lives are in danger. However, with my Lord Douglas imprisoned, I do expect our lands and possessions will be taken.'

'My Lady, if that were to happen, we would arrange for your safety and well-being to be provided elsewhere. There are many who would offer up their life and relinquish all of their possessions in the name of Douglas,' said. Fullerton. Lady Eleanor held out her hands and touched the heads of the two loyal servants. Her complexion was still pale but her lips widened in a soft smile as Fullerton and Cuthbert bowed and gently retreated.

Several years after the imprisonment of Sir William Douglas, a tall, well-built clergyman made his way through a busy French village square. The market traders made several glances in his direction. However, no one could identify him or recognise his status due to the long dark-blue cloak that covered his large frame. His striking appearance attracted a small group of begging children, who followed behind him, requesting his help to end their aching pains of hunger. As he made his way past the traders' stalls he gestured for their support to satisfy the needs of these less fortunate souls. A portion of stale bread was thrown to the ground and immediately seized upon by the desperate urchins.

Having broken free from his band of followers, the stranger was able to proceed to his destination in a more discreet manner. A few minutes after knocking at the small door of the priory he heard footsteps followed by the loud clanking of the securing bolt being slipped aside. 'My name is Lamberton,' announced the Bishop in French tinged by his broad Scottish accent.

'We have been expecting you for some time now,' replied the old monk, as he gestured for his visitor to enter into his sanctuary.

'I have had a long and hazardous journey,' declared the Bishop.

'We will have quarters prepared for your stay, your Excellency. Please rest, and I will bring you refreshment,' offered the monk, as he pointed towards a small table positioned below the only window in the otherwise dark room.

'I greatly appreciate your kindness and offer of hospitality,' replied Lamberton. 'However, I must urgently speak with your young guest.'

'He is being tutored at the moment, but I will have him called to you,' said the monk.

"Lamberton thanked the monk, then sat down and breathed a sigh of relief that the first stage of his journey was over. Bishop Lamberton, the most prominent church figure at that time in Scotland, carried a great deal of responsibility on his tired shoulders, and it clearly showed on his depressed and weary face. His country was clinging on for survival during desperate times of relentless battles against the English and constant treachery and internal strife from its own nobles.

'Can I go on?' he asked himself. 'Perhaps my next conversation will be the beginning of the end.' He did not look forward to delivering the message he carried. His head bowed in despair, he prayed for the strength to continue, for an end to death and destruction, for peace in his homeland, and for the safety of the young man he was about to meet. In the name of the Lord, he prayed for God's help to guide this young man towards his destiny.

The sound of footsteps broke into his silent prayers. 'Your Excellency!' exclaimed a slim, dark-haired, handsome youth. Lamberton woke from his meditation with a startled look. 'Young James,' he cried out, as he looked into the bright and innocent face of the young man standing in front of him. With outstretched arms, he rose up and embraced his young friend. The sad, depressed look of a few moments earlier was now replaced with a smile and an expression of delight and joy on the face of the Scottish Bishop.

'How you have grown,' he declared. 'How are you my dear boy?'

'I am well, thank you,' young James replied.

'Have they been looking after you, as agreed?' asked Lamberton.

'They have, sir, they have fed my mind with abundant nourishment. However, I would say that the nourishment given to my body has lagged behind a little,' answered young James with a cheeky smile, as he patted his flat stomach, and then gestured to the bulk that Lamberton carried around his waist. The room echoed with the sound of laughter, as the two of them continued to exchange greetings and affection for each other.

'They have taught you well, my son,' said Lamberton as he sat back down.

'What news do you have for me?' asked young James. 'I have been away from home for ages, there must be lots to tell!' Excitement was written all over his face. At his question, the look of sorrow started to reappear on Lamberton's face.

'Please sit down, young James,' the Bishop requested. 'There is much to say and do.'

'What of my mother?' asked the excited young James.

'Lady Eleanor and your brothers are all safe and well and looking forward to your return,' answered Lamberton.

'My brothers?' young James called out. 'When I left my mother was with her third child, but I did not know …' Lamberton interrupted him. 'Yes, I am delighted to say that you have a second younger brother. I believe his name is Archibald.'

'And my father?' asked the boy more tentatively, and added, 'I am greatly appreciative of your visit to me today, your Excellency, but I don't believe that you have come all this way to bring me only good news. I am well aware of my father's reputation in the cause for freedom. I am aware of his stubbornness and anger and that he would not hesitate to raise arms against anyone who threatened his family or nation.'

'You are very astute for someone so young,' answered Lamberton. 'Your father is indeed the reason for my visit,' he added, as he looked into the face of the young Douglas.

'I heard that he had been captured by Longshanks and taken to London. I also heard, that because my father had supported Wallace, he would not be freed. London is not far from Paris and I have been kept well informed,' said the young son, who then took a deep breath and waited for the reply that would break the bad news.

'James,' Lamberton reluctantly continued, 'I regret to say that your father, Lord Douglas, has died whilst imprisoned in London by Longshanks.' Expecting an emotional reaction, Lamberton reached over to embrace and console the young James. The boy's reaction was quite different to what Lamberton had expected.

'We must prepare to leave now, we must plan, I still have much to learn, I must visit my mother, our lands, the English, I will ...,' young James cried out in an agitated manner.

'My son, please sit for a while, there is more to discuss,' said Lamberton, as he tried to assess what was going on in the young man's troubled mind. 'Longshanks has confiscated all of your father's estates. He has given what was yours to his most loyal noble, Lord Robert Clifford. Lady Eleanor and your brothers have been taken into safe keeping.'

'I am now the Douglas!' James shouted out. 'I may not yet be ready, but I ask your Excellency to please assist me in my preparations for achieving my destiny, for by the grace of God I will achieve it!'

During the remaining daylight hours, the two voices could be heard continuing their conversation. There were periods of silence and soft whispers, followed by bursts of laughter which could be heard from outside the small refectory. Discussions continued into the early evening. Their conversation was finally broken by the entry of several monks who acknowledged young James, whom they had grown to love and respect over these last few years.

'I hope you will not be taking our best student away,' one of the elderly monks asked, as he greeted Bishop Lamberton. The monk smiled. 'Are all the sons of Scotland as eager to grow up so quickly and learn so much in such short time?' he continued, and he looked admiringly at James.

'You will be joining us for supper?' asked one of the other monks, as he sat down nearby. 'Yes, please,' replied Lamberton, 'And with your approval I would appreciate shelter tonight. Young James and I must leave in the morning'

'You are most welcome your Excellency,' said the elderly monk. 'We are honoured by your visit, and we wish you a safe return journey. However, first I have a message for you from Monsignor Francis. He has asked to meet with you, after you have eaten.'

'Thank you, I would appreciate a few moments of his time, for I must pay my respects and extend my gratitude for the good deeds you have all performed in tutoring young James,' said Lamberton, rubbing his hands with anticipation as he waited for the promised meal to be brought out.

After supper was over, Lamberton was taken to meet with Monsignor Francis.

'Welcome your most holy Excellency, and may I add, my good friend' said the grey-haired priest, as Lamberton entered the private room. 'My humble pleasure to meet with you again, Monsignor Francis,' replied Lamberton. 'I come to thank you, for the safe-keeping and tuition which you have provided for my young friend. He has flourished under your care.'

'It has been a pleasure your Excellency. Young James is a very remarkable young gentleman,' the Monsignor added, with a proud smile that suggested his monks had indeed performed a valuable role in helping to develop and mould the personality of this young student. 'He shows great potential, as well as fine qualities of compassion and tolerance towards others. He has applied himself to his studies with great diligence and dedication,' Monsignor Francis continued, as he gave his brief assessment of the young Douglas's progress.

'His father would indeed have been proud,' replied Lamberton. There was a pause, before Lamberton continued 'You have spoken of his virtues. Does he have any weakness?'

'There do not appear to be any, other than impatience,' replied the Monsignor. 'There is one small concern; he appears to be suppressing a burning desire to assume his father's role. I would not like to be on the wrong side of this young man when he reaches full adulthood.'

'Why do you say this?' asked Bishop Lamberton, in some consternation.

'Look into his eyes when you mention his father, or mother, or anything to do with the troubles in your lands,' replied the observant Monsignor. 'There is a look of cold, controlled vengefulness that appears to be waiting for the right moment to be unleashed.'

'I have seen those same eyes,' replied the Bishop. 'There is much learning and much work still to be done to help him achieve his destiny,' the Bishop concluded.

'Your Excellency, please pardon my interference, but as the Holy Father's representative in your homeland, there are limitations to your involvement that would be pleasing to him' the Monsignor cautioned.

'I agree,' answered Lamberton, with surprise that this subject has been raised. He continued, 'Yes, I have loyalties to our Church in Rome, but I also have loyalties to the people of my own nation.'

The Monsignor interrupted. 'But you must be careful, your Excellency, there will be many of young Douglas's enemies who will most likely be giving generously to our holy church, we must not ...' Lamberton interrupted impatiently. 'What I do, or say, will first always be to the pleasure of our Lord Jesus Christ, and to all others second,' he declared, in a manner indicating that he would not hesitate to challenge his church's wishes if provoked.

'Anyhow, a very important matter is at hand, I must pay my dues to you for the keep of young James,' said Lamberton, producing a leather pouch from beneath his cloak. 'I hope this meets with your approval?' he asked, as he handed the payment over to the Monsignor.

'We have already received payment for young James's upkeep,' declared Monsignor Francis.

'From whom?' asked Lamberton. 'I cannot say,' replied the Monsignor, 'It was a condition of the generous payment.'

'We will be leaving in the morning, and I thank you most sincerely for your kindness and hospitality,' said Lamberton, as he offered an embrace to his good friend. 'I must have time to pray now,' he added.

'I also,' replied Monsignor Francis. 'May God bless you and all of your people,' he continued, as he bowed his head and made the sign of the cross.

'Thank you, and may God guide you, bless you, and reward you and your good Order with the fruits of heaven,' replied Lamberton.

4

MEETING WITH LONGSHANKS

THE FIRST CROP of the autumn harvest was being cut, and all who were able-bodied, young and old, were assisting in the urgency to complete the task before the end of the recent dry days that followed weeks of drenching rain along the Fife coast. Outside the residence of Bishop Lamberton of St Andrews, two young men were loading bales of barley and oats onto a cart, in preparation for transport into town.

'Young James!' called Bishop Lamberton. 'I'm in receipt of some very important information which requires your attention,' he added, with great seriousness. The younger of the two men approached the Bishop. 'Your Excellency?'

'King Edward of England is at this moment making his way to Stirling to meet with the nobles of Scotland. I have been asked to attend,' explained Lamberton. Young Douglas listened with total attention.

'Can I please come with you, your Excellency?' he asked. 'I would like to see the face of the man who killed my father and stole my inheritance.'

'You may accompany me, but only in support of my plan. It is a simple and honourable plan,' answered Lamberton, adding 'We can discuss it further whilst we journey.'

The other young man, who had continued working during this conversation, stopped and approached the Bishop. 'Your Excellency, might I accompany you?' he requested, with head bowed.

'Of course my dear Cuthbert, your protection and loyalty will be most appreciated,' replied the Bishop. 'You are a dear friend and loyal servant, and I am sure that Sir William and Lady Douglas would be most proud of your dedication and support to the upbringing of young James over these last six months.'

The rain continued to fall relentlessly as the three riders made their journey south-west to Stirling. A break in the clouds lifted their spirits as they finally approached their destination. They were requested by a stable man to leave their horses at the bottom of the long steep road leading up to the heavily armed fortress. He offered food and water for their tired beasts. Having been on his horse for some considerable time, Lamberton was glad of the offer and welcomed a chance to stretch his legs before his important forthcoming meeting.

As they made their way up the muddy pathway, young James caught his first sight of an English soldier since his father was taken. Both Cuthbert and Lamberton observed the expression on his face. 'James!' cried Cuthbert. 'Remember what I told you, control and discipline,' 'I'm only looking!' replied the young Douglas with an expression on his face suggesting that he would dearly love to have a go at the English sentry.

As they came nearer to the castle gates, more English soldiers were visible, as they patrolled the road leading up to the entrance. One group of three was engaged in a hostile argument with a roadside trader who was trying to make a living selling fresh fruit to passers by. 'How can I make a living if you lot keep stealing my goods? I have a wife and children to feed,' he cried out. 'Shut up,' answered one of the soldiers, who grabbed the trader by the neck. 'Another word out of you and it will be your last,' he threatened.

On arrival at the gate, young Douglas and Cuthbert were left behind, while Bishop Lamberton went inside to join other senior members of the church along with key Scottish nobles. After an hour had passed, young Douglas turned to his friend and asked, 'What do you think is going on?' 'Probably more treachery, more threats, and more wars,' Cuthbert replied.

'I want to see King Edward, that Longshanks,' spat out young Douglas, as he paced up and down the square, 'and I want him to see me.'

'Is he really as cruel as they say?' Douglas asked, as he stopped pacing for a moment, and turned to look at Cuthbert. 'Yes!' replied Cuthbert. 'He is the most ruthless of all who have sat on the English throne. You must be patient my young friend, above all else you must maintain control of your feelings, and not show any fear,' advised Cuthbert.

As the two lonely figures sat waiting, a loud cry was heard coming from further down the muddy roadway. Both Douglas and Cuthbert turned to see another trader being abused by the same English soldier. As the soldier repeatedly kicked into the body on the ground, his two partners were helping themselves to the freshly baked bread laid out on the trader's stall. Douglas and Cuthbert turned and looked away, since there was nothing to say, and nothing they could do at this moment, but the anger within them was painful, suppressed, and desperate for the day when it could be released.

A short time later, a guard appeared at the main doorway accompanied by Bishop Lamberton. The Bishop raised his hand and gestured to Cuthbert that they were safe before beckoning young Douglas to come forward and enter. As they entered the wide torch-lit corridor, the young Douglas walked behind Lamberton. He stared up at the faces of each of the guards, who were positioned at regular intervals along the long walkway. Douglas wondered if any of these guards were involved with the capture and death of his father. 'If they were, some day they will pay,' he thought to himself. The guards paid no attention to the young boy walking behind the tall, elderly Bishop.

As they approached the dark oak door at the end of the corridor, the two guards blocking their way moved aside. Douglas could feel his heart pumping faster than he had ever experienced in his young life. The intense fear forced him to take a deep breath, as he took the final steps towards the door. He regained his composure, bowed his head, and followed the bulky frame of Lamberton.

As they both entered the large hall, young Douglas maintained his self-discipline. With eyes focused on the floor in front of him, he remained behind his protective Bishop.

'Lamberton!' cried the King of England, his voice echoing through the large stone-walled hall. 'You have requested my time. Be quick!' he demanded, in the loudest voice that young Douglas had ever heard.

'Sire, I present to you this young man. He is of sound and noble character, and now seeks to be your most humble and loyal servant. I pray, Sire, that you receive him here today to accept his homage and to grant him the return of his rightful lands,' announced Lamberton.

The young Douglas, still with head bowed, came out from behind his protector and took several steps to the side, his movement suggesting independence in purpose.

'Lands! What lands does he request to be returned?' barked the King.

'Sire, I pray that you will correct that which is wrong and unjust. I beg your kind consideration,' replied Lamberton.

'Stop wasting my precious time and come to the point,' roared the agitated King.

'Sire he claims the estates of the name of Douglas, for his father was the Lord of all Douglasdale,' answered Lamberton.

With his head still bowed, young James Douglas heard the King hiss 'Douglas!' The King's rage was fearful to behold as he continued, 'Sir Bishop, your position protects you. If you are to show any allegiance to my crown, make no such request upon me. His father was always my barbarous enemy, who supported and fought alongside the savage Wallace. It was right and just that he finally died for his actions in my prison. He was always against my sovereign position; therefore, I am entitled to take what was his. The boy can have his inheritance, but not the lands or titles of his father.'

Young Douglas raised his head and for the first time looked into the ferocious face of Longshanks. Douglas's pacing heartbeat had now slowed down, and his face appeared expressionless as, without fear or anger, his eyes pierced into the eyes of Longshanks. The King looked back at the son of Douglas, and saw a look of startling directness which, if coming from someone older, could have provoked a hostile response. 'Clifford has been given the lands that you speak of, for he has always been a loyal and trusted servant to my crown,' Longshanks concluded, and curtly turned away.

The young Douglas felt his stomach churn, as if he had been forced to eat the most vile and distasteful of all decaying foods. The sudden agonising internal pain and discomfort caused him to bend his young body forward and prevented any words from being uttered. If he were to find the strength to overcome the crippling stomach pains, and somehow summon the courage to speak back, who knows what this unforgiving King, who everyone yielded to, would do. He knew that to plead justice, to argue for fairness, or to seek forgiveness for his father's doings would all be to no avail. He chose silence instead.

Nor did Bishop Lamberton speak further, but ushered his young page to a hasty retreat. As they both walked towards the doorway, the son of Douglas turned his head for one last glance at Longshanks. King Edward caught the cold glare in the young man's eyes as they made parting contact. The King's eyes were puzzled, for he was not sure what to make of that most unusual expression coming from the eyes of one so young.

The travellers from St Andrews made their way out of the castle and down the muddy pathway leading out of the town.

Douglas and Cuthbert noticed that the three soldiers were continuing to harass and abuse the street traders. The soldiers appeared to be drunk from excessive consumption of free ale and were staggering as they approached Bishop Lamberton.

'What do we have here?' asked the more aggressive of the group. 'For your penance, my dear Bishop, you must give me all your possessions, or you will not go to heaven,' he demanded, while laughing and threatening the Bishop.

'If you don't get out of our way, I will give you the back of my hand young man,' replied Lamberton. 'We are messengers of King Edward and if you don't let us pass, I will call the Captain of the Guard.' Lamberton added, as the cowardly bully backed down.

The soldiers stood aside and let the travellers pass. In a final act of drunken rage, the ringleader lashed out at one of the traders standing by. Bishop Lamberton quickened his pace, and quickly disappeared round one of the many buildings that lined the steep twisting roadway. Cuthbert followed quickly behind, but sensed a slight hesitancy in young James, who appeared to pause and kick at the ground in front of him. 'James, please hurry,' urged Cuthbert, as he also disappeared round the tall building.

Young Douglas bent down as he turned round the corner and out of sight. He swiftly picked up the granite stone chip that he had dislodged and kicked round the corner. His left hand held the piece of hard stone, while his right hand undid the leather belt around his waist. On looking back he could see the abusive soldier staggering across the roadway and saw too that the others had their backs to him as they walked up towards the castle. The son of Lord Douglas now unleashed his first act of revenge. In a few seconds the belt was swirling above James's head and the drunken soldier dropped to the ground without a sound, blood pouring from the wound above his left temple. With a few quick paces, young James quickly caught up with his companions. Cuthbert, on noticing his young friend redoing his leather belt said, 'A dangerous move, but well done.'

As the three tired travellers made their way back to St Andrews, Lamberton said to his young squire, 'My dear young James, our diplomatic plan of approach did not appeal to the compassion of King Edward. We must now go home and live in peace.'

'I say this, there will be no peace with me as long as Longshanks lives, and until my inheritance is restored,' answered Douglas, who appeared to have grown in stature over these last few days.

Douglas continued to grow in both body and mind. He spent many long days hunting and learning the art of survival and living off the fruits of his land. He mastered the art of archery and the use of the sword. He became an excellent horseman. He spent many hours learning these skills. When congratulated on his progress and success, instead of resting and enjoying the praise, he would respond with more practice and dedication. In the evenings he would talk and debate many issues to challenge his ever-inquiring mind.

'Why do you apply yourself with such determination and dedication,' Lamberton would ask, in order to prompt a debate. 'To defeat the enemy,' Douglas would reply. 'Who is the enemy?' Lambert would ask, with a smile indicating a trick question. 'The English of course, your Excellency,' came the reply from the young man, thinking the Bishop's questions too easy. 'Would that be the good English or the bad English?' asked Lamberton. 'The bad English of course,' answered Douglas. 'And what of the good English?' asked Lamberton. 'Are there any?' replied Douglas, with yet another question.

'Are there good and bad Scots?' Lamberton would ask. 'I would say yes,' replied the young student.

'If there are good and bad Scots, could there also be good and bad English, Irish, French or any other nation?' Lamberton finally would ask.

'I conclude that the point being suggested is that I should apply myself to the defeat of evil rather than the elimination of any particular race?' answered the young Douglas, with a hint of sarcasm that suggested he knew all along.

One evening Lamberton was in the company of young James when he recalled a question that he had been meaning to ask him since bringing him back from France. 'James, tell me, when you were being schooled in France, did anyone other than me come to visit you?'

'No, you were the only one that came to see me during my stay' Douglas quickly replied.

'Did anyone enquire about you while you were there? Think carefully,' asked Lamberton.

'No, not that I was aware of,' answered Douglas, but he added, 'There was an unusual situation when provisions were in short supply, and strangers unexpectedly arrived. It was claimed that they provided funds that enabled the priory to meet its needs. It was also stated by one of the junior monks that my keep was fully paid up for many years.'

'Did you see those strangers?' asked Lamberton.

'I saw riders; I think there were six of them. They looked like knights, all except one of them. I did not see or hear any more,' replied Douglas.

'The one who did not look like a knight, what in fact did he look like?' asked Lamberton, who would not let go of this enquiry.

'It was several years ago, about two years after I arrived at the priory. The one who did not look like a knight, he was very tall and broad shouldered, he had long reddish hair and carried a large broad sword, which he refused to remove, strapped to his back. He appeared to give instructions to the others,' replied Douglas.

'Are you sure he did not say anything to you?' asked Lamberton.

Douglas became impatient. 'Your, Excellency, I do not want to appear to be rude, but I have already said that I did not speak with anyone. Let me ask *you* a question. Do *you* know who these men were?'

'James, as I was not present, I cannot say for sure. However, there is only one man that I can think of who would perform such a considerate act, and who would fit your description.'

44

Who is that?' asked Douglas.

'Someone who was the closest friend to your father, and who was in France at the same time as you,' answered Lamberton.

'But who?' asked Douglas again, with more frustration in his voice.

'Someone, who, like your father, was always at war with Longshanks,' declared Lamberton.

'Do you mean Wallace?' asked Douglas. Lamberton ended the conversation without giving an answer but with a smile.

Over the next few years, as the young James Douglas slowly matured into manhood, he saw less of Bishop Lamberton, his guardian and protector through his childhood years. When he did encounter his presence, the good Bishop would tell him tales of his distant travels, and of the significant events taking place during these war torn times.

'My dear young squire,' Lamberton began, as he gave his young friend the latest news. 'We live in very troubled times; the internal strife, treachery, hatred and evil that exist in our land are festering and poisoning the minds of many of our Lord God's children. I fear for the safety and future of our nation.'

'What can we do?' asked Douglas.

'We? Perhaps very little,' replied the Bishop.

'There must be something that can be done!' cried the ever eager and innocent Douglas.

'There is some hope and expectation in my heart, and I pray to God that some day we may live to see an end to it all,' the Bishop announced. 'Since the death of Bruce, Earl of Carrick, I have met and talked with his son Robert. He has acquired a reputation of deceiving the English into thinking that he opposes our cause. There are also many Scots who wrongly believe that this Robert supports the English, which adds to the deception. But most significant is his claim to the crown of Scotland.'

Young Douglas listened eagerly to the Bishop's words, inspired by the thought of a Scottish King whom he could support.

'If this Robert Bruce is as you say, what's holding him back?' asked Douglas, as he detected a possible opportunity to join this interesting noble.

'It has been agreed that John the Red Comyn be given lands in return for supporting the Bruce into kingship. It has also been said that King Edward has suspicions regarding the intentions of Bruce.'

'I hope the lands of my father are not being offered as exchange,' declared Douglas.

Bishop Lamberton sighed deeply. 'I'm afraid, though, that I have further bad news for you,' he said. 'As you were aware, Wallace, to whom your father, Lord Douglas, was a most loyal follower, has been hunted by the English during these recent years. I regret to say that news has reached me of his death; he was betrayed, they say, by one of our very own, captured and then taken into custody by Lord Clifford and finally executed at the hands of Longshanks. Hung, drawn, and quartered they say, a most horrendous, evil, public execution.'

Douglas stood up, and, burning inside with rage, he clenched his fists. 'This Lord Clifford, he was the one who captured my father, and now the same fate for Wallace. He is the one who now holds my lands.' Douglas paused for a moment. 'I want to join with the Bruce,' he cried out impatiently. 'I have waited long enough, I want to join with him and fight for our cause.'

'How very gallant and courageous of you, James, but you have waited this long, and you must still be patient,' urged the Bishop. 'I would, however, ask that you come with me to a place of refuge close to your home estate.'

'Where, your Excellency?' asked Douglas.

'Somewhere in the forest of Selkirk,' Lamberton answered with a smile, an answer that lit up the face of the young Douglas.

5

RETURN TO MOTHER

THE LOW-LYING AUTUMN sun projected slender streaks of light through the gaps in the gold and russet trees lining the road, while the ground underneath them was still dark, soft and moist from the overnight dew. The leaf-covered pathway stretched out like a speckled carpet cushioning the footfall of travellers on their journey south. Three riders approached a junction. 'Are you sure you don't want me to come with you?' asked Stuart Cuthbert, turning to the younger of the other two men.

Douglas shook his head. 'My most dear and loyal friend, you have already given more than you pledged. The time has come for me to acknowledge your service. I say thanks to you on behalf of my father, Lord Douglas, on behalf of my mother, Lady Eleanor, and in the name of Douglas, I say thank you. I regret that I cannot yet offer payment or reward for your good deeds and loyal services. However, I do promise to repay my debts to you when I regain my inheritance.'

The three men reined in their horses as the time finally arrived to part company. After dismounting, Bishop Lamberton approached Cuthbert, the good friend and obedient servant who had assisted him in raising the Douglas from young child to manhood. 'I too must thank you my dear Cuthbert,' he said with great affection, as he embraced his dearly loved companion. Cuthbert bowed his head and then knelt down on one knee in front of his most holy Bishop. 'May God bless you, and guide you safely, in the name of the Father, and of the Son, and of the Holy Ghost,' the Bishop recited, as he made the sign of Christ on the head of his friend.

Cuthbert re-mounted his horse, raised his arm in the air, and let out the fearsome, ear-shattering cry of 'A Douglas! A Douglas!' The sound sent a thrill of excitement through every nerve in the body of the young Douglas. It was the first time that he had heard the ancient battle cry of his family clan being shouted, the same clan of which he was now the true leader as Lord of all Douglasdale. He raised his arm in acknowledgement, and smiled proudly, as his dear friend Cuthbert turned and rode off eastwards along the forest road.

The two remaining riders swiftly made their way southwards, into a place of refuge in the Selkirk Forest. They rode until the dwindling late afternoon sun lent the landscape a warm glow that suggested peace and tranquillity falling across the borderlands. A vertical pillar of smoke could be seen above the distant trees as the two riders approached. 'We have arrived,' declared Lamberton, then cautioned 'Please be careful, James. We must be prepared for the unexpected.'

As the two men rode into the clearing, their eyes and ears scanned every corner. The only movement was that of a small boy trying to cut wood with limited success. Struggling to raise the large axe above his small frame, he tried to chop the stubborn log that refused to submit to someone so frail.

'What do you want?' asked the young lad.

'We are friends,' replied Lamberton, as he looked down at the boy's dirty face.

'What is your name?' asked Douglas.

'I'm not telling you,' came the cheeky reply. 'Are you English?' the youngster asked, as he attempted to raise his axe in a threatening manner.

Douglas dismounted 'If I help you cut these logs, will you tell me your name?' he inquired of the child.

'That depends,' replied the youngster, looking up at Douglas with a suspicious frown.

'Depends on what?' asked Douglas.

'Well, if you cut all of them, and carry them back for me, and tell me your name, then maybe I will tell you my name,' answered the young boy.

'That sounds like a good Douglas deal,' replied Douglas, as he quickly severed the stubborn log.

With a surprised look, the youngster stepped back. 'How do you know my name?'

'I don't,' answered the laughing Douglas. 'Douglas is my name.' He turned to the pile of logs. 'I will cut enough wood to see us through the night, and then you can take me to see your mother.'

'Fine,' replied the youngster. The young boy appeared to be mesmerised by this tall, dark-haired stranger. In a short while sufficient wood had been cut. Each person carried a portion under their arms as they made their way towards the central building in the farm complex.

As they approached the complex, a figure, who had been watching these events from the side of the building, came towards them. The first few steps were taken with extreme caution, then, as the faces started to be recognised, the pace quickened. 'My God! Your Excellency! Is it really you?' shouted Fullerton, as he ran towards the two visitors. 'I had given up hope of ever seeing you again. This is truly a wonderful event to be honoured by your presence!'

Lamberton dropped his pile of wood, and embraced his old friend. 'I too am honoured to be in your presence,' replied Lamberton.

Fullerton, looked towards Douglas. 'Is this he?'

'Yes, my friend, this is he,' said the Bishop, with a proud smile.

As they approached the door of the building, voices could be heard from within.

'Perhaps you should go and help him,' a female voice called out.

'But mother he needs to learn' came the reply.

As the door opened, a stocky youth rushed over to see who was entering. 'My dear lad, we have visitors, very special visitors. Where is your mother?' asked Fullerton.

'She's inside,' answered the youth, with a puzzled look on his face.

'Hugh! Who are you taking to?' asked the female voice from within.

'My good Lady, I bring someone here to meet with you,' Fullerton called out.

A small woman, no longer young, slowly walked towards the doorway. As she approached, she saw that there was someone standing behind her son and Fullerton. 'Who is that with you?' she asked. There was no reply, only silence, broken by the soft footsteps as the woman approached. As she came closer, her son Hugh moved to the side. Fullerton still blocked her view. 'Who is with you?' she asked again. Fullerton did not reply, as he also stepped aside to be replaced by the large frame of Lamberton in the doorway.

Surprised by the sight of the figure that now stood in front of her, she nervously called out, 'My Lord Bishop!'

'My good Lady Douglas, I come to pay you respect and give comfort,' answered Lamberton, as he walked towards her, and greeted her with an embrace.

'This is a great day for us all. That you have travelled so far and to be so kind to us is a remarkable gesture of your faith and love of God,' declared Lady Eleanor. 'What news do you bring?'

'No news, my lady, but I bring you … James,' answered the Bishop, as he stood aside to reveal the silhouette of a tall, broad-shouldered young man standing at the entrance.

Lady Eleanor froze with shock and looked towards the doorway. The young man's face was in shadow; she could not recognise him. But her face lit up, a smile appeared, and tears of joy started to flow as he called out 'Mother,' and stepped towards her. Her composure was temporarily lost as her emotions took control. She ran towards him. 'My beloved James!' Arms wrapped around each other, mother and child embraced in a sudden wave of released love and affection.

'My dear James, I can't believe it's you. How you have grown! You are so tall and broad. You have your father's looks! Oh, your father would be proud!' Words tumbled out of Lady Eleanor's mouth.

'Mother, I love you with all my heart. I missed you and I regret that I did not come to be with you before now,' said Douglas, as he continued to embrace his beloved mother.

To Lady Eleanor's soft query 'You are here now, and you will be staying?' Douglas gave a firm 'Yes!'

'James, let me introduce you to ...' said Lady Eleanor. 'Let me guess,' interrupted Douglas. 'This young gentleman must be my brother Hugh, who was only a baby when I left.' Douglas shook hands and embraced his younger brother, who although pleased and surprised to see this very special visitor, appeared to find the occasion rather awkward and embarrassing.

'Now let me think, who could this possibly be?' asked Douglas as he knelt down in front of the small dirty-faced boy and stroked his chin.

'Archibald!' the little fellow cried out, as he poked his finger in the left eye of Douglas. For the first time in his life, Douglas felt pain, and his younger brother was the perpetrator. As he stumbled back, he cried out in agony. The loud bursts of laughter that followed drowned out his cry of discomfort.

'James, you will remember our good friend Robert Fullerton, a very loyal follower of your father and appointed guardian and protector of our family,' Lady Eleanor announced, as she gestured towards the battle-scarred Fullerton.

'My dear sir, I am truly in your debt. Your kindness, loyalty and support to my family have been truly astounding. I make my pledge to you that some day I will reward your kindness,' declared Douglas, as he shook hands with the loyal family friend.

Prior to the evening meal being served, the Bishop said a short Mass. Those around him bowed their heads as they prayed together and were comforted by the kind words and holy presence of their spiritual leader. The evening meal was then served in an atmosphere of joy and celebration. Many stories were exchanged. The missing years were recounted. Family love and affection filled the air. The Douglas family were together as one in peace and happiness. Conversation continued as the flames from the log fire flickered deep into the night. As the last embers faded away, the sun slowly awoke with a soft radiant glow that rekindled the warmth and joy from the previous night.

Bishop Lamberton was already prepared for departure when James awoke. 'My dear James,' said the Bishop, 'I must leave now. I intend to reside at Berwick during the winter months ahead. I ask that you come to me when I send for you.'

'Your Excellency,' answered Douglas, 'I will spend the winter with my mother and family. I will be ready to join you in the spring.'

'Enjoy your stay, my young friend,' answered the Bishop, 'for there is much ahead for you to achieve.'

Lamberton smiled as he looked back at the happy family he was leaving behind. As he rode out, he gave a final parting wave. He knew that the next few months would pass very quickly for young Douglas, and that it might be the last time that the ambitious James would spend with his loving family.

During the winter months, Douglas took the opportunity to renew his love and acquaintance with his family. He worked in and around the farm complex, supporting his own and other families during the harsh winter days. In the evenings, he would exchange stories with his mother, brothers Hugh and Archibald and the family friend Fullerton.

'Robert!' Douglas asked of Fullerton one day. 'What can you tell me of the one they call the Bruce?'

'Now there's a man of mixed reputation,' replied Fullerton. 'Those who are not close to him see a man of many moods, a man who changes sides, a man who can't be trusted.'

'What do *you* see?' asked Douglas.

'I see, as your father, Lord Douglas, also saw, a man who is tormented by the state of his nation at war, a man who is disgusted by the cruelty and treachery of his fellow Scots.'

'Is there anything else?' asked Douglas with great interest.

'Yes, I see a man who has the potential to become our rightful King, a man, who, if given the support, could become the saviour of our nation,' answered Fullerton, who then asked, 'Why do you ask me about the Bruce?'

Douglas answered in a more serious tone 'Based on what I have heard, he sounds like the man I should be joining up with.'

'A good choice young Douglas,' declared Fullerton, 'But only when you are ready.'

As the winter months closed in, food started to become scarce across the borderlands. The relentless summer rains had resulted in poor crop yields to support the needs of a war-torn nation, and the family of Douglas began to suffer with the rest.

'Young Douglas!' cried Fullerton, 'Let's see what you are made of,' as he handed him a short bow and pouch of arrows. 'There is game aplenty in this forest, but only to those who are skilled hunters.' Douglas eagerly took up the challenge.

Several hours later, with frozen hands and legs numbed from wading through the deep snow, the two hunters made their way up to a small hilltop. As they approached it, Fullerton silently signalled that there might be prey on the other side. An overhang of snow on one side of the hill, created by the prevailing winds, had built up over the last few days. This white barrier slowed their final steps to the top. Fullerton put his hands to his mouth, indicating that total silence should be observed.

The two hunters moved silently and cautiously. Looking slowly over and down the eastern side, they spotted a small herd of forest deer that were grazing on the only patch of vegetation in sight. Sheltered by the protection of the steep side of the hill, this tiny green oasis in the forest had remained untouched by the snow-bearing winds which had passed over it. With synchronised precision both hunters released their frozen fingers and let loose their arrows to the right and left of the herd.

The arrow from Fullerton embedded itself into the haunch of the beast on the left of the herd. Immediately the stunned creature dropped down on its knees. The arrow from Douglas entered into the neck of the beast on the right hand side of the herd, causing it to immediately drop and fall over on its side without a hint of life left in its body.

The rest of the herd bolted in panic. The victim of Fullerton's arrow started rising to its feet in one last attempt to flee only to be brought down by an arrow in the side of the neck from Douglas. Fullerton looked at Douglas, smiled and said 'Well done, young man, Cuthbert has taught you well I see.' Later that evening, the families in the farm complex, including the Douglas, dined on the efforts of the two huntsmen.

During the remaining winter months, Douglas and Fullerton continued to partner each other in stalking and hunting forest game. Both hunters complimented the skills of each other. Douglas thanked Fullerton for what he had learnt from him over these few months.

'My dear friend, I ask that you also help my brothers to become skilled in these fine arts,' Douglas would ask of Fullerton.

'Your brother Archibald shows promise, but Hugh is disturbed by the sight of blood and killing. He appears to be unusually unsettled by the taking of life' Fullerton commented.

'Perhaps, like me, he has a purpose in life,' said Douglas.

'Perhaps, but he does not possess your sharpness of mind,' replied Fullerton.

As the year 1306 arrived, Douglas would spend long hours in the company of his brothers. He would excite and inspire them with tales of the past, and also of his plans for the future, and the revenge he would seek in order to retake their stolen inheritance. 'Can I come with you to kill the English?' young Archibald would ask. 'They are all thieves, very cruel and bad,' Archibald would add, as he punched the air in excitement.

With a smile and a laugh, Douglas would recall the similar conversations he had with Bishop Lamberton. 'I only intend to fight against evil,' Douglas would say. His mother, Lady Eleanor, looked over at her boys with a proud gentle smile, as she listened to her eldest son's tales.

6

MEETING THE BRUCE

THE ARRIVAL OF SPRING caused the lingering winter snow to melt and gradually the bitter cold staleness which had existed throughout these dormant grey months was replaced with the comfort of warming air and the sweet scent of nature's fresh life. On the forest floor, the lake of bluebells nodded their heads in approval as they danced in the gentle breeze.

A stranger arrived in the early afternoon. 'I have a message for the one called Douglas,' he announced.

'From where do you come?' asked Fullerton.

'Bishop Lamberton has sent me,' answered the tired rider. Fullerton led the messenger to Douglas who was inside talking to Lady Eleanor. Douglas received the messenger graciously and asked him to be seated while he delivered his message.

'Dear sir, I bring you news from his most holy Excellency, Bishop Lamberton.' the messenger began. 'He has requested your presence at Melrose Abbey. He begs to inform you that John the Red Comyn has been killed by Robert Bruce of Carrick at Dumfries. The good Bishop asks that you meet with him for discussions on how you may join with the Bruce in his quest to claim the crown of Scotland. The Bishop asks that you join him immediately.' Douglas thanked the messenger, and asked Fullerton to offer him food and refreshment before leaving.

'Mother, have you met the Bruce?' asked Douglas, when the messenger had departed.

'Yes, I have,' said Eleanor, 'and I have something to tell you. When your father, Lord William, was away with Wallace, Robert Bruce led an attack on our castle at Douglas. However, when he reached our walls he decided to follow his conscience and oppose our invaders. He loudly called out. "No man holds his own flesh and blood in hatred, and I am no exception." He then stated that he must join his own people, and the nation that he was born to. Those who opposed his stance left. Those remaining joined with us and supported his cause. I have heard very little of him recently, until now.'

'Thank you, mother,' said Douglas.

'May God be with you and guide you in your quest, my beloved James,' said Lady Eleanor.

Douglas swiftly made his preparations for departure and bid a final farewell to each member of his loving family, but as he walked towards the doorway to leave Fullerton called him to stop. 'Douglas!' he shouted, 'before you leave, I have something for you.' Douglas turned to see Fullerton standing with a battle-worn broad sword, which he held out in front of him.

'This belonged to your father; he was forced to surrender it when he was taken by the English knights Clifford and Percy at Irvine. I'm sure he would want you to carry it with you,' Fullerton declared.

'There would be no greater honour for me than to carry my father's arms against those who took his life,' Douglas answered, as he took hold of this precious item and placed a kiss on the sword's cross-shaped handle.

Hugh, the young brother of Douglas, stepped forward. 'I also have a gift for you; please take this long dagger which belonged to our father. Use it, not to harm others, but use it only against evil, in order that you can achieve your ambition.'

As Hugh handed over the gift he embraced his older brother, who then replied 'Thank you, my dear Hugh, you are truly a remarkable person, and a kind and loving young brother. I will cherish this gift and use it as you have requested.'

Lady Eleanor asked her beloved James to stop for a moment. 'I would like to present a parting gift to you,' she said, indicating a pleasant surprise was in store. From inside an old wooden storage box she retrieved an object which was contained within a dark protective cloth. As she untied the cloth and rolled out the contents Douglas saw a large white garment that was decorated with a coat of arms.

'This is the Douglas coat of arms, which belonged to your father; wear it with pride, respect and dignity. When your day arrives to wear this garment, you will officially be the protector of the name of Douglas.' Douglas took hold of the precious coat and held it against his chest. The front was embroidered with the outline of a white shield with three stars sewn onto a blue background along the top section.

'I pledge that I will always honour the name of Douglas by wearing this garment in the pursuit of my destiny,' he declared proudly.

'I too have a gift for you, James,' said cheeky-faced young Archibald. Everyone looked at the boy in surprise. 'What gift could he possibly have?' they thought to themselves. Douglas braced himself and prepared to be on the receiving end of another poke in the eye, or kick in the shin, or some other painful surprise gift from his youngest brother.

The young Archibald ran over towards Douglas, and with outstretched arms jumped into the embrace of his older brother. As the two brothers hugged each other young Archibald kissed his hero on the cheek, and said in an embarrassed voice 'I love you, James.' Tears began to well up in the eyes not only of Douglas, but also of everyone present.

This gift from the young child was the most precious of all, thought Douglas.

'Are you not taking the horse you brought with you?' asked Fullerton as he pointed over towards the field where the animal was grazing. 'No!' replied Douglas. 'I have no method of payment to you or my family, all I can give is my horse which you may use to work the fields or sell to support your needs. Please consider this as a token of my appreciation.'

'I am grateful,' answered Fullerton. 'But your journey will be longer now. You will need to take extra care.'

'I'll be fine,' smiled Douglas.

As he made his way along the forest trails, Douglas moved with great speed for someone travelling on foot. He kept his head up, looking all around him, watching for danger, yet still admiring the many beauties of the forest. The fresh flowers of spring brightened up his pathway as he made haste along the lonely journey. His sudden appearance startled many of the creatures of the forest. A young deer stopped grazing, looked up, and bolted with fear as he appeared from nowhere. The forest birds feeding on the fresh buds of spring cried out with fright as he passed near.

Many hours had now passed since Douglas had said farewell to his beloved family. He had not stopped. He maintained a constant pace. Doubts started to enter his mind. 'Will I be able to complete my journey?' he asked of himself. He had never been on his own before. 'What if Bruce does not want to associate with me?' 'What if I fail?' 'What of my family?' he repeatedly asked of himself. These conversations with himself continued to eat away at his confidence, as the yards, and the miles quickly passed by.

The twilight hours gradually turned to darkness, and Douglas's tired legs began to falter. He decided to stop for a few moments. Sitting down under a large beech tree, he closed his eyes for a short rest. The self-doubts began to change to gentle dreams. As he drifted into a deep sleep, the recurring dream that had haunted him since childhood returned once more.

He tossed and turned, and saw the same two faceless female figures, both adult, and both dressed in long white robes. One would always be coming towards him, the other drifting away. Each figure was holding a sleeping child. They would gently call out his name, 'James, James,' in a soft, warm whisper. He called back, but they did not reply. He would look back and forward from one to the other, but he could never see both figures at the same time. His dream would end with both figures drifting away. The dreams continued to occupy his sleeping mind. They were dreams of the past, dreams of the future, dreams of happiness and peace in his lands, dreams of good deeds. The dreams became intense, the happiness changed to anger, the peace changed to horror, and the good changed to evil.

The creatures of the night broke the still silence with their ghostly cries. He awoke with a startle, his eyes unable to focus in the darkness. He was lost, he cried out with fear as his terrified body shook with the anguish of a lost soul in an unknown world. Still confused, and in shock, Douglas rose to his feet. He rubbed his eyes and slowly regained his composure. Unable to shake off the demons of his dreams he knelt down and prayed for guidance.

'Dear God, I beg you to give me strength during these hours of darkness. I have thanked everyone but you for the safety and welfare of me and my family during these treacherous years.' As the intensity of his prayers deepened he said, 'My Lord God, I put you above all else, as your child I pledge to follow the way of your son Jesus, who gave his life in honour of you.' Douglas closed his eyes and continued in silent prayer.

Throughout the night, Douglas lay beneath the shelter of the large beech tree. He slept silently and at peace with himself. The early sun arrived, illuminating the forest and removing the darkness around where he had slept. Douglas had gone. The fast pace continued as he made his way in the early morning sun. His renewed determination and confidence propelled him effortlessly along his way.

As he continued his thoughts were focused on the beauty around him. Mother Nature put on an impressive pageant at the start of this spring day. The early morning light penetrating through the soft, low-lying mist provided the atmosphere. The birds of the forest provided the sweet dawn chorus. The trees, hills and rivers were the main characters, their costumes being the many coloured leaves, flowers, grasses and ferns.

In the afternoon, Douglas reached the top of a small hill which offered him a clear view for many miles ahead. As he scanned the horizon, he spotted the smoke rising in the distance. Focusing his eyes towards the distant haze, he could vaguely make out the rooftop of the magnificent abbey, about which he had heard many a tale. The view gave him a fresh burst of energy. He accelerated his pace and made good progress down the hillside pathway.

About a mile outside the town, Douglas stopped and gazed at the magnificent river that had become the backbone of life in these borderlands. Its awesome power and beauty were unmatched by anything he had seen during these last few years. As he observed the creatures that made this place their home, he recognised that some divine intervention must have taken place to create such a sanctuary for life. 'The richness of life generated by these waters must be an extension of the hand of God,' he thought to himself as he washed and refreshed his tired body in the cold clear waters of the Tweed.

As he approached the abbey, his pace slowed down. The magnificent building, with its splendid towers and round-headed arches, appeared too magnificent for such a quiet countryside location. The late afternoon sun bounced off the sandstone walls, creating an illusion of a palace of gold in a land of poverty. 'How could such a creation be made by man?' Douglas thought to himself. Over his short life he had witnessed many things. He had seen the destruction and evil that man could inflict, yet here in front of him stood the opposite, a creation of amazing beauty, made by man, for worshipping the giver of life.

On arrival, Douglas announced that he wished to meet with Bishop Lamberton. A few minutes later Lamberton came out to greet his young friend. 'You have arrived much quicker than I expected, I'm once again very glad to see you my young friend.' They both made their way to a small vacant annex room normally used by the lay brothers. 'You may stay here tonight young James. After you have eaten we will talk of the message I have received relating to Bruce.' Douglas thanked him and he entered the small austere room.

After he had eaten a well-earned meal consisting of fresh fish from the Tweed, bread from the Abbey's grange, washed down with wine made from the fruits of the local orchard, Douglas felt tired and in great need of rest. He closed his eyes and was about to drift off into a deep sleep when suddenly his guardian Bishop entered. Seeing that his young squire was so tired, the Bishop decided to keep his conversation short.

'My dear Douglas, while I was at Berwick I received a message from Robert Bruce. He is about to make his way to the palace of Scone to be crowned King of Scotland,' Lamberton announced, in a manner suggesting something serious and sinister had happened.

'Why do you convey such good news with despair and sadness in your voice?' asked Douglas. Lamberton replied in a tone more serious than Douglas had ever heard from his longtime friend and guardian.

'Robert Bruce, Earl of Carrick, has taken the life of John the Red Comyn in the sacristy of Greyfriars Church in Dumfries. There is great fear for the future of our church in Scotland. Our leaders in Rome will consider this act of Bruce as sacrilegious, and may consider excommunication.'

'Excommunication for whom?' asked Douglas, as he patiently listened to his knowledgeable friend.

'We look forward to his crowning, and with great hope and expectation for our suffering people. However, it may lead to our whole nation being expelled by our church leaders.'

'Will that really be such a bad thing,' asked Douglas with a hint of sarcasm.

'If Scotland were to be excommunicated, and our church in Rome supportive of England, it could be disastrous for the future of our nation,' replied Lamberton with great seriousness.

'If that were to happen it would appear unjust to me, considering the many evil deeds that the English have perpetrated upon on our nation,' declared Douglas. Lamberton looked at his young squire realising that the boy he had raised had matured not only in body but in mind also. He could sense that his young friend's devotion was first to God, then to his nation. Loyalty to his church was of lesser importance.

Taking a few seconds to collect his thoughts, Douglas gave his reply to the good Bishop. 'Your Excellency, the English have, by force, disinherited me and my family and taken our lands. The message you are in receipt of states that the Earl of Carrick claims to govern this kingdom, and because of his slaying of Comyn, all Englishmen are against him. Nevertheless, it is now time for me to join him. Therefore your Excellency, if it pleases you, I will meet with him and offer my support to his cause, and through him, I may, with the grace of God, recover my lands from Clifford and his kin.'

'Then I'm unable to help you any longer,' the distressed Lamberton declared. 'My sweet son,' Lamberton continued quietly, 'whom I have grown to love over these years, may God help me. It would be pleasing to see you take up with Bruce; however, I can no longer assist you in any way.'

'I will need a horse if I am to ride with him,' said Douglas.

'Then you must take mine, but do not ask for my permission for I cannot be seen to give you my approval,' answered Lamberton. 'There is no horse so fine in this country. Take him without my consent, and if anyone should challenge you, take the beast in spite of them.'

Lamberton placed a pouch of money in front of his friend. 'Here is a sum of silver which would be of benefit to our future King. Take this also.' James knelt down in front of his most gracious and holy spiritual father. Lamberton blessed his young friend and offered up a prayer. 'Almighty God, grant he who kneels before you that he may be enabled to defend himself against your enemies, and grant safety and guidance to the one he is about to join up with, and that they pursue their cause in your good name.'

The early morning sun struggled to break through the clouded skies as it attempted to deliver the first light of life into the new day. The abbey was already busy with the industrious residents as they quietly went about their religious disciplines in the dull grey early hours. Young Douglas had wakened from a sound sleep, and was now prepared to leave this holy place. Nervously he approached the stable where the Bishop's horse was resting. He recognised the creature. It was indeed a magnificent animal, exactly as Lamberton had stated. 'Ideal for a long journey ahead,' Douglas thought to himself, as he walked over towards the peaceful looking creature, which stared at him.

The stable groom was going about the business of performing his duties. 'Good morning my man,' he said, as Douglas approached. 'Looks like another wet day in store for us.'

'I have to get the Bishop's horse ready,' Douglas informed the stable worker. 'Fine by me,' came the reply. Once he had saddled the well-rested animal, Douglas quickly mounted and attempted to make off.

'Hold on! I have to account for this horse,' shouted the stable groom as he lunged forward to grab hold of the horse's reins. With deep regret, Douglas drew his sword; the shocked groom instinctively covered his face with his arms, as Douglas suddenly brought the handle of the sword down on him. The groom immediately fell stunned to the ground.

'May God forgive me!' cried Douglas, as he rode out of the abbey grounds.

For the first hour, Douglas rode his borrowed horse with great speed and purpose. He deeply regretted the action he had just taken against the innocent stable worker. 'I had no choice!' he continually repeated to himself. The dark clouds hung over him, as he made his way westwards. His destination was the road at the head of Annandale. Lamberton had advised him that Bruce would head north along this road in the next few days. He finally reached his destination at the place called Tweed's Well, in the area where the waters draining down from the high mountain moors form the source of the great river that he had followed. He rested here for the night, watched, and waited for the travellers from the south.

Douglas examined the markings on the road; no large groups of horse riders had passed by in the last few days. He hoped that was not too late. By mid-afternoon of the following day, Douglas noticed riders approaching from the south. He could not identify the exact numbers, but guessed around fifty. Douglas mounted his horse and took cover in the protection of the forest edge. As the riders came into clear view, he recognised the group as that of Bruce.

The nineteen-year-old Douglas immediately rode out of the forest, and unintentionally startled the front riders, who viewed him suspiciously, as he came towards them. Although the riders at the front of the group had arms drawn, they did not consider this lone rider a serious threat. Positioned slightly back from the leading riders was Robert the Bruce, who was flanked on either side by two riders with arms also drawn.

The sight of Bruce riding towards him filled the young Douglas with excitement. Here was the man that he hoped would help him in the pursuit of his destiny. Douglas and Bruce's party finally came together. Douglas, unable to control his emotions, immediately called out, 'My dear Lord Bruce, I wish to be your most obedient, trusted aid and ever loyal servant. I present myself, my name, and my lands in protection of your name and in support of your cause.'

The party of riders stopped to listen to this young stranger, who in his first few words had given a more genuine pledge of support and loyalty to Bruce than most other Scottish nobles had in a lifetime.

'What name are you known by?' asked Bruce. 'Douglas, my Lord!' young James answered. 'A Douglas! Tell me more,' requested Bruce.

'I have been under the guardianship of Bishop William Lamberton of St Andrews, ever since my father, Lord William, was taken by the English lords Clifford and Percy at Irvine' replied the exited young James. 'I come to do homage to you as the rightful King of Scotland, I come to avenge my father's death at the hands of Longshanks, I come to fight to reclaim my lands, and my inheritance from the English Lord Clifford.'

Bruce replied. 'Young Douglas, I am honoured by your presence. Your father, Lord William Douglas, was a courageous and honourable man who supported our cause and gave his life in exchange for you and your family's safety. As his son, this company most welcomes you. Your guardian, Bishop William Lamberton, is a close friend and a great spiritual leader to our nation; he also is an honourable man. There could be no greater honour for me today than to have the son of Douglas, who has been advised and guided by Lamberton, join me as I lead this nation forward.'

Taking the pouch of silver from his belt, Douglas handed over the valuable gift offered to him by Lamberton and said 'Sire, I present you with this gift as a token of the friendship and loyalty of his Excellency, Bishop William Lamberton. Please accept this gift in support of your good cause.'

'I gladly accept, with humble thanks and appreciation,' replied Bruce. 'Please join with me as we ride to Glasgow and then on to Scone in order that I be crowned by our people as King of this once proud nation.'

7

THE CROWNING OF BRUCE

DOUGLAS RODE WITH the rear group, as Bruce's party made their way north towards the town of Lanark. He was proud to be in such fine company and he wished his mother and brothers could witness this event. A short time after Douglas joined the party; the group passed by a roadside marking. The front riders took no notice of the sign and Douglas himself did not notice it until he was almost on top of it. The wooden sign, which pointed to the west, had the name 'DOUGLAS' carved on it.

An uncontrollable force suddenly overtook Douglas. Confused and shocked, he had to stop. He pulled up as the other riders rode on. 'I will catch up,' he shouted, as the puzzled riders glanced round. Douglas turned his horse to the left, and faced the direction that the sign was pointing. He looked over to the lands in the west and stared. His face was expressionless, but his eyes soon reddened not with tears but with rage which began to build up within his young body; it was a raging anger that he was not accustomed to experiencing.

In spite of all that had happened to Douglas, Lamberton had raised him in a life of love, kindness and consideration for others. His thoughts abandoned these good qualities, as he looked towards his homelands of Douglasdale. An uncontrolled fire burned within him. Hatred, revenge and death were the thoughts that now resided in his angry mind. At that moment he made a pledge to himself. 'The next time I come here, it will be to restore the name Douglas as the rightful owner. Anyone, who stands in my way will perish.'

Douglas quickly caught up with Bruce's party and regained his position with the rear group of riders. Some time later the group by-passed the town of Lanark and headed alongside the dominant River Clyde and onwards towards Glasgow. As they passed along this route, they marvelled at the lush growth of vegetation. The whole landscape appeared to be several weeks ahead of the rest of the country, in terms of producing the fruits of the land.

'Why are we not heading directly to Scone?' asked Douglas, to the rider on his right.

'Other nobles will be joining us and we need to recruit more followers, as keen as you I hope,' answered the rider.

The band of riders stopped to rest for the night in the ancient woods alongside the banks of the Clyde, a few miles from the castle of Bothwell. Several members of the party started cursing as they openly expressed their frustration.

'Why are they angry?' asked Douglas.

'Bothwell is in English hands,' answered Davidson, a twenty-two year-old follower of Bruce, who had joined the party at Dumfries. 'They would like to be in a position of strength of numbers that we could take it back,' he added.

'I would like to see this castle,' said Douglas.

'You can't, we will have to keep well clear, there are too many English troops,' answered Davidson.

'Is that right?' asked Douglas with a grin on his face.

A short time before dawn, Douglas was awake and silently walking his horse through the woods. The sound of the powerful river on his left assisted him as he slowly made his way in the patchy moonlight. A short time later he came to the edge of the wood. The clearing in front of him stretched for about half a mile, and in front of him stood the magnificent castle with its thick stone walls illuminated by the many burning torches that flickered in the wind, high up on the tall towers, outshining, it seemed, the dull sky above. 'Even with the largest of armies, taking this place would be a difficult task,' Douglas thought to himself.

As the dawn started to come up, Douglas gazed at the majestic building. The sound of wildfowl disturbed from their roost along the steep riverbank startled him. He remained silent and still, as an old man and young boy came along the track pulling a cart towards the castle. Confident that there was no danger, Douglas gently called out, 'Good morning my friends,' to the surprised strangers as they approached.

'Good morning to you, sir,' was the reply from the old man.

'This is an early hour to be out and about,' said Douglas.

'Yes it is, but a safe time to deliver my goods,' the old man answered, as he relaxed after looking into the kindly face of the smiling stranger.

'What goods do you deliver?' asked Douglas.

'I deliver payment for being allowed to live in safety with my family in our home a short distance from here. I bring provisions to feed the bellies of Aymer de Valence, Earl of Pembroke, and his English army,' answered the old man.

'To bear such a burden for the welfare of your family is a sure sign of a very honourable and loving father,' said Douglas.

'I thank you kind stranger, but this is an honour I would rather not have,' replied the elderly man.

'How long will you be inside the castle walls?' asked Douglas.

'Only for a few minutes to unload my cart,' came the reply.

'I would like to see inside, may I be allowed to go in with you?' asked Douglas.

'Yes, you look like someone I can trust. My son will watch over your horse. You will of course have to leave your sword, as there are many English troops inside, and they would not take too kindly to seeing an armed stranger at such an early hour.'

As Bruce and his party awoke from their rest, Davidson was surprised to notice that his new-found friend Douglas was missing. There was no time to look for him; the party had to make immediate departure. In the early light of dawn, the riders made their way onwards. On the other side of the estate of Bothwell, they rejoined the main route towards Glasgow. A short time later a lone horseman could be seen waiting in the distance; as the party approached, Douglas was recognised.

'Sire, I must speak with you,' he asked as he approached the surprised Bruce. 'This morning I was inside Bothwell. As you are already no doubt aware the great castle is in the hands of the English, under the control of Aymer de Valence, Earl of Pembroke, Longshanks's Warden of Scotland; he has a large army, several hundred at his disposal. They are well equipped, and ideally positioned to quickly respond to any rebellious activity that should occur.'

There was a look of astonishment on the faces of Bruce's followers. 'Who is this Douglas? A young stranger, who, without being noticed, silently disappears in the night from their very own camp and then enters the most secure English held fortress in all of Scotland without any fear'?

'I'm very impressed dear Douglas, you have taken a great risk. The information you have provided is very useful, we must be careful of Pembroke and his forces. We must make haste, we will be in Glasgow very shortly,' replied Bruce.

As the riders covered the last few remaining miles into Glasgow, Davidson, the young friend from Dumfries, looked at Douglas and smiled. 'I don't know why, but when I saw that you had disappeared this morning, I suspected that you might be up to something. I have a feeling that interesting times may be ahead.' Douglas smiled back, he felt good that he had contributed in a small way.

'Have you eaten this morning?' Douglas asked.

'No, we had no time, we will eat when we get to Glasgow,' replied Davidson. Douglas pulled out a portion of cooked wildfowl from inside his coat and threw it over to Davidson. 'A gift from Aymer de Valence,' shouted Douglas, laughing out loud.

By mid-morning they had entered the outskirts of Glasgow. Bruce had requested a lone rider to go on ahead to announce their arrival. The rider was also instructed to ensure the way ahead was safe and free of English troops. Their destination was the large cathedral that stood impressively above all other buildings. As they made their way through the busy streets, word started to spread of their arrival.

Many locals stopped and stared, young children ran alongside the party of riders. It had been a long time since such a large gathering of Scots had been seen riding through these streets. Many came out and cheered, street traders shared food with the riders as they went by. The air was filled with excitement. One old man waved, as he wiped back the tears of joy at seeing hope for his country in the smiling faces of Bruce and his brave band of followers. 'We want to join you,' cried a group of young men who ran alongside the proud group of strangers.

Bruce and his followers approached the large cathedral. He could see the messenger that he had sent on ahead had arrived safely and was now standing alongside the elderly Bishop in front of the doorway of the great place of holy sanctuary. As Bruce dismounted, the Bishop stepped forward. 'Your most holy Excellency, my dear friend Bishop Wishart, I come to seek God's forgiveness for my sins,' declared Bruce.

'My dear son, my Lord Bruce,' said the Bishop, 'I am honoured that you have come to the house of God to seek his forgiveness. You have caused very serious concerns amongst the leaders of our holy church. Please come inside.'

Bruce gestured to a few of his followers to join him inside. The intimate nobles and close friends of Bruce had not yet invited Douglas into their inner circle, and he therefore waited patiently outside.

Inside the splendid cathedral, Bishop Wishart took Bruce aside into the sacristy while his close followers waited in the large nave. 'My dear Bruce we have a very difficult situation to overcome. No doubt there was provocation, and reasons for your actions against Comyn at Greyfriars. However, I must state that our Holy Fathers in Rome will be supportive of Longshanks in condemning your actions.'

'Your Excellency, my actions, albeit regrettable, were for the sole purpose of ridding this nation of the evil, treachery and suppression that Longshanks and his henchmen have inflicted on our people. I ask you to accompany me to the historical palace of Scone, and support me in my coronation as King of Scots, in order that I may lead our people to achieve the freedom and liberty that is theirs by right.'

Wishart could see the genuine concern, love, and affection in the heart of Bruce. 'My son, let me absolve you of your sins.' The Bishop took out his sacred stole and placed it over his neck. 'In the name of the Father, and of the Son and of the Holy Ghost …'. Bruce knelt down in front of the Bishop and received the sacrament of confession.

Outside a large crowd were forming. 'So if we join you, what's in it for us?' asked one eager youth, who was considering if he should give his pledge to support to Bruce.

'You will have the satisfaction of being part of our cause. Your family and friends will be proud in knowing that you are prepared to take up arms for the freedom and future prosperity of them and our nation,' answered one of Bruce's elderly followers, as he tried to attract more young men to take up the cause.

'All right,' said the young man, but I don't want to die at the hands of the English.'

'No more do we!' answered one of Bruce's followers.

A short time later, Bruce, along with his inner circle of friends, emerged from the tall building.

'Have you been able to encourage any more followers?' he asked of those around him.

'Yes, Sire, we have spoken to many who wish to join us,' replied one of his men.

A short time later, after his band of loyal friends had finished eating, they were ready for the next part of their journey. Bishop Wishart came out with a large bundle under his arm and joined them. 'Are we all ready?' Wishart asked. 'Yes!' came the reply. 'Let's go and celebrate the crowning our new King,' declared Wishart.

Bruce, accompanied by Douglas, Bishop Wishart, his close noble friends and party of followers headed to Scone. 'We must split up,' declared Bruce. 'We must avoid Stirling.' Two routes were identified: one that would enable the main body to avoid the garrison of English troops based at Stirling, the other to pass through areas that would enable them to recruit more followers. The main body headed north and over the hill pass behind the small village of Lennox, and onwards towards the place called Doune and then eastwards into the estates of Kinross. The smaller band took the route past Falkirk and Stirling, recruiting more followers along the way.

On 27 March 1306, Bruce and his men arrived at their destination of Scone. With great anticipation, they made their way to the Moot Hill, the ancient crowning place of the Kings and Queens of Scotland. Word had spread of this great day. The many friends and nobles who had come here to demonstrate their loyalty greatly impressed Bruce.

Bruce finally addressed those who had honoured him by their presence. 'My most holy Bishops, Wishart, Lamberton, and Moray. My dear Earls of Lennox, Atholl, Errol, Menteith and Mar, I thank you for your presence. I am honoured by your support. My dear loving brothers Edward, Thomas, Alexander and Nigel, my loyal nephew Randolph, I am overjoyed that you are with me this day.' Bruce greeted each loyal family member and friend in turn. 'To everyone, who has put themselves at risk by being here with me today, I thank you and I solemnly pledge that I will repay the faith and trust that you place in me today.'

'My Lord Bruce,' the Abbot of Scone called out, 'Can we really do justice to your coronation? We have no crown, the English have stolen our sacred Stone of Destiny, we have no ancient robes for you to wear, and there is no Earl of Fife to perform the customary ceremony of your crowning.' Much discussion and arguing took place amongst the prestigious group that surrounded Bruce.

'I have a circlet of gold that could take the place of a crown,' announced Sir Christopher de Seton, brother-in-law of Bruce.

'I thank you, my brother,' replied Bruce. At this moment, Bishop Wishart stepped forward and produced a set of regal robes and vestments, which he had brought from Glasgow. 'I think you will find that these are appropriate,' he called out. Bruce expressed surprise and thanked his good friend.

A voice from the back of the group then called out, 'I don't have a sacred stone but I am skilled and accustomed to performing sacred blessings.' Bishop Lamberton stepped forward to loud applause.

Behind the wooden throne was placed the great banner of the Kings of Scotland with its lion and scarlet lilies that had for so long lain concealed. Bishop Lamberton performed the simple ceremony. Few words were spoken. As Bruce knelt before Lamberton, a short prayer was said. Finally, the gold circlet was placed on the head of Bruce. 'Arise Robert, King of Scots!' Lamberton called out, as he stood back to loud cheers and applause from everyone present. Bruce rose to his feet, smiled and waved to those around him.

James Douglas stood at the back of the gathering of nobles; he was not one for mixing within large crowds. He looked around and wondered how genuinely loyal were the individuals who paid homage to their new King. He had heard so much gossip of treachery and treason over these last few days that he was not sure whom he could really trust.

Lamberton approached Douglas and asked, 'You are deep in thought, my young James, what troubles you?'

'I'm pleased to see you, your Excellency,' responded Douglas with deep concern. 'I hope you are well? If I look troubled, it is because I have some doubts about the genuineness of the loyalty being expressed here today. Only a few hours ago I overheard words of betrayal and now I hear the opposite. What am I to believe?'

'Believe both!' declared Lamberton. 'In times of joy, safety and wealth, expect to see loyalty and happiness, in times of despair, danger and poverty expect to see betrayal and anger. It is merely good versus evil my young friend. If you can maintain your loyalty when evil is all around, then you will truly be a loyal friend to our new King and a good servant to our lord God.'

'I thank you for your wisdom, your Excellency, I will do my best,' answered Douglas, as, reassured, he smiled and nodded his head.

King Robert and his party stayed at Scone until the following Sunday. Just before midday, a woman rider came into their presence, and while still on her horse shouted 'I am Isabel, Countess of Buchan, sister of the Earl of Fife; it is my brother's right to perform the ancient tradition of the placing of the crown on our new King. As he is too afraid of your enemies to be seen performing this honourable task, I have come to offer to carry out this ceremony, in the name of my family, and in keeping with tradition.'

'I thank you, my Lady, but there is no need,' replied King Robert.

'Sire, as you are aware, any little thing that your enemies could produce to discredit you, believe me they will, and they will use it against your good name,' the Countess replied.

'She is correct, my Lord,' declared Bishop Wishart.

The coronation ceremony was repeated on Palm Sunday, with the Countess of Buchan performing the ancient royal tradition. Everyone again paid homage and joined in the joy and celebration of a Scots King at the head of their nation. Again the cry rang out 'Hail the Bruce! King of Scots!'

8

FIRST BATTLE, FIRST DEFEAT

WHEN EDWARD, KING OF ENGLAND, heard of the killing of Comyn, and the support Bruce had received from his fellow Scots in being crowned King, his anger was intense. 'Go to Scotland, take men at arms, burn, slay and raise the Dragon, for I promise all of Fife as a reward to the man who should take or slay the Bruce!' screamed Longshanks.

The Earl of Pembroke, Aymer de Valence, cousin of Longshanks and brother-in-law of Comyn, was immediately ordered to lead an army and hunt down those rebellious Scots. Sir Henry Percy and Sir Robert Clifford, the two main enemies of Bruce and Douglas, and currently in possession of their respective lands, were ordered by Longshanks to join with Valence.

'We must teach those Scots a lesson they will not forget,' cried Longshanks. 'No quarter shall be given, no mercy shown. All who have taken up arms, and given their support to that murderer Bruce, shall be put to the sword.'

Messengers were sent to all of the English garrisons in Scotland. 'All forces were to make themselves available to be led by Valence in pursuit of Bruce and his followers'. King Edward then prepared a letter for Pope Clement V and petitioned him to have Bruce excommunicated for committing the sacrilegious murder of Comyn, on the consecrated ground of Greyfriars Church in Dumfries. During the month of May of that same year the order of excommunication was duly passed.

The late spring warmth of 1306 allowed nature's jewels to sparkle across the fertile land. The flowers of field and forest presented an abundant display of beauty and life, projecting the smile of the great Creator.

The peace and tranquillity that existed in these glens was halted abruptly that spring by the thunderous noise of many riders, as they headed northwards towards Perth. It was the noise of three thousand horsemen, led by Valence, along with many of Comyn's grieving followers who sought their revenge, in pursuit of Bruce and his supporters.

With a combined force of six thousand, the English army arrived with such speed and determination that their Scottish prey was taken by surprise. Bishop Wishart of Glasgow was one of the first of Bruce's closest followers to be captured, with the sudden arrival of the English forces as they entered Cupar Castle in Fife. Bishop Lamberton of St Andrews encouraged the people of his local parish to join with Bruce, and was then forced to surrender himself. Both bishops were cast in chains, taken and imprisoned in the dungeons of English castles. Their lives were spared only because of their position within the church.

By mid-June, Bruce had managed to attract sufficient support to give him the confidence to meet with Valence at Perth. With an army of four and a half thousand, Bruce arrived outside the protective walls of the town.

'There is no way that we can take this place,' advised Thomas Randolph, nephew of Bruce, as the Scottish nobles and their King looked at the massive task in front of them. 'I agree,' replied Bruce. 'We have neither the equipment nor the manpower for such a task.'

Accompanied by a small band of knights, Bruce rode towards the city gates, and issued his challenge. 'Valence, Earl of Pembroke, King Edward's Warden of Scotland, hear this. I, Bruce, King of Scotland, hereby challenge you to uphold the traditions of chivalry. I offer you the challenge to surrender this town immediately, or to meet with me in battle this day.' A short delay occurred, as Bruce and his knights remained outside awaiting the reply.

'Do you think Valence will come out?' asked Edward, brother of Bruce.

'I do,' answered Bruce. 'I believe Valence to be a man of honour; I believe he will come out for battle.'

A messenger from inside the town of Perth appeared at the gates. 'Your request has been considered, King Edward's Warden of all Scotland, the noble Earl of Pembroke, Aymer de Valence, will meet your army in battle at midday tomorrow.

'So be it!' shouted Bruce, as he and his band of knights rode off to rejoin their army.

Inside the town walls, Valence and his company of nobles, including several Scots, were busy discussing the implications of the decision that they had just taken. 'My Lord, let me make a suggestion,' announced Sir Ingram de Umfraville, a Scottish noble and supporter of the murdered Comyn. 'I would advise not to wait until tomorrow. Bruce and his army are desperate to rid their nation of your presence. I fear that if they are given time to prepare their battle tactics we may have a difficult task ahead.'

The other advisers to Valence all agreed. 'What do you then suggest?' asked Valence.

'I say we attack now!' cried Umfraville. 'Bruce and his army will be spending the remainder of this afternoon, and into the late evening, setting up camp. Some will be foraging for food, others will be sleeping after their tiring journey. They will be unprepared and not expecting us.'

'You talk good sense,' answered Valence, with a cunning smile. 'I will ensure that King Edward is made aware of your loyal support in bringing an end to this pointless campaign of Bruce. 'Let us get our army ready. We leave within the hour!'

Bruce and his army had withdrawn a few miles and camped for the night outside Methven. No sentries were posted; no guards were placed along the road from the town of Perth. The army of loyal followers went about their own business. The last few hours of daylight were taken up looking for food and preparing for the well-earned night of rest in preparation for tomorrow's battle.

Douglas, however, more alert than his fellows, looked around the immediate area and felt uncomfortable and insecure. 'What would I do if I were Valence?' he asked of himself. He approached Bruce, and nervously stated, 'Sire, I'm very uneasy about this situation. I fear that Valence may not be the honourable and chivalrous noble that you credit him for. He speaks for Longshanks, and we have all learnt, to our regret, not to trust his word or intentions.'

'My dear Douglas, I appreciate your concern, you are very protective of me, but also very young and inexperienced in these matters. Trust my judgement on this day,' replied Bruce.

'Sire, I know that I have not as yet earned the right to your close company, but I ask that you allow me to be your personal guard through these next few hours,' requested Douglas.

'Very well my young friend, you may become one of my immediate guards.' They both smiled at each other as their friendship took yet another step forward.

Nervous of the events that tomorrow's battle would bring, Bruce's army quietly settled down for the night. They would be up before dawn; an early night of rest was essential. The last daylight hours started to drift away. Many of them, including Douglas, had never before been engaged in any form of combat. Like a mother protecting and nursing her young children during a storm, the surrounding Perthshire hills provided a comforting bosom to the bodies and minds of this army. The lonely individuals put their faith in God for their protection, as they lay on the dry ground in the woods beside the River Almond. Some prayed aloud, others in silence.

Douglas was on edge. He could not rest, and he sensed that danger was imminent. He positioned himself on the ground beneath a tree slightly higher up the hill from where Bruce was resting. The smoke from the various burning fires that were being lit to cook the evening meals restricted his view of the surrounding area.

The first indication that Valence had broken his word was the eerie cry of someone in pain, which occurred when an English sword penetrated the defenceless body of a follower of Bruce, who was resting at the edge of the wood. In the next few moments others were asking themselves whether they had really heard a noise, or whether it was only imagination.

Douglas was on his feet, sword drawn, and now more nervous than he had ever been in his life. He rushed towards Bruce, as the cries of pain and horror of many loyal Scottish lives being slaughtered started to fill the evening air. English foot soldiers lodged the first surprise attack, as they cut their way through the unprepared Scottish forces. Bruce's followers, many without their weapons, rose to their feet in response to the sudden cries of terror, only to be immediately cut down by the blood-hungry attackers. Shock and panic immediately spread amongst Bruce's forces, as English horsemen rode through the unprepared camp and scattered the terrified residents in all directions.

On realising what was happening, Bruce cried out 'To arms, everyone!' His call was too late; his army had been caught out, unprepared, unarmed, disjointed and now running for their lives. A few of the followers of Bruce started to regain their composure, while groups of armed Scottish soldiers began repelling the horrific attack. Instructions were coming from all directions. Total disarray and confusion existed throughout the Scottish camp. The bloody bodies of the slaughtered Scots lay all around. Many of the victims lay motionless amongst the burning remains of the campfires that had been scattered throughout the wood. Many were dead; many were maimed and cried out in agony only to attract the attention of their executioners who gave no mercy and finished off their gruesome task.

Douglas kept his focus of attention on the safety of his King. With both sword and dagger drawn he moved forward and prepared himself to meet the first victim in his quest for revenge. An English soldier came running towards him, striking out in all directions with a blood-stained battle-axe. Douglas calmly stood his ground and raised his sword as the determined soldier charged at him. With unexpected speed, Douglas twisted his body to the side and coolly thrust his long dagger into the lower neck of his attacker with deadly power and precision, severing the English soldier's main artery, and causing blood to spurt out over both victim and executioner. The soldier's life immediately ended. 'I pray that my brother Hugh would have considered my action as one against evil,' Douglas thought to himself. The coldness in the way he had carried out this execution took Douglas by surprise; he had made his first kill; he had no remorse.

The desire for revenge now began to burn inside Douglas like a wild, blazing hillside fire. He continued to make his way across the few yards of ground to aid Bruce, who was surrounded by his loyal knights. Several determined attackers, their faces blood-stained and full of hatred, attempted to block his path; one by one, their lives were clinically ended, as Douglas effortlessly brought them down with the same controlled precision as his first victim. The lethal combination of speed, strength and skill, along with his sense of purpose and passion, proved to be unmatched by anyone who came towards him.

The knights who were guarding Bruce were outnumbered and uncoordinated as the English swarmed all over them. The spilt blood continued to flow over the Methven hillside. The battle continued as the brave supporters of Bruce made a superhuman effort and fought desperately for the safety of their King. Bruce gave encouragement when, on seeing his army falter; he charged into the battle and called out his war cry. He cut down many of his enemy with great strength and resilience. His actions inspired his men and brought out the last ounce of effort from every one of his dedicated followers.

The desperate fighting continued to take its toll as more and more of Bruce's army collapsed, either at the hands of the English soldiers or through sheer exhaustion. Many started to flee, because staying surely meant death. Like a mountain stream that very quickly gathers momentum, more and more followers of Bruce deserted their cause, encouraging others to lose faith and flee for their lives. The true loyal followers stood firm and battled honourably in a patriotic show of strength towards the rightful King of Scotland.

Out of the black smoke-filled evening air, a band of bloodthirsty English knights rode towards Bruce and his close protectors. One carried the emblem of the Dragon, indicating that no quarter would be given. Bruce's loyal band of knights knew that this would be a battle to the death, and that no opportunity would be presented for negotiation should they lose. Valence led the charge towards Bruce, who was now surrounded by a group made up of his brother Edward, Christopher Seton, Neil Campbell, Gilbert de la Haye, James Douglas and the Earl of Atholl.

The first charge of English knights took place. Bruce gave the instructions to spread out and for each man to defend himself. With sword drawn, Valence galloped straight towards Bruce; the other Scottish knights paired off against their attackers. Douglas moved in closer on the right side of Bruce. On the left of Bruce, Christopher Seton provided protection. Valence's horse panicked as it came upon the rigid group of determined Scottish nobles. At the final moment before impact, the beast pulled up, only to be slain by a direct thrust from the sword of Bruce. Bruce became unhorsed in the chaos that followed, as the other knights engaged in battle with their attackers. As Bruce remounted, the English knight Sir Philip Mowbray managed to grab hold of his bridle and cried out 'Help, I have him, I have their new King, I have Bruce.'

Douglas was engaged in his first experience of combat against an English knight, and was in the process of delivering yet another thrust of death from his father's sword, when he heard Mowbray call out. Douglas had waited a long time for the chance to experience taking the life of one of Longshanks's nobles. He had taken no pleasure in the slaying of his first English soldier a short time ago. However, on this occasion he felt the killing was justified. But he had no time to dwell on his mixed feelings. As soon as he had pulled his blood-stained sword from the side of the dying knight, Douglas turned to help his King. He looked round and saw Seton coming to the protection of Bruce, striking Mowbray to the ground and releasing the Scottish King's horse in the process.

Bruce remounted, raised his sword and called out 'On them! On them!' Many of Bruce's knights were taken prisoner, amongst them Thomas Randolph. With his numbers dwindling, Bruce called to his knights 'Sirs, since fortune runs against us here today, it is best we pass from this danger, till God presently sends us grace, and it may happen yet, if they pursue, we shall requite them in turn.' They all agreed and retreated. The English forces, also exhausted, made no chase after them but rounded up the many significant prisoners and made their way back to Perth.

Into the darkness of night, Bruce and his reduced band of exhausted followers headed northwards. A gentle rain started to fall, slowly at first in the soft wind, but building up pace as the wind grew more and more powerful. The forces of nature were now taking their turn to assault the defeated riders, but, tired and wet, they still headed onwards. The lashing rain drenched their garments and penetrated their numb bodies with its ice-cold sharpness. Their heads were bowed; they did not know where they were going. Their only desire was to distance themselves from their attackers. Those on horseback proceeded at walking pace through the cruel and unsympathetic night. Those on foot walked behind, heads bowed in hopeless desperation.

As the night wore on, their numbers were further reduced as some decided to make their own way to a safe place. First, Sir Christopher Seton left their company, followed a short time later by Sir Simon Fraser.

The main group continued onwards towards the mountains of Atholl. The rain fell on them with relentless force. Underfoot the sodden mud sucked at every forward step, adding to their already heavy burden. Their hope was gone, their faith in their creator's protection was all but lost, as they questioned, 'Why us? Why dear God?' They could not understand why all was against them. 'Were the ones who perished a few hours ago at Methven the lucky ones?' they repeatedly asked themselves, in dejection and despair.

Douglas too was dejected. 'Is this really worth fighting for?' he said to himself. He thought of those Scottish nobles who had recently fought against him. 'Have they made the better choice,' he asked of himself. He thought of his father, Lord William, who had given his life, and of his mother, Lady Eleanor, and brothers who were still in hiding in the forest of Selkirk.

He raised his head and cried out 'For the sake of our families, our nation and our King, let God guide us safely through this night.' Those around looked up and a faint glimmer of hope appeared on the desperate faces. Douglas dismounted from his horse and offered its service to a foot soldier who was on the verge of collapse. Others who saw this good deed were comforted and humbled by this gallant gesture offered in such treacherous conditions.

The sun did not break through the following day; instead, a thick, low-lying mist hung over the hills and glens of Atholl. An eerie atmosphere prevailed, created by the silence of the still, damp air and the sight of the many injured soldiers taking refuge amongst the heather, bracken and shelter of the forest. No one moved, no animal came within sight, dawn had failed to arrive, and no birds were singing.

Beneath a group of protective trees, the hot breath of life could be seen slowly rising through the cold air as someone awoke from a nightmare. Douglas rose to his feet. He looked around him and saw the tragedy of defeat. Poor souls, loyal to the last minute, dedicated to the freedom of their nation, lay there in front of him, having collapsed with exhaustion. They had given everything to the cause of their King.

Douglas was concerned. 'When these sons of Scotland waken from the safety of their peaceful sleep their pains will surely return. Despair, hunger, cold, defeat, and isolation .... Many are sure to leave,' Douglas thought to himself.

Douglas approached Bruce, who was awake and going over in his mind the events of the previous day and night.

'Sire, I fear for our followers. We do not have the resources to protect or care for them. As they awake many will want to leave and return to their homes.'

Bruce replied with distress and anxiety in his voice. 'I share your concerns, Douglas; I am ashamed that I have led these good men into such tragedy. We cannot support them; some may be better off leaving us. Their safety and welfare is of far greater concern than my selfish cause.'

'Sire, there can be no greater cause than to seek our freedom and to return this land to its own people. At this moment their bodies may not be able to support your cause, but their hearts and minds will always be with you,' replied Douglas, as he knelt down in front of his King.

'For one so young, and inexperienced, you speak with great comfort and wisdom,' said Bruce, as he put his hand on the shoulder of his young friend. 'Perhaps I would be best to let these good people go back home and allow myself to be accompanied by a few loyal close friends,' continued Bruce, defeat and sadness in his voice.

'When they awake we can discuss it with them,' answered Douglas.

Over the next few months, Bruce's followers had vastly reduced in numbers. Those who remained sought refuge in the mountains of Atholl. A small band of loyal knights, including Douglas, provided their King with close protection and words of encouragement. The summer months brought comforting warmth to their bodies. The band supported themselves by foraging for food from nature's larder.

Frequent news came their way, always depressing, always of friends or loved ones who had been taken by the curse of evil that scourged these lands. Horrific tales of death and destruction inflicted upon those who had supported Bruce were being received from various sources. Many of those who had fought alongside them had been captured, hung, drawn and quartered. Longshanks had given the orders, under the banner of the Dragon, to give no quarter and to show no mercy. Anyone who was suspected of supporting Bruce was to be punished.

A wave of murder, rape and pillage swept the country. One messenger brought news of Sir Simon Fraser who was captured shortly after the battle at Methven. 'Fraser has suffered the same fate as Wallace, hung, drawn and quartered, his head cut off and placed beside Wallace's shrivelled skull on London Bridge,' the messenger announced. Disgust and revulsion spread though the ranks of Bruce's band of followers.

News arrived that the two good Bishops, Lamberton and Wishart, had been taken prisoner and were being held in chains in the dungeons of some English castle. Douglas, on hearing the fate of Lamberton cursed and swore that he would inflict pain unimaginable on those who committed these evil deeds. 'I have sworn vengeance to my father, my mother and family. I now swear to God Almighty that I will avenge his holy servants who are held by those who perpetrate such evil.'

Those around him looked on in silence; they had seen many a brave man make boastful statements of revenge that were way beyond their ability. However, when Douglas spoke, many took notice. His plans for vengeance, although extremely ambitious, were considered achievable by those who had come to know him over these last few months. 'I'm glad he's on our side,' someone whispered.

As the weeks passed, the battle for survival was not just limited to seeking food and shelter but also waged against the destructive thoughts that attacked the weakened minds of the fugitives. The despair continued, isolation and loneliness sapped the spirit and confidence that they had once abundantly possessed. News was received that Isabel, Countess of Buchan, had been captured and caged for performing the task of placing the crown on the head of Bruce. More followers, worried about the safety of their families, decided to leave the cause and go home.

'Something needs to change,' Bruce declared to his close protectors.

'What do you advise, my Lord?' asked his brother Edward.

'I suggest we head further north, there will be greater distance between us and our hunters.'

'Do you mean we should run further away?' asked Douglas, indicating great impatience and frustration of not being able to do anything.

'My brother Nigel, my beloved Lady Queen Elizabeth, many of the wives and ladies of your good selves are in refuge and in danger of their lives if captured. We must bring them into our protection. We surely know what will happen if they are captured,' declared Bruce.

Neil Campbell voiced the feelings of many. 'It will cause us great effort to provide their safety, but I agree they will be at greater risk if we do not. I long to see my wife, Mary.'

They all agreed to head north and meet with their loved ones.

Their sense of purpose, along with their respect and dignity, was immediately restored when the small group of women joined the company of nobles. The warm, healing power of female love and affection overcame the coldness, despair and dejection of these long drawn out months. Smiles and laughter returned to uplift the spirits and restore hope to this band of Scottish rebels.

A great deal more time would need to be spent hunting and foraging for food. With more mouths to feed, and ones that might be selective in what they eat, the task of hunting had to be more efficient and effective than before. Douglas, impatient as ever, asked his king, 'Sire, if it pleases you, I would ask that I be allowed to lead the hunting and searching for food. It would please me to be of such service to you and your ladies.'

'Are you skilled in these things?' asked Bruce.

'We will not go hungry,' replied Douglas.

A voice called out 'He only wants an excuse to kill something.' Douglas turned around, smiled, and replied 'You may be correct my friend, but I don't think I need an excuse. The rumbling coming from your belly is surely a good enough reason. Why don't you join me?'

'I would be delighted to show you how to hunt,' replied Davidson, who had kept close to Douglas since meeting him at Tweed's Well. Douglas laughed; he looked forward to this challenge.

Over the next few weeks Douglas accompanied by Davidson and a small band of hunters returned repeatedly with fresh game. First venison, partridge and grouse then fish such as salmon and trout were hunted, snared and caught. Douglas provided a mixture of foods, rich in nourishment and energy-restoring properties that fed life back into the band of followers. The late summer months started to yield their riches in wild fruits, nuts and fungi. Douglas shared his skills with others in order that they could assist. However, none could match his hunting skills.

Having recovered from their defeat at Methven, and with the passing summer months aiding the healing of their worn bodies and distressed minds, Bruce and his followers made their way west towards the lands of Argyll.

'We must get away from these treacherous mountains before the onset of winter,' advised Neil Campbell of Kintyre.

Bruce agreed. 'We should head towards the Kintyre peninsular. I would be happy if you could lead us towards your homelands. From there we will be within sailing distance of Carrick,' Bruce suggested to Campbell.

'I would be honoured,' replied Campbell.

They arrived at the north of Strathfillan and rested near Tyndrum. They felt safe here; they lit their fires and enjoyed the comforts of peace and tranquillity.

Bruce approached Douglas. 'I wish you to come a short distance with me.'

'Where?' asked a puzzled looking Douglas.

'Only a short distance. We will be safe,' replied Bruce.

At sunset Bruce paid homage at the nearby holy shrine of St Finnan. Douglas stood guard, as his King knelt in silent prayer. No words were spoken, as Bruce sought forgiveness, and asked for guidance from his creator.

As Douglas looked up at the surrounding hills, he felt uneasy. 'This place is too wide open, we could be observed from miles away,' he thought to himself. As Bruce and Douglas made their way back to their camp Douglas still felt uneasy.

'Sire, I fear for our safety, something does not feel right.'

'My dear Douglas, I have learnt from my misfortune to listen more carefully to what you have to say. What is wrong?' asked Bruce.

'This place is too quiet. Look around you; there is no sound, no movement of any kind. I would expect to see more life in a place such as this; I feel that we are being watched.

'I think you must be mistaken; there are no English for many miles,' stated Bruce, plating down Douglas's concerns.

'Sire, if I am wrong, I apologise.'

'If you are correct, I will never let you out of my sight,' replied Bruce as he laughingly made his way back to camp.

The following morning the small army of Bruce moved on and made their way through a narrow pass at Dalrigh. Large stones littered the surrounding hillside, placed there by the powerful forces of nature in bygone days. The first sign of trouble was when some falling rocks startled one of the leading horses. Several large stones came hurtling down the steep slopes and rolled across their pathway. The riders were severely restricted by the narrowness of the pass and were struggling to protect themselves and their horses. No one showed any concern, other than a respect for the dangerous landscape that they now passed through. Douglas rode up beside his King. 'Sire!' He had not finished his words of concern, when the warrior cries were heard coming from above.

They came out from behind the large boulders; they appeared from nowhere, semi-clothed and with painted faces. Crying out 'Death to the Bruce' they came swarming down upon them, battle-axes waving above their heads. MacDougall, Lord of Lorne, and his clansmen went into battle against Bruce and his party. The wild highlanders lashed out at the bodies of the horses carrying the followers of Bruce. There was confusion and disarray.

Once again, Douglas was immediately beside his King, providing his protection. They instinctively reacted and fought back with great strength and courage. Horse after horse started to fall, brutally slaughtered, as the razor sharp axes cut into their unprotected legs and bodies. Many of their riders suffered the same fate as they also were brought down.

Douglas cut down one attacker who threatened his King with a wild lunge. When a second attacker came up from behind Douglas moved to deflect the blow only to be struck side on by the screaming warrior. A counter-thrust from the injured Douglas ended the life of yet another ill-advised attacker. The main band of MacDougall's warriors was a few seconds away. To stay here meant death. Bruce called out 'Retreat! Retreat! We must go back, protect our ladies.' The group quickly withdrew. Bruce accompanied by his few remaining knights, including the wounded Douglas, protected the rear as the main body made a prompt exit.

Bruce glanced at the wounded Douglas. He owed this young man an apology for not accepting his earlier advice. Several attackers chased Bruce's party. Bruce turned round to meet them head on; there was more room to manoeuvre now that they were out of the tight pass. He charged and brought his sword down on the two leading attackers bringing them to a halt. Those behind them stopped in their tracks, aware that to proceed any further meant death at the hands of Bruce.

MacDougall was raging. Here in front of him was Bruce and his followers who represented less than one quarter of his warrior force of a thousand men, and yet he was unable to prevent Bruce, the focus of his revenge, from cutting down each wave of attack that he sent forward. Bruce continued to stand his ground, the wounded Douglas not far behind watching in admiration every move of his beloved King.

Others glanced behind to see their brave King performing these heroic acts to protect their lives. MacDougall issued instructions to two of his band, the MacIndrosser brothers, who were desperate to have their go at Bruce, to quickly make their way around their prey and ambush him as he retreated. They set off on horseback, accompanied by a third warrior, and attempted to get in front of Bruce and wait in ambush.

As Bruce made his way further into retreat, the three ambushers pounced upon him. The first one leapt towards his horse's bridle, but before he could touch the leather strap, Bruce's sword came down upon him, severing his arm at the shoulder. The second brother grabbed at Bruce's leg, and tried to force him to dismount. Bruce lashed out; the attacker lost his balance, and was then dragged along the ground with his hand caught up in Bruce's stirrup.

The third attacker came at Bruce, screaming obscenities and abuse. With the greatest effort that he could gather, Bruce violently slashed his sword down onto the head of the doomed warrior who immediately fell to ground with blood spurting from his crushed skull. As Bruce made his way back his sword was used for one final act of execution as it pierced the back of the neck of the brother who was caught up in his stirrup. He too fell to the ground lifeless.

MacDougall and his followers immediately stopped in their tracks. This mighty Bruce, who they had just witnessed kill three of their most feared warriors with the greatest of ease, claimed to be the King of Scotland. They looked on in awe. Was he really their true King? Although greater in numbers, they were all afraid to renew the attack. Bruce and his band continued to make their retreat.

Since their enemies blocked their immediate route west, Bruce and his followers made their way towards the Loch of Dochart. The small island castle would provide temporary refuge for their women. As they rested for the night, there was panic in their conversations. Many wanted to leave, many were confused.

'Sire,' asked Douglas. 'I have no difficulty fighting our English enemies, but those warriors today were our own people. Why do they hate us so much, and want to attack us?'

'They don't hate you,' replied Bruce. 'They attack us because their leader, MacDougall, is the son-in-law of John the Red Comyn whom I killed.'

Douglas felt disgusted with himself, as he wiped the blood of the slain Scotsmen from his sword.

The injury to Douglas was not serious, but would take several days to heal. Others were less fortunate as they lay in great pain with crippling wounds that would prevent them taking any more part in this campaign. Many grieved over their dear friends that lay dead back at the pass of Dalrigh.

John, Earl of Atholl, was becoming disillusioned with the King's cause. He looked around him. 'This is not an army, this a group of good loyal servants of our King, who are prepared to suffer blindly as they follow him from one defeat after another in search of their freedom,' he thought to himself. Atholl approached Bruce. 'My dear King, I would like to talk with you. We live in so much fear and pain, we are always journeying without food or rest, and we constantly live with death and injury. We are always in retreat from defeat by our enemies. These sufferings I can no longer bear. I would die for your cause, but I must have rest. I beg you therefore to let me leave your company.'

Bruce appraised Atholl's words keenly. 'Am I asking too much of these loyal sons of Scotland?' he asked of himself. He turned to Atholl. 'Sir Earl, we shall discuss what may be best,' adding kindly 'Wherever you may be, let God grant you defence from your enemies.'

Bruce called those closest to him to discuss their situation. All agreed that they were in great peril if they continued as before. They agreed that the women should go north to Kildrummy accompanied by Atholl and Nigel Bruce. 'We shall continue from here on foot.' Bruce declared. 'Let the ladies have the remaining horses.' They all embraced. They might never meet again but the decision had to be taken. Tears flowed down the faces of the King, the women, the knights and the nobles. The commoners who had come so far felt honoured that they would all be as one from here onwards.

The small party on horseback rode off along Glen Dochart and then headed northwards towards the safety of Kildrummy. Bruce was left with about two hundred men on foot. They dare not go back west to the lands of Lorne. They must also avoid the lands of Perth in the east where Valence, Earl of Pembroke, would still have troops searching for them. To the north lay the treacherous highland mountains. They agreed to head south and made their way around the steep slopes of Ben More. They made their way on foot over a high pass.

When they arrived at Loch Voil near Balquhidder they felt better. The beauty of the magnificent braes lifted their spirits. There was safety, food and shelter to be had in this region. Bruce took refuge in one of the many caves along the steep north shore. From here, they would plan the next stage of their campaign.

9

JOURNEY TO KINTYRE

DOUGLAS WAS SITTING with his back resting against a large boulder. His injury was all but healed; there was no open wound, only bruising from the blow received at Dalrigh, which had resulted in the numbness and swelling of his left arm. The only inconvenience was that for the next few days he could not use his short bow for hunting.

As he sat he gazed over the still waters of the loch, which reflected the mirror image of the surrounding hills. The beauty of this land captivated him. Since he had set out on his quest, he had been inspired and amazed by the sight of the magnificent creations that Mother Nature had provided to this country.

'God has been very generous to us, the rich resources and beautiful lands that we are privileged to live amongst are truly proof of his presence,' he thought to himself. 'Why can't the minds of man be in harmony with this beauty? Why does man not respect our creator and behave accordingly? Why does man have to be so selfish, so cruel and so evil?'

As the word evil went through his mind, he pulled out the long dagger that his brother Hugh had given him. 'Only to be used against evil,' was the request that his brother had gently whispered to him when he gave him this weapon. Douglas started to sharpen the long blade. 'I guess that since it looks like you're going to be very busy, I must keep you in good order.'

Bruce was engaged in deep conversation with Neil Campbell. 'Do you think you would be able to do it?' asked Bruce.

'Yes, if I leave now I would make my way to my homelands by the sea and there I would arrange for your voyage to Kintyre.'

'Where and when shall we meet?' asked Bruce.

'In twelve days time,' replied Campbell. 'Rest for a few days, and then take your men and head south-west towards Stronachlachar and over to Loch Lomond. Do not go north. The loch can be crossed by small boat or raft at the place called Inversnaid. Once on the west bank of the loch make your way south to Tarbet. At Tarbet, there is pass, only a few miles long, that meets with the sea at Loch Long. I will meet you there with ships and provisions.'

'My dear loyal friend, I am deeply grateful for your courage, your support and loyalty. I will not forget your good deeds,' declared Bruce as he embraced Campbell. 'You must take men to assist you,' requested Bruce.

A few days after Campbell had left; Bruce and his remaining army made their way along the route that Campbell had described. It was late afternoon when they finally arrived at Inversnaid on the east bank of the mighty Loch Lomond. A gentle rain had been falling for the last few hours, soaking the small weary army, as they finally stopped at the bank of the deep loch.

Douglas noticed that his King was exhausted from the long journey that they had taken; he also appeared a little dejected. 'Sire, please rest here until we find suitable shelter for you,' Douglas suggested. 'Let me organise a local search of this area to find somewhere safe.'

'Thank you, Douglas, as you can see I am much more suited to travelling on horseback. I appreciate your concern,' said Bruce.

Several men were sent in both directions along the steep loch side to search for a suitable place of shelter. A short time later one returned to say that a cave was found that could accommodate several men. It was agreed that Bruce should take the opportunity to rest; two guards went with him for protection. As he walked Bruce said 'Please search for a way across this loch. I don't advise that we cross during the daylight. However, by morning I would like us all to be on the other side.' Douglas said that he would see to it. The evening hours crept by as Douglas, accompanied by several others, searched for a way to cross this large stretch of open water.

Although the gentle rain continued to fall there was no wind. 'Crossing the loch should be easy,' Douglas suggested to his fellow men.

'Easy! Yes, if you're a bloody duck,' replied one soaking wet companion. They all burst out laughing. 'Shall we make a raft?' asked another. 'If we have no other choice then I would agree that we build a raft. However, I am suspicious,' replied Douglas.

'Suspicious of what?' asked Davidson who never seemed to be far away from Douglas.

'Look around you,' said Douglas. 'There is obviously a great deal of activity in this area. Many people appear to have used this location to cross the loch. Look at the remains of the burnt out fires, look at those markings on the ground. I suspect a boat of some sort may be hidden nearby.'

They continued their search, looking in and around the many bushes and thick bracken that surrounded the loch side.

A loud splash startled them. They all turned to see Douglas wading into the loch. He continued until the water was up to his chest. His head disappeared under the water, submerged for such a long time that it appeared impossible for someone to survive. They ran down to help him. A few moments later, the wooden hull of a small upturned boat rose to the surface and moved slowly towards the shore.

As the upturned bow came nearer, the legs of Douglas could be seen underneath. Helping hands grabbed at the boat and assisted it and Douglas ashore. 'How on earth did you know that it was in there?' asked Davidson.

'Could you have thought of a better place to hide it?' asked the smiling soaking-wet Douglas. Once again, Douglas had amazed those around him with what appeared to be the gift of a sixth sense.

With the daylight hours all but gone, a partial moon in the cloudless sky illuminated the calm waters of the loch. The rain had stopped. Douglas had managed to dry himself from the heat of a small fire, which he and several others were huddled round. The still evening silence was frequently broken by the sound of tawny owls as they intermixed their calls of 'hoo-hoos' with squeaks of 'ke-wicks'.

Bruce approached and apologised to those present. 'I deeply regret that I have been a burden to you all. The next stage of our journey will hopefully see our fortunes change.' Several spoke up in support and offered words of encouragement.

'Douglas has found a small boat. We can now cross the loch,' declared the brother of Neil Campbell. 'My brother will honour his promise to arrange boats to take us to safety. If we cross the loch tonight we can make good progress.'

Bruce looked at Douglas and smiled. 'Another good deed my young friend. You are beginning to make a reputation of yourself, one of which your father would be very proud.'

'Thank you, Sire. If it pleases you, I would advise that we start crossing now; it will take many hours to get everyone over.'

The small boat was only large enough to carry three men along with their belongings. Several volunteered to swim alongside with the protection of a safety rope should they get into difficulty. The plan was agreed. Bruce asked Douglas to join him in the first crossing. A short time later, the two of them set foot on the opposite bank. The third man returned with the boat to the bank at Inversnaid. Douglas lit a small fire in order to guide the returning boat back to the same spot. The whole process was repeated many times throughout the long night and into the dawn.

Once the whole group were dried out and safely assembled on the west bank of the loch, they made their way south towards Tarbet. They headed along the west pass that dropped down to the sea at Loch Long. When they first caught the sight and smell of the seawater their hearts lifted. They could sense that a new and hopefully more successful part of their journey was about to commence. Their view of the loch improved as they drew nearer, and they saw that the tide was out and that no ships were visible.

They continued to head south and agreed to take refuge up in the glen above Craggan. From here, they would have a clear view down the loch, and would be able to watch for Campbell's approaching ships. The glen would also provide an escape route to the east if required, as well as a place for shelter and possibly good hunting for those with the right skills.

Campbell was not expected to arrive for several days. Bruce and his small army needed to continue to hunt to support themselves. Bruce was feeling more positive and cheerful than he had for a very long time.

On hearing that they were to go hunting, Douglas approached Bruce and asked. 'Sire, let me take some men in order that I can provide for you.'

'My dear Douglas, is there no end to your kindness and loyal support. I feel that I could be accused of taking advantage of your excellent hunting skills,' replied Bruce.

'Sire, there is nothing on this earth that I would rather do,' answered Douglas.

'Let me then make a suggestion to you, young Douglas. Let us both take a party of men each, and spend the whole day hunting. Let's see who has been the most successful come dusk.'

Early the following morning, Bruce and Douglas, accompanied by a few helpers, set out to hunt either side of the glen. It was dry with a slight breeze blowing from the north-east. The King headed up over to the south ridge, and with the wind at his back his party were confident that their day would be fruitful. Douglas asked his men to stop and sit down. 'Are we not supposed to be trying to beat them?' asked one of them. 'Please be patient,' replied Douglas. 'Let's sit here for a moment, look at the clouds above, which way are they moving? Feel that breeze, where is it coming from? Look up the glen, where would the deer be most likely grazing? Where would they find water?'

No one answered, but they understood what Douglas was suggesting. Rushing up the glen, without due thought, would frighten every living creature for miles. Taking their time to study the surrounding conditions and anticipating the behaviour of their prey would prove to be more productive with less effort. The first few hours of preparation proved to be effective for Douglas and his party. They slowly and cautiously hunted their prey with great efficiency; they brought down a young buck, caught grazing by the small burn that flowed down the glen. They stalked several wildfowl feeding on the nearby grassy banks. Other unsuspecting creatures became the targets of Douglas's deadly archery skills.

Bruce and his men had long disappeared over the south ridge. Their success was limited, the wind at their back signalling their presence on several unsuccessful attempts to bring down a grazing deer. They circled round a small herd. 'This looks better,' whispered one of them as they crawled forward on all fours. Suddenly the heads of the beasts were up in the air. Something had startled them; the sound of a horn being blown could be heard in the distance.

'What the hell was that?' asked one of the frustrated hunters. The sound of the horn could be heard again, only this time getting closer. 'Let's wait, and see who comes our way. Stay under cover,' ordered Bruce. A short time later, a band of about ten hunters with horns blowing came in the opposite direction. As they approached, Bruce and his men tried to see who they were, without giving away their own presence.

'It's Lennox,' shouted Bruce in excitement. The unsuspecting band of hunters, led by the Earl of Lennox, were taken by surprise when Bruce and his small band jumped out in front of them. 'My King, my Lord, may God be thanked, you are alive,' cried Lennox as he ran towards his beloved Bruce. Full of joy, they embraced, embarrassed in front of their men as they wiped tears of happiness from their smiling faces.

Lennox introduced his King. 'My dear men, this is Robert Bruce of Carrick, the rightful King of Scotland who will unite and lead our nation against our enemies.' Lennox's men knelt before their King and expressed their loyalty. Bruce and Lennox exchanged news.

'We are camped down the glen,' said Bruce. 'My men are in need of food, hence the need to hunt.'

'Why are you, our King, out hunting? Surely you have good men who could perform this task?' asked Lennox.

'We are resting here for a few days, and I have challenged one of my most loyal protectors to a day's hunting,' replied Bruce. 'Who would that be?' asked Lennox. 'James Douglas, son of Lord William,' answered Bruce. 'If he is anything like his father, you will have great difficulty matching his skills,' replied Lennox. 'I have already discovered that I have no chance of matching his hunting skills,' answered Bruce.

'May I suggest that your hunting for today be now over?' requested Lennox. 'My men and I have ample food to offer you and your men'

Bruce thanked them. 'Please join us in our camp,' he requested. As they made their way back down the glen, Bruce and Lennox continued their conversation.

'What is this glen named?' asked Bruce. 'I don't believe there is a specific name,' answered Lennox. 'It's been very good to us today,' replied Bruce.

Towards the end of the day, Douglas and his small band of men returned to their camp with the fruits of their highly successful day's hunt, full of self-pride and admiration of their own skills in the search for food. There was no way that anyone (King or otherwise) could have been more successful hunting in that glen that day.

As they walked into the camp, they were amazed at the sight that greeted them. Bruce and his men were eating and drinking their fill. An abundance of food had appeared. Had Bruce and his small group been more successful?

Bruce approached Douglas, as his men delivered to the camp enough food to feed many. 'My dear Douglas, we have good news.' Bruce went on to describe the meeting with Lennox and the provisions that had been given. 'You have surely won today's hunting competition,' announced Bruce. There were cheerful cries of, 'Well done, my lords,' as the small army felt comfortable that they had sufficient food for a few days.

Still feeling excited about the success of the day's hunt; one of Douglas's men was overheard stating, 'Douglas appeared to know every inch of that glen like the back of his hand.' Bruce, on hearing these comments, and feeling that he had slightly cheated his young noble friend, called him over. 'Douglas, once again you have proved yourself, and in recognition of your achievements I name this glen in your honour. From this day on, this place shall be known as the Glen of Douglas.' Douglas bowed his head; he was deeply humbled by such a simple act of recognition from his beloved King.

Bruce and his army continued to take refuge in the safety of Glen Douglas. From several hundred feet above the sea level they watched and waited for the return of Neil Campbell.

Several days later, the midday sun shone down on the west coast of Scotland. The warm wind sent pulsating waves of continuous movement up the sea lochs, and onwards to penetrate the nooks and crannies of the Argyll hills and glens. The long grasses and ferns were bending over, twisting and turning in harmony as if being stroked by a giant invisible comb that appeared to be sweeping the country with a powerful but gentle force. In the skies above, the irregular flow of small clouds were rushing by, casting their gentle shadows down below, and stimulating the many colours of this magnificent land to spectacularly respond to the changing rays of light from above.

A lone eagle appeared from over the north ridge of Glen Douglas and could be seen soaring effortlessly above, as it hunted in the delight and pleasure of these magnificent surroundings. Its yelping 'Kaa' could be heard from below. Many looked up and marvelled at the beauty and awesome power of this unique and magnificent creature.

'A ship!' a voice called out, 'I can see a ship!' The lookout pointed down towards Loch Long. They all rose to their feet, excited with the prospect of heading towards the safety of their destination in Kintyre. Bruce requested Douglas to arrange for a signal in order to identify their position to the ship. The other nobles were asked to round up the men and make their way down to the edge of the sea loch. Several more ships could be seen on the horizon.

Douglas, accompanied by his good friend Davidson, built two fires about fifty yards apart. As the fires started to ignite, they collected and prepared fresh green vegetation, which was still damp from the overnight dew. 'Shall we throw it on now?' asked Davidson, as he prepared to start the signal. 'Not just yet,' replied Douglas. 'We don't know who could be watching.' As the ships came up the Loch, they waited. 'Not long to go now,' declared Douglas.

The first ship was a few hundred yards from passing by the glen, when Douglas shouted over to Davidson 'Now!' The pillars of white smoke shot straight up as they both piled the damp vegetation on top of the fires. A cloud of smoke caught Douglas's breath and caused him to cough violently. 'Here take this and if you can blow louder than me then you may keep it,' said Douglas, as he handed Davidson his hunting horn. Davidson took a deep breath and blew as loud as he could. The haunting sound drifted across the loch. 'It's now yours my good friend. Let's go!' cried Douglas. As they both headed down towards the loch side, they could see that the first ship was turning in towards them.

Several hours later, Bruce and his diminished army were heading down the Firth of Clyde, as the ships brought by Neil Campbell took them to the safety of Kintyre. The wind that had aided the speedy arrival of these good friends and their mighty ships now became a burden. Bruce's army took to the oars. With the Argyll hills fading in the distance, and the rugged Arran mountains appearing on the horizon, the fleet made its way in between the islands of Bute and Cumbrae.

Their arms started to ache, as the pain of stretching and straining the infrequently used muscles started to take is toll. A rotational system was agreed where each man got a period of rest every hour. As the fleet passed by the little island of Cumbrae, they turned and headed west to the Cock of Arran.

'We must not go down the east coast of Arran,' advised Neil Campbell as he spoke with Bruce.

'I agree,' replied Bruce. 'We could be easily spotted from the Ayrshire coast. Best to keep to the west.'

The wind took a turn for the better as they headed down the Kilbrannan Sound. They were able to ease up on the oars as the powerful force of nature carried them southwards. The men were in cheerful spirits, some singing, some laughing. Their aching arms and blistered hands were a small price to pay for the pleasure of this journey through paradise.

Douglas, who had taken his turn at the oars, sat quietly alone. His mind was elsewhere. He thought to himself 'Since I have joined with these good men, I have been in constant retreat from our enemies.' He looked uncomfortable and ill at ease with his present situation. 'Now that we head to Kintyre, more retreat, more hiding. When will we take the initiative and become the pursuers of those who invade our lands and take our freedom?'

The ships had turned west and were now heading into the Mull of Kintyre. Douglas stood up and looked back. Across the sea to the east, he could see the outline of the Carrick hills, and far beyond these hills was his home in Douglasdale. As he looked out into the distance, he gently touched his only three possessions: his sword, his dagger and his coat of arms. 'Will I ever return?' he asked himself sadly, and sighed.

The fleet arrived at Kintyre in the late evening. A small band of friends and relations of Neil Campbell, who were also loyal supporters of Bruce, waited to greet their visitors. Angus MacDonald of Islay and Lord of Kintyre came out to meet his prestigious guests.

'My Dear King, Robert Bruce,' I welcome you to these lands. You and your party are most welcome here. I offer you the safety of Dunaverty Castle, I offer you food and provisions, and I offer you my men for your protection.'

Bruce thanked his host for his kindness and humanity, for the gifts, which he gladly accepted, and for the loyalty demonstrated to his crown.

A few days later Douglas approached Bruce. 'Sire, what plans do you have as the winter months are nearly upon us?'

Bruce, concerned, answered 'My dear, Douglas for one so young, you are a credit to your father and to the good name of Douglas. As you can see our numbers are small. Even with your great determination and courage there is very little that we can do until we acquire greater resources. MacDonald has been very kind and supportive to us, but we can't rely on one man alone.'

'Do you plan to stay here?' asked Douglas.

'No, we must move on. I wish to head over to the island of Rathlin where I may be able to gather support from our Irish neighbours. I also wish to send out messengers to all parts of our lands to seek additional support. I am concerned also for the safety of our ladies who went north to Kildrummy. I need to find out about their welfare.'

Bruce looked into the eyes of Douglas. 'James, you looked troubled. What do you wish to do?'

Douglas looked back at his King with a serious look in his face, yet one not without a hint of mischief and devilment. 'From now on, I stop retreating from our enemies. The next time I see the English they will be running away from me in fear of their lives.'

Bruce, with a wide grin, replied 'That's something I would dearly like to witness. Why don't you wait here for my return in the early spring?'

10

RETURN TO CARRICK

DURING THE WINTER months, Douglas remained at Kintyre where he earned his keep by offering his skills to support the efforts of his kind hosts. His impatience continued to cause him great restlessness and uneasiness. His thoughts were constantly returning to the welfare of his family and to his good people of Douglas. He had great difficulty in sleeping and burnt up his excess energy by hunting and performing some of the many manual labouring tasks necessary during the cold winter months. His suppressed anger was partially released each time he made a kill whilst out hunting. His hosts were delighted with their guest, who more than paid for his keep.

As the first sign of spring arrived, Douglas was no longer the innocent, shy reserved youth that had joined up with Bruce and his band almost a year ago. He had grown stronger and broadened out, his tall frame filled with solid, flexible muscle that had been earned by hard work and nourished by his productive hunting skills. He had also grown in maturity, astuteness and awareness of everything around him. His perception and ability to anticipate the behaviour of others provided him with a weapon that was more lethal than his deadly sword or bow. Others marvelled at the fine qualities that this young man possessed. His gentleness, consideration and kindness towards others humbled those who knew him. Children would flock to him for attention; he would spend many hours entertaining their young minds with tales of travel and adventure. Other men wanted to be in his friendly company. The elders looked to Douglas as a perfect role model for their youngsters to follow.

The young women too were attracted to Douglas. He was the most desirable of all the single young men in their company. He gave them the same attention and kindness as others. However, those who were looking for more intimate affections had arrived too early in his life. Douglas had to fight within himself, as the desires of nature battled against the will and determination of his destiny.

In the early spring of 1307, Bruce returned to Kintyre. Sir Robert Boyd had also arrived, having escaped capture at Kildrummy. He had news for the King. Other messengers too had arrived with news from around the country. As each one took his turn to speak with their King, Bruce grew more and more concerned.

First news of his brother Nigel, taken to Berwick, hanged and beheaded. The Earl of Atholl, taken to London, hanged and beheaded. Christopher Seton, captured not long after the battle at Methven, hung, drawn and quartered. The Countess of Buchan who had placed the crown on the head of Bruce, along with his beloved sister Mary Bruce, the wife of Neil Campbell, both taken and hung in cages from the battlements of Berwick and Roxburgh castles. Marjorie, the daughter of Bruce, imprisoned in a nunnery in England. Christina Bruce, wife of Christopher Seton, imprisoned in an English convent. Finally Queen Elizabeth, wife of Bruce, taken to England and placed under house arrest at Burstwick-in-Holderness.

Bruce's distress and grief for his lost loved ones was visible, and those close to him offered such kind words of comfort as they could. Their King needed their support more now than at any other time. Douglas quietly stood nearby. He had no words of comfort to offer to his King. His desire for revenge against the perpetrators of these evil deeds filled his head and breast with constant anger. His frustrations were added to when he heard the many tales of treachery and treason from his own fellow Scottish nobles. 'How could they? How could they betray their own people? And take sides with the English?' he thought to himself.

News had arrived that English forces had heard of Bruce's whereabouts and were ready to set sail to Kintyre. There was great discussion and intense argument about what they should do next and where should they go.

Douglas spoke. 'The poor folks of this country have great hope and expectations of us, and yet we lie here idle. I hear that the castle of Brodick, situated on the isle Arran, is occupied by an English garrison. Let me go and remove them, for it is does not belong to them.'

'I agree,' cried out Sir Robert Boyd. 'There is little reason for staying here longer. I know that island very well and I have been inside the castle.'

Bruce gave his approval.

'Who wishes to go with me?' asked Douglas of those around him.

'You can count on me,' shouted Davidson as he walked over to stand beside his friend Douglas.

Suddenly a stranger, someone who had recently arrived and who was standing in the background, called out 'Why do you need anyone to go with you, after all you are the Douglas?' Everyone turned round to look at this stranger. Douglas had briefly heard the words but was unable to recognise the voice or to see the face.

'Who are you Sir? Please announce yourself,' someone asked. The stranger walker towards Douglas as others moved out of the way. 'Let Douglas answer,' said the stranger.

'Cuthbert!' cried Douglas. The two friends rushed towards each other and embraced. Tears, which were strangers to the face of Douglas, filled his eyes with the happiness of this reunion.

'My Lords, my friends, this is my good companion Stuart Cuthbert, loyal servant to my father and guardian to me during my early years. There is none other that I would have beside me in battle. He taught me most of what I now know.'

'You embarrass me, young James,' replied Cuthbert, whose battle-scared body commanded the rightful respect for such a proven warrior. Douglas stood between his two good friends Cuthbert and Davidson. 'I believe that I have all the men that I need; however, should anyone else wish to join us they would be most welcome.' Several stepped forward and pledged their support to the task of taking Brodick Castle.

Douglas knelt before his King. 'Sire, I pledge to fight for the return of your rightful lands. First I will take Brodick. In ten days time, please join me, when we can then prepare your return to Carrick.' Bruce thanked his loyal friend, and granted his leave to perform this heroic task.

It was late afternoon when the small party set off for the island of Arran. Douglas, accompanied by Cuthbert, Davidson, Sir Robert Boyd and two other loyal men, set sail with determination and total commitment that they would succeed in their planned raid on the stronghold of Brodick Castle.

The wind direction was to their advantage, as they cut across the Kilbrannan Sound and headed towards the southern end of the large island. They paused for a short time against the protective shadow of the small Holy Isle. As darkness descended on the Firth of Clyde, they lowered their sails, and took to the oars. They quietly passed around Clauchlands Point, and slowly entered into the still waters of Brodick Bay. Silently and with gentle movements of their oars, they pulled against the tidal currents and slowly passed under the torch-lit battlements of Brodick. They could hear shouting and laughter from the castle above as they quietly rowed towards the shore, and landed on the edge of Merkland Wood.

Without uttering a single word they all got out and pulled their boat out of the water. They covered it up amongst the protection of several thick gorse bushes at the edge of the wood. They then hid the rest of their equipment close by, and took refuge in the wood within sight of the castle.

Douglas agreed to take the first watch, and then to pass the same task on to each one of his party in turn. In the darkness he gazed out from the camouflage of the dense wood and scanned the moonlit bay for any sign of movement, then looked forward towards the tall castle. No sign of any life existed.

After several minutes of repeating his observation checks, something caught his eye. It was not a movement but a stillness, high up on the sand bank, and about fifty yards away he saw the outline of three boats. There was something strange about the way these boats were positioned. They looked as if they had been dragged up the beach as far as humanly possible. They appeared to have been taken right up alongside the rocks at the foot of the castle. Douglas wondered why. In the darkness of night, he strained his eyes and tried to avoid his imagination taking over.

He crawled out from his hiding place, silently making his way towards the three boats. He gently made his way along the edge of the rocks, then, on all fours, he slowly inched towards his target. As he got closer, his suspicions grew stronger. 'There is something in those boats,' he thought to himself. Finally, as he came in touch with the first boat, he heard voices from the castle and immediately lay flat on the sand beside the first boat. The two guards stood on the battlements and talked for several minutes before moving on. Douglas stood up and checked the contents of the first boat. He repeated the same exercise with the other two.

When he returned to the safety of the wood, Douglas finished the remainder of his watch and then woke the next member of his party. 'Davidson,' whispered Douglas. 'Listen very carefully. You must keep a close eye on those boats. Do not go near. Pass the message that should anyone come out of the castle we are all to be immediately wakened. Do not fail me.'

The outline of the three boats started to become more visible as the hours of darkness began retreat. The tide was in and almost touching the first boat. Cuthbert was on watch when Douglas crawled up beside him.

'Can you see anything?' he asked as he rubbed his sleepy eyes.

'No,' replied Cuthbert. 'But I do suspect that those boats appear to be full of something.'

'They are full of provisions for the English garrison,' replied Douglas. 'I suspect that they may have arrived just before us last night, and have still to empty the contents. I would expect them to come out while the tide is high to finish their task and possibly return to the mainland.'

'Shall I waken the rest?' asked Cuthbert.

'What do you think?' replied Douglas, who felt uncomfortable giving orders to his partial guardian of many years.

'I say yes.'

The remainder of Douglas's party were wakened and alerted to the situation. They all lay in wait for the castle gates to open.

A short time later, while the twilight hours were melting into dawn, shouting could be heard coming from the castle battlements. 'All clear!' cried the sentry guard. The solid castle doors swung open and then a group of about ten English soldiers came out and made their way down towards the boats.

'Wait!' whispered Douglas as he put his hand on the shoulder of Davidson who was desperate to bolt out and attack. 'There will be more troops still to come out. Let's wait till they empty the first boat,' advised Douglas, as he calmed and prepared his men for battle.

As the first group started to unload the provisions from the nearest boat, a second group of about twenty joined them. This group consisted of mainly English troops but also contained several Scots who had joined the other side. They proceeded to carry back the goods to the castle. The first boat was almost empty when Douglas got ready to give the signal. 'Look! Take notice, many of them don't have arms, and those who do, when their hands are full, that's when we go in.'

Several of the enemy soldiers were inside two of the boats when Douglas and his men charged. But when they sprinted forward towards their prey, they did so silently. The normal custom of shouting and yelling battle cries was abandoned, as Douglas and his men tried to make the most of the advantage of surprise. They were helped by the soft sand which muffled the sound of their footsteps as they closed in on their targets.

The bulk of the English troops had their backs to their attackers, and it was not until one of the men in the nearest boat looked up as he was lifting a large bundle that Douglas was spotted. By then he was almost upon them. The cry went out 'Look out!' It was too late, as Douglas lunged in with his sword. The first victim collapsed dead on the spot, before he had time to realise what was happening. Cuthbert also caught his targeted victim unawares as he too brought instant death to an unsuspecting enemy. An armed English soldier turned to meet Davidson, but the momentum and determination from the Dumfries-born warrior carried his sword straight into the chest of his victim, who became the third casualty.

With the element of surprise now gone, Douglas and his men shouted and screamed as they cut down their terrified enemy. The others, inspired with the confidence of seeing the first of their enemies falling so effortlessly, also brought down their chosen targets. The scene became more of an execution than a battle, as Douglas and his small fearless band of warriors took their vengeance.

The Scots who had joined up with the English garrison ran for their lives. The English panicked and split into two groups. A small handful of unarmed troops rushed to push the empty boat towards the water's edge and attempted to make their escape to the sea. The others ran towards the castle gates. Douglas called out, 'After them! Don't let them reach the gates!' His men immediately responded and chased after their enemy. Many were caught and slain before they could reach the safety of the castle.

The noise and bedlam of the slaughter had attracted the attention of those inside the castle walls. More troops, followed by Sir John Hastings and other English knights, blindly rushed out to deal with the small number of attackers. Douglas and his men did not let up, the combination of dead bodies and sight of English troops running in fear of their lives further fuelling their confidence. Douglas called on his men to rush the castle gates. When Hastings and his knights saw these fearsome, ruthless warriors continue to slay those who stood in their way, they retreated into the sanctuary of the castle walls. The doors were slammed shut before Douglas and his men could enter.

Douglas and his victorious band of men turned and made their way back to the shore. The small group of English troops who had a short time ago escaped by boat were drifting in the tidal currents. Without oars or sail, they were unable to control their craft and drifted helplessly out to sea.

Douglas gathered his men. 'This day we have taken a small step on the long journey to achieving our purpose. We have proven to ourselves that brave hearts alone will not win victory. Today we beat our enemy as result of cunning and surprise; from now on these tactics will be our main weapons of war.' They all cheered and congratulated each other on their magnificent victory.

The remaining boats were launched out to sea. The group split in two and rowed south back across the thick mist of Brodick Bay. With ample supplies of food, clothing and other essential items, they were delighted with the results of their captures. Their pace had considerably slowed down as the efforts of the morning battle started to take its toll. As they approached the south side of the bay, and being well out of sight of the castle, Douglas gave the instruction to pull into the estuary leading into Glen Cloy.

The band of successful warriors made their way up into the head of the glen where they set up camp and waited for the arrival of their King. They feasted on the good food and wines that they had acquired from their enemy. They each relived the excitement and great satisfaction that this rare taste of victory had given them. Sir Robert Boyd, who had played a significant part in the victory, but had not said very much, called out. 'My dear fellow Scots, today I am immensely proud to be in your good company. We have not just beaten our enemy; we have become united as one, in the joy of victory, which I have not experienced for a very long time.'

They all nodded in approval. Douglas, spoke up: 'Our enemy is ourselves, our lack of faith and confidence in what we can achieve has held us back on many occasions. Together and with the guiding grace of God we can achieve much more.' There was a still silence as each member of the band quietly reflected on the meanings behind these words. Cuthbert said nothing, but his eyes lit up, and a proud smile spread over his face as he looked towards his good friend Douglas.

Several days later Bruce and his fleet arrived on the other side of the island. As they sailed up the Kilbrannan Sound, they scanned the coast for a suitable place to land. The bay at Drumadoon appeared to offer the best shelter and protection for the many boats. Bruce, and a few close loyal protectors, took refuge in a cave a few miles north of the bay. Several messengers were sent out in search of news of Douglas and his small band of men.

A few days later, two of Bruce's messengers, accompanied by a local woman who lived on a small farm midway between Brodick and Drumadoon, arrived at the cave entrance. 'Please tell our King Robert that we have news for him,' requested one of the men. 'What news do you have?' asked Bruce. One of the messengers gestured to the local woman, who appeared to be mesmerised by seeing the King of Scotland for the first time. 'Tell me, my good lady, have you seen any strangers in these parts in the last few days?' asked Bruce.

'Yes, Sire,' said the woman in a quiet voice, 'I can indeed tell you of strangers who have arrived here. About one week ago, they attacked the castle at Brodick and were victorious in slaying many of the garrison. These were no ordinary men. They silently came out of the early morning mist, terrifying and scattering the traitors who had joined the English. Many of the garrison were killed. Very few remain. These men fought with great courage and strength that this island had not seen before. Many tales are being told of their victory. The people of this island are more fearful of these Scottish warriors than they are of the English.'

'The people of this island have nothing to fear from these men, for they fight for my cause,' replied Bruce, 'Can you take me to them?' Without further delay, Bruce, along with about ten armed followers, accompanied the woman as she made her way back over the island. A few hours later, they stopped at the top of a small hill midway across the island.

'Down there,' said the woman, pointing, 'in the wooded glen. It is in there that they camp.' Bruce thanked the woman and gave her a generous reward for her help.

Bruce and his men continued down the glen. As they approached, Bruce blew his horn. Douglas was the first to recognise the sound. 'That's our King's horn,' he called out. A second blast was heard. Robert Boyd, who had missed the first call, immediately called out. 'That is surely our King; I know the sound of that horn.'

Both groups made their way towards each other, careful at first in case they were being led into a trap. 'Let me go look first,' suggested Douglas. As he looked out from the protection of the wood, he could see his King and the small band coming down the glen. Douglas waved for the others to follow him.

When the King saw his loyal friends, he was delighted; they embraced and congratulated each other on the success of their journey. Sir Robert Boyd, who was full of praise and admiration of Douglas and his brave men, started to tell his King of the successful victory. 'No need to tell me about your victory,' declared Bruce. 'The whole island is aware of your success; word has spread. What you have achieved at Brodick will be remembered as the first successful battle of our campaign. Well done to all of you.' They all stood and thanked their King for his appreciation. Douglas gently moved into the background, for he felt uneasy about the possibility of acquiring a fearsome reputation.

Douglas and his band invited the King into their small camp in Glen Cloy, where they showed him the plunder from their victory. He was pleased that what they had acquired would feed his men for many days. Feeling safe in their numbers, and with their reputation having spread throughout the island, they decided to remain in this camp for one more night.

The next morning Bruce gathered his close followers and advisers around him. 'My dear friends and good people, whilst spending time in the cave, north of Drumadoon, I have had time to think on where we go from here. I do not want us to continue to roam our country in retreat from our enemies. What you have achieved at Brodick must be repeated elsewhere.'

'What do you wish us to do?' asked one of his followers.

'We will sail over to my homelands of Carrick, and enquire as to how the people feel about me and our cause,' answered Bruce.

Douglas spoke up. 'Sire, may I suggest that someone go on ahead and enquire as to these things you seek. If the land is safe, we can then all proceed. If not, then we do not put you or ourselves at risk.'

Bruce smiled. 'Who amongst you will take upon themselves this task? It will have to be someone who knows that land and can find out these things for us.'

Cuthbert stepped forward. 'Dear sirs, my King, if it please you I would go, for I am from that land. My father was from Galston to the east, my mother from Ayr. I have dwelt many years in that part of country. I have many friends who would aid me.' Bruce looked at Cuthbert. He did not know him very well, and was unsure if he could be trusted. The King glanced at Douglas for approval. Douglas answered with an approving nod of his head.

'My friend Cuthbert, as you are true to Douglas you are true to me also. Please prepare for your journey. Find out these things for me. When you are satisfied as to the safety of that land, I would ask that you signal by lighting a fire at Turnberry Point. Allow yourself one week from now. We will watch for your signal.'

Cuthbert thanked his King for the trust placed in him, and requested that he be allowed to leave now. Douglas approached Cuthbert. 'Please be careful my friend, for I will have much need of you in the future,' he said. Both friends embraced for a short moment before Cuthbert took his leave.

The King, along with Douglas and most of the others, agreed to make their way to the south of the island. The castle of Kildonan, which belonged to MacDonald of the Isles, would provide the ideal sanctuary and the perfect viewpoint to wait for the signal from Cuthbert. A small handful of troops were sent back to advise the rest of the fleet to await their instructions.

Cuthbert landed at Ayr. Here he spent time amongst many old friends that he had not seen since the time he rode with William Douglas, the father of young James. He avoided talking about Bruce and his cause, but enquired as to the loyalty of these people. He sensed that their allegiance was to their King. However, the fear and retribution that had been inflicted by their enemies had torn them apart. There was now disarray and treachery. Their first loyalty was in protecting their own lives, and whoever provided them with safety and security would be repaid by their support.

Sir Henry de Percy, who had been given these lands by Longshanks and who garrisoned at Turnberry Castle with around three hundred men, provided that forced and costly protection.

Cuthbert heard many stories of great cruelty inflicted on these people by Percy, such that all in these lands obeyed him.

Cuthbert headed south, visiting many villages. In Maybole, Girvan, the feelings of the people were the same: fear dictated who received their loyalty. He made his way to Maidens Bay, a short distance from Turnberry Point. Cuthbert's mind was in turmoil. These people of Carrick lived in fear, and there was only one solution for their salvation. However, his loyalty to his King and to his good friend and almost brother Douglas meant he could not light the fire, for to do so would surely lead Bruce and his followers to their death. 'What do I do?' he asked of himself.

As Cuthbert stood on the beach at Maidens, the daylight hours passed away, and a full mood illuminated the calm seawaters of the Firth of Clyde. He could see the glow of fires in the distance from dwellings on the island of Arran. He still did not know what to do; no solution entered his mind. He thought of his good friend Douglas. 'What would he do?' he asked of himself. He looked south down the coast to Turnberry and with immense horror realised that the decision had been made for him. Someone had lit a large fire at the tip of the point. The flames leapt up a great height, and would surely be seen by Bruce and his men on Arran.

On Arran, a guard on the castle of Kildonan spotted the fire and duly informed his King. Each of Bruce's nobles felt sure that this was indeed the signal from Cuthbert. The nobles advised their King. 'We must make our way now, in order that we arrive during the darkness and without being discovered.'

'I agree,' said Bruce 'Get ready, signal to the rest of our fleet.' With their belongings, already prepared in anticipation of the signal being given, they quickly made their way towards their boats.

As Bruce made his way towards the vessel, his hostess, a relative of MacDonald of the Isles, came towards him and whispered to him. 'My King, take good heed of my words as you pass forth on your voyage to avenge the harm and outrage inflicted by those who invade your lands. Be assured that no force or strength of hand shall cause you to leave this country. You shall endure many sufferings before your campaign has ended, but you will overcome each one.' Bruce thanked her for her kind words of comfort and reassurance.

About an hour later, the full fleet was making its way across the Firth of Clyde and heading towards the bright burning fire at Turnberry. God was with them, as the skies clouded over and blocked out the light from the full moon.

With the distant fire burning bright over on the mainland, Bruce's fleet held a straight course as they headed towards Turnberry Point. A gentle breeze helped them make good progress and the clouds above continued to obscure the full moon. They sailed on blindly; guided by the fire which they assumed had been lit by Cuthbert.

The situation that Cuthbert found himself in caused him great anguish. He continued to fear for the friends and loyal countrymen who sailed towards him. He immediately collected driftwood from along the sandy shore. 'If I light a second fire, I may be able to warn them off,' he thought to himself. In the panic he was unable to determine how far out Bruce's fleet might be, and had no idea as to when they might arrive. 'If I light this fire too early, they may not see it, too late and they may not be able to do anything,' he thought to himself. In the darkness he searched along Maidens beach and found a small sheltered cove out of sight of Turnberry Point. Here he would light his fire, which would only be seen by those approaching from the sea. He continued to throw more driftwood onto the small pile, and had it prepared and ready to ignite.

Cuthbert walked a straight line down to the water's edge; he repeatedly glanced between the fire at Turnberry and the darkness out at sea. He waited and waited. The gentle breeze of the last few hours was starting to pick up speed. He looked up to the skies above, and saw that there was turbulence as the clouds passed over. Suddenly there was gap, and for a few seconds the moonlight partially illuminated the seas below. He saw what he was looking for. About two miles out to sea he could see the sails of many ships heading towards him. He quickly ran back to the pile of driftwood and turned round.

As he prepared to ignite the small fire, Cuthbert looked out again; the clouds had once more blocked out the light from above. As he waited a second break in the clouds occurred but, on again looking out to sea, Cuthbert was shocked when he saw nothing. The ships had gone. Had he imagined them? He knew he had to regain his composure. 'Why would they disappear? Where are they? I did see them,' he thought to himself. As he tried to find an explanation for the disappearance, he thought what it would be like to be on one of those ships. A smile of relief passed across his face. 'They don't want to be seen in the moonlight. They have dropped their sails. They must be rowing from now on.'

Cuthbert waited for a short time and then decided to light his fire. The flames started to take hold and generate light around the secluded cove. 'I need to signal,' he thought to himself. He took hold of his woollen shawl and as the flames grew stronger, he stood in front of the fire and intermittently blocked its view from the sea with the unrolled garment. As he continued to signal, the first boat arrived. He ran down to the shore's edge. The men were rowing with extreme caution. The other boats were further back out at sea and waiting on the signal to come in. With swords drawn, Bruce, Douglas, and other armed nobles carefully stepped ashore.

Cuthbert ran into the shallow water to meet his King and friends. Bruce approached him first. 'Sire, I tried to warn you. These lands are not safe. The locals all appear to be siding with your enemies. Lord Percy has a garrison of well over three hundred men outside that castle above the bright burning fire.' In the panic and desperation, Cuthbert was losing his breath. 'They all hate you more than they hate anything else,' he nervously gasped.

'Traitor! Why then did you light that fire?' shouted Bruce, as he made to grab hold of Cuthbert. Douglas rushed forward and stood between his two good friends.

'Please take time to explain,' requested Douglas.

'Sirs, as God is my creator, I swear I did not light that fire, nor know why, or who has done so. However, from when I first saw it, I was sure that you would all be sailing towards it with great haste. I did light that small fire to enable me to divert you away from the dangers that await you over there.'

Bruce placed his hand on the shoulder of Cuthbert. 'My good man I was wrong to doubt your loyalty, for you have truly performed a good deed this night.' The King turned to his close council of nobles and asked for their advice. Sir Edward, brother of Bruce, spoke out. 'I will not be driven back to sea. I say that we go on; my fortune I will take here, good or bad.' 'Hear, hear!' others called out.

Cuthbert asked to speak. 'Sirs the people of these lands live in fear of their lives; the cruelty inflicted by Percy and his men is the reason for them not supporting their rightful King. If we can weaken Percy's stronghold over them, then I say this, my Lord Bruce, you will start to regain your support and your lands.' Without further debate, the decision was agreed.

Bruce made one final comment. 'Percy, under Longshanks's instructions, has terrorised our lands with his cruel deeds, and filled our people's minds with hatred. With the blessing of our Lord God, let goodness be done. While Percy and his garrison sleep nearby let us go now and avenge our people.'

The signal was given for the rest of the fleet to come ashore. As the army assembled, the instructions were given for the task ahead. Bruce's disciplined troops moved silently in the darkness. As the night wore on, the silence was broken by the screams of terror as the doors of buildings outside the castle walls were broken down and the garrison occupants put to the sword. Without mercy, the avenging executioners slew the invading occupants who had brought so much sorrow and evil to this country.

Lord Percy was wakened by the bedlam outside his fortress. Along with the few men inside, he was unable to do anything. As they looked out and saw the carnage below, they were filled with such fear that they dare not go to assist. The execution continued into the early morning hours.

Everyone, at the request of Bruce, shared the plunder. 'It is a small reward for their efforts,' he declared, as he watched his men celebrate the victory of the night.

Bruce and his army remained in these parts for several days. In spite of the garrison being overcome, the good people still lived in great fear of Percy. 'They will only come back and do more harm to us once you are gone,' cried an old man, who came through Bruce's camp. 'One victory in battle does not win a war,' declared a friend of Cuthbert, who had offered his support.

Several days after the assault on Lord Percy's garrison, Bruce and his army withdrew into the safety of the Carrick hills. Percy and the few men who remained with him took advantage of the departure and fled back to their homelands in the north of England.

11

THE DOUGLAS LARDER

A FEW DAYS AFTER Bruce and his men had taken shelter in the Carrick hills, Douglas approached Bruce. 'Sire, we have performed a great deed for the people of Carrick by removing the evil forces of Lord Percy. I now fear for the people of my own lands, for it troubles me, that just as you had Lord Percy enjoying the fruits of your lands and inflicting great suffering on your people, my people too have been suffering these horrors. I fear that Lord Clifford will be oppressing the good people of Douglasdale. Sire, with your leave, I would wish to go and inquire.'

'My dear Douglas, I can't see how it can be safe for you to go. The English will be many, and you will not know who your friend is. I can't offer you any men, for what I have I need to protect Carrick,' Bruce replied.

'Sire,' said Douglas, 'I must go, it is my destiny. With the good fortune that I pray God will give, I will take my chance, whether it be to live or die.'

'Douglas, I give you my blessing. Do as you desire, and if you find danger which you can't resolve, I ask that you return to join with me again. Your support for my cause and your fine qualities are always welcome in my company.'

Douglas thanked Bruce, bowed his head and stepped back.

As he was about to walk away, Douglas turned towards his King. 'Sire, there is one small favour that I may ask of you. My good friend Cuthbert, who knew my father and knows my people, would be of great help to me.'

'So be it. A good choice, I may add,' said the King. 'I too have a favour to ask of you. There is one who looks to you with great respect and admiration. I believe he would learn much in your company.' Bruce turned, and looked over at the young follower Davidson, who was observing this conversation. This young man had joined up with his King at Dumfries, and had been loyal to him ever since.

'A good choice also,' declared the smiling Douglas.

With a spring in their step, the three good friends made their way eastwards and on towards Cumnock, their final destination being the beautiful valley of Douglasdale, about forty miles from Ayr. The sight of these three friends, laughing and telling tales as they walked past, appeared to present no threat to anyone, enemy or otherwise, who might cross their path. The reality, however, was much different. As they made their way along the trails and talked of their adventures, these three men knew that they were the most skilful warriors of their time. They knew that they would not encounter difficulty, even against a force ten times their size. The combination that they presented, in terms of skill, tactics, cunning, strength, experience and youth, would be unmatched by anything they would be likely to meet.

Having started their journey late in the afternoon, they did not expect to cover any great distance in the remaining daylight hours. 'I have relations living not far from here,' said Cuthbert, as they approached the village of Cumnock. 'There is a small farmhouse, a few miles to the east; we can rest there for the night.'

'Who lives there?' asked Douglas.

'A good cousin, Paterson, the son of my father's sister,' replied Cuthbert. 'He can be trusted, and may have news of your lands to the east.'

'I look forward to meeting him,' replied Douglas.

'I hope he has plenty to eat,' said Davidson, 'I'm absolutely starving!'

'You've been getting spoiled by the rich foods which we have acquired from our very generous enemies,' replied Douglas.

'That's a habit I would like to continue with,' laughed Davidson, as they finally approached the home of Paterson.

They made their way up to the humble dwelling house. It was a long farmhouse, built on a slight slope and consisting of three separate accommodations. The lower barn was used to accommodate the cattle. The middle one was used for the storage of grain. At the top was a third, which was used for the shelter of the inhabitants.

'I hope we're not given the offer to sleep in there,' Cuthbert remarked, as he held his nose on the way past.

'It's a good thing that those animals are kept at the bottom of the slope,' replied Davidson.

'I'm glad,' said Cuthbert, 'that shit doesn't flow upwards.'

'Who knows, with a good strong wind and some typical Scottish rain you two might be out of luck,' commented the laughing Douglas.

As they came over to him, Paterson did not recognise the three strangers. Cuthbert called out to him. 'Cousin Thomas, my good family friend, I am in need of shelter for myself and my two friends for the night. Can you help?'

'That's nice, haven't seen you for years, you don't ask about my wife, or me, you don't ask about our health, you come straight to the question, and ask for lodgings. A typical selfish Cuthbert,' cried Paterson, with a serious look on his face.

126

'All right then, how are you?' asked Cuthbert.

'Fine,' replied Paterson.

'Can you provide us with shelter?'

'Of course,' answered Paterson with a smile. 'You know you don't need to ask.' The two cousins greeted each other with the hidden affection that their conversation had earlier disguised.

A short time later food was prepared and served by Paterson's wife. The guests enjoyed a simple meal of broth made from cuts of mutton and served with thin cake made from oats. When they had finished, the visitors thanked their hosts. Davidson spoke. 'Sir, my Lady, I doubt that I have been served such an enjoyable meal from such kind hosts since my own mother and father fed me many years ago.' There was a pause, and then a burst of laughter, as they all looked at Davidson, who had greatly overstated his compliments. 'I think he enjoyed it,' said Cuthbert as he bowed his head in embarrassment.

As they drank the small quantity of ale offered by their hosts, questions were asked of Douglasdale.

'What have you heard?' Douglas politely asked.

'Many enemy troops, people living in fear, murder, rape and pillage,' answered Paterson, as the others listened silently. 'The stories are the same wherever one goes. Douglasdale? I doubt if it's any different from anywhere else.'

'Anything else?' Cuthbert asked.

'Oh, in case I should accidentally forget, treason, treachery and betrayal, all by our own fellow Scots,' added Paterson.

'Fear can change many a good man's heart,' commented Douglas.

'You sir, appear to be a good man. Do you come from Douglasdale?' asked Paterson, as he looked at the friendly face of this young man.

'No offence, my good friend, but best not to ask,' said Cuthbert, as he answered Paterson's question and then glanced at Douglas. They continued to talk for many hours.

In the morning, the three guests thanked Paterson and his kind wife for their hospitality. Douglas, although he did not have anything to repay the hospitality, approached Paterson. 'Sir, there are many like you who have kindness in their hearts for their fellow men. I can only pay you with my own words of thanks in appreciation for your good deeds. I thank you, and I wish you and your lady good health.'

Several hours later, the three travellers made their way past Muirkirk, and on through the narrow pass at Glenbuck. As they came out from between the steep slopes and into the wide, open moor, they marvelled at the sight of the two distant hen harriers performing their majestic acrobatic aerial dance in the distant sky. As they continued, they glanced down at the shallow river that flowed to their left, several feet below the trail. No one made any comment, as they tried to make good speed, in order to get to their destination before darkness. The fun and laughter of the previous day had disappeared as the serious purpose of their journey and their destination drew closer.

A few miles further on, they came to a point where the trail cut across the twisting river as it flowed eastwards, carving out its gentle gorge. Cuthbert and Davidson jumped from boulder to boulder, and managed to keep their feet dry, as they successfully reached the other side. Douglas stopped; he stared into the clear sparkling water. His two companions looked back.

'What's up?' they asked.

'Nothing,' replied Douglas, as he bent down, cupped his hands, and drank. 'Only the sweet beautiful taste of Douglas Water,' he loudly called out.

The trail headed onwards along the high ground. The Douglas Water gathered pace, as other streams flowed down from the Douglasdale valley, and joined the journey through this magnificent land. There were few hours of daylight left as the path they followed came over a small hill. They saw the smoke of Douglas rising in the distance. 'Let's wait until darkness before we go in,' requested Douglas. They rested for a short time on the outskirts of the village.

Douglas, looking concerned and unsure, spoke. 'I am sitting here excited in that I am about to enter my home village and will finally see and meet the people of Douglas, and yet I won't know a single soul, nor will they know me. Will I be made welcome?'

Cuthbert leaned over and patted his good friend on the shoulder. He did not say anything; the comforting touch was sufficient to express his sympathy and support.

'What if they reject me, just as Bruce's people of Carrick rejected him? Will they be too afraid to give me their support?'

'My dear good friend James,' replied Cuthbert, 'I will enter first, for I know several people who were loyal to your father. Believe me; they will be glad to see the son of Douglas. Believe me also, every man, woman and child in yonder village, when they hear who you are, they will give you their undivided loyalty and support. You are the Douglas, you are the true Lord of Douglasdale, and the people of Douglas will be overjoyed with your return home.'

'I hope you're right,' said Douglas as he looked over towards the village.

As the darkness descended on the valley of Douglasdale, Cuthbert made his way through the narrow streets. A few suspicious glances came his way as the villagers made their final preparations for the end of day. The sense of urgency in his stride indicated that he knew where he was going. Individuals moved out of his path as if to confirm that people will make way for those who have purpose and know where they are going in life.

The glow from the fire inside illuminated the window of the house that was the destination of Cuthbert. 'I wish to speak with Mr Thomas Dickson,' declared Cuthbert to the young girl who opened the cottage door. 'Uncle, someone wants to speak to you,' called the girl passing on the message without moving from the doorway.

A short time later, and in the darkness of night, three figures made their way through the narrow village streets and arrived unnoticed at the house of Thomas Dickson. The young girl, without speaking, gestured the three strangers to enter. Cuthbert stepped towards Dickson and announced. 'Sir, this is him, this is James Douglas of Douglas, eldest son of Lord William of Douglas. He has spent the last year supporting our King Robert the Bruce in his campaign to reclaim our nation from the English. He is the rightful heir to the estates of Douglas; he comes here to seek your support, and to rid our lands of Clifford's reign of terror.'

Dickson walked over towards the tall, dark-haired, twenty-year-old man who stood in front of him. His eyes were full of emotion as he stared into the face of the young son of the late Lord Douglas. Douglas smiled and moved closer 'Sir, I am deeply honoured to meet with you, a loyal and trusted friend of my father. I am privileged to be in your good company. I come here not with an avenging army, for I have none. I come here with my two most trusted friends, and with the determination of my father's blood, I will avenge those who have inflicted so much pain, evil and cruelty on the good people of Douglas. Sir, I humbly ask for your support.'

Dickson fell to his knees, his arms tightly wrapped around the waist of James Douglas. Trembling with emotion, the elderly friend of the Douglas family cried out 'My Lord James, this day I thought I would never see again, I am your most obedient, humble and loyal servant. I offer you all that I possess; what is mine is yours.'

Douglas helped his loyal servant to his feet. 'Sir, I seek neither wealth nor fortune, only justice for those who have been cheated, robbed and cruelly treated by he who invades our lands. Will you be able to gather support from others to assist us?'

'There are many who are not afraid,' said Dickson, 'and will be as glad as I am to see you here. There are many also, who are afraid, and have been terrorised into supporting our enemies. We must be careful.'

After they had eaten, Dickson suggested that he be allowed to go speak to other villagers who he was sure would give their support. The young girl showed the three guests to a secret resting place at the rear of the cottage. Tired after their long journey, Cuthbert and Davidson decided to settle down for the night.

Douglas sat by the burning log fire, staring into the dancing flames. 'What does the future hold for me?' he asked of himself. As he quietly meditated, the young niece of Dickson coughed to seek his attention as she handed him a cup of water. 'Sir, this may help you stay awake until my uncle returns,' she said, as she stood beside the fire with outstretched hand.

Douglas raised his head and looked into the face of the young girl. Her large dark eyes were sparkling from the reflection of the bright flames. Her pretty young face was the picture of innocence, full of kindness, love and tenderness, a beauty that he had not seen before, illuminated by the warm glow from the burning fire.

'Thank you, you're very kind,' replied Douglas, as he took the cup. 'I think my Uncle Thomas likes you,' said the young girl.

Douglas laughed. 'You could be right,' he replied. 'Tell me, what name does such a beautiful girl like you be known by?'

'I am called after my mother. My name is Sophia,' she answered.

'Ah! Sophia, the Goddess of Wisdom,' replied Douglas. 'A beautiful name for a very beautiful person,' he added, with a wide smile. Sophia blushed with embarrassment and rushed away giggling.

A short time later, the peace of the evening was interrupted, as Dickson, accompanied by a stranger, entered the cottage.

'My Lord James, please let me introduce you to this good man,' announced Dickson, as the stranger stood before Douglas and paid homage. Over the next few hours, and into the late night, the situation was repeated, as one by one, the good men of Douglasdale came to pay respect to their true

Lord of Douglas. In the morning, the situation was repeated, as more and more came to pledge their loyalty to the one who was to lead them to freedom within Douglasdale.

By mid-afternoon of the following day Douglas asked his friends to join him for discussion. Cuthbert along with Davidson were always by his side, Thomas Dickson and three other men from the valley of Douglasdale were in attendance. Douglas addressed those present.

'My dear friends, in the few hours that I have been home, I have been deeply honoured and humbled by your truly magnificent loyalty and support. The kindness that has been expressed to me would have made my late father a very proud man indeed. I thank all of you for your continued loyalty to the name of Douglas.'

'Sir, what plans do you have?' asked Andrew Young, a close friend of Dickson and one of the prominent figures in the local community

'Give the man time to get to know the place first,' replied Dickson.

'It's all right,' answered Douglas. 'We must not rush. However, each hour that we sit doing nothing is one more hour of our lives that we give to our enemies.'

'Have you had any experience of actual fighting?' asked Andrew Young. It was Cuthbert who replied.

'Sirs, I have seen many great warriors in my time, I could name many names. Let me say this, there is none that this young Douglas who stands in front of you today fears. In battle he has no equal.'

'But there are only three of you,' commented William Craig, another local prominent figure of Douglasdale. This time Davidson spoke.

'Sir, I too have seen many a battle. I have played my part in large armies, and I have suffered defeat. Numbers alone will not guarantee victory. Douglas, who stands here before you, has many things to offer other than strength of numbers.'

'Tell us more,' requested Dickson.

Douglas quietly spoke. 'My dear friends, our enemies come with great numbers which we cannot hope to match. They have great wealth and endless supply of troops and provisions. However, they can be defeated, not by strength of force, which we have not, but by cunning, by entrapment and by stealth. Our enemies are so because of their greed, their selfishness and their desire for power. We will bait our traps with these attractive morsels which our enemies will find irresistible.'

The three local men of Douglasdale sat in silence, their faces expressing their astonishment at the words of wisdom spoken by one so young.

Douglas asked for information. 'Tell me, how many men are garrisoned in the castle?'

'About thirty, all armed,' replied Dickson.

'When do they come out?'

'They send out regular patrols of around ten men, about three, sometimes four times each day.'

'Is there any time when they all come out?' asked Douglas.

'No,' replied Dickson.

'Well, there is a time when most of them come out,' commented Andrew Young.

'When is that?' asked Douglas.

'Sunday, to attend mass at St Brides,' replied Young.

There was a silence while the minds of those present started to consider this possible opportunity.

'Today is Friday,' commented Douglas. 'This coming Sunday is Palm Sunday, a day of celebration of our Lord's triumphant entry into the holy city of Jerusalem. Let this day also be a day of celebration of the triumphant return of Douglasdale to its own people. Let us arrange for this holy day to be one of great celebration, let us entice our enemies to come join us in celebration.'

'The people of Douglas are all behind you,' declared Dickson.

'Then let us discuss the detail of our strategy in order that we can prepare our people,' said Douglas.

Over the next few days there was an air of excitement about the village, as small groups of people huddled together whispering as they shared the plans for Sunday's event. Everyone was made aware of the plan to hold a procession and celebration of the holy day. There was not much to celebrate during these days of occupation by the invading enemy; the thought of a joyous Sunday of celebration filled everyone with feelings of happiness and pleasure. Only a few knew of the sinister plan involving the English garrison.

On the Saturday evening Thomas Dickson and his niece Sophia prepared a final meal for their guests. After they had eaten, Douglas, Cuthbert and Davidson all thanked their host for his hospitality and kind generosity.

'Will you be going away tomorrow?' asked young Sophia, who was unaware of the secret events planned for the Sunday morning. She looked towards Douglas, with a look that indicated a very special affection was developing towards this handsome young man, whom everyone in the village appeared to worship.

'I am afraid so,' replied Douglas. 'We have much to do.'

'Will you be coming back?' asked Sophia with a look of sadness in her face.

'I suspect that we will be coming back many times,' answered Douglas. Young Sophia said nothing and smiled in Douglas's direction.

'Sophia,' called her uncle. 'I think it's time you were in bed. Our guests and I need to talk alone.'

'Yes, uncle, good night everyone,' replied the young girl, as she quietly walked to her room, glancing back with special a smile at Douglas. 'Good night Sophia,' everyone called back. As the door closed, Dickson commented. 'Looks like you've got yourself a young admirer there.' 'One of many,' added Davidson.

'She does appear to have taken to you, James,' declared Dickson. ''

'Tell me about her, what of her parents?' asked Douglas.

'Her mother was my cousin. She became ill a few years after Sophia was born, and sadly died while still a young woman. Her father, a good man, also from these parts, he got involved in an argument with a group of English soldiers. The argument started when they tried to take some of his cattle, which he was herding at the time. He objected, and a fight started, he was killed in cold blood. I was Sophia's only living relative, so I took her in and she has remained with me ever since. She is a wonderful person, a girl who has suffered so much anguish and yet constantly gives so much kindness and comfort to others. She is my wee angel.'

'You are very fortunate to have such a treasure,' replied Douglas.

As the hours passed, the final plans and preparations for the Sunday service were discussed in detail. 'It would be best to give the signal as they start to come out after Mass,' declared Cuthbert.

'I agree,' answered Douglas. 'I have heard of too many stories of the vengeance that follows the act of sacrilege. There must be no blood spilt in the sacristy.'

The three guests retired to their secret room for their night's rest. Dickson wished his friends good night and quietly said. 'My friends, whatever happens here tomorrow, I thank you for the hope that you have given us. I will pray for your safety. Should anything untoward happen to me, I ask one thing. I fear for young Sophia. Please ensure her safety.' Douglas placed his hand on the shoulder of the elderly friend of his late father. 'Sir, you have nothing to worry about, and you have my solemn word, she would be well cared for, that I promise.'

During the hours of darkness, Douglasdale was at rest. The only movement was that of the castle sentries, walking back and forth, as they guarded their protective fortress. Along with the rest of the village the residents of Thomas Dickson's house were at peace with the world as the early hours of Palm Sunday approached.

Douglas was restless in his sleep. The heavy concentration of the previous day and the responsibility of the day ahead were disturbing his rest. He tossed and turned, and kicked out in his sleep. His mind was drifting in and out of dreams. The recurring dream of his childhood returned once more to haunt him. The two faceless female figures, their images floating in and out of his vision. To the left, to the right, above and below. He could never see the two of them at the same time. The white robes, the faceless figures, their heads, each covered with a veil, the calling of his name. James! James! The dream continued on and off throughout the night.

Palm Sunday arrived with bright rays of sunshine that cast their smiles across the land of Douglasdale. The unblemished clear blue sky above projected the purity that nature is capable of producing. A thick low-lying mist hung over the length of the Douglas Water and dispersed itself on either side of the valley. The hot breath of the grazing cattle could be seen pulsing out as the heavy overnight frost continued to chill the air around them.

The early risers had already started their preparations. Several people could be seen making their way to the church of St Brides, where the local priest was busy making his own preparations for the important service that was about to take place. The smell of freshly baked bread filled the air, as helpers prepared their offerings. In the castle, the garrison had awoken and were preparing their own feast, which would be enjoyed on their return from church. The fasting, in force since the night before, was starting to encourage healthy appetites amongst the local residents.

As the time for Mass approached, the many paths leading to St Brides started to become busy, as the local people made their way to the church. The gates of the castle opened and troops started to make their way along the quarter mile path towards their place of holy worship. That morning the village of Douglas and the sounding area looked one of perfect peace and happiness. The clear beautiful spring morning scene projected an image of perfect harmony, as everyone slowly made their way to worship their creator.

The church started to fill up, as the local folks arrived in procession with green boughs in their hands, as they demonstrated their faith in their creator. The rows in front of the altar were quickly occupied, while the early arrivals positioned themselves for the best view. Many women and children had made their way to the front section. Standing behind them were several groups of men who had managed to get in before the English garrison had entered. The troops from the castle occupied the middle section. At the rear of the church, several groups of men could be seen standing together. The coldness of the morning was kept at bay by the heavy coats and shawls that the congregation wore.

The door of the sacristy opened, and a lone priest, dressed in red garments, made his way towards the altar. At the same time, the last three men entered the church, closing the door behind them.

Standing facing the congregation, the elderly priest raised his hand, made the sign of the cross, and called out 'In nomine Patris, et Filii, et Spiritus Sancti. Amen.' The service continued as the priest performed the blessing of the palms in front of him. 'Bless, we beseech thee, O Lord, these branches of palms. And grant that what thy people today bodily perform for Thy honour, they may perfect spiritually with the utmost devotion, by gaining the victory over the enemy, and ardently loving every work of mercy. Through Our Lord...'

The blessed palms were then distributed to all present. The priest beckoned for the hymn, 'To Christ the King,' to be sung. A short time later the Gospel, the passion of our Lord Jesus Christ according to St Matthew, was read aloud. As the reading ended, the words 'Eli, Eli, lamma sabachthani?' – My God, my God, why hast thou forsaken me? – echoed within the stone walls of the church. The Mass continued. The three men who had come in last rose to their feet and made their way out through the door. A short time later, the women and children at the front of the congregation also rose to their feet and began their slow exit precession.

As the singing procession passed out through the church doorway, two men were standing outside, one on either side of the exit, issuing instructions to everyone to quickly make their way away from the grounds. 'Keep singing, but go quickly, don't wait, you must hurry,' whispered Cuthbert and Davidson, as they ushered the local women and children away from the horror that was about to unfold. Several yards from the doorway stood a lone man. Anyone coming out from the shadows of the church would have difficulty focusing on his darkened face as the sun shone from behind and over his shoulders, illuminating the silhouette of his long dark hair. His bulky dark robe appeared to be ill fitting on his large frame.

The last of the women hurried round the side of the church and out of sight. Just a few seconds later the first of the men came out and gathered against the church wall on either side of the doorway. The English troops then emerged, rubbing their eyes as they tried to focus in the bright sunlight. They stood talking as their comrades came out from the church. The two groups of Douglasdale men stood quietly talking on either side of the Church doorway; they constantly glanced at the lone figure that stood a few yards further off. Several of the local men began to show signs of panic as they struggled to overcome their fear.

A group of English troops, along with a number of locals, were still inside the church building, and were about to come out, when the premature call was heard. 'A Douglas! A Douglas!' screamed one of the locals, as his nerves failed to hold back the tension and excitement that had been building up inside him. The troops outside looked around in amazement.

'What the hell's happening? Where are the women and children?' several called out.

'It's a trap,' shouted one of the troops.

Sandwiched between the local men inside and those outside the church building, the English troops rushed to re-enter the sanctuary of the church walls. Thomas Dickson, who was still inside the church, was the first to draw his weapon, as he lunged at the troops who blocked the doorway.

The lone figure, who had been carefully watching every move, suddenly removed his dark robe to reveal underneath the coat of arms of Douglas. The flash of steel was all that the first victims saw, as they were slain by the lethal Douglas blade. He ran at them, his sword severing limb upon limb, plunging into one body after another, as he cut his way through the bloody mess that fell on the ground of St Brides.

Cuthbert and Davidson led the local men. They came at their enemy from either side, cutting into the shocked troops with the same ruthlessness as their leader. The sight of Douglas wearing his coat of arms, and slaying his enemies with such ease, lifted their confidence and inspired the hearts of the locals. Each man joined in the attack on the enemy, as more and more of the invading troops were brought down. Douglas fought with a wild passion that had never been seen before. His flashing blood-stained blade cut through the almost helpless troops as if they were water.

Douglas pushed his way to the doorway. Those who had not fallen victim to his lethal sword quickly got out of his way, as he re-entered the church. There he found several fights in progress. He looked round for his Dickson, friend to two generations of his family. Attacked, Douglas cut down two more soldiers with short plunges from his sword. The fighting stopped as a handful of troops dropped their weapons in surrender.

While the locals, with their weapons drawn, held them at bay Douglas looked around again for Dickson. He found him among the bodies on the floor, alerted by a slight movement from an injured man. Turning this injured and unknown man over, he saw beneath him the bloody face of Thomas Dickson. He saw the gaping wound on Dickson's neck. He had lost a great deal of blood and was unable to talk, but he looked up into the face of young James. Although he could not speak, the expression on his dying face told the story. He was dying a free man of Douglasdale; there was sadness, and great peace in the victory that had been achieved. Douglas bent down and kissed his good friend on the forehead.

Dickson tried to speak, but the words would not come out. 'So… So… So….,' he whispered. Douglas placed his hand on the side of his friend's face and with tear-filled eyes said, 'Have no fear. I will look after Sophia.' Thomas Dickson closed his eyes for the last time and left this earth a free man.

Douglas lifted the body of Thomas Dickson and carried it out of the church. Several local men rushed to his aid. 'Please take care of him. He was a great man,' he requested, as they took his friend's body away. Douglas stood still, and looked around the grounds of the church. The slain lay everywhere. His Douglas coat of arms was drenched in blood. The locals surrounded him, silent at first, their minds refusing to believe what their eyes were telling them. With the leadership of this young warrior of Douglas they had retaken their land. They were free, they were proud. They called out and cheered, 'A Douglas! A Douglas!'

Cuthbert, Davidson and many others approached Douglas. 'What's next?' asked one of the locals. Douglas turned his back on the church and looked over towards the castle of Douglas, which was a short distance along the narrow track. He thought of the loss of his friend Thomas Dickson and grew hot with anger.

'Let's go,' he called. 'Bring the prisoners.'

The prisoners were brought together and marched at sword point towards the castle gates. Douglas and his men were immediately behind them and prepared for any counter-attack that might come from the castle. As they approached, they noticed that the gates were open. They quietly entered, shielded by the prisoners who were pushed in front.

No sign of any life existed as they spread out and searched the castle premises. Three other prisoners were taken, a porter, a cook and a stable lad. The feast that was waiting for the return of the garrison troops was shared out. What was not eaten, and there was plenty, was sent back to the village to be shared among the villagers.

Cuthbert approached Douglas. 'Today, with your leadership, we have achieved a great victory. However, the result of this victory is that this castle is now in your hands. It may have been a difficult task to take it, but it will surely be an even greater task to defend it.'

'My loyal friend, we have been together for so long now that I believe we are starting to think the same. I do not have the resources to hold this castle of my family. I also do not intend to walk away and let our enemies just march straight back in. If we allowed that, then there would surely be no purpose in today's efforts and loss of lives.'

'Does that mean you don't plan to stay?' asked Davidson. To which Douglas replied, 'I would prefer to be free, and hear the lark sing, than to be locked up in that place and hear the mouse squeak.'

Douglas instructed that the castle belongings be raided. 'Everything that can be taken, will be taken. Leave nothing,' ordered Douglas. Provisions, clothing, weapons, armour and silver treasures, anything that could be carried was gathered up and removed from the premises. The stable lad was called and ordered to prepare three of the best horses. The remainder were slain, their bodies thrown into the deep castle well and covered with salt. The wine cellar was forced open; all the grain stores were brought in. Wheat, flour, malt and meal that could not be taken were thrown in among the smashed wine urns.

'What of these prisoners?' asked Andrew Young who stood alongside William Craig and many other good local men who had performed magnificently this day.

'What would you have done with them?' asked Douglas.

'If they live to tell the tale, Clifford will surely take his revenge upon us with a vengeance,' replied William Craig.

'It cannot be right in the eyes of our God to take the life of a prisoner,' declared Andrew Young.

Douglas spoke. 'You are good men who are caught between protecting your own lives and that of your families

141

and at the same time doing what is right in the eyes of God. I ask that you take no further part in today's events. Should anyone ask, say that I, James Douglas, son of Lord William, who was imprisoned and executed by the hand of Longshanks, have this day taken my first step towards avenging my fathers death. Any man, English or otherwise, for there are many traitors within our own nation, who perpetrates the evil that this nation has witnessed, will suffer the same fate by my own sword. Tell them that I have no family, no army and no friends. Tell them that the torture of others to avenge me will only result in their sure death. Tell them that if they retake this castle, I will simply take it back again. Tell them that my enemies should fear me more than any other.'

The local men were shocked and silenced by these words, and quietly made their way back to the village with the plunder that was rightfully theirs.

Douglas, along with Cuthbert and Davidson, stayed behind. 'Let me perform this unfortunate task' asked Cuthbert. 'No,' answered Douglas. 'If I have to answer for my actions before God, then so be it. Bring them in one at a time.'

Douglas slowly entered the wine cellar. One by one, each of the prisoners were taken inside. Several minutes later Douglas came out, pale and with an expression of disgust and revulsion written all over his face. It was evident that he took no pleasure in his actions.

'Burn it,' ordered Douglas. 'Burn all of it!' he shouted. 'If it *can* burn, burn it.'

Cuthbert and Davidson went around the castle, torching everything that they could. When he was alone Douglas sat down, and held his head in his hands. 'Why can evil only ever be destroyed by more evil?' he asked of himself. 'I must seek forgiveness. I must go to St Brides, and I must seek my penance.' His eyes filled with tears, and in his heart were tears that no one could see, tears of sorrow that only he and his creator could witness. 'Are we all possessed by evil? Are my enemies and I really any different? How can good overcome evil, without becoming evil? How can evil be destroyed?'

A short time later Cuthbert and Davidson had completed their task. 'We must go now,' ordered Cuthbert. 'The smoke will be seen for miles. It may be observed by others.' Douglas looked at his two loyal companions. 'You both know that I was not telling the truth earlier when I said that I did not have any friends, I have two of the best. Thank you for helping me achieve what we have done today. I must perform two tasks before we leave. I will tell you as we make our way back to the village.'

Now on horseback, the three riders arrived back at St Brides. Douglas quickly dismounted and entered into the church; he made his way to the front of the altar, and immediately dropped to his knees. Head bowed and in silent prayer, he repented for his acts of murder and asked his maker for forgiveness. One by one, he relived each of the executions that he had administered. 'Am I just as evil as they?' he asked. He looked up at the crucifix sitting on top of the altar and begged for forgiveness. He bowed his head once more in silent prayer.

Preparing to leave the church, Douglas raised his head and looked up. A cold shiver shot through his entire body, his throat went dry, and he could not swallow. He felt a tightness in his chest that he had not experienced before. The sight above him almost paralysed him with fear. Behind the altar, mounted in each of the top corners of the church, he recognised the two images from his childhood dreams. Two identical statues of the Virgin Mary, one on each side, their heads covered with the light behind them projecting their shadows across the church ceiling. From where he knelt, only one could be seen at any one time without turning his head. The only difference from his dream was that they did not hold a child in their arms. 'What did this mean?' he asked of himself. 'I must have been here as a child,' he said to himself, 'but what of the voices?'

Douglas mounted his horse and informed his trusted companions that there was one important thing to complete. 'We must go to the house of Thomas Dickson.' When they arrived at the cottage door, Douglas commented 'I won't be long.'

The house had many visitors, for there were many who had come to pay their respects to the man who had played a great part in the day's events. Many women of the village had come to offer their services of help and support.

Douglas entered, and was greeted by comforting words of praise and recognition for his heroic actions. He said nothing as his eyes scanned the crowded room. The body of Thomas Dickson was being prepared in the secret room that had been his shelter for the last few days.

'He's in there,' gestured a small elderly woman. Douglas nodded, and continued to look round the room. She was not present.

'She's in there,' said a young girl, who had come to offer support to her friend. 'She has told me about you.' Douglas went over to the room door, and softly knocked to attract her attention. 'Who is it?' a voice called out from within. Douglas slowly opened the wooden door.

Sophia was sitting on the edge of her bed, still crying. 'Sophia, I am deeply sorry.' She bowed her head, as the tears continued to flow. 'I promised your uncle that I would....'

She lifted her head and interrupted, 'I know, he told me.'

'Will you come with me?' he gently asked. 'I will take care of you. You will be safe.'

Sophia stood up and wiped her tears. She did not hesitate. 'Yes. We can leave now.' Douglas embraced the little girl who had just lost her only relative. There was no one that she would rather be with than James Douglas.

As they made their way out, they met many more who had arrived at the door of Thomas Dickson to pay their respects. Douglas mounted his horse and lifted young Sophia up alongside him. The large crowd that had gathered thanked Douglas for what he had achieved today, and wished him and his companions a safe journey. Douglas offered his appreciation for their support, and pledged that he would return many times to ensure their safe protection. He called out 'The day will come when Clifford and his men will not want anything to do with Douglasdale. They will hear of what happened today when the castle of Douglas became the Douglas Larder, and they will consider it too dangerous a place for them.' There was loud cheering and applause for these words of hope.

The small party of riders made their way down towards the Water of Douglas. A short time later, Douglas gestured for his men to stop. 'There is something that I must do before we go any further,' he called out. Sophia proudly remained on her hero's horse as Douglas dismounted and made his way into the flowing waters. 'I cannot cleanse my soul of my sins, but I can cleanse this garment of the blood of those who I have slain in Douglasdale this day,' he thought to himself, as he submerged the crimson-stained coat of arms into the precious source of life that flowed through this valley. The stains of his sins dissolved and dispersed into the slow running currents. He prayed quietly to himself 'Let the water of life cleanse my cloth of the evil that brought me here, and, I pray, my soul from the evil that I have succumbed to this day.'

12

THE ORPHANED CHILD

PASSING BY THE TINTO hills to their north, the three horsemen
and the child made their way eastwards towards the sanctuary
of the Selkirk forest that covered vast acres of the borderlands.
For the first few miles, Douglas kept looking back to ensure
that they were not being followed. 'Where are we headed?'
asked Cuthbert. 'I would like to know also,' commented
Davidson.

'To safety, my friends, and to rest for a short time,' replied
Douglas.

'I don't like not knowing where I am going,' declared
Cuthbert, who was feeling concerned and agitated.'

Douglas pulled up and asked his companions to stop. 'I
apologise if I appear to be taking your loyalty and support for
granted. However, for your own safety and that of others I
would ask that you put your blind trust and faith in me once
again.'

'My loyalty and support, you will always have, but please give me some credit,' declared Cuthbert, who had just uttered his first words of discontent towards his good friend.

'I understand your reaction to my apparent secrecy. However, let me say this, I am taking you to a place that if our enemies knew that you had knowledge of, they would commit the most horrendous acts of evil to extract from you. I don't want you to carry that burden,' replied Douglas, as he tried to reassure his companions.

'If you can't tell us where we are going, can you tell us who we are going to see?' asked Cuthbert.

'Can't you guess?' asked Douglas. Cuthbert suddenly realised, smiled and shook his head as if angry with himself for doubting his good trusted friend.

'Will someone please tell me?' shouted Davidson. 'Patience my man, patience please, for goodness sake be patient,' answered Cuthbert, as he laughed aloud. Sophia had to grab a tighter hold of Douglas's waist as he urged his horse to pick up more speed.

They achieved good progress as they made their way east and on through the hill passes south of Biggar. Preferring to avoid contact with anyone, they were forced to make a detour around Tinnis Castle, which they could see standing out in the distance on the steep rocky hillside. They entered into territory that was familiar to Douglas, the River Tweed flowing through these glens brought back the memories of when he first started out on his long journey to regain his inheritance. They kept to the south side of the river, which twisted and turned as it made its way east, each bend in the river signalling to him that he was not far from his destination. They continued on and passed south of Peebles, avoiding contact with any of the locals.

A few miles to the west of Peebles, they turned and headed south along the forest trail at Cardrona. They continued south and made their way over the pass between the hills of Dun Rig and Deuchar Law. Their horses strained as they climbed the steep hill slopes. Onwards they climbed, as their clothes started to dampen with the wet mist that hovered below the two thousand feet tops. They reached the top of the ridge on the north-west side of Deuchar Law and then made their way down the drovers' path that followed the trail of the small burn that flowed south-east to join up with the Yarrow Water down below.

The sound of the mountain stream guided them in the semi-darkness as it turned eastwards making its way below Deuchar Law and down into the vast dense protective forest of Selkirk. This forest had provided shelter and protection to Douglas and his family before and would, with God's good will, continue to do so.

Darkness had fallen. The three riders and their young companion had survived a long and hectic day. They needed to stop and rest for the night.

'Do we have far to go?' asked Cuthbert?'

'We should arrive any moment now,' answered Douglas. 'Please be careful, and prepare to expect the worst.'

They stopped at a clearing in the forest. 'What do you see?' asked Davidson. 'I see the same as you,' answered Douglas. 'Why do we stop then?' asked Davidson. 'What do you smell?' replied Douglas taking a deep breath.

The smell of burning wood lingered up the hillside track, and carried with it just a slight hint of the smell of food being cooked which could be detected with the minimum of concentration. As they continued down through the forest trail the smoke grew thicker and the smell stronger.

The glow from the burning fires could be seen as Douglas and his men dismounted and made their way silently forward. Douglas looked to Cuthbert 'I would be grateful if you could wait here with Sophia, while we go ahead to check if all is safe.' 'She will be safe with me,' answered Cuthbert. 'Call out if you need me,' he added.

Douglas and Davidson continued to make their way on foot towards the group of farm cottages that surrounded the Blackhouse Tower. The silence of the evening was disturbed by the barking of dogs who pre-warned the inhabitants of the approaching strangers. As they came towards the first cottage,

Douglas was surprised that the loud barking of the dogs had not prompted anyone to come to the front doorway. He looked around and then realised why.

Standing in the shadows at the side of the cottage, he could barely make out the outline of a man watching them. 'Who are you?' The voice from the shadows called out.

'Someone who has failed again to approach you unawares,' replied Douglas.

'With the noise you were making, even the dead could hear you,' answered the voice from the shadows. 'I doubt even the spirits of the dead could sneak up on you without being discovered,' called Douglas, as he approached the side of the cottage.

'Do you know him?' asked Davidson. 'About as well as a son knows a father,' answered Douglas. 'Let me take your horse. Please go call Cuthbert, tell him that it's safe for us to enter.'

When Davidson returned with Cuthbert and young Sophia, the cottage door was wide open, and both Douglas's and Davidson's horses were tied up at the side. They could hear people talking and loud laughter coming from inside. Douglas's three companions entered one at a time.

'Let me do the introductions,' declared Douglas. 'This is my good friend David Davidson whom I first met when I joined up with our King Robert Bruce at Tweed's Well about a year ago. He has been a very good and loyal friend to me over this last year.' Davidson stepped forward and shook hands with the stranger.

'My pleasure to meet you sir, any friend of Douglas is a friend of mine,' announced the stranger to Davidson.

Douglas then took the hand of young Sophia, who had just completed this day's long journey without uttering a single word of complaint. 'This beautiful young lady who stands before you is the niece of someone that the family of Douglas will always remember and be indebted to. Her uncle, Thomas Dickson, gave up his life to assist me in regaining the castle of Douglas from Clifford's army. A truly remarkable man, who leaves behind a remarkable young niece. I have given my pledge to be her guardian and protector.'

'Such beauty I have not seen for many a year,' declared the stranger as he bowed and kissed the small delicate hand that was presented to him. 'I also knew your uncle Thomas Dickson. He was indeed a very good and honourable man.'

'My final introduction requires no announcement,' declared Douglas as Cuthbert entered the cottage. The two friends and companions who had been separated for many years finally saw each other again. 'Robert!' declared Cuthbert as he stepped towards his dear friend. 'Stuart!' replied Fullerton as they both embraced. It was ten years ago, not long after the imprisonment of Lord William Douglas, that these two friends, who were almost brothers, had parted company. Fullerton had stayed true to his pledge to Lord William and had protected Lady Eleanor over these years. Cuthbert had also remained true by being ever at the side of James Douglas. Douglas introduced Fullerton to Davidson and to young Sophia. He had many tales to tell of his good family friend.

'Has he performed well while looking after you all these years?' asked Fullerton, as he inquired of Cuthbert's standard of protection towards the young Douglas during the recent battles.

'I owe my life to him,' answered Douglas. 'Without his advice and subsequent support I would not have come this far.' Douglas smiled, as he put his arms round his two friends and embraced them both. 'My father, as I am today, would surely be proud of you both,' said Douglas, as his face filled up with joyful emotion.

Fullerton looked at Cuthbert and expressed relief at seeing him alive. 'My good friend, you had us worried. We have heard of what happened at Methven. We have heard of the terrible loss of life and of those who were injured. We have heard of truly terrible tortures and the cruel deaths of those who were taken prisoner. We have heard of things unimaginable that have been inflicted on those who supported our King Robert Bruce.'

'But why were you worried about me? I was not present at Methven. I first caught up with Douglas at Kintyre,' Cuthbert explained.

'The drove road that you have just come down, whilst not used by strangers, does get used by the men of the forest of Selkirk as they take their cattle to market at Peebles. Many stop to give us news.'

'What news have they told of me?' asked Cuthbert.

'Obviously not of you, but the name of Cuthbert has been mentioned,' replied Fullerton.

'My father, a good man from Galston, who amongst other things was a valet to the Knights Templar, may have been at Methven, but he would not have been engaged in battle. I have not heard of him this last year,' said Cuthbert, as he anticipated that some bad news might be about to unfold. Fullerton gave him the story.

'A few months ago two men came over the pass with their cattle. They stopped and told us that they had heard of many things. They told us they had heard of a man who had not even been carrying arms, a man who was a servant to the Scottish nobles and who was captured at Methven and then taken to Newcastle.'

'What happened to this man?' asked Cuthbert.

'When he arrived at Newcastle he was executed,' replied Fullerton.

Cuthbert felt shaken. 'And his name?'

'I am sorry to say,' Fullerton replied, 'the man they spoke of was known as Cuthbert. I believe they said there was some mention of him being a valet, but they could not say for certain.'

Fullerton placed his hand on his friend's shoulder. The shock of this tragic news stunned Cuthbert. He felt prepared for many things but not to hear of the death of his own father. 'I wish to go outside to be alone for a while,' said Cuthbert. Douglas embraced his bereaved friend and expressed his deepest sympathies as he accompanied him to the doorway.

Douglas felt guilty and disgusted with himself. He said to the others, 'Please excuse me. All I appear to talk and think about is my inheritance, my lands, my father, my family. It's all about Douglas, Douglas, and then more Douglas. Today, two good people, young Sophia and now my good friend Stuart Cuthbert, have lost close family members. I am deeply sorry for my selfish, self-centred view of this world. Please forgive me.'

Young Sophia, who had not said a word since she left Douglasdale, walked over towards Douglas. 'Kind sir, you are the most considerate and compassionate person I have ever known. Please don't chastise yourself with those words of self doubt. The tragic loss of our loved ones has been at the hands of our enemies, against whom you seek your revenge. Please maintain your commitment to the good cause of removing these men of evil from our presence.' Fullerton and Davidson both replied. 'Hear, hear!' and, 'Well spoken, young lady!'

Douglas said nothing, but he thought to himself 'There is something about this young girl that touches feelings within me that I have not experienced before. Is it because she has lost her father just as I have? Or is there something else?' Whatever the reasons, Douglas felt soothed by her kind words of comfort. Sophia smiled at him. Her beautiful little face, with a smile that would melt the heart of anyone, brought Douglas back from his feelings of self-pity. He smiled back, not just his usual gentle smile, but a sincere smile that told a story to the one whom it was directed at. Sophia blushed in embarrassment.

Douglas looked towards Fullerton and asked. 'Are they all in the Blackhouse Tower?'

'Yes, they are safe and well. Do you wish to meet with them now?' said Fullerton.

'Yes, I would like to introduce my mother to Sophia.' The tall stone tower, known locally as the 'Blackhouse', stood proud above the surrounding cottages. It was positioned at the bottom of the glen below Deuchar Law, and adjacent to the burn that flowed into the Yarrow Water, a short distance to the east of St Mary's Loch. This secure sanctuary within the forest of Selkirk presented a safe haven for the protection of the Douglas family.

Fullerton made the introduction. 'My Lady, a very welcome guest has arrived.' 'Mother!' Douglas called out. 'Oh! My son,' was the shocked reply, as she rose from her fireside seat. Lady Eleanor and James embraced and kissed.

'This is wonderful, it's good to see you again my son, I'm so happy, my prayers have been answered.'

'Mine also,' replied Douglas. 'I'm glad to see you're safe and well. How have you been?'

'I'm fine. Please sit down and tell me all that has happened to you since you were last here.'

'Mother, to tell you everything would take another whole year, please be patient. First let me introduce this young lady to you.' Fullerton gestured Sophia to step forward, before he himself departed and left them on their own.

Douglas took the hand of young Sophia and brought her over to his mother. 'Let me introduce you to Sophia of Douglasdale. Sophia is the niece of Thomas Dickson, a good friend and loyal supporter to my father.' Sophia stepped forward and performed an elegant curtsy in front of Lady Eleanor. 'I'm honoured and pleased to meet you, my Lady.'

'I too,' replied Lady Eleanor. 'How is your uncle? He was a very good close friend and most loyal supporter of my husband.'

Sophia trembled, and looked at Douglas for help in answering this most difficult question. Douglas interrupted. 'Mother, I regret to say that Sophia's uncle was unfortunately killed during a skirmish involving myself and Sir Clifford's men at St Brides Church a short time ago.'

Lady Eleanor paused for a second, then reached forward and lifted young Sophia's right hand, grasped it in both of hers and gently pulled it towards her bosom. With a tenderness that only a mother can give, she replied 'My dear child, I'm deeply sorry to hear such tragic news. Your uncle was well liked by the family of Douglas, and you have my deepest sympathies.'

The warmth and consideration shown by Lady Eleanor deeply touched Sophia. 'My lady, I am deeply saddened by the loss of my only uncle. He was my one and only guardian after my father's death, also at the hands of Clifford's men, some time ago. I wish to say, however, that through the courageous efforts of your son James, Clifford's men have now been removed from Douglasdale. My uncle has died for a good cause. The freedom of Douglasdale has been won by the efforts of your brave son and my good uncle.'

'You are brave for one so young. I am sure your uncle and your father would have been proud of you,' replied Lady Eleanor.

Douglas interrupted the conversation between his mother and Sophia. 'Mother, I have a request to make of you. I ask that Sophia be allowed into this house for her safety and protection. I gave my pledge to her dying uncle that I would be her guardian and protector.' With a wide smile that indicated her answer before she spoke, Lady Eleanor replied. 'I would be honoured and delighted to have such a lovely young lady grace our home with her presence.' She embraced young Sophia and added 'I could be doing with some female company around this house.'

'I will earn my keep,' declared Sophia.

Lady Eleanor laughed out loud. 'Although not a requirement, such a kind gesture would of course be greatly appreciated. Welcome to the house of Douglas.'

Over the next few weeks, Douglas stayed with his family. He spent time with his young brothers, Hugh and Archibald, who were spellbound by his tales of adventure. They were fascinated by the tale of the Douglas Larder. He introduced them to Sophia, with whom they immediately became good friends. They had much in common, and yet they had many interesting differences. Sophia was warmly accepted into the family and assumed the role of daughter to Lady Eleanor and sister to Hugh and Archibald.

Many evenings were spent with the three youngsters sitting round the fireside listening to James tell them of his adventures. He described his stay in France; he talked of the friendly people who all appeared to like the Scots, the magnificent buildings, the rich variety of food and the delicious wines. He described the feeling of the hot sun, very different from the cold damp climate that they were used to. His two young brothers and their adopted sister Sophia stared at him, as they were transported to each of the far off places that Douglas described.

As he talked to his loved ones, Douglas felt immensely proud of himself and what he had achieved. He liked this feeling; it gave him a purpose, and it gave him faith in himself and motivated him to do more. When he described the hardship that he had endured, the memory of the pain and suffering of those times disappeared, and was replaced with an inner strength that made it all seem worthwhile.

Young Archibald, who was now eleven years old, asked his older brother 'James, were you not lonely? Did you not want to cry?' Douglas replied. 'Yes, I was lonely, but I had a very good friend who was always with me, and yes I did cry, many times.'

Young Sophia, who was almost the same age as Archibald, sat with an intense look upon her face. She interrupted. 'I know who was with you.'

'Who?' asked Archibald.

Sophia did not answer, but repeatedly pointed her index finger upwards as if to mention his name was a sin.

Douglas told the children that one morning they would waken and he would be gone. 'For I have to continue my journey,' he apologetically declared.

Douglas also spent a great deal of time in his mother's company. He shared with her the adventures of the last year. She expressed great concern over the many dangers that he had faced and was very proud of his successes. During one late evening conversation, when they were on their own sitting in front of the burning log fire, Lady Eleanor turned to James. 'My dear James, tell me this, you have retaken the castle of Douglas. You have avenged your father's name many times over. You have shown your loyalty to our King, Robert the Bruce. If you were to do no more you would still have achieved more than was ever expected of you. Tell me, what is your final destiny? And when will your journey end?'

Douglas looked into the face of his mother, a face that was full of love and kindness. He was twenty years old and yet he did not really know his own mother. During his short hectic life, he had only lived in his mother's presence for a few years as a small child, before his father's imprisonment. As an adult, she was almost a stranger to him. He was feeling tired and his mind drifted away from the questions she had asked. She awaited his reply. He stared deep into the glow of the burning fire, and was entranced by the dancing flames. Lady Eleanor sat patiently. 'James…, James.' He awoke from his trance with a startle. There was a feeling of déjà vu. The familiarity of the situation puzzled him.

Douglas continued to stare into the burning flames as, without looking in his mother's direction, he gave his answer in Latin. *'Dei gratia, sic vis pacem, para bellum'* – By the grace of God, if you want peace prepare for war. Douglas then looked at his mother. 'My destiny has been born from the events of my father's death. If I were to cease now I would cause my family no shame. My destiny goes beyond my father's good name and I believe now comes a Deo et rege – from God and King.'

Lady Eleanor sat quietly as her son continued to explain. 'During the last year, I have lived in constant fear. I have had cold, hunger and despair as my everyday companions. These are the sacrifices that I must make. I do not know where it will all end, if at all. However, I intend to devote my whole life to ridding our nation of evil.'

Lady Eleanor interrupted. 'And the English?' Douglas looked at her keenly. 'They are misguided, they are not the enemy. They are forced by the evil King Edward to commit those horrendous acts of evil. Yes, they invade our lands, but only with the assistance from those Scots who betray their own people. A united Scotland would have no difficulty in repelling our enemies. Our weakness is our lack of unity. The greed, the selfishness and treachery that are consistently practised by our very own nobles makes us constantly vulnerable to our enemies.'

Lady Eleanor spoke. 'My dear James, I am immensely proud of you and your achievements. It saddens me to think that you will not stay at home and live with your own family. I respect your very gallant and noble ambitions and I will always give my support to your destiny. I ask only one thing, promise me that you will come to visit us often. Please don't lose touch with us.'

'I will never be far away,' replied Douglas in a tired voice. 'Tomorrow I must leave.' Douglas kissed his mother and bid her good night.

'Good night my dear, I will pray for you,' replied Lady Eleanor as Douglas left her company.

As Douglas made his way out of the room, there was something that he could not understand. During the weeks that he had been here, he had noticed that his mother and brothers always appeared to have provisions aplenty. Apart from the services of Fullerton, there were only a few servants who worked at supporting his family. No one appeared to go hunting, and there was ample supply of livestock being farmed around the premises. The furnishings of Blackhouse Tower, although humble, still required funds to purchase and maintain. His own clothes were practically rags, yet the garments worn by his mother and brothers appeared appropriate to a more affluent lifestyle.

As he lay in bed, he thought to himself. 'I am the oldest of this family and yet I have not provided a single penny to its upkeep. There must be some source of income that is supporting them.' These thoughts, in a land full of corruption, betrayal and treachery made him feel very uncomfortable as he drifted off into sleep.

Back at Fullerton's cottage, Cuthbert had regained his composure since hearing of his father's death, and was full of enthusiasm for the way in which young James had succeeded his father, Lord William. Fullerton had enjoyed the company of his guests, and was keen to hear more from Davidson about the adventures that young James had been a part of. 'So tell me, what sort of a man is he turning out to be?' asked Fullerton.

Davidson replied first. 'He has become our good King's right hand man. King Robert has taken him into his confidence, and looks to him as his adviser in all matters of warfare. In battle, he has no equal. I have seen him scatter vast numbers of enemy troops single-handed. He fights with a cold ruthlessness that is lethal and terrifying to his enemies.'

Cuthbert then commented. 'Our people are inspired by him; he lifts their hearts and souls and gives them hope. He applies all the qualities that we instilled in him. Gallantry, honesty, kindness and compassion, he has them all in abundance. His heart is the bravest in all Scotland.'

That night, only those who were sound sleepers managed to survive with their dreams uninterrupted, as the driving rain lashed down on the forest of Selkirk. The wind gathered momentum as it leapt over the border hills and swept up the length of St Mary's Loch and onwards deep into the heart of the immense forest. The trees creaked with the strain as they bent and swayed to the invisible force that attacked their deep-rooted positions. The fires that burned through that night flickered as the powerful draughts caused the flames to intermittently catch their breath.

Lady Eleanor checked on the welfare of her two youngest sons. They both slept soundly. She looked in on young Sophia. The little angel was also sound asleep; the tragic events involving the loss of her uncle appeared to be now fading into the distant past and she seemed to be at total peace with this cruel world. Comfortable that all was well, the mother of the house returned to her own bed.

Douglas had been enjoying a deep sleep until the wind started to let itself be heard. His broken rest caused him to drift into dreams. The dancing flames from the earlier evening reappeared in his mind. The open-air fires that he had shared with Bruce and his army flashed in and out of his dreams. The recurring dream of his childhood returned, with the two faceless figures, each carrying a child. They drifted in and out, but he could only visualise one at a time. The figures started to appear amongst the burning flames of the fire. One of them gradually became clearer as the bright flames surrounded her. She started calling out his name. 'James ... James.' He recognised that voice. She called out again, 'James ... James.' 'He called out who are you?' In his dream he reached into the flames to save her, and called again 'Who are you?' 'James ... James.' Her face appeared.

Douglas partially awoke in a state of shock, panicking and covered in perspiration. He heard the same voice. 'James ... James.' His mother, Lady Eleanor called out, shaking him as he tossed and turned on his bed. His glazed eyes stared right through her as she shook him again. This time he came round. 'James, it's all right, it's only a dream,' his mother called out.

'Yes,' replied Douglas, as he regained his senses. 'It was a dream.'

'Was it a bad dream?' she asked.

'I don't know,' he replied.

'Do you want to tell me about it?' she asked.

Douglas took his time in answering. 'It's about two women who each carry a child. I can only ever see one at a time.'

'Do you know who the women are?' asked his mother.

'Until tonight I did not know,' said Douglas. 'However, just before I woke I saw the face of one of them.'

'Who was it?' Lady Eleanor asked. Douglas rubbed his eyes.

'It was you mother, you. I have been dreaming about you.'

'And the other woman?'

'I don't know,' answered Douglas.

Lady Eleanor put her arms round her son and quietly whispered. 'Perhaps now that I have appeared, your dream will disappear.'

'I hope so, but I feel that it will return. I sense that I am the child in the dream. I need to know who the other woman is,' replied the confused Douglas. Lady Eleanor covered her son and reassured him by saying 'Do try to get some rest; you will have a long journey ahead of you tomorrow.' As she did so there was a worried look on her face.

The morning sun had still to show itself when Douglas quietly got his horse prepared for an early start to the next stage of his journey. Fullerton had been wakened by the noise of his young friend as he attempted to depart without a goodbye.

'Sneaking off then are you?' called Fullerton.

'Time to stop relying on others,' answered Douglas.

'Maybe others want to be involved through their own free will.'

'Maybe,' answered Douglas.

'Don't you think you're being selfish, taking this crusade all on your own shoulders?'

'I don't want any others close to me to lose their lives or the lives of their families.'

'So you're going to take on the whole bloody English army and every traitor to the Scottish cause all on your own?'

'If need be,' answered Douglas as he continued to get his horse ready.

'James, if I did not know you any better I would say you were not serious. Listen to me, you may appear to be on your own, but the vast majority of our people will join up with you if they see strength in leadership.'

'I *can* provide leadership, but I don't want an army to follow me,' answered Douglas, with a look that suggested that he did have a plan in his mind. 'We don't have the strength of numbers to defeat our enemies on an open battle field.'

'How then do you plan to defeat them?'

'The way you taught me: stalk them, trap them, surprise them. If we were to go hunt a wild animal we would not ride out into an open field and shout charge!'

Fullerton smiled. 'Good answer. I notice you say, "we".'

Douglas responded with a similar smile.

'Shall I give them a shout?' asked Fullerton. Douglas nodded his approval.

The four of them sat together, Douglas, Fullerton, Cuthbert and Davidson. Douglas spoke. 'I leave this morning to go join up with our King Robert. I have pledged my support to him. However, I will soon come back amongst you. I ask this of you; any man who is willing to fight for our cause will be most welcome to join me, not as part of an army that will march to war, but a disguised army that goes about its business without being noticed by the enemy. I wish to create an army that will attack silently at night without being visible; an army that the enemy does not see, hear or even know exists. An army that spends a great deal of its time at home and can strike at a moment's notice when called.'

Cuthbert asked. 'What do you want us to do?'

'Spread the word, seek good men whom we can trust,' answered Douglas.

'I will do as you say, for there are many who would want to join us,' declared Cuthbert.

'I don't know the men of these lands. I would rather go with you to follow the Bruce,' said Davidson.

'So be it. Be ready for my return,' said Douglas as he made his way over to his horse.

Douglas turned round, looked over at Fullerton and called out, 'Robert, thank you. The pledge that you gave my father has been honoured many times over. I hope I can match your kindness and your loyalty.' Douglas turned to Cuthbert. 'Stuart, my good friend, there is one man I would not want to meet in battle, and that is you. If you can find others who possess even one of your qualities, tell them they will be welcome at my side.'

13

DOUGLAS CASTLE, SECOND ATTACK

THE SHADOW OF TINTO HILL provided partial shelter from the south-west winds as the two riders headed towards the trail that would follow the source of Douglas Water. Their destination was the home of William Craig of Sandilands. As they headed towards the south Lanarkshire village, both riders slowed down and moved with great caution. A pair of buzzards soared above, scanning the ground below in search of prey to feed their latest brood, the mewing 'pee-oo' calls signalling their presence to those creatures capable of recognising such unique cries.

Based on the events of the last time they were in Douglasdale, both riders were prepared for a hostile reception. They did not want to enter the main village of Douglas until they were able to assess the situation regarding any vengeance that Clifford might carry out. Sandilands lay a few miles to the north-east of Douglas, and contained the home of William Craig. He was considered a trustworthy man who played a valuable part in the planning and recovery of Douglasdale, yet at the same time an individual who stayed in the background and did not command any significant attention.

Darkness had set in by the time Douglas and Davidson arrived at William Craig's house. He greeted his two friends with great affection. 'It's good to see you again; I did not expect you to return so soon. You have become a legend,' he said to Douglas, as he shook the hand of the true Lord of Douglasdale and warmly invited him into his house.

'It's good to see you also. Tell me, how have things been in Douglas since we last left?'

'Patience my dear friends,' replied Craig. 'First you must eat and drink.'

A short time later, the serious conversations began. Craig spoke first. 'When Longshanks heard of what had happened he went into yet another of his mad rages. He gave money to Sir Robert Clifford and ordered him to immediately restore Douglas Castle. This he has now done.'

'Have there been any reprisals?' asked Douglas.

'No, which is quite a surprise. Many thought that Clifford's men would seek their revenge against us, but it has not happened,' answered Craig.

'Maybe they have still to look in the castle well,' suggested Davidson.

'What's in the well?' asked Craig.

'The slaughtered remains of the last garrison,' replied Davidson, as he looked towards Douglas. 'After what Douglas did, they may be too frightened to take revenge against you.'

'Well I can say that their tactics have changed,' declared Craig. 'They never come out. They appear to have come here, restored the castle, and locked themselves in. Previously they would come into the village and helped themselves to whatever took their fancy. They now rely mainly on provisions being brought in to them.'

'There is one other story that I have heard that is a serious concern,' continued Craig. 'When Longshanks heard of what had happened at Douglas Castle, and also of the events at Brodick and Turnberry, he expressed anger with Aymer de

Valence, Earl of Pembroke, who he had expected to deal with this uprising. Valence, along with John of Lorne, has been ordered to deal once and for all with the situation. He has collected a large army and has been seen in the low-lying hills around Cumnock.'

'In that case we must be careful and consider this situation in any plans that we may make,' commented Douglas.

'What plans do you have?' asked Craig, who was excited about the prospect of giving the invaders of his country another bloody nose.

'None,' replied Douglas. Craig looked rather disappointed. 'The best plans are those that are created by the people who will be executing them,' added Douglas, with a suspicious look on his face. The smile returned to Craig's face.

'I take it that you do actually have something in mind then?' said Craig.

'I need more information,' replied Douglas, looking thoughtful.

'What information do you require?' asked Craig.

'Any information you have about those who currently occupy the castle. Who is the captain of the garrison? How many men do they have? When do they come out? Do they have horses? What provisions do they have? When would their next supply of provisions be due? Are there any locals who are allowed to enter the castle?'

Craig and Davidson looked at each other in amazement. 'Would I be correct in assuming that if we supply you with these details, you will produce a plan that would involve retaking what belongs to you?' said Craig. 'Give him the information and watch him go knock at the door and ask for his castle back,' commented Davidson, as the three friends laughed and looked forward to what was hopefully going to be another successful exercise involving the castle of Douglas.

Over the next few days, word spread throughout the area of Douglas's return. His good friends and supporters all pledged their loyalty and stated their readiness to help him. This undivided support gave Douglas a problem. He expressed his concerns to his close friends. 'We must be careful. Such popularity, which I am not accustomed too, can be a dangerous thing.'

'What would you advise?' asked Craig.

'You have done well my good friend,' Douglas congratulated Craig. 'Based on the information that has been provided, I have a plan. However, I don't wish to share the whole plan with anyone.'

'If you don't share your plan, does that mean we are not part of it?' asked Davidson.

'Each man will be informed of the part he has to play, but no one, other than myself, will be aware of the total plan. This may cause our men to feel not trusted, but the risk of treachery will be minimised, thereby protecting their safety. I want our men to feel confident that I will protect them when they give me their support.'

Craig and several other key individuals organised various meetings with small groups of men throughout the area. In secret, and in Douglas's presence only, they were informed of the part they were to play in the plan.

Douglas addressed them. 'My good friends of Douglasdale, I put my trust in you once again. You have shown yourselves to be loyal men, and I ask once more for your commitment. You have seen how our last victory against our enemies has caused them great discomfort and that they no longer take advantage of you. Yet they still reside in our land in the home of my family.'

'We will all fight with you!' cried one supporter, who was loudly applauded.

'I thank you my good friends,' replied Douglas. 'However, I must mention one detail; you have been given specific instructions on your involvement. These instructions must remain only with you. No others should be given this information.'

'You can trust us,' called one man. 'Yes, we can all be trusted,' several others called out.

Douglas held his hand up to quieten the group and spoke more seriously than they had ever heard him speak. 'Trust is a fine quality that you all possess. However, our enemies have ways of making you break that trust. Believe me, when I say that I have seen sons betray fathers, wives betray husbands, and brothers betray brothers. There is no end to the corruption and betrayal, driven by greed and ambition, that exists within our nation. The plan that I have created has only been shared in part amongst you. I will know of any man who discloses this detail to others. Any man who does so will become my enemy and the enemy of Douglasdale and will be slain by my own sword.'

A voice called out from amongst the group 'No man of Douglasdale will ever betray you my lord.' There was again loud applause as every man present stood up and called out 'A Douglas! A Douglas!' Douglas was greatly humbled, and wished he had not been forced to use threatening words to seek their secrecy.

Around mid-morning of the following day, John Graham, a local man of Douglasdale, accompanied by his young son, led a lame sheep along the path that passed between the castle and the adjacent woods. Graham constantly tugged at the rope, as he pulled the sheep along. His young son was gently stroking the back of the beast with a thin stick, urging it on its way. The sentry on guard saw the passers-by and called down to those below. 'Dinner anyone!' Several more soldiers appeared on the castle battlements and looked out. A few moments later, the castle doors opened.

'Hey! You there! Stop!' called out the soldiers as they walked over towards the passers-by. Just then a flock of rooks that were parading in a straight line as they searched for food in the field along the edge of the wood, cried out with loud cawing 'kaah's' as they took to flight. Thinking that they had caused the birds to startle, the soldiers had no cause for concern.

'Where do you think you're going?' asked the first guard as he approached Graham. 'Nowhere Sir, I am merely taking this animal home for slaughter in order that I can feed my family.' 'Oh you are, are you,' replied the soldier. 'Only after you have paid the toll fee for passing along this road.'

'What toll fee?' asked Graham.

'The fee is one sheep per person who passes by. We will give you a discount, since we are in a good mood today. We will not charge for the boy.'

'Sir, I beg you, please be reasonable, my family will starve, I must provide for them,' pleaded Graham, as he made to get away.

'Then you will have to steal something else to feed your hungry brats,' answered the soldier, as he laid his sword against the neck of the nervous Graham. A second soldier grabbed hold of the rope and pulled the docile beast away from its owner.

'Be off with you both,' he shouted.

Graham's young son immediately yelled out, 'Leave my father alone!' The boy lunged at the soldier, whacking him across the wrist with his stick, and causing him to yell out, as his sword dropped to the ground.

'You little bugger! I'll kill you!' shouted the soldier, as he grabbed the stick, broke it in two and delivered a vicious slap straight across the boy's face. The soldiers laughed as they walked away with their prize. Graham picked up his weeping son. His mouth was bleeding, but fortunately he was not as badly injured as at first appeared. Father and son hastily made their way along the road and headed out of sight.

Douglas released the tension in his hunting bow, and allowed both soldiers to live another day. He was comfortable that the first part of his plan was complete. Both he and Davidson had witnessed this event from the edge of the wood.

'They did as you said,' commented Davidson.

'Yes, greed got the better of them. I wonder what they will say when they see the beast that they have stolen is being eaten alive by maggots and has a stomach full of worms,' replied Douglas.

'It should motivate them to come out when a good healthy stock of cattle next passes by,' said Davidson, as a mischievous smile appeared on his face.

The people of Douglasdale went about their business as normal during the next few days. There were no unusual occurrences. It would soon be a full week since Douglas had arrived and nothing had happened. Many started to wonder if any real plan had in fact been drawn up. Those who were not informed of the fine detail did not ask any questions; those who did kept silent.

On the morning of the fifth day after Douglas's return to the area, a small herd of cattle was rounded up to be taken to the market at Lanark. Several horsemen were involved; they quickly got their beasts ready and started out on their journey. The field that the beasts had been grazing in lay on the south side of the village; the road to Lanark lay to the north-east and involved passing along the trail in front of the castle. The beasts were prime cattle, only a few years old, and could be herded at a fast pace.

As they rode past the castle, the riders shouted at their animals. 'Come on, move it, move it,' and the cattle responded by picking up speed and entering into a fast trot. The noise disturbed the sentries on duty, who called out to Thirlwall, the captain of arms who had been assigned responsibility by Clifford following the massacre the previous month. The garrison had been running low on provisions and was in great need of fresh meat. Thirlwall gave the order to ten of his men to pursue the cattle on foot. Then another five soldiers mounted their horses and rode out to follow the pursuit. A few minutes later, the riders from the castle overtook their men on foot and led the chase after the cattle.

The cattlemen continued to drive their beasts at maximum speed along the forest trail. The route twisted and turned as it ran parallel with the flow of Douglas Water. About a mile from the castle, Thirlwall's riders had their quarry in sight. The young herd, although moving fast, were now beginning to tire from the exhausting pace that was being set. The cattlemen did not look back; instead, they continually glanced from side to side along the trail.

The cattlemen continued to drive their animals at great speed and were now not far from the point of exhaustion. Ahead of them, the trail turned sharply to the right and out of sight from the pursing troops. Only a few seconds separated them as the five garrison horsemen sped one by one round the turning, expecting to be immediately upon their prey.

The sound of thundering hoofs was replaced by horrific screams as the horses galloped straight onto an array of wooden stakes that had risen up from the ground immediately after the cattlemen had passed. A flight of arrows penetrated the unprepared bodies of the front riders. One rider survived the hail of arrows only to be executed by the sword of Douglas as it cut deep into his chest. Swordsmen on either side of the path threw themselves upon the rest. Outnumbered and unable to defend themselves, the remaining garrison horsemen fell to their deaths one by one. The suffering of the injured horses was immediately stopped as their lives were compassionately ended. The whole execution had taken place in a few minutes. An eerie silence filled the damp morning air as Douglas and his men looked around them.

'They're only a few minutes behind,' called one of Douglas's men as he gestured that the foot soldiers were on their way. 'Stick to your instructions,' shouted Douglas.

Davidson gave his signal as the soldiers came running along the path. Douglas's men, who had been lying in hiding on either side of the trail when the horse riders had earlier passed by, suddenly sprang up from the thick bracken and pounced on the unsuspecting soldiers.

Taken by surprise and vastly outnumbered, the garrison soldiers were quickly overcome. Those who were at the rear panicked at what they saw, turned and started running back along the trail towards the castle. Douglas, along with several horsemen, gave chase and caught up with the terrified men, who were still not in sight of the safety of the castle walls. One by one, each of the fleeing soldiers was run down. Douglas's men struck at their unprotected bodies and terminated their desperate lives.

Impatience was getting the better of Thirlwall as he paced up and down along the castle battlements. 'What is keeping them? Hopeless, every last one!' he shouted. 'Get me my horse.'

Meanwhile, Douglas and his riders were waiting on either side of the trail, a short distance inside the camouflage of the forest. 'Let's wait to see if any more come out, curiosity should be getting the better of them by now,' he said to his men, who were pumped up with the excitement of what they had achieved so far this morning. 'Remember, I want a few to be able to escape and get back to the castle gates. It's the only way we will be able to get in,' instructed Douglas as his men waited silently.

A few minutes later, Douglas and his men heard the signal from their lookout. A group of horsemen, led by Thirlwall, came galloping out of the castle gates and followed the trail in pursuit of their own men. A short time later Thirlwall's riders had entered the forest. Douglas and his men pounced upon them.

Thirlwall's men appeared to be more prepared than the others and put up a brave fight; several of Douglas's men were wounded. Douglas, on seeing one of his men fall, immediately made way towards Thirlwall and struck down the garrison captain with a single sword-slash across his head. For a split second Thirlwall looked stunned, then dropped from his horse like a stone, blood pouring from his fatal wound.

Panic immediately spread amongst the reminder of Thirlwall's men. They scattered in all directions, pursued by Douglas's men who continued to give no quarter and relentlessly executed their revenge.

Several garrison horsemen turned and made their way at full speed back towards the castle gates. Douglas and his men followed. Some were caught and cut down by Douglas as they desperately tried to reach the safety of the castle gates. As they galloped at full speed, two riders managed to get inside the castle gate ahead of Douglas and his men. Unable to keep the gates open any longer, the gatekeeper slammed the large gates shut in front of their own approaching men, who were then trapped outside. The final slaughter took place outside the castle gates. The only survivors of the castle garrison were the few terrified souls who had locked themselves inside.

Douglas, along with Davidson, William Craig and the many men of Douglasdale who had joined in this morning's attack gathered outside the castle gates. Once again, they had inflicted great losses on their unsuspecting enemy. They all roared and then called out. 'A Douglas! A Douglas!' as they cheered their support once again for their leader.

Douglas addressed his men. 'You men of Douglas, I am proud of all of you, for you have proved once again that our enemies may come with their armies, but together, and with determination, skill and cunning, we can defeat them. I thank you again for your support and I promise to keep returning until our enemies finally decide that Douglasdale is too dangerous for them to invade.' The cheering continued.

Douglas rode over to the castle walls and called out. 'You inside, give this message to your Lord Clifford. Tell him, I, Douglas of Douglasdale, will no longer accept his occupation of my lands. Tell him that I do not have an army of soldiers, but that the good people of this nation are my army and they will always follow me. Tell him that I will come in the dark of night when he sleeps. I will not be heard nor will I be seen. I will not rest until he has left these lands for good.'

The frightened men on the battlements stared down with dejected faces, defeated, confused and bewildered. They were safe, but they knew they were really prisoners in this now dangerous castle. The change that had occurred in their lives in the last hour had been too much for them to grasp in such a short time.

Douglas announced that he would leave. He thanked all those present, and offered any that wished to follow him the opportunity to fight with King Robert the Bruce. Many men raised their hands and then declared amongst themselves that they would gladly follow him, for he had once again shown himself to be a true leader of men. Douglas spotted one man, whom he recognised, standing amongst the crowd in front of him. He dismounted and went over to him.

'Sir what is your name?' 'I am John Graham, my lord,' answered the man whose sheep was stolen and whose son was slapped. Douglas inquired after the welfare of the boy.

'My lord, he is well. He carries a thick lip, which can be a good learning experience for one so young,' said Graham.

Douglas laughed. 'You and your son both put your lives in great danger, I thank you my good man and I will not forget either of you for being part of our plan.'

Douglas asked those who wished to follow him to prepare to leave the following morning. He called out 'At the request of Longshanks, Aymer de Valence, Earl of Pembroke, is at this very moment camped outside Cumnock and prepares to attack our King Robert the Bruce. Our King is in desperate need of our help. Please prepare to come with me.'

14

CONFLICT IN THE SOUTH-WEST

WITH THEIR LUNGS filled with the freshness of the chilly early
morning spring air, Douglas and his band of fifty men left their
families and homes in Douglasdale and made their way west
to join up with Bruce. An intermittent grey frosty mist hung
over the low-lying areas of their beloved valley, as the loyal
men, some on foot, some on horseback, followed behind their
inspirational leader.

Those on horseback, although about to have the easier
journey, shivered as the cold morning air passed through
their bodies. Those on foot had quickly warmed up, and were
chatting and laughing as they slowly and proudly jogged
alongside their comrades of Douglasdale. There was no better
feeling that morning than that experienced by the men of
Douglasdale.

Douglas rode at the front of the band of enthusiastic
men. He felt good. He was proud of these men. They were
his people, his friends, and he loved every one. He knew they
were prepared to die for him, and he also knew that although

they were making their way to give their support to their King, without him there would be no such loyalty. Being their leader filled Douglas with great pride and satisfaction. He thought of the father that he had not really known. Only a few childhood memories existed from those very early years. 'What would my father think, if he could see me today, leading his men to join our King, in the fight for our freedom?' he asked himself. The cold air was making his eyes water, disguising the tears of sorrow, joy and happiness that were generated by the mixed emotions that filled his gallant heart.

Douglas spoke with his men as they journeyed. They told him of their families, and their mothers and fathers, many of whom had supported and fought with Lord William Douglas. They spoke of their wives, sons and daughters who had cried on the doorsteps that morning as they waved goodbye. As they spoke, Douglas realised that he was not alone; these men also had suffered many losses, of their freedom and of their possessions, at the hands of their invaders. They had the same cause for revenge as he. He felt guilty and selfish in thinking that he was the only one who had been the subject of such misfortune.

Douglas was glad to have these men beside him. As he listened to them talking about themselves he got to know them even more. However, there was a price to pay for this good friendship. The duty of responsibility that went with the leadership and friendship that he had for these men caused him concern. He recalled from his early education the French maxim *Noblesse oblige* – Rank imposes obligations.

'How will I feed them? How can I protect them? What of their families?' These and many other questions filled his head with doubt. It was good to have them with him; their strength of numbers would be invaluable. However, there were many benefits of being on his own; the success that he had achieved so far with small numbers of men had proved to be highly effective. He made a pledge to himself that he would lead his men alongside Bruce, but he would one day soon return them to their families and homes in Douglasdale.

By mid-afternoon, Douglas and his men approached Cumnock. A few miles outside the village they met a lookout whom Douglas recognised. The lookout was pleased to see Douglas and his men, and gave them directions to the secure place where Bruce was camped. As they made their way into the camp, Douglas was pleasantly surprised by the size of the force that Bruce had gathered.

Bruce welcomed Douglas with open arms, and greeted him by saying 'James, my good and loyal friend, I am pleased and proud to have you join me once again,' to which Douglas replied 'I am honoured by your welcome, Sire, and I bring with me my good men of Douglasdale, who also pledge their support to your cause.'

Bruce was delighted with this demonstration of loyalty. 'For such a small place as Douglasdale, you have presented many men. I am deeply grateful, friend,' declared Bruce.

Douglas asked his men to bring their gifts to the King. They did so and brought in many weapons and provisions, which they laid out in front of him. 'With the compliments of the garrison at Douglas,' declared Douglas.

'Well done,' said Bruce. 'I did hear a story that you had caused them great pain. I also hear that your name is being cursed, not just by Lord Clifford but by Longshanks himself. I hear that he considers you to be the ghost of your good father, who was his most hated enemy. They say that they refer to you in discussion as the Black Douglas.'

Douglas laughed. 'Black Douglas? I must be doing something right if I am starting to get under their skin.' They both laughed aloud.

'Sire, you also appear to have acquired many more men,' commented Douglas.

'Yes, I have. They started arriving in ones and twos, then the numbers grew; more and more have been arriving over the last few days. I am glad to say that word has been spreading and more will be coming to join us.'

Douglas asked Bruce for a private word. 'Sire, I have been informed that Sir Aymer de Valence has a great army and is currently close by in search of your camp. You say that word is spreading. I would advise caution. That word may also be spreading to the ears of Valence.'

'Your advice and words of caution are greatly appreciated. What would you suggest?' asked Bruce.

'I would advise that you move camp soon. To stay so long in one place is dangerous. I would advise that a few men be left behind to organise those who may wish to join with you. I would caution against telling anyone of your destination. You now have many men, and thus it is also much easier for enemy spies to enter our midst,' answered Douglas.

'James, your advice is very wise; I will order that we move further south to Galloway, where we will be midway between the lands of Carrick and Dumfries. There are many secure places where we can shelter and establish a base. That will enable us to send out men to recruit more followers, who I know will be loyal to our cause. I suggest we move on in a few days' time.'

Later that evening, word came to Bruce that Valence was close by with a larger army of troops. The messenger who brought this information also announced further concerning news that John of Lorne, a nephew of the murdered John Comyn, had joined with Valence and that he brought with him around eight hundred men, many of them local men of Carrick and Dumfries. The most disturbing news was when the messenger announced that Thomas Randolph, a relation of Bruce, who had been captured by Valence's men at Methven, had switched sides and was now supporting him and that he had recruited many Scottish followers.

'Isn't he related to you?' Douglas asked of Bruce. 'Regretfully I have to say yes. He is my nephew, from my mother's side,' Bruce sadly replied.

'If we ever meet in battle, what would you have me do?' asked Douglas.

'I would prefer for him to be taken prisoner, for he is a good man, although perhaps misguided by greed and the false promises of those who advise him,' answered Bruce.

Information on Valence's advancing army continued to arrive. 'Sire, they have much greater numbers than we,' announced the latest messenger to arrive at Bruce's camp. 'They appear to have many hundred on horseback and over one thousand on foot, we are vastly outnumbered,' added the bearer of this alarming news.

Bruce gathered his close nobles, including his brother Edward and the ever-loyal Douglas. 'My Lords I did not come here to run away. However, we do not at this moment have the men to stand and meet with Valence's much larger advancing forces. I therefore propose that we split up into three groups and meet later at a suitable place.'

'There is one other piece of information that I must make you aware of,' declared the latest messenger. 'Speak my man, what have you not told us?' demanded Bruce. The messenger was beginning to panic; he regained his composure and answered, 'It's John of Lorne, my Lords; he has a pack of hounds. They say that one of them once belonged to our King, they say it has the scent of Bruce permanently in its nostrils.'

Douglas interrupted. 'My Lords, may I, with your approval, make the following suggestion. Let us all take a piece of cloth belonging to our King, and let us lead those hounds in a merry dance in all directions.'

'Agreed,' replied the delighted Bruce.

Douglas continued. 'May I also advise, that a few good archers follow behind each of our three groups, and attempt to bring down those hounds that have your scent.'

'Agreed again,' shouted Bruce.

The next few days were spent on the run, confusing the hunting hounds and avoiding capture. The sharing of Bruce's clothes amongst his men had worked for a few hours, but the hounds that pursued Bruce did in fact have his scent truly recognised and well established. Bruce was concerned. The proud force which he had such great difficulty in gathering was now scattered around Carrick and into Galloway. The constantly barking hounds could be heard in the distance as they closed in on his scent. He did not want to make his way to the agreed meeting place until the hounds had permanently lost his trail.

With desperation taking over, Bruce stopped running. He spoke to the archer who was always by his side. 'My good man, there is no other way to resolve this problem. You must wait here and when that hound comes into sight you must bring it down with your first arrow.' 'Sire, I would be honoured to perform this task,' replied the young archer who welcomed this challenge.

Bruce, continued on his own, while the archer waited, camouflaged by the dense cover that a group of gorse bushes presented. The barking continued as Bruce made his way south. Suddenly squeals of pain replaced the mad barking as the deadly first arrow penetrated the body of the hound that once belonged to Bruce. He stopped. It did not take long for his archer to catch up. 'Thank you my good man, you have done well today,' said Bruce.

After a few miles, Bruce sounded his horn. Two short blasts were all that was required. His men gradually came out from their hiding places and were delighted to rejoin him. Bruce continued his journey south, leading his men over the moors as they made their way deep into the heart of the hills of Galloway, an area that would offer unrivalled shelter and protection for his forces. Ensuring that they were unnoticed, they passed by the village of Straiton and followed the source of the Water of Girvan and onwards deep into the dark shadows of the Carrick forest. They finally reached their destination in the tranquil oasis of Glen Trool. Bruce informed his men that they would rest here and wait until his brother Edward and good friend Douglas came with their men to join them.

In the meantime, Douglas and his men had circled Dalmellington. They headed south, and down the west side of Loch Doon. They secretly passed unnoticed alongside the English-held island castle and continued south, following the stretch of water known as the Gala Lane. They continued onwards in the shadows of the steep cliffs of Mullwharchar,

Dungeon Hill and Craignaw. To their right, high above them, hung the spectacular granite cliffs.

As they continued onwards, the narrow trail underfoot became softer and eventually petered out. They found themselves at the edge of the Silver Flow, a massive floating bog that had devoured many a lost traveller and would certainly prevent any pursuing army from following behind them. Davidson, who came not far from these parts, led the way. 'It's about to get dangerous, please make sure you keep right behind me, follow my footsteps, on no account wander off my course,' he instructed them, as they cautiously followed behind him.

As they slowly moved forward, they eventually came to a gap in the cliffs at Snibe Hill. Davidson stopped, and called out 'We must head over this pass and up onto the hill tops.' A short time later, they were on solid ground again as they headed across the ridge known as the Rig of the Jarkness. Darkness was descending fast as Douglas and his men traversed the high ridge. One of the men called out 'Look! Fires!' Douglas turned and looked south.

In the area at the top of Loch Dee, several large fires could be seen burning bright and illuminating the skies above. Douglas agreed to go down and check. 'Be careful, they will surely have sentries posted,' advised Davidson. Douglas did not answer but replied with a look that said he was well aware of the risks. 'We will wait for you at the head of Loch Trool,' said Davidson as he led Douglas's men down the side of the Gairland Burn.

A few hours later darkness had descended on this remote place and hid from view the rich natural beauty that the magnificent glen possessed. Douglas, who had managed to acquire important information on those who were camped not far from Loch Doon, had rejoined his men.

'What news do you have?' asked Davidson.

'Information that I would rather keep for the ears of our King,' replied Douglas.

They continued on their journey and carefully made their way along the narrow trail that followed along the loch side. They finally arrived at the place where Bruce had established his temporary base. Suddenly one of the men called out for the party to stop. 'Listen!' he whispered. As they stood silently in the partial darkness, they heard the sound of horses a short distance away. Davidson went closer to identify who was near by. 'It's the King's brother, Edward, and his men,' shouted Davidson. The two groups of men greeted each other and were grateful that they had arrived safely at their destination.

When Bruce heard of their arrival, he was relieved that they were safe, and expressed his appreciation that they had brought many men with them. Both Douglas's and Edward's men were exhausted from the long journey that they had just completed.

'What do you know of our enemies?' asked Bruce. Douglas allowed Edward to reply first. 'I have no information to tell, I suspect that Valence and his men may not be far away. They have many spies who have previously entered our camps.'

Douglas requested that he be allowed to speak with only Bruce present. The others were asked to leave their company. 'Sir, I regret to inform you that Valence has his army only a few miles east of here. I am concerned that several days ago, when he was close to us at Cumnock, we took avoiding action and agreed in secret to meet here in this glen and yet he is still nearby. I have no doubt that one close to us has informed him of your plans.'

'Your assessment is very accurate, my good Douglas. Our enemies have many spies. Earlier today, an old woman entered our camp begging for food. I personally took her into my care and gave her food from my own table. I offered her decent clothes to replace her worn rags, and I offered her shelter for the night. I offered her kindness and protection. When I looked into her eyes, I saw the eyes of treachery. She knew that I saw through her disguise and she broke down. She cried on her knees before me and claimed that Valence knew of our camp and that he had sent her here to find out about our strength of numbers and our intentions. Valence intends to send his army to attack us at dawn,' replied Bruce.

For the next hour Douglas and Bruce shared suggestions on how best to cope with this situation. 'I will not run any more. It is time I led my men to victory over these ruthless invaders and the traitors who have joined them,' announced Bruce.

'I agree,' replied Douglas. 'I would also suspect that all we require is one good victory. Success in battle will encourage greater support from your people.'

Bruce smiled and quietly spoke. 'I have a plan, but once again I require your cunning skills and continued loyalty for it to be successful.'

'Sir, you cannot doubt that I am your loyal servant and will honour your request,' said Douglas.

It was a few hours before dawn when Douglas and his men crept out of the camp and settled into their positions on the steep slope above the narrow loch-side path. Their chosen ambush point was at the top of the glen overlooking the route that Valence's men would soon be forced to come along in single file. The chilled night air numbed their bodies as they nervously lay in wait. The many rocks lying on the steep ground prevented them from getting too comfortable. Several men were startled by the sudden ghost like appearance of a hunting barn owl, which silently glided above their heads and down the edge of the loch side in search of voles to feed its hungry young. A short distance away, Bruce, along with his brother Edward and their men, waited at the point where the path opened out into a wider area.

Silently they waited. About an hour before dawn, they heard it. It was the sound of approaching soldiers, making their way along the path towards Bruce's camp. No matter how carefully they trod, they could not disguise the metal clanking of their armour that disturbed the stillness of the night, nor could they dull the sound of hooves on the stony ground. Douglas whispered to his men to be patient. Bruce stood at the edge of the path with his back to his own men and waited for the enemy to appear.

A single arrow was lit by one of Douglas's men; it hit its target, and ignited the dry material that had been laid along the darkened path. The first invading soldier heading towards him was visible for Bruce to see. An arrow from the bow of Bruce penetrated the throat of this leader and appeared out of the back of his neck. Before the unfortunate soldier had dropped dead to the ground, a cry from Bruce of 'Upon them!' had broken the still silence.

Douglas and his men rose to their feet, and a wave of burning arrows screamed down and hit their targets on the narrow path below. The panicking invaders were now visible to those who had waited in ambush. Showers of large boulders, dislodged from above them, poured down on the enemy. Their screams could be heard throughout the glen. Their crushed bodies, with broken limbs and smashed skulls, lay scattered along the pathway. It seemed that the only route out was the deep waters of Loch Trool, but the ice-cold depths showed no mercy and instantly devoured those who could not swim, while those who could were slowly picked off by the precision of the archers above.

Bruce and his men attacked from their side of the pathway. They easily picked off each defenceless man in turn. Bruce inspired those behind him as he killed three more with his sword. At the other end of the trail, the army of Valence was in a state of panic and disarray. They stumbled on top of each other, as they desperately tried to retreat back through the narrow pass and away from the ambush.

Amongst the English force, Sir Aymer de Valence and Sir Robert Clifford pleaded with the men to go back and fight. Sir John Vaux argued that the situation was hopeless. 'You, Sir, are a coward, and you encourage others also,' shouted Sir Robert to Vaux. On hearing this, Vaux drew his sword to slay his accuser. 'If you are so brave, sir, why don't you yourself go along that trail and have your head crushed to pulp,' he riposted. Valence tried to separate the nobles. 'Sirs, our men see you fight, they lose heart and desert us. Your squabbling has caused a loss of faith. Our situation now appears hopeless.'

As they argued, Douglas and his men appeared on the pathway. With bloodcurdling screams they rushed at their enemies, attacking them with relentless force in revenge for past events. Although vastly greater in numbers, Valence's force scattered in all directions.

As the dawn started to break, Douglas could see Sir Robert Clifford in the distance. This was one man he would dearly love to meet in battle, for he was the one to whom Longshanks had given his father's lands. He considered the possibility of pursuing him. However, although the enemy was retreating, with daybreak arriving and the fact that he was vastly outnumbered, Douglas wisely recognised that this was one confrontation that must await another day.

Valence meanwhile, realising the hopelessness of the situation, had fled for his life. There was a danger that his own men might turn against him. He made his way back towards Loch Dee and then northwards to the safety of Bothwell Castle.

A short time later, the fiery red sun cast rays of dazzling light across this magnificent glen, activating the full spectrum of nature's splendid colours and stimulating the rich display of spring life for the pleasure of those who stood there to witness it. The sun's warmth lifted the hearts of Bruce's supporters and gave them renewed energy.

Looking round, every man marvelled at the inspirational beauty of this breathtaking glen. The still waters of the loch reflected the purples, reds, gold and greens as the mirror image stretched down the length of the glen. This was a place of unique splendour, an oasis, where one could stand and admire the outstanding artistry of the creator of life. There could be no greater contrast than that between the magnificent scenery that lay before them and the eerie silence and darkness of a few hours ago. This was a prize which they considered had been well worth fighting for.

Bruce called all his men together. This event was a turning point for them, they had taken the battle to their enemy, they had outwitted them, and, with a much smaller force, they had won. His men felt good.

Some of Valence's men whom they had defeated approached them. Many of the enemy force came from these lands and requested to be allowed to support their King Robert Bruce. This was agreed, and Bruce's army began to grow from this success. Douglas stood with his group of fifty men. He was proud of them, and glad that there were no casualties. He praised them for their courage and thanked them for their brave efforts.

Bruce spoke. 'My good men, today we have achieved a major victory, we have proved to ourselves that together we can defeat our much larger enemy. Our achievement this morning is significant in that success will encourage more of our own people to join us. We will head northwards, others will see our strength, and we will not hide. We will go to Carrick, Kyle and Cunningham. We will grow in numbers. We will eventually meet our enemy again, and we will again defeat them.'

Over the next few weeks, Bruce and his army travelled throughout the lands of Carrick. They recruited many men. They soon became the dominant force in this area since their enemies either had moved on or had joined with them. To the north, the people from the lands of Kyle and Cunningham switched their support to the cause of Bruce. The confidence of Bruce and his men had never been greater; their support continued to grow.

Douglas, always alert, was anticipating the next move of his enemy. He requested that many of his men spread out throughout the south-west of Scotland and form a network of observers that would monitor and report on the movement of Sir Aymer de Valence and his armies. In compensation for the risk that they would be taking, Douglas offered these men the opportunity to be based at home in Douglasdale. They agreed that all information on the activities of their enemies would be reported back to Douglasdale; from there Douglas could easily be contacted. With Valence based at Bothwell, two observers were sent to monitor and report back to Douglas on any activity.

Having made his way to the safety of Bothwell Castle, Valence was becoming more and more concerned; his continued failure to capture Bruce was causing King Edward of England great impatience. Edward had made threats against Valence if he failed to deliver Bruce. The humiliating defeat by Bruce's inferior numbers at Glen Trool had still to reach the ears of Edward. Valence knew that it had been a year since he had scattered Bruce's army at Methven and he had still failed to capture him. He knew that if he failed to capture Bruce in the next few months, King Edward would remove him from his post, but there were other possibilities of the King's anger being displayed that Valence could not bear thinking about.

News reached Valence that the men of Kyle and Cunningham had joined Bruce in considerable numbers. He immediately ordered Sir Philip Mowbray to take one thousand men and to start at Cunningham and seek revenge as they headed south. Word reached Douglas within a few days of Mowbray's movements. Douglas requested his leave from Bruce and headed north with his band of forty men. They stopped at the forest on the north side of Kilbirnie Loch and waited for further news of Mowbray's movements.

One of Douglas's men had been observing Mowbray and reported back that he was close by and would be coming this way the following morning. Douglas and his men repeated the tactics of the success at Glen Trool. They identified the route that Mowbray would be following, a trail cut alongside the large marsh that lay in front of them. This trail made its way through the boggy terrain and came into a narrow pass that would only allow single file movement. On either side the marsh split in two, separated by the Maich Water, which flowed down from Misty Law in the high moorland country above. The deep, black, boggy ground made it impossible for horse riders to cross. The trail lay on the north side of the pass, and so Douglas and his men agreed the position of their ambush on the south side; from here they would be able to observe their enemy unnoticed.

Douglas, accompanied by his men, lay hidden throughout the night. As dawn broke, he could see Mowbray's men approaching. The colourful banners of the English army glowed in the early morning sunlight. The bright low-lying morning sun was an advantage to Douglas that morning. Douglas and his men remained hidden; Mowbray's men, with the sun in their eyes, could not see those who waited in ambush as they entered into the narrow pass. Douglas's men remained patient, waiting until a good many of Mowbray's force were positioned in single file within the pass. Mowbray and his men felt safe and confident that morning, reassured by their numbers and rigorous training.

A battle cry broke the stillness of the early morning. 'A Douglas! A Douglas!' cried one of the men who lay in hiding. The first flight of arrows hit their targets with such devastation that almost every one penetrated deeply into its intended victim, causing them to fall to the ground. The leaderless horses panicked and reared in terror. Subsequent waves of arrows were targeted at a mixture of riders and horses.

As the broad-barbed arrows penetrated deep into the horseflesh, the unfortunate beasts fell to the ground and blocked all progress along the trail. With their swords and axes drawn, Douglas and his men leapt down upon their frightened enemy. The sharp steel blades cut deep into the bodies of the panicking enemy and removed all life from those who remained in that narrow pass.

Once again, a small force led by Douglas had injected total panic and disarray into a vastly superior enemy. Mowbray's men could not go forward, nor could they make any progress over the steep sides of the narrow pass. There was only one way out and that was to retreat. However, the trail was so littered with fallen horses and slain troops that progress was greatly impaired. The slow retreat enabled Douglas and his men to continue the slaughter.

The remainder of Mowbray's troops, who had not yet entered the narrow pass, heard the screaming of their own dying men and saw the carnage that lay in front of them. Once the first few started running away in terror many more followed. No one stopped to count the numbers of Douglas's men who had performed such a ruthless and efficient execution. All that mattered to them that morning was to flee for their lives. Douglas and a group of his men chased after them and continued the process of executing those that they could catch.

Mowbray, who had been at the front as he led his men into the pass, was still desperately trying to defend himself. His troops had fallen all around him. He had been fortunate that he was able to use his shield to avoid the deadly arrows that had slain many of his men. There was no way back for him. He dug his spurs deep into his horse's body. The animal screamed, leapt forward and trampled over the bodies of his dead men. Several of Douglas's men blocked his way; they swung their swords and axes to prevent his escape. One of Douglas's men leapt from a boulder and grabbed Mowbray's sword belt. The terrified horse continued forward and the belt broke and came away in the man's hand. Mowbray continued to dig his spurs into his petrified beast, which now broke free, and made its way out of the narrow pass taking its rider to safety.

Mowbray rode with great speed; he had come with a thousand men and was now fleeing on his own from Douglas and his band of forty men. In fear of his life he headed for Kilwinning and then sought safety amongst the few coastal places still occupied by English troops. The rest of Mowbray's army had split up and scattered in all directions. Those who were not afraid of the embarrassment and consequences of this defeat headed back to the safety of Bothwell Castle. Meanwhile, Douglas and his successful warriors were looting the bodies of over sixty men whom they had slain in the pass that morning.

When Sir Aymer de Valence received the news of what had happened, he struck his messenger. He went into a wild rage and pledged that he would shortly lead his army against Bruce and finally put an end to the rebel's campaign.

'But please, my lord, if I may speak?' asked one of the men, who had returned.

'Speak, sir,' shouted Valence.

'My lord, the ambush of Mowbray did not involve Bruce; it was the one known as the Douglas, some call him the Black Douglas, it was he who planned and executed these attacks,' replied the man.

Valence picked up on two words, 'You say 'Black' Douglas and you imply that he has been involved in more that one occasion?'

'He is known as the 'Black' because of his long dark hair and pale features, but also because of his battle tactics. He fights without a large army. He hides during the day, and comes forth in the night; he lays ambushes for our armies, he is the most skilled of the warriors who associate themselves with Bruce,' answered the man.

'Where is he from? Does he have a price?' asked Valence.

'He is the son of Sir William Douglas who fought with Wallace. His father was taken prisoner by King Edward and died in the Tower of London. The lands of Douglasdale were confiscated by Edward and given over to Lord Clifford. They say that he does have a price. It is the full return of all his lands,' replied the man.

Valence paused for a moment and then said 'I have not yet met a Scotsman who did not have a price that was negotiable. I must talk with this Douglas.'

Douglas and his men returned to join their King, Robert the Bruce, who was based at Galston. On hearing of the victory over the large force led by Mowbray, the King was overjoyed. Bruce spoke, as he greeted Douglas's return. 'My Dear Douglas, you never fail me, I know of no other Scot who has your courage and determination. Today your actions have sent out a clear message to those who may be undecided on which side they should offer their lives. I say this, they would be well advised to fear us more than our enemies.'

'I agree,' replied Edward Bruce, who was also delighted with Douglas's success. 'If they don't, the Black Douglas will come and get them.' Everyone cheered. There was confidence amongst their men that had not existed before. Bruce felt more positive than ever, but he also knew that many battles would have to be fought before he would be fully recognised as the King of a united Scotland.

Valence continued to hear many tales of how Bruce and his men controlled the south-west lands and how more men were joining him each day. He feared the popularity that Bruce was building, and became concerned that if left unchecked, Bruce's army might grow to become a very serious threat. A few days later Bruce received a message from one of Valence's many spies. Bruce asked the messenger to deliver the message in the presence of his close nobles.

'Sir, as the one who states his claim to the crown of Scotland, your action is deplorable. To carry such a prestigious crown on your head, while behaving as a wild animal with no sense of chivalry or honour, is a gross insult to the people that you seek to lead. You lead your men like a pack of wild savages. Your tactics are to hide, then ambush and slaughter those who are unprepared for warfare; you appear to avoid any form of clean, honest battle at all cost. If you were to meet with me in open battle, your honour, reputation and nobility would be restored. Your people would respect you and you would wear your crown with dignity. I therefore offer you this challenge. I, Sir Aymer Valence, Earl of Pembroke, hereby challenge you, Robert Bruce, to meet me in battle on the 10th day of May in the year of Our Lord 1307, at Loudoun Hill.'

'Let's take him on,' cried one of the many nobles who had just heard the challenge.

'He will have several thousand men at arms. It would be dangerous,' commented Edward Bruce.

'No Scottish army has ever defeated the English in open battle,' called out one of those present. 'We have many good men, who will give their lives to our cause,' said another, as the views and opinions continued to be shared.

'Douglas, what do you think?' asked Bruce, as he looked towards Douglas and attempted to read his cunning mind.

Douglas had been sitting quietly listening to the various comments being made. He was not a man of many words; however, on this occasion he needed to speak his mind. 'Sirs, much of what has been said is true, and I agree with many of you. However, let us not forget the cruelty that King Edward's men have inflicted upon our nation. Valence speaks of a clean, honest battle; does he mean a battle like Methven? When he broke his word after agreeing to meet us in the morning, and then came upon us unprepared the previous evening? He mentions chivalry and honour, yet he has slaughtered many innocent people because of their association with us. He has imprisoned our clergy, Bishop Lamberton and Bishop Wishart. He speaks of nobility. Where is the nobility when they hang our Scottish noble ladies in cages suspended from the battlements of English castles? The message that Valence sends is that we are winning; our tactics are having a serious impact upon our enemies. His greatest concern is the selfish shame he has suffered in not being able to capture our good King during this last year. The message that he sends is, in my mind, a last desperate attempt by one who has failed miserably to capture our King, Robert the Bruce.'

Silence fell over the gathering. The words that Douglas spoke had reminded them of the immense cruelty that they had suffered, and also of the cause for which they were fighting. To Bruce's question 'What would you have us do?' Douglas replied 'I would advise that you reply to Valence and tell him that you will gladly meet him in battle on this requested day,' replied Douglas.

'My young James, do you have anything else to add? Plans perhaps?' asked Bruce. Douglas smiled and looked around at the faces that were staring at him. For the first time since joining Bruce he felt that he was a key adviser in battle tactics. 'I have two plans,' he said. 'The first is to find out what detailed plans Valence is at this moment drawing up; the second, well let me say I would only share it in secret with you, Sire,' 'We can talk later,' said Bruce.

A short time after the messenger had been sent back to Valence, Bruce, along with Douglas and a small band of men, made their way secretly to Loudoun Hill. It was not far from Galston and could easily be reached on horseback in a few hours. Loudoun Hill sat proud above all else in the surrounding area. The narrow pass that embraced the River Irvine as it cut through the rough terrain looked like the best place to meet with Valence's forces. Higher up on the south slope the road followed the curve of the pass and provided travellers and merchants easy access between the south-west coast and the lowlands of central Scotland. As he looked around the area, Bruce spoke to his men and asked their thoughts on the best strategy.

Douglas appeared to take a back seat in the planning and preparation for the meeting with Valence in battle. He had previously given his advice to Bruce. The narrow pass looked like the best place to wait and meet the enemy force. It was also agreed that ditches should be dug at specific locations around the area.

Douglas spoke to Davidson and took him into his confidence. 'My good friend, you have been of immense support to me and have provided me with much encouragement. I have a request that I must make of you. I suspect that Valence may have my name in his mind, for I have caused him great pain and embarrassment.'

'What can I do for you?' asked Davidson.

'I want you to get word to Valence that I wish to negotiate terms with him,' replied Douglas, but before Davidson had time to realise the horror of what he had been asked, Douglas explained 'I want to find out what's in his head and what plans he has for the 10th May.'

'I understand,' said Davidson. 'I will go myself and present your request.

Davidson was allowed to deliver his message to Valence. 'Sir, I bring you a message from James of Douglas,' declared the nervous Davidson as he faced Sir Aymer de Valence.

'Ah! The Black Douglas, the young rebel who advises the Bruce, now sends me his messenger. What does he want?' asked Valence.

'Sir, he is young and he has only been involved in this campaign for just over one year. He has advised the Bruce on tactics that have caused you great pain and I am sure embarrassment. He has also led his men to inflict revenge on those who steal his lands,' said Davidson.

Valence did not like being reminded of these things and started to lose his patience with this messenger. 'I know all that you say. Let me tell you this, his father was a brutal savage who terrorised my King Edward's loyal and innocent servants and he deserved all that he got,' shouted Valence. 'Now tell me, what does he want?'

'Sir, he simply wants the return of his father's lands. He wants Douglasdale and the other estates of his father returned to his name,' replied Davidson. 'And?' asked Valence. 'And in exchange, he will support you in the defeat and capture of Bruce at Loudoun on the 10th May.'

Valence, suspecting that the truth was not being told, asked 'Will this James of Douglas, meet with me and look me in the face and pledge this promise?

'He is an honest and honourable man. I am sure we can arrange for the two of you to meet and discuss your terms,' replied Davidson.

A few days later, Valence and a small number of guards made their way to Gillbank House, a tower-house situated two miles south of Strathaven, which was owned by the Auchinlecks. This family had been active supporters of Wallace, but had suffered such great losses that they were no longer able to raise arms against anyone. Douglas and his men had already arrived. He had agreed to abide by the truce of this meeting. However, not one to trust his enemies, especially Valence, he had his men positioned around the building. Several were also inside disguised as Auchinleck family members.

The two loyal servants to their own respective Kings finally came together for discussion.

'So you want to negotiate?' said Valence.

'I ask for the return of what is rightfully mine,' answered Douglas.

'And what, sir, do you claim is yours?' asked Valence.

'I am well aware, sir, that you already know the answer to your own question,' declared Douglas.

'Douglasdale is not mine to give,' answered Valence. 'Sir Robert Clifford has been granted that land by the rightful owner, King Edward of England.'

'Sir, I have twice defeated the invading garrison at Douglas. I have defeated your own men at Glen Trool and more recently at Kilbirnie. I now offer you the opportunity to avoid further defeat and humiliation,' declared Douglas.

'Sir, I have much greater strength of numbers than you or your Bruce possesses. In King Edward's armies I have unlimited resources that will surely crush the untrustworthy rabble that claims to follow you and the sacrilegious, cowardly Bruce that you call your King,' replied Valence.

Douglas raised his voice. 'Sir, that rabble, as you describe them, has achieved many successes against greater numbers. We can repeat that success many times over.'

Valence sat down and paused to collect his thoughts. The words that Douglas spoke rang true in his head. What Douglas had said was correct. However, he was not in a position to negotiate the ownership of Douglasdale. There was, however, one possible opportunity. Valence looked at Douglas; he saw the eyes of a very determined young man. He knew that if he could persuade Douglas to desert Bruce, then this uprising would be dealt a serious blow and the capture of Bruce, which had evaded him for the past year, would be achieved.

Valence came nearer and aggressively put his face up close to Douglas. 'Sir, let me present to you an offer for consideration. I do not have the authority to return your lands to you. However, should you aid me in defeating Bruce's army, I will grant you, in the name of King Edward, and without fear and without reproach, retrospective pardon for the actions you have taken against him. I will also grant you the freedom to reside in Douglasdale as a servant to Sir Robert Clifford.'

Douglas's face was unreadable. It did not convey any emotion as he replied to this proposition. 'Sir, I have seen much cruelty and suffering, and like most men, I wish to live in peace and safety with my family. If I am not to have my lands returned, then so be it. Sir, your offer is acceptable to me. What do you wish me to do?'

'Douglas, you have exercised good judgement today, and you will, I am sure, be justly rewarded,' said Valence. 'Tell me, what plans does Bruce have, as he prepares to meet me in battle?'

'Sir, I have no knowledge of the detailed plans that Bruce has drawn up. He wishes to demonstrate his warfare and leadership qualities to his men, and he has chosen to plan this event alone. I only know that the rabble will consist of untrained and ill-equipped men, who will quickly lose confidence if charged by your horsemen. They will be easily scattered,' said Douglas.

'What role will you play in these events?' asked Valence.

'I will lead my men as I normally do; they are only fifty in number. I will ride alongside Bruce. If your vanguard is destroyed, Bruce's men will acquire false confidence and will charge your main body. This action I suggest you allow,' said Douglas.

'What! You want me send my men to their death?' shouted Valence.

'Please be patient, let me finish. This action will be a small sacrifice, which will reap significant rewards,' replied Douglas.

'And what of you and your men of Douglasdale?' asked Valence.

'We will ride into your main body. You must let us through and allow us a gap to turn and join with your men. Together we will take Bruce and his army,' declared Douglas.

'Can your men be trusted?' asked Valence.

'They will follow me to my death,' replied Douglas.

'Let us shake hands and agree to this plan,' declared Valence, holding out his hand.

'Sir, I would rather shake your hand when we celebrate our successful victory,' replied Douglas, his hands behind his back, close to the long dagger that remained hidden there.

As he rode with his men past Strathaven and on to Galston, many thoughts were going through the mind of Douglas. If Bruce wins the battle, there would still be much to achieve before his lands of Douglasdale would be returned. He would still be a fugitive, as he had been all his life, and would still be hunted by his enemies. If he stuck to the plan that he agreed with Valence, then Valence would surely win. He asked himself the question, could Valence, who had previously gone back on his word, be trusted? If everything went as discussed, he could go back to Douglasdale and live in peace with his family.

Over the last few days, Bruce's men had been busy digging several ditches across the narrowest section of the pass at the foot of Loudoun Hill. The digging had taken place at night in order to avoid the observing eyes of Valence's lookouts. The ditches, which were dug at right angles across the pass, were dug deep, with the soil piled high on the east side from which Valence's army would approach. Many measurements were taken to ensure the depth, width and distances between ditches were exact and according to plan.

On the evening of the 9th May, Bruce assembled his men a few miles to the west of Loudoun Hill. From here lookouts, who were positioned on the top of Loudoun, could easily observe and signal the approach of Valence's army. Bruce had managed to assemble over six hundred trained fighting men. He also had the support of the same number again of local men, who although not skilled in warfare, were prepared to risk their lives in support of their King and in pursuit of their freedom. Bruce walked among his men, asking their names and where they came from. He was proud of their support and humbled by what they possessed. Their confidence and determination to win inspired him.

Douglas sat with his men. There were a few conversations taking place. 'Where to after this one?' asked Davidson, indicating yet again total confidence in his youthful leader. 'Perhaps we could go home to Douglasdale, retake the castle again, see our families, get drunk, and have a good time,' replied Douglas, as his men all cheered loudly with the thought of seeing their loved ones very shortly.

Sir Aymer de Valence, meanwhile, had been marching his well-equipped and trained army of nearly three thousand men from Bothwell, on past Strathaven, and was now close to Loudoun. They were camped for the night and ready for an early start, and hopefully an early and successful conclusion to the following day.

On the morning of the 10th May, the warm Cunningham air was clear and scented with the perfumes of the late flowers of spring. The rich green-rolling countryside which stretched out on either side of the River Irvine provided a comforting landscape to those who made this place their home. There was much beauty in these parts, not just from the many colours and splendid creations of nature, but also from the resources that this land yielded to his inhabitants. Those who cared for these lands were richly rewarded with the fruits of the fertile soil. Over the years, many trees had been cleared to make way for necessary crops that fed both man and his prized beasts.

On the top of Loudoun, lookouts on both sides signalled the presence of their respective opponents. The approaching English army shone bright in the mid-morning sunshine. The gleaming shields, colourful pennons and many large banners produced a spectacular display, as they moved in unison along the road towards Loudoun. The rhythmic beat of thousands of marching footsteps resonated along the pass, as they pounded the dry ground. The grand sight, so spectacular that it resembled a Roman legion being led by its emperor, looked a powerful and fearsome sight to the enemy, as Valence and his men, with the sun sparkling off the bright steel swords and high held lances, proudly marched towards the agreed battle site.

Bruce mounted his horse, turned towards his men and called out 'My lords, my good men, the time has arrived once more for us to unite in battle. Our enemy now approaches intent on killing us and taking our lands by their great power, and if we allow them, they will surely do so. Since we know of their intentions towards us, let us go now and meet them hardily, so that the strongest amongst their company can be discouraged by our brave encounter. If their vanguard can be halted, the rest will surely falter. Although they are more numerous than we are, we should not be disheartened, for when it comes to fighting, in battle there is none better than us. Therefore, my lords and men show again your courage and your great valour to build our reputation. Think what pleasure awaits us if we achieve victory over our enemy here this day. For there will be no one in all of our lands that we now need fear.' Amidst the loud cheering that followed, Edward Bruce called out. 'Sir, with God's will, we shall act as you desire, and no blame shall be cast upon us.'

Bruce's army, which was six hundred strong, made the first move. Leading his men towards the foremost ditch, he shouted out instructions for them to take up their positions. Valence, observing the movements of Bruce and his men, called on his own army to make their move. He shouted out encouragement, and declared that rich rewards would come their way should victory, which was expected, be achieved here today. The English army moved forward and then stopped. Silence, which is a precious thing for men as they prepare to go into battle, existed for a few moments. They all waited, and no one spoke. They thought of their loved ones. Many were down on bended knee, deep in prayer. Their creator was asked to provide protection and to take sides.

The English trumpets broke the silence as they sounded the charge; those alongside Valence rode to the front of him and with spears held level, charged at the Scottish King's position. As they advanced at speed, however, the vanguard unexpectedly plunged into the first deep ditch. Terrified horses, limbs broken, brought their riders down and exposed them to the waiting Scots. The spears plunged deep into both man and beast as the first casualties were inflicted. Bruce and his foot soldiers charged forwards, with swords, axes and spears cutting, slashing and penetrating into the enemy flesh, as no man was spared.

Douglas and his men, coming from behind Bruce, charged forwards on horseback as they rode through the narrow gap between the disguised trenches. The remainder of the English vanguard opened up, as the small but powerful band of determined men cut their way though and into the heart of the enemy ranks. A good two hundred or so of Valence's men now lay between the men of Douglas and Bruce. Those amongst the English vanguard felt defeated and trapped. Those within the main body of Valence's army moved back as they prepared to meet the charge of Douglas's men. Meanwhile, Bruce's men were inspired, as their leader and his brother Edward continued to attack with fearless determination and cut down every living thing in their path.

Suddenly, without warning and against the movement of attacker and defender, Douglas and his men turned. There was a pause of only a few seconds when very few knew of what was going to happen next. Douglas's men charge again, only this time towards Bruce. The powerful English vanguard had their backs towards Douglas as they desperately tried to break through Bruce's ranks. The swords and axes of Douglas and his men cut unexpectedly into their victims as they closed the gap between the two groups of determined Scottish warriors. Attacked from both sides, they were slaughtered as they hopelessly attempted to defend themselves. Those in the middle of the English vanguard, knowing that in a few moments they also would be slain without mercy, took their only option and ran. Some dropped their arms as they plunged into the River Irvine; others scrambled up the south-sloping hillside as they desperately tried to escape.

With the gap almost closed, Douglas and his men turned once again, and accompanied by many more of Bruce's horsemen, charged towards the main body of Valence's army. With their confidence being shattered in such a short period, many from this invading force had started to run. Despite their greater numbers they lacked the determination that their attackers possessed. They were overpowered by the superior courage and resilience of a nation fighting for its very freedom and existence. Bruce remounted his horse, and along with his men joined in the bloodthirsty pursuit. The pass was littered with the slain bodies, the spilt blood covered the whole ground and coursed downwards into the slow-flowing river.

The deserters from Valence's army grew in number as they tried to flee in all directions. Just as he did at Glen Trool, Valence tried one last time to get his men to turn back and face the army of Bruce. No persuasion could convince them, no bribery or threats were being listened to as more men ran past and deserted his once mighty army. As Bruce and his men continued to cut down his forces, Valence had no choice but to save his own life. He dug into his horse and galloped off at full speed leaving his army beaten, dejected and in total despair.

As the pursuit of the fleeing enemy ended, Bruce, Douglas and the other nobles gathered together with their delighted and victorious men. They took time to express their gratitude to God, praising him diligently for bringing them this magnificent victory. They were grateful that their own lives had been spared and that their cause had received a most significant boost. Bruce addressed his men, congratulating them on their courage and emphasising again that together, as a united Scotland, they could achieve so much more.

Over the next few days, as word spread of this victory, many more came to join the army of their King. The success of victory had clearly shown its attraction to those whose support had so far been lying dormant.

Douglas and his men were pleased that the part they had played in these events was appreciated by their good King and that others would be encouraged to join with them.

Meanwhile Valence, ashamed, humiliated and embarrassed by his failure to capture Bruce over the last year, and now with this defeat at the hands of a inferior army, had made his way south to meet with King Edward and offered him his resignation as Warden of Scotland. As was predictable, the King of England went into one of his many rages. He cried out for the head of Bruce as he physically struck the warden who had failed him repeatedly.

During the spring of 1307, the men of Kyle, Carrick, and Cunningham, along with their courageous neighbours from Douglasdale, had come together in unity. They had bonded under Bruce as never before, demonstrating their allegiance to the Bruce, their noble King and inspirational leader. They would gladly follow him into battle against a force of ten times their own size, and they would expect to achieve victory.

Several days after the battle at Loudoun Hill men were still arriving to join with Bruce and pledge their support to his cause. Like an uncontrollable plague, word of what was happening spread throughout the land, as more men arrived each day. Previously restricted by the fear of the horrendous reprisals taken against anyone who supported Bruce, these same men now refused to be terrorised by the threats of reprisal from King Edward. They now had leadership, they felt protected, and they were inspired by the recent victories. They had made their choice. They knew that some day they would die; however, they themselves could choose the where, when and why. They had chosen to fight with Bruce, and if they must die, to die free men.

Bruce let them know that he recognised their courage and their loyalty. He openly praised them, and he spoke to many individually and made them feel more than just nameless members of his army. They felt appreciated and proud to be part of his following.

Bruce had concerns, however; he knew that their numbers were still insufficient to achieve the ultimate victory. He addressed his men. 'My dear lords and men, I praise your contribution, I greatly admire your bravery and I am proud of the fighting spirit which you have demonstrated. However, I must ask for your patience. We need to increase our numbers in order to further our cause. We are but a small part of a much larger nation. For us to succeed, others throughout this land must join with us. I have decided therefore to go north and seek their support and I pray that some day soon we will all be united as a nation in pursuit of our cause.

Bruce discussed his plans with his close nobles, many of whom would go with him. Edward Bruce, Sir Robert Boyd, the Earl of Lennox, Sir Gilbert de la Haye, Sir Alexander Fraser and his brother Simon, along with many others, immediately offered their continued commitment, and agreed to follow him. Douglas, although he had developed a close friendship with Bruce, was not recognised as a noble and was not involved in this inner circle of political conversation. Douglas was by himself, deep in thought, and he made no comment. Bruce approached him, assuming that all was well and knowing that there was no need to ask for the support of Douglas, as it was always given. However, some assumptions should not always be taken for granted.

Bruce smiled at his most loyal servant. 'Would your good men be ready to come with us?' he asked, as he made recognition of the special skills that these men possessed, men who under Douglas's leadership had became his most efficient and effective fighting force. Douglas, with his head bowed gave his answer. 'No,' he said. The reply was firm, clear and precise. Bruce was stunned and shocked by such a short and direct answer. He asked that the other nobles leave their presence.

Bruce spoke alone with Douglas. 'My good James of Douglas, throughout this land many men now come to join us; our numbers have never been greater. You now say that you will not come with me. What's bothering you my friend? Please help me understand, please explain,' said Bruce, as he tried to understand the reason for the devastating answer.

Douglas raised his head, and with the most serious look that Bruce had seen on the face of this young man, replied 'Sir, your success has been magnificent, many men come to join you each day. I have felt privileged to have played a small part in your campaign, but neither I nor my men will go north with you.'

'Why?' asked Bruce.

'Sir, you request your nobles and your army to go north. If you do so, your protective forces will be away for some time. We have inflicted great defeat and embarrassment on our enemy the King's forces. Revenge will surely come from he who invades our lands. To leave our southern borderlands unprotected will mean exposing our defenceless people to unimaginable horrors. I cannot allow that to happen.' Douglas paused for a moment. 'Sir, I ask that I be allowed to stay and protect these lands, for Longshanks will surely come here. I may not prevent him, but I can cause him losses and inconvenience that will delay his forces until you return.'

Bruce was deeply humbled by the answer from Douglas. He realised that he had been selfish in only thinking of building on his success and recruiting more men to his cause. Ambition and power were becoming the driving forces of this campaign. Yet here, in front of Bruce, stood a young man of twenty years old, who was showing more thought and unselfish concern for the people of this nation than their own King was.

As Bruce looked at Douglas both men's eyes filled up with the emotion of affection. Bruce spoke softly. 'James, you have humbled me with your unselfish concern for our people. For that I have great respect and admiration. You have been in my company for one year. No man has given me more support than you have. Many of my achievements have only been possible because of your skill, loyalty and determination. I would not refuse any request that you make, for I know that it would be intended for my own good. You have made such requests in the past and I am sure you will continue to do so in the future. With my blessing, you may go as you please and do as you see fit.'

'Sir, I will defend your borderlands with my life,' replied Douglas.

Bruce embraced his young friend. 'There will, as you quite rightly say, be great danger. I regret that I cannot give you any more men. May God be with you and your good men of Douglasdale.'

15

CASTLE DANGEROUS

THE MORNING RAIN was gently falling across the Douglasdale. There was very little wind. The small rain soaked everything, as it silently fell on the residents of Douglas. This grey, bleak morning was one that caused a dilemma, not severe enough to stop the inhabitants who wished to do so from going about their business outdoors, but miserable enough to help make up the minds of those who did not want to do anything other than rest inside in the dry warmth. There were many in Douglas that morning who fell into the latter category.

Those who were up and going about their business that morning were doing something different, which strangers to these parts would not have noticed. No two people would pass by each other without talking; everyone who was up and about was putting the village gossip to shame. The conversations were all very similar. 'Have you heard? Did you know? Were you aware?' all were enquiring questions to determine if the latest news was correct. 'They arrived in the middle of the night,' said one young woman as she spoke to her neighbour.

'How did they get on?' asked one old man who wished he was younger and could have joined them. 'Is he with them?' asked a young girl, as she enquired about the gallant leader. Final word of confirmation came from one of the mothers. 'They have all come home, every last one of them, a few injuries but they are all home safe.'

That morning the people of Douglas wanted to celebrate. They were in the mood to recognise this day and show how proud they were, because this was a joyous occasion if ever there was one.

Douglas had woken from his deep sleep. He remembered that he had dreamed the dream again, but this time it was different. There was only one faceless woman. 'Some day perhaps it will be explained,' he thought to himself. He was glad to be home, but there was sadness. A good friend with whom he had developed a very close relationship had parted company with him. David Davidson had made his choice and decided to go with the Bruce. He was glad that his King attracted such good men, but he was sad that a man that he had grown to trust with his life would no longer be by his side. 'Someday, perhaps we may meet again,' he thought to himself.

By midday the rain had stopped and the sun had broken through. A bright colourful rainbow appeared in the distance and presented an enormous smile across the face of this valley. The gossip had stopped only to be replaced with factual information. What these fifty men had achieved was at first not believed. However, the stories were consistent and matched the tales that messengers had been bringing. Every man who had returned with Douglas was a hero. Douglas himself had become more than a hero. He was the leader, he inspired them, his cunning, skills and tactics of warfare were unbelievable for one so young. Those who had fought in battle knew that Douglas had no equal. He did not need a permanent army, as no man at any time would refuse to join him should he be called.

An army that can suddenly appear from nowhere is a highly prized possession; likewise, one that can disappear just as quickly will be a major concern to any enemy. Within a few moments of returning to their homes, every one of Douglas's men had fully blended back into their community. His small army of devoted followers had come and gone in only a few months, during which time they had inflicted great damage on the enemy forces.

The priorities over the next few days were to have a good rest and to allow plenty of time for war wounds to heal. There was a dormant, sleepy atmosphere throughout the village and across Douglasdale. No one appeared to be bothered about anything; people simply went about their business in a quiet, confident and contented way. In the past, there was always an element of fear and intimidation due to the occupation by the invading foreign force. Today that fear was being reversed, as the invaders were now the ones being intimidated and harassed.

Douglas was approached by one of the elderly men of the village. 'They're back, this time led by a man called John of Webton. He's a bit like yourself, young and fierce, he commands the castle garrison.' Douglas shook his head. 'Will that lot never learn?' he sarcastically replied. There was laughter, as everyone knew that yet another plan to retake the castle was about to unfold.

The following morning many of the locals were collecting their stock and preparing for transportation to Lanark market. A few had already started out, hoping to arrive early in order to allow their beasts time to rest and feed before being put on display for sale. As time wore on many more could be seen making their way towards the Lanark road on this bright fresh May Day morning. This was an event not just for the men, but for their families; wives and children would also make the journey, as they looked forward to the long trip and the excitement of the interesting goods being sold at the market. The opportunity to buy new clothes or any of the wide range of unusual goods that would be on sale would be the main topic of conversation during the length of the journey.

Within the castle, Sir John of Webton had been informed of what was going on outside, as the folks passed by with their many desirable goods. 'What do you think?' he asked of his men. 'They would not set a trap using the women and children,' said one of the guards. 'I agree,' said another. 'They go to Lanark this time every year, it's a regular event,' declared one of the men, who had survived from the last attack.

'What do we need most?' asked Webton. 'Anything! We are in short supply of almost everything,' replied the man, who along with his assistant was responsible for the keep of the provisions. 'Let's wait for a little while and see what comes by,' instructed Webton.

The slow procession continued, as the folks of Douglasdale, with their attractive stock, made their way, in full view, past the castle and on towards the road to Lanark. Webton called out to his men 'I have seen enough, let's go, we can't let this opportunity pass us by. They appear to have plenty, I'm sure they won't grudge us if we help ourselves to a few items.' There was no need to go out on horseback, as the trail was not that far from the castle.

As the gates opened, three fully loaded wooden carts, along with a few packhorses, were being led past by several men on foot. John of Webton accompanied by about twenty of his men rushed out. As they approached the convoy, Webton called out 'We want to help you.' The men of Douglasdale stopped, waited and said nothing. Webton called out again. 'We want to offer to lighten your load.' As the men of the garrison finally approached, they drew their weapons and aggressively pointed them at their surprised victims who remained still and silent. 'Your journey to market will be much easier with a lightened load,' declared Webton, as he gestured his men to seize the plunder.

The men of Douglasdale stood back and offered no resistance. They said nothing as Webton and his men simply walked back towards the castle with the stolen goods. 'That was easy,' said Webton. 'If the one they call the Black Douglas' ever reappears, I will demonstrate to you how easy it will be to take him also.'

As Webton and his men made their way back, they pulled at the reins of the stubborn beasts that were reluctant to follow their new masters. They were about half-way back when they heard the sound of horses. They looked towards the stone walls that provided their safety and place of sanctuary. Their stomachs churned in panic and fear stopped them in their tracks as they saw what awaited them. In front of the castle gates were two groups of horse riders, six on either side; they had swords drawn and were now slowly coming towards them. On their own, these riders would not normally present a fearsome sight. Terror was engendered by the thirteenth rider, the one in the middle, the one with the long black hair, the one who wore the Douglas coat of arms.

The garrison troops let go of their plunder. They turned to look behind to where their victims had stood when they had robbed them just a few minutes earlier and received another shock, for their victims were now only a few yards behind them, having followed them silently back towards the castle. Webton and his men stared at these men of Douglasdale. Their next move was critical; they wondered if they should attack their defenceless victims. The men of Douglas immediately cast off their robes to reveal their weapons; their sharpened swords and axes gleamed in the morning sun. It would be unwise for Webton's men to take these men on.

Webton instructed his troops to group on either side of the three carts, as Douglas and his men began their approach. The fearful tension was made worse by the slow deliberate manner in which Douglas and his men approached Webton's force. Petrified, the men from the castle garrison looked back and forward, unsure who would make the first move. The tension reached its climax as the cry was finally made, 'A Douglas! A Douglas!', and the charge began.

The first blood to be drawn was neither by Douglas's men on horseback, nor by the men of Douglas who came from behind, but by the men who had remained hidden in the three carts. They burst out, plunging their swords into the backs of the nearest soldiers. Webton had failed his men, who now ran for their lives, to the left and right, chased by Douglas's riders who quickly cut them down. A few stayed with Webton, only to be slain.

Douglas dismounted and walked over to face Webton.

'Do you know who I am?' asked Douglas.

'Yes,' replied Webton, attempting to thrust his sword at Douglas, narrowly missing his stomach as Douglas twisted to the side to avoid the lethal strike. As he twisted, Douglas used his momentum to immediately turn back, drawing his sword across the open neck of the outstretched Webton. The split-second delay was all that Douglas needed, as his sword penetrated the side of Webton's chest and ended his period as occupier of Douglas Castle.

Within a few minutes, Webton's men were no more; all those who had tried to steal from the people of Douglas that morning now lay slain. As his men removed the weapons of the dead, Douglas, along with his companions on horseback, made their way back to the castle gate.

'What shall we do now? Do we take the castle?' asked one of his men. Before Douglas could give his answer, he was called by one of his other men. 'Sir, you may be interested in this,' called the man, as he handed over a letter. 'It was found on the body of Webton.'

Douglas read the bloodstained letter. It was from a lady in waiting, a woman who was the love of Webton, the man he had just slain. She had written to him stating that when he had successfully held the dangerous castle of Douglas for a period of one year she would be so impressed by his bravery and strength in leadership that she would accept his offer of love and would be glad to become his wife.

Douglas stared at this letter. He read over the words again, he looked at the blood that stained this message of love and affection, the blood that he had drawn with his own sword. He realised that these men who invaded his lands were ordinary men, with lovers, parents, wives, families who were concerned for them and hoped and prayed for their safe return. He realised that every time he killed an enemy there would be someone somewhere who would be grieving for a lost loved one. A mother, who had lost a son, a son or daughter who had lost a father.

He could feel that grief, and he shared that pain, as he himself had lost his own father in much the same way. He had no sympathy for those who come here invading his land and inflicting such cruelty on his own people. However, he felt great sympathy for those who were the real victims of war, the ones whose pain would remain for the remainder of their lives. 'How can I fight this bloody war without hurting the innocent?' he quietly asked of himself.

'Sir, are you all right?' asked one of his men who noticed that Douglas appeared to be in a deep trance. 'Yes, just thinking, that's all,' replied Douglas. 'What about those in the Castle? There's about another twenty of them in there,' asked one of the others.

Douglas called to his men. 'Listen to me, all of you. You have given me your trust, which I cherish and will always honour. I am about to do something which many of you will oppose. This action which I am about to take will end the occupation of this castle by a foreign force once and for all.'

'What do you want us to do?' asked one of the men.

'Simply do as I say and don't question my reason,' replied Douglas.

Instructions were issued to bring horses and provisions for twenty men. The dead were taken away to be buried in a Christian manner. Money was collected, but the reason why was not given.

Douglas mounted his horse and approached the castle gates alone. He called out 'You men inside, listen to me, I am Douglas of Douglasdale, and I am the one you fear most. I offer you a choice. You may stay inside and try to defend yourself. If you do, you will surely die, just as Webton and his men have done this morning. Or you may leave now and return home to your loved ones. I have provided horses and provisions; I will give you money and a letter of safe passage should anyone challenge you. I give you my solemn word, leave now and you will live to be with your families.' Douglas raised his voice louder still and called out. 'Talk amongst yourselves, take your time, this is no trap, do what is right for you and your families.'

Douglas asked all his men to move back, and requested them not to return home yet. He pleaded for their absolute trust in him. Reluctantly, they did as they were asked and pulled back out of sight, leaving Douglas alone in front the castle entrance. He patiently sat on his horse in front of the closed gates. Behind him stood the twenty horses, gently grazing on the short lush grass, oblivious to what was going on. To the side lay the pile of provisions that had been freely donated by the folks from the village.

There was a silence and nothing moved as Douglas awaited their answer. He expected to hear discussions inside or even possibly arguments, but no sound came from within. He continued to wait. His horse was becoming restless. The first sound he heard was the squeak from the rusty hinges of the large gates, as they were slowly pushed open. Eventually the noise came to an end as the doors of the castle of his inheritance were opened wide enough for a man to pass through.

A few seconds elapsed before the first face appeared in the narrow gap at the gate.

'Do you really mean what you say?' the voice called out.

'Yes, I do, and I give you my word, as the true Lord of Douglasdale, that no harm will come to you.'

'Why do you make us this offer of unconditional release?' called the nervous voice from behind the gate.

'I don't want you to remain here, the people of Douglas don't want you here, your families don't want you here. Therefore I suggest you defy your King Edward, and in the name of God return to your homelands.'

There was a short pause before the doors were pushed wide open. The twenty troops stood together, frightened and insecure. They had lost their leader to this fearsome warrior who now stood a short distance in front of them.

'Please, come on out!' called Douglas. The garrison men slowly walked out, huddled together and petrified as they moved towards him. The polite and confident manner in which Douglas presented himself added to their fear. Douglas gestured towards the horses and provisions as they made their way past.

The first group of men who passed by Douglas paused and hesitated before finally helping themselves to the provisions and grabbing the reins of the nearest horse. As the last few men walked slowly past, Douglas called out 'Stop!' Those closest to him expected the worse; they looked round in terror and anticipated yet another trap. 'Take this,' he said, as he held out a letter and a purse of money, and placed it in the trembling hand of the soldier nearest him. 'As I promised, this should ensure you have a safe passage home.'

The men all looked at Douglas. They did not know what to make of him or this situation. As grown men, they had never at any time in their lives felt so vulnerable and so petrified. The situation was made worse by the fact that it was only this one man, the Black Douglas, who had now retaken this castle three times and who now stood on his own against their twenty.

Douglas stood back as the men mounted the horses they had been given. 'I have one last request,' called Douglas. They turned round and faced him. 'I wish you a safe journey. If you meet with Longshanks or with Clifford, tell them what has happened here. Tell them that it would be unwise for them to send any more armies to invade this land. Tell them that you were the fortunate ones that I decided to let go. Should others come they will not be so kindly treated.'

The defeated garrison men made their way slowly at first, and then at a fast gallop, as they left Douglasdale for the last time.

Douglas slowly made his way through the large gates and into the castle of his family name. He looked around at the high, thick walls that had provided shelter and protection to his forefathers. He felt regret that he had been unable to live here with his own family. He could only imagine a small portion of the pleasure that had been denied to him, the pleasure of growing up in this homely place, rather than the drab French abbey that had been his temporary accommodation during those distant early childhood years. As he looked around, he thought of his own two brothers, who were in hiding along with his mother, and were being denied the same rights. How wonderful it would have been had they all been able to live here in peace. The sound of horse riders arriving at the gate broke his reverie about the wonderful life that could have been.

'Sir, are you all right?' called Andrew Young, who arrived with three other riders. Douglas turned towards them.

'Thank you for returning, I am fine.'

'Is there anything you require of us?' asked Young. Douglas looked around the inside of his castle once more and then answered 'Tell the men to come in and take all that they can. When they are finished I have one final request.'

'What would that be, sir?' asked Young.

'Destroy it. Pull it down. Make sure no one, especially Clifford's men, ever occupies this place again.'

'We will carry out your wishes,' answered the sympathetic Young, who understood Douglas's dilemma.

As more help arrived to carry out Douglas's request, he stood back and watched the first actions of these good and loyal men as they proceeded to demolish this precious place.

Andrew Young approached to offer him comfort.

'I am leaving now,' said Douglas. 'This part of my life is now over; Clifford's men will not be back. I must now go to my family. I thank you for what you have done for me.'

Andrew Young put his hand on Douglas's shoulder and said 'My Lord, I thank you for what you have done for us. You have restored our pride, you have given us back our dignity and you have helped us obtain our freedom in our own land of Douglasdale.'

'Some day I may be back and I may have cause to call upon your good services again,' answered Douglas with a gentle smile.

As Douglas mounted his horse the men stopped working for a moment and all looked at him. He had made many emotional speeches to them in the past, but this time there were no words that could convey his feelings. The look from Douglas was all that was needed to express his genuine love and affection for these men. They in turn replied with that same look. It was the look of total respect and admiration for this great man, who they were proud to have as one of them. Douglas pulled on his reins, turned his horse and disappeared out of the castle gates.

16

HUNTED BY THE SCOTS

THE LONE RIDER made his way across Tweeddale and headed towards the outskirts of the great Forest of Ettrick. Staying in the shadows and avoiding contact with anyone, and without being noticed, Douglas quietly passed through the few small villages that lay on his route. He did not head for Blackhouse Tower, where his family was in hiding, but instead continued east in the direction of the Tweed. As he followed the flow of this splendid river, it felt like many years ago that he had first come this way. His destination was the same as last time, Melrose Abbey, a place where he would seek some answers. He did not want to arrive during the hours of darkness, but instead rested on the edge of the forest until morning.

About an hour before dawn, he quietly approached the side door of the abbey. Several knocks were required before any response could be heard coming from within the massive building. The door was carefully opened by a young monk who asked if he could be of help.

'I wish to be allowed to speak with Brother Michael,' replied Douglas.

'And who may I say wishes to see him?' asked the monk.

'Please tell him that I am a good friend of his Excellency Bishop William Lamberton, of St Andrews,' answered Douglas, as he stood in the doorway.

The monk asked Douglas to enter and wait. As he looked around, he felt safe in this place, cocooned by the thick sandstone walls, the absolute silence and the smell of burning incense. The atmosphere of this place was like no other.

'So you are a friend of Bishop Lamberton,' called Brother Michael as he approached Douglas. 'And who, sir, are you, if I may ask?'

'I am James of Douglas. I was raised by his Excellency Bishop Lamberton and I come here to seek any news you may have of his whereabouts.'

'Please sit down James and I will tell what I know,' answered Brother Michael, as he gestured to Douglas to sit beside him. 'Tell me, without being disrespectful, how do I know if you can be trusted with confidential information relating to our mutual friend?' asked Brother Michael.

Douglas looked at him. 'Brother, I am no fool. You know who I am, and you will no doubt be aware of my association with Bishop Lamberton. I am short of time and I must say that I am well aware of the secret communication network that exists within our church. I expect there is very little that you do not hear about. So if I may ask again, what can you tell me of Bishop Lamberton?'

Brother Michael smiled at Douglas. 'You are just as Lamberton described you. I can see why he referred to you as being impatient. The latest information that I have is that he is still being held prisoner by King Edward.' Douglas gave out a loud sigh of frustration as Brother Michael continued. 'However, all is not bad news. I have heard that he has been released from the dungeons of Winchester Castle, and has been allowed an element of freedom on the condition that he remain within the diocese of Durham. His full release is

216

expected soon.' This answer eased the concern that had been burning in Douglas's mind towards his good friend. He felt guilty that he had not done anything to assist his escape.

'And how is his health?' Douglas asked Brother Michael. 'He is fine considering the conditions that he has had to endure. A lot better may I add than Longshanks.'

'What do you mean?' asked Douglas.

'They say that not many survive being chained in those dungeons. The conditions are said to be very demanding, even for one of such strong faith as Lamberton,' answered Brother Michael.

'I meant, what did you mean about Longshanks,' asked the ever-impatient Douglas.

'Longshanks is very ill, and lies on his death bed at Lanercost Abbey,' said the monk.

'Why is he at Lanercost Abbey?' asked Douglas, concerned. 'That's just over the border.'

'He originally came north because of the reports he had been getting about Bruce and the damage being done by his followers,' explained Brother Michael 'You have certainly been getting a name for yourself. Some say that Longshanks is more concerned about you, the Black Douglas as you are now known to your enemies, than about King Robert the Bruce. Longshanks has suggested that you may be your father reincarnated.'

'Do you know what plans he had?' asked Douglas.

'He has apparently dismissed his Scottish Warden, Sir Aymer de Valence. Whatever you did to that man it worked, as his reputation and name have been completely destroyed. Longshanks decided to come into Scotland himself and deal with Bruce's uprising in the south-west.'

'How ill is he?' asked Douglas, who now had a look of delight on his face.

'We should not take any pleasure from the suffering of others, no matter who they may be,' chided Brother Michael. 'However, in answer to your question he is reported as being seriously ill and not expected to live much longer.' Douglas tried hard to remove the smile from his face, but in spite of his strict Christian upbringing it would not disappear.

The two men spent the next hour discussing many things. Douglas's motive was to seek out as much information as possible. Any news on the movement of King Edward's troops was of specific interest. Where were they based? What routes did they take? These and many other questions were asked. Their friendship grew as these two mutual friends of Lamberton discovered that they had much in common.

Recognising that he had overstayed his visit, Douglas announced that he had to leave. However, before he left Brother Michael supplied him with a great gift, the names of many contacts who would be able to help him. These were the names of individuals who had also chosen to lead a humble life devoted to the worship of God, dedicated laymen who resided in other holy places of worship and meditation. These men could be contacted at Jedburgh, Dryburgh, Kelso and many other places of sanctuary. Of all the riches that existed in these times, knowledge and information were the most valuable. Douglas's meeting with Brother Michael that morning provided him with the locations of such riches.

'What are your intentions after you leave here?' asked Brother Michael.

'There is much that I have to do. However, I would like to meet with some of the men you have mentioned,' replied Douglas.

'Please wait for a moment,' Brother Michael asked, as he left Douglas alone for a short time. Douglas was pleased that he had come here. He had made a good friend and had acquired good information that would be of use to him. A few minutes later Brother Michael returned and handed Douglas a long brown robe and a pair of leather sandals. 'Please accept these humble gifts. They may not be of much use to you in battle; however, they will enable you to be less conspicuous when you visit the places you intend.'

'Thank you my dear friend, I greatly appreciate your assistance,' said Douglas as he made his way out of the abbey.

Over the next few weeks, Douglas visited many places. Dressed in the robe Brother Michael had given him he called upon the contacts whose names the monk had supplied. Many were helpful and supportive to him; others were reserved and not prepared to offer any help or disclose any information. The monk's clothes had been useful, and had enabled him to check out those who were not prepared to help him, while at the same time protecting his identity.

During these weeks, he acquired much information on the movement of English troops throughout the borderlands. On his own, he was able to seek out their camps, and identify the many routes that they used to transport their supplies to support the northern garrisons. He quickly recognised that if he were able to stop, or even delay these supplies as they headed north it would have a major impact on the English forces that invaded his country. With the first stage of his plan now complete, Douglas was ready to return to those who were closest to him.

It was about midday as Douglas made his way through the Selkirk forest and along the stretch of the Yarrow Water. The route that he followed headed onwards towards St Mary's Loch. As he approached the turn off that headed up the glen towards Blackhouse Tower, several men, who had been sitting as the edge of the wood rose up to observe him. He did not recognise any of them.

'Good day, sir,' one of them called out.

'Good day to you,' replied Douglas, guardedly. 'Are you from these parts?'

The men were unsure how to answer this question. Douglas grew even more concerned at this hesitation and was now extremely worried about the safety of his family, who lived just a short distance up the glen. A voice called out. 'We better answer him, or we will be dead meat.' Just then, one stood up and turned round to face him. It was his friend Cuthbert. The two men smiled and embraced. In Cuthbert, Douglas had not just a good friend, but also someone who could not have been more loved had he been his own brother.

Cuthbert introduced Douglas to the men who had come to join him. 'This is him, the one they are all taking about, the true Lord Douglas himself' Cuthbert called out. The men stepped forward to greet Douglas, and to pledge their loyal support to him. 'Please come with me,' said Cuthbert, before turning to the men and ordering them to 'Continue as you were.'

Douglas and Cuthbert made their way up the glen towards the Blackhouse Tower. 'What's going on?' asked Douglas as he looked back towards the new men. 'Better to be careful,' answered Cuthbert. 'We have heard that Longshanks is heading north and is not far away. We hear that he is determined to seek out the Bruce and his followers, including you, once and for all. We have recruited many good men who have come to help protect your mother and family.'

'Longshanks will not be coming here. That I can guarantee,' said Douglas firmly.

They made their way towards the Blackhouse Tower. 'I want to see how they are,' said Douglas as Cuthbert escorted him the short distance to his family's home.

'Fullerton has been gone for a few days. He asked that I keep guard,' said Cuthbert.

'Once again you have done well my good friend,' said Douglas. As he entered the tower building, his mother was not surprised to see him; she had been expecting his arrival for several weeks now. Lady Eleanor greeted her beloved James. 'I am glad you kept your promise to return so soon,' she stated, as she embraced the eldest of her sons.

'How are you, Mother? I hope you are well,' asked Douglas. 'I am as well as can be expected,' she answered. 'Where are the others?' asked Douglas.

'They are safe. It was felt that it would be appropriate to split up and not stay in the one place.'

'Exactly where are they?' asked Douglas.

'Archibald is safe. He is with distant relatives,' answered Lady Eleanor.

'And Hugh, where is he?' asked Douglas, who was becoming more concerned with what he was hearing.

'Hugh is with friends of Bishop Lamberton,' came the short and rather abrupt reply from his mother. Once again, Douglas had to repeat the same question. 'Where is he?'

'He is at Melrose,' his mother answered. Douglas did not like the way in which this information had to be extracted in order to find out about his own brothers, especially from his own mother.

'Mother, there has always been danger, so what's so different this time that our family has had to split up?' Douglas demanded to know.

'My dear James, please don't mistrust good intentions. We have been informed of possible dangers that we must prepare for.'

'What new dangers have forced these actions to be taken?' asked Douglas.

'We have heard that King Edward is at this moment making his way into Scotland and seeks out those close to you and King Robert,' answered Lady Eleanor.

Douglas laughed. 'Mother let me tell you this. Longshanks is dead; he died last week at Lanercost Abbey; he had been seriously ill for some time. Yes, he was coming north as you say, but he won't be coming any longer. His reign of terror has now come to an end.'

'Oh! I did not know,' cried Lady Eleanor.

'So now that the danger that Longshanks presented is no more, Hugh and Archibald can return,' commented Douglas. His mother hesitated.

'No! There is another danger,' Lady Eleanor quietly announced.

'What other danger?' Douglas asked.

His mother paused. He had never seen her like this before, and something appeared to be causing her even more concern than the fear of Longshanks. She spoke in a gentle voice, but her worry was evident. 'There is a group of English troops, Clifford's men I believe, who are planning to hunt you down. They know what you have achieved with Bruce, and of what you did in Douglasdale. Clifford has stated that the castle is too dangerous for his forces to occupy; they now call it Castle Dangerous as a direct result of what you did. They are now determined to hunt you down. You have caused them great losses.'

There was nothing new in what his mother was telling him. Douglas still suspected that the full truth was not being told.

'Mother is there more that perhaps you may not be telling me?' he asked with a raised voice.

'That no way to speak to your mother,' called a soft but firm voice from the doorway behind him.

'Sophia! How are you my dear?' asked Douglas in pleased surprise, as he turned and looked at this sweet young girl again. He had thought little about her in his travels and at no time had expressed any concern for her well-being. He felt ashamed and guilty that he had troubled himself so little about her welfare. Sophia walked towards him; beauty and elegance were two qualities that he was not accustomed to, yet here, as she moved across the room, in this young lady they were in rich abundance. 'I am fine, and I have been well looked after by your good, kind mother,' replied Sophia. Although pleased to see James, she was not pleased by the manner in which he had raised his voice against his mother.

Lady Eleanor spoke. 'My dear Sophia, thank you for the support, but I would be extremely grateful if you could leave us alone for a short moment. I will call you when we are finished.' Sophia left the room, closing the door as she went.

'James, there is a problem, one that is most serious. Several Scottish nobles accompany the English troops who are now hunting for you. These men know more about you than you realise,' said Lady Eleanor, as she tried to comfort her son and at the same time inform him of this worrying news.

'Who are these Scottish nobles, do you know their names?' asked Douglas. Lady Eleanor could no longer hold back, she had to tell him. 'It's Thomas Randolph and Alexander Stewart,' she said quietly.

Douglas shook his head, which was fast filling with rage, and shouted 'One, a relation to our King Bruce, the other, a bloody Stewart of all people. When will this country ever be at one? The real enemy, as we have said many times before, is not the English but the treachery of our own people, those who are driven by greed and blind ambition, those who betray their own kin for their selfish gains, those who seek power only to abuse it. Will it ever end?'

'Please be patient, James. At this very moment our loyal friend Fullerton has sent out trusted men with false information to see if he can entrap them and track them down. He has already reported back that he has picked up information on their whereabouts. We can then keep one step ahead should they come too close.'

Douglas, still raging, continue to shout. 'These times amaze me. Thomas Randolph was considered a loyal supporter of Bruce. He was captured by Valence at Methven. He is the nephew of our King and yet he takes sides with the enemy. Do these men not have any decency or principles?'

'James, please, don't spend too much time trying to understand the actions of those who hold different views. As you have said, greed and ambition is what drives these men.'

Douglas slowly regained his composure. He rarely lost his temper, yet here in front of his own mother he had just done so. 'If I am going to lose my temper,' he thought wryly to himself, 'perhaps it's best to do so with a loved one who will offer forgiveness and advice ... a long as I don't do so too often.' He smiled at his gentle mother and gratefully received her answering smile of forgiveness.

'Perhaps fear is also a factor to consider as an explanation,' said Douglas.

'You could be right. Many good men have been forced to change sides as a result of fear,' commented Lady Eleanor.

'Yes, perhaps that is the reason. However, they will shortly fear me more than anything else in these lands,' declared Douglas. His mother looked at him. At first she had not believed the many stories of his successes in battle that had been arriving regularly. However, they were coming from different sources, and were proven correct. She had heard of his reputation and was immensely proud of him. She knew that the enemy already feared him; that in fact he was fast becoming the most feared man in the country. However, she had her own fears about James – not of the English, nor of those who hunted her beloved James, but of a secret which she hoped James would never discover.

'Where exactly is Fullerton at this moment?' asked Douglas. 'James?' said Lady Eleanor. 'What, Mother?' 'Be patient,' she said with a smile.

Later Douglas spoke with Cuthbert. 'What progress have you made in recruiting more men?' he asked his friend.

'We have done well; we have a good twenty local men who have joined us. Some have gone with Fullerton, the others you see around you.'

'Any more?' asked Douglas.

'No, but we believe that we could get at least a hundred more if there was less fear in their minds,' replied Cuthbert.

'What is the main cause of such fear?' inquired Douglas.

'It's Stewart and Randolph, who own lands around Berwick and Nithsdale. They are spreading fear amongst those whom we wish to recruit. These are no ordinary men; they are powerful nobles who have available to them significant resources on either side of the border. The blood connections that those two men have with the family of Bruce are discouraging many Scots from raising arms against them. There appears to be a waiting game being played.'

'What do mean, waiting game?' asked the confused Douglas.

'Who makes the first move. If Stewart and Randolph capture you, then many who are simply waiting on the outcome will take their side and we will only have the men you see around you today. Our campaign would then be hopeless.'

Douglas thought for a moment. 'And what if I capture Stewart and Randolph?'

Cuthbert shook his head from side to side, laughed, and said 'You never give up, do you?'

'No!' said Douglas, as he also shook his head.

'If you capture those two traitors, all hell will break loose. You will have more men following you than you will know what to do with. You will have the control of the borderlands in the palm of your hand. You will have the resources at your disposal to stop the movement of English troops. With Longshanks now dead, you could not pick a better time. You may even be able to exercise greater control over our nation than our King Robert Bruce,' said Cuthbert.

'What you say makes good sense my friend,' answered Douglas. 'However, Stewart and Randolph are not only skilled warriors, they are fellow Scots, whom I don't want to kill, and they do have many men. They will not be taken easily.'

The two good friends continued with their discussion. They agreed that with Longshanks now gone, the time for action was now.

'Where is Fullerton?' asked Douglas.

'I don't know,' answered Cuthbert. 'What? Why don't you know?' asked the surprised Douglas.

'Your mother knows. She requested that all information regarding Fullerton's whereabouts be for her ears only,' answered Cuthbert, who did feel uncomfortable about this situation.

'I will consult with her and come back to you,' said Douglas, who hid his embarrassment, but who was becoming more confused and concerned about his mother's unusual reactions to these dangerous times.

Lady Eleanor was sitting alone in front of a south-facing widow. There was sadness in her face, a face that normally conveyed maturity and wisdom within its beauty, and always showed warmth and affection. She stared out across the Yarrow countryside, looking down across the treetops that covered both sides of this glen. Her mind was elsewhere, her face, drawn and worried-looking with a worry that could not be shared, and therefore could not be eased. No one in her family had ever seen this look on her face before.

Douglas knocked and entered. As his mother looked round, he saw that look, and it shook him. A cold shiver ran down the whole length of his body. She seemed someone else. 'Mother, you look … .' He did not finish what he was going to say, but instead put his arms around her and embraced her.

'James, my dear James,' she whispered, as she hugged him tightly. 'I don't want to lose you, you are so precious to me.'

'Mother you will not lose me, I promise. I also promise that we will shortly all be together again. I don't want my family to be scattered in all directions.'

'James, I don't want you to go after Stewart and Randolph. It's too dangerous,' she said as she wiped tears from her eyes.

Douglas grew impatient. He had only been here a few days, and yet he was desperate to go seek out those who it was claimed were hunting him. His impatience was brought to an end when word finally arrived from Fullerton. The messenger, tired after his long return journey, was not allowed to rest until the information had been given. 'Has he found them? Does he know where they are? How many men?' Douglas asked, without allowing time to answer.

'Give him time, for goodness sake,' said Cuthbert, as he put a reassuring hand on the shoulder of the messenger.

'I'm sorry,' replied Douglas, who realised his impatience was getting in the way.

'Stewart and Randolph are getting closer. They were last seen in Selkirk. They had about thirty, possibly forty men,' replied the messenger.

'What of Fullerton?' asked Douglas.

'He is following them, but he needs more men; he has left a marked trail for you,' answered the exhausted man.

In less than an hour a small band of men had left their place of hiding. The loved ones left at Blackhouse Tower would be safe with the few trusted men who remained to guard them. Douglas and Cuthbert, accompanied by ten other riders, travelled fast as they headed alongside the Yarrow Water and on towards Selkirk. The blistering pace set by their impatient leader caused all but the best riders to panic as they struggled to control their beasts along the narrow trail, which repeatedly twisted and turned as it followed the Yarrow through the colourful glen.

Their first stop came at the point where the Yarrow merges into the waters of the Ettrick. A welcomed short rest by the gentle flowing river was followed by a slower, more deliberate pace, as they searched for the first sign.

'What are we looking for?' asked one of the men, mumbling 'I thought we were supposed to be in a hurry!'

'You will know when you see it,' shouted Cuthbert.

'Look for something unusual,' cried Douglas.

They continued the slow searching pace for about half a mile until they arrived at the point where the castle of Selkirk stood proud on the other side of the Ettrick. Cuthbert broke the silence. 'Look! Up there!' he called out as he pointed to two short strands of wool that were tied to a branch that overhung the trail ahead.

'How do you know it was Fullerton?' called one of the men.

'Well it wasn't a flying sheep,' shouted Cuthbert.

'Where to now?' asked Douglas.

'The Tweed,' shouted Cuthbert.

The fast pace resumed as the riders headed past Selkirk and onwards to where the Ettrick meets the Tweed.

The next marker was spotted by one of the men as they crossed the wide shallow Tweed below Rink Hill. A small pile of stones sitting a few feet above the trail was the signal they were looking for. Two pieces of wool, under the top stone, one twice as long as the other, told Cuthbert all that he needed. 'Innerleithen,' he called out. The riders sped on. 'How far?' asked Douglas. 'About twelve miles,' replied Cuthbert. 'Where do you think they are heading?' Douglas shouted over to Cuthbert. 'Not sure, could be Peebles,' he called back.

The riders continued as they followed the Tweed westwards through the dense forest of Traquair and onwards towards Peebles. 'We'd better slow down,' shouted Douglas. 'If we come upon them we won't be in a fit state to fight.' When they approached the River Leithen where it flowed down and into the Tweed they continued their slow search for the next sign. A loud voice took them by surprise, when someone from the hillside above them shouted down 'Who are you looking for?'

'Friends, they came past here not so long ago. Have you seen them?' Douglas called back. The stranger stood up and pointed towards Peebles. 'Yesterday afternoon,' he shouted. Douglas waved. 'Thanks, friend.'

On arrival at Peebles, they rested for the night. Several men went out in search of information. After making friendly conversation with the locals, they inquired if any strangers had come past. No one had heard or seen anything. Cuthbert and Douglas wondered if their journey had been a waste of time. The following morning, as Douglas discussed with Cuthbert which direction they should take next, a shepherd came past as he herded his small flock towards the town centre.

'I don't know how many,' he replied when asked. 'All I can say is that there are strangers in that house at Lyne. They were coming and going,' he added.

'Did you see any horses?' asked Douglas, as he tried to help the man remember.

'I think there were about a dozen, tied up at the side, the bloody things frightened my sheep.'

'Thank you, my friend,' said Douglas as he handed the shepherd some coins as compensation for the interrogation.

The house they were looking for stood high up on the hillside above the banks of the Lyne Water, a few miles west of Peebles. Anyone approaching from the lower levels of the Tweed would be easily noticed during daylight hours. 'Where is Fullerton?' asked the nervous Douglas, as he stood with Cuthbert gazing up at the distant building and observed several people walking about. 'He can take care of himself,' replied Cuthbert, as he tried to reassure his concerned friend.

'We need to wait until darkness,' said Cuthbert, sensing that Douglas appeared to have lost his initiative on this occasion.

'Let's go back!' declared Douglas, who up until now had been extremely ill at ease with this situation.

'What! Go back! We can't just leave them,' shouted Cuthbert who was fast losing patience with his good friend and leader. The smile that had been missing for some time from Douglas's face reappeared.

'Yes, go back, but not to leave them alone. Let's go back in order that we can go up and over. When that sun goes down, I want to be dropping in on those up there.'

A few hours before darkness, Douglas and five of his good men made their way up and over the hill of Lyne. As he peered over the large moss-covered boulder, he looked down into the glen and thought to himself 'Two hours to get up, and a quarter of the time to come down.'

There was about one hour before dusk when Douglas, having crept closer with his men, looked down again. The sight below him caught him unawares, striking him like a vicious blow to his body. At the rear of the house below, two soldiers could be seen carrying out a body from the rear door and dumping it on the open ground. A third soldier approached a small group of men who were on their knees and were tied together in a huddle. Douglas could not hear what was being said, but could well imagine, as the next victim was selected and taken inside.

They came down on all fours, directed by the glow from the smoking fire. The sharp stones, irregularly scattered throughout the hillside, dug into their knees as they slowly and painfully crawled down, unable to express any sound of discomfort. The dilemma of balancing speed with caution was difficult, due to the irregular patterns of movement from down below. One of Douglas's men spotted the lone guard who sat at the front watching the route up from the glen below. 'He needs to be taken first, and then we give the signal to Cuthbert,' Douglas instructed two of his men.

The captives knelt on the cold damp ground, their heads bowed in a gesture of defeat and humiliation. 'Where's Fullerton?' the voice of Douglas quietly whispered into the ear of the nearest captive. The man startled, taken unawares by Douglas's silent approach. Douglas immediately gestured for total silence. The captives looked up at him in relief and silently gestured towards the rear door. Further down the glen, Cuthbert had spotted the signal and was fast approaching.

The relieved men were untied, but the ropes were left loose around their shivering bodies. Douglas and his men waited. There was only one way into the building and that was to wait for the rear door to open again, when the next victim would be brought out. 'I hope Cuthbert arrives before that door opens,' whispered Douglas to one of his men. The muffled sound of men shouting, jeering and laughing could be heard coming from within, but no sense could be made of what was going on. Cuthbert had still to arrive when the rear door suddenly opened.

'Who's next?' called the guard, bowing down to grab the nearest man, as his two companions proceeded to dump yet another body.

'Me!' said Douglas, as he stood up and stabbed his long dagger into the upper abdomen of the astonished guard. The dying guard put both his hands on Douglas's right hand. Douglas's left hand was covering the man's mouth to silence any cries for help. The guard dropped to the ground, dead. The other two guards were dealt with equal precision and they also dropped silently to the ground.

Douglas was first to enter; those inside had their backs to the door and were oblivious to what had just happened. 'Talk,' a voice at the far side of the room roared out. 'Tell us where he is and you will live,' called the same voice again, as the cries of someone in great pain echoed throughout the room. Three guards and a dead body had gone out; three guards and a bound prisoner were expected to come back in. The disguises could have been easily spotted by anyone paying close attention; however, they were only required to cover those first few yards.

Within the room, the centre of attention was the far wall, where someone was being beaten. Douglas went berserk. He knew who it was that was being tortured and he knew why. An almighty swipe from his sword cut through the right forearm of his first victim who screamed in pain as he and his sword hand parted company. The momentum of Douglas's sword struck deep as it cut through the collarbone and across the bare neck of the next. A third had the lethal steel penetrate through his chest and puncture his heart. The others turned. Douglas's men were instantly upon them.

'A Douglas! A Douglas!' The terrifying battle cry, roared out by Douglas's men, filled the room and injected a paralysing fear into the enemy guards. The element of surprise was no longer a benefit as more guards came rushing through from the next room. Cuthbert, followed by his men, came blindly charging in, his sword slashing in all directions to stop them getting at Douglas and his group.

Several more were cut down before Douglas could reach the tortured prisoner. Horror and anger raged within him as he glanced at the half-naked figure that was crouched on the floor against the rear wall, his hands tied behind his back, face and upper body covered with cuts and bruises. The sight of the distressed Fullerton was too much for Douglas, as he rushed at the two guards who were positioned in front of his injured friend. With both hands tightly gripping his broad sword, and with the maximum force that he could muster, he swung left and right as he cut his way through. Both guards put up a good defence, but nothing could stop the determined Douglas, as he ruthlessly cut through the last hurdle that stood between him and his injured friend.

Douglas bent down to comfort his beloved companion. Fullerton, in obvious pain, his face covered in blood, looked up at his young lord. There was great sorrow in his eyes, but there was no time for sympathy or much needed comfort. Fullerton gestured for Douglas to continue what he had started as he nodded his head in the direction behind Douglas. More enemy guards had appeared. A single thrust from the sword of Douglas immediately ended the progress of the one behind him.

Cuthbert and his men were engaged in heavy fighting along the corridor and towards the next room when Douglas and his men joined them. The sound of the vicious fighting had alerted those above as several figures came running down the spiral staircase and joined the mass brawl at the end of the corridor. However, these men were not guards; these men were the Scottish nobles who had been hunting for Douglas. First to come down was Alexander Stewart, son of Sir John who was killed at Falkirk. Stewart killed one of Cuthbert's men by stabbing him from behind. After Stewart came Thomas Randolph, the nephew of King Robert the Bruce. Randolph appeared shocked by what he saw in front of him. He defended himself but appeared reluctant to attack any of Douglas's men. The third noble to come down was Adam Gordon, a knight of the Earl of Dunbar, who seized the opportunity to run through a gap in the fighting and head for the front door, which he burst open with a wild kick and then ran for his life.

The others were hemmed in within the large front room as Douglas and his men gradually overcame their enemy. Alexander Stewart fought for his life as he wounded another of Douglas's men. Cuthbert's target was Thomas Randolph. 'If I get him they will surrender,' he thought to himself. The fight reached its peak as Cuthbert faced Randolph and Douglas faced Stewart. The clash of steel against steel echoed throughout the building as both sets of men paired off against each other.

Douglas drew blood first, as he slashed his sword across the left arm of Stewart, temporarily disabling him and causing him to momentarily back off. Cuthbert exchanged blows with Randolph, who still appeared to be defending than attacking. The remainder of Douglas's men, having dealt effectively with their tasks, stood back and watched. Douglas struck Stewart again, this time on the upper right arm, causing him to drop down in pain. Douglas seized his opportunity and instantly thrust his sword against the throat of his victim. Thomas

Randolph, who still appeared only to be defending himself, immediately dropped his sword and pleaded for mercy.

Douglas, still burning with revenge for what these men had done to Fullerton, took a deep breath. As he was about to plunge his sword through the neck of this now terrified Scottish noble traitor Stewart looked up at him, his eyes now pleading for mercy, and dropped his sword. 'Have mercy on your own kin,' Stewart called out.

Douglas hesitated as he looked at the petrified face. 'What do you mean, kin?' shouted Douglas.

'Stop! Stop!' shouted the voice at the door. It was Fullerton, who had crawled from the other room. He called out again 'Stop, no more!' Fullerton, cut, bruised and battered, lay on the floor, and requested mercy for those who had tortured him.

Douglas turned to look into the face of Stewart, his sword still pressing against the noble's neck. 'What did you mean, kin?' Douglas asked again. 'Ask your mother,' replied Stewart. Douglas was stunned by this answer and eased his firm grip on his frightened victim. His searched in his mind for an answer, but none would come that made sense. 'Let him go,' shouted Cuthbert, who then instructed the rest of Douglas's men to seize and bind their captured enemy.

Several hours later Fullerton lay resting, still in great pain and very weak from his injuries. Douglas sat with him, thinking about what Stewart had said, and still unable to understand his remark. 'What did Stewart mean, kin?' he asked Fullerton.

To Fullerton, still suffering in agony in body, this question struck a more painful blow that any inflicted by his torturers. He gently shook his head in reply. 'Do you know?' asked Douglas. Fullerton did not answer but grasped his stomach and passed into unconsciousness. Douglas was at a complete loss as to the behaviour of Fullerton. 'How had he got himself into this situation? His friend was the most skilful and experienced warrior that he knew. And why had he wanted to save his torturers' lives after what they had done to him?' 'None of it made any sense. Douglas left his friend being tended by one of his men and made his way to speak with his prisoners.

'Why do you give your support to the English?' asked Douglas, as he sat down beside Randolph and Stewart.

'Why not?' replied Randolph. 'We still have our lands; our titles and our estates still belong to us. The English are not as bad as many make out.'

'What of the torture that they have inflicted on our people?' asked Douglas.

'All due to one man, Longshanks, and he is now dead,' answered Randolph.

'What of your uncle, King Robert the Bruce, why don't you give him your support?'

'He fights like a coward,' replied Randolph.

'Bruce is no coward,' replied an angry Douglas. 'Why then does he not come out into the open and fight like a true honourable noble?' asked Randolph.

'I put it to you, sir, that the coward is he who comes with an army ten times in size to defeat in battle a much smaller nation.'

Douglas's answer closed the conversation, as Randolph paused to reflect on his situation.

Douglas then turned to Stewart and asked 'Sir, do you wish to explain what you meant by being my kin?' Stewart, glad that those earlier words had saved his life, now regretted that he had been forced to utter them. 'I can't add any more. It's something that I was told many years ago. As I said, you must ask your mother,' he mumbled.

Throughout the night Douglas and Cuthbert shared the watch over the injured Fullerton as he drifted in and out of consciousness. They tended his wounds and provided comfort during the hours of darkness. Douglas could not stop thinking of Stewart's suggestion that he was his kin and of Fullerton's strange behaviour. 'Perhaps my mother is the only one who can explain,' he thought to himself.

In the morning, Douglas announced that he would take some men and escort Randolph and Stewart into the possession of Bruce. 'They can both explain to him why they are traitors. I am sure that he will deal with them accordingly.'

Fullerton had recovered a little from his injuries, and although still in great pain, he was helped onto his horse. Douglas turned to Cuthbert. 'Please take good care of him; he has been as much of a father to me as my very own.' Cuthbert clasped Douglas's hand and acknowledged his request. Douglas leaned over the arched body of Fullerton. 'Robert, my friend, and dear friend of my family, I thank you for the years of care and protection that you have given us. Please allow us to repay that debt and care for you now. I will return shortly to be with you.'

A few days later Douglas delivered his prized prisoners into the hands of Bruce. 'These men, who were hunting me down have now surrendered into your keeping. Please do as you see just,' declared Douglas, as he handed over his prisoners. The King addressed his good friend. 'My Dear Douglas, you have done well. By showing mercy to these nobles you have demonstrated that we have forgiveness in our hearts and seek to unite our nation. Their capture will discourage others who may oppose us.'

Bruce thanked Douglas many times for his good efforts and wished him good fortune on his return to the borderlands.

Bruce turned to Randolph, the son of his sister, and said 'For a while you have refused your allegiance to me. This I now demand.'

Randolph, confident that he, as the King's nephew, could say as he pleased, replied 'Sir, you rebuke me, but rather you should be rebuked and prove your nobility in open fighting and neither by cowardice nor cunning.'

Bruce laughed. 'Perhaps one day it may come to that,' he replied. 'But since you speak so forcefully, it is wise that men should rebuke such proud words until they know the truth, as you should some day.'

Douglas asked for permission to depart and to continue with his struggle to regain control of the borderlands. 'It should be easier now that Longshanks is dead,' he declared.

'For the moment maybe, but his son Edward II possesses much the same desire to rule over our nation,' replied Bruce, with a word of caution for Douglas not to become too confident.

A few days later, Douglas and the three men who had travelled with him made their way into the narrow glen where the Blackhouse Tower was located. Douglas looked around in concern. 'Where are the guards?' he asked as they made their way up the trail. There was no sight or sound of anyone. Some horses were tied up opposite the tower house, but there was no sign of the riders. Douglas entered his temporary home. There was no one in the house, but also no sign of any disturbance.

'It's as if everyone just got up and walked away,' said Douglas to his men. As he thought of what he had just said, the unthinkable went through his mind. 'Surely not, I pray to God no, please God don't let it be so,' Douglas called out. His men were alarmed by the sight of his extreme anxiety. 'Sir, what's wrong?' asked one.

Before Douglas could regain his composure, the answer came slowly walking down the glen. It was his mother, accompanied by young Sophia and comforted by Cuthbert, at the head of the returning funeral procession. Douglas wept. He knew what had happened, and he blamed himself. Cuthbert was the first to approach him. Douglas's anguished face spoke the question. 'Yes, I'm afraid he did not make it. They must have beat him very badly,' said Cuthbert. Lady Eleanor, her eyes red from crying, still had her head bowed when Douglas approached her. 'Mother,' he said. She looked up and held out her arms. Shaking, they both embraced as they shared in the grief at the loss of their true friend, Fullerton.

'I'm sorry. Mother. We did not get to him in time,' said Douglas.

'He was a good man, a wonderful person. Your father trusted him.'

'Why did he go after them? I don't understand,' said Douglas.

'We can talk later,' replied Lady Eleanor.

Douglas spent a few moments with each of the men. These were men who also respected and held a great deal of affection for their common friend. Although Douglas was the leader of these people, Fullerton was the elder common man who put the family of Douglas before all else. In him, they saw a role model. He would be sadly missed but not forgotten.

Sophia stayed beside Lady Eleanor as they went inside to grieve in private. The adopted daughter was proving to be a tower of strength during this tragedy.

As the hours of darkness descended, Douglas approached his Mother. 'Can we talk now?' he asked.

'Yes, if you wish,' she replied.

'Mother, I want to ask two questions. First, why did Fullerton risk his life and go after them?'

'To ensure our safety, of course. They were hunting you down, and were getting too close,' replied Lady Eleanor.

Douglas paused for a few seconds. The second question he wanted to ask was a simple one, but the answer could be devastating.

'You said two,' said Lady Eleanor. 'Pardon?' said Douglas, who was deep in thought. 'You said that you had two questions. So far you have only asked one.'

Douglas drew a deep breath. 'Alexander Stewart claims to be my kin. In what way are we related?' he asked.

Lady Eleanor froze on hearing the question that she had dreaded being asked. Unable to hide her emotion, her head bowed, she wept, and shook with fear.

'Mother, what's wrong?' asked Douglas, as he put his arm around her.

'Give me a moment,' she asked.

'He's your cousin,' she finally declared.

'My cousin! How can he be my cousin?' asked the surprised Douglas.

Lady Eleanor looked up into the face of her tall handsome son. 'Oh, James, please don't,' she said, with a trembling voice.

'Mother, please, I beg you, tell me the truth,' said Douglas 'Is he a cousin from my father's side?'

Lady Eleanor shook her head and wiped her eyes.

'On your side then?'

Lady Eleanor shook her head again, and then covered her face with both hands.

Douglas stared at her. 'If not my father's and not my mother's, how are we related?' he asked.

Lady Eleanor reached out and firmly held her son's hand, but her voice trembled as she answered him. 'He is your cousin on your mother's side.'

Douglas paused for a moment. 'But you just said that he was not related on your side.'

'That's correct, not on my side, but on your mother's side.'

'Mother, this does not make any sense. What are you saying?'

'James, please sit down, and I will explain everything to you,' said Lady Eleanor. She realised that the time had come and the story would have to be told. After a short pause, she began her explanation.

'Alexander Stewart is the son of John Stewart, a good noble who, like your father, fought with Wallace. John Stewart was a good friend of your father; he died in battle at Falkirk.'

'What's this got to do with me?' asked the impatient Douglas.

Lady Eleanor braced herself. 'John Stewart had a sister, Elizabeth, a kind and loving woman. She died of a painful illness two years after you were born.'

Douglas caught his breath and quietly whispered. 'Do you mean ...?'

'Yes, she was your mother,' replied Lady Eleanor in a soft apologetic voice.

Douglas stood up. Lady Eleanor braced herself for his departure, as he turned away and composed himself, wiping the tears from his eyes. But he turned back, and came towards her. 'You are my mother, what has happened in the past and what happens in the future will never change the feelings that

I have for you. I want, with your permission, always to be able to call you my mother.'

Lady Eleanor stood up and embraced her son like never before; she had dreaded this moment for many years and had expected the worst. The happiness she felt at the continuing love he had expressed filled her heart.

'Tell me more, Mother,' said Douglas. 'Tell me about yourself. After my natural mother died, when did you meet my father?'

Lady Eleanor smiled, and spoke now with ease. 'I was the daughter of Mathew Lord of Lovaine and relict of William de Ferrers, Lord of Groby. I had a handsome dowry from several English estates and was also in possession of five Scottish counties. One time, 1288 if I'm correct, when I was in Scotland collecting rents, I had cause to stay in the castle at Tranent, a few miles east of Edinburgh. One morning, a force under your father, Lord William, beset the castle. Some said that this was a cruel and barbaric attack, but that was not the case. Your father was a kind and considerate man; even in time of warfare, he showed true nobleness and gallantry. It was said that he abducted me. Well, if falling in love at first sight and wanting to go with him is abduction, then I admit I was abducted. King Edward, Longshanks, was outraged by this event and ordered all of your father's lands to be confiscated and ordered that he be imprisoned should he be caught.'

'And was he?' asked Douglas, who was spellbound by this story. 'Yes, he was, but he had powerful friends at court, James the Stewart, the brother of your mother Elizabeth, arranged his release and for his lands to be restored.

'And what of you? Did Longshanks harm you?' asked Douglas.

'I was fined one hundred pounds for marrying your father without the King's permission. However, due to circumstances, I was unable to pay and my manors in Essex and Hereford were confiscated. After your father was taken prisoner at Berwick, you will remember being sent to France. At the same time I had your brother Hugh taken care of by distant relatives in Essex. However, during the period that your father fought with Wallace the Sheriff of Essex found out about Hugh and had him imprisoned.'

'Mother, are you saying that Longshanks fined you one hundred pounds for marrying my father and imprisoned my two-year-old brother?' asked Douglas, who was starting to disbelieve this story.

'Yes. It's true, every word.'

Douglas paused. This story might be true, but even in this cruel world was still difficult to believe. He took the opportunity to resolve a mystery that had been bothering him for some time.

'Mother, there is a question that I have been meaning to ask for some time. Do you still collect rents for any lands?'

'Yes, my dower was returned. It has provided a small income that has supported us over these years.'

'What of Hugh, do you think the imprisonment caused him any harm?' asked Douglas.

'If you mean his backwardness and slowness of learning, yes it's possible,' replied Lady Eleanor.

'Was there anything else?' asked Douglas.

'Your father was also fined by Longshanks. I think he still owed about eighty pounds for abducting me. However, the Sheriff of Northumberland was ordered to levy off your father's estate of Fawdon and as you already know his lands of Douglasdale were bestowed upon Sir Robert de Clifford.'

'Mother,' asked Douglas, smiling cheekily, 'what does it feel like to be English?'

'Fine really, apart from a few embarrassing moments. And what does it feel like to have an English mother?' asked Lady Eleanor.

'Has its advantages,' replied Douglas, as he put his arms around his beloved mother and embraced her tightly.

That night, as Douglas slept, the recurring dream from his childhood days reappeared. However, this time there was only one face, the face of Lady Eleanor. He slept peacefully and at ease with the world.

17

CONTROL OF THE BORDERS

THERE WAS A PEACEFUL atmosphere at the Blackhouse Tower. It was a time for reflection, accompanied by a feeling of sanctuary that had followed the rescue and tragic loss of Fullerton. Knowing that the noble traitors Stewart and Randolph no longer presented any danger, Douglas and Cuthbert took time to rest and rethink their strategy and of what should be their next challenge.

'What's in your mind?' asked Cuthbert as he approached Douglas, who was calmly sitting outside in the warm sunshine.

'We have seen how men react when confronted by fear,' commented Douglas. 'How will they react if that fear is removed?'

'Please explain,' requested Cuthbert.

'If we quickly spread the word that we have captured Stewart and Randolph, if we say that we already have a large army hidden throughout the forest, what will happen?' asked Douglas.

'Many will come and join us, prepared and eager to fight for you,' answered Cuthbert.

'I share the same thoughts. My plan is to spread good news that will remove fear and encourage many others to join us,' declared Douglas. 'However, people need more than words, they need to see us. We will ride throughout the border towns and villages. People will see us, we will talk to them, they will feel safe and they will want to be part of our success,' explained Douglas as he stood up and stretched out his arms. 'Our period of rest is over. Let's get ready.'

That summer was constantly wet and miserable. Throughout these months Douglas and his men continued with their plan to visit many places. With heads held high, they first entered Selkirk. They presented their strength not in numbers but in confidence and daring. They spoke to the locals. 'I am Douglas of Douglasdale, these trusted men who follow me have offered their support to rid these lands of our invading enemies. We are here to protect you,' declared Douglas, as he addressed the crowd who gathered around him.

'How do we know that we can trust you?' shouted a local man, who was suspicious of these strangers.

Cuthbert gestured that he be allowed to answer. 'This man before you, is the one that the English call the Black Douglas. He is the one they fear the most. He comes with the full support of our own King, Robert the Bruce. Along with Bruce he has defeated Sir Aymer de Valence and sent him back to England.'

The crowd had heard of these stories, but were suspicious of their accuracy. They had heard of a warrior called Douglas, who was indeed developing a reputation of being feared by the English.

'It's not the English that we fear. It's our own treacherous nobles, who have betrayed us so often that we don't know who to trust,' said one elderly local, who stood directly in front of Douglas and his men.

'Sir, I too have been betrayed by those that you speak of,' replied Douglas.

'What of Stewart and Randolph? They have many men who follow them, English and Scots,' shouted the same elderly man.

Douglas dismounted and went over to stand beside him. 'Sir, Alexander Stewart and Thomas Randolph were captured by me and these men who you see riding with me today. I have delivered them both to King Robert. There is no one to fear, other than ourselves,' declared Douglas.

'How do we know that you won't be just like the rest of them,' shouted an aggressive younger man who stood with a group youths.

'What do you mean when you say "like the rest of them"?' asked Douglas.

'They ask us to join them, only to keep the riches that we win for them,' shouted the same young man.

'Douglas got back on his horse. 'Listen to me, I have lost more than any man among you. I promise you this, join me and any plunder, wealth or riches that come our way as a result of victory will be shared by you all. I give my solemn word,' declared Douglas.

'But they are not soldiers,' shouted a attractive young newly wed woman who did not want to see husband go off to war.

'Yes, you are not soldiers. But I don't come here for soldiers, that is not how I intend to defeat our enemies,' answered Douglas.

'How do you intend to defeat them?' shouted a suspicious voice from the crowd.

'You are men of the forest, you are hunters, you are farmers, you know these lands, and you know every hill, glen, river, trail and pass. With your knowledge, and a cunning strategy, we can defeat any enemy. We will hunt our enemy as we hunt down any wild animal that threatens our families or our livestock,' shouted Douglas.

The questions stopped. Huddled discussions took place, and many heads were nodding in agreement. Some, who were lacking in confidence, were not sure and shook their heads hesitantly. One older man, his aged body bent and twisted from the years of hard labour, approached Douglas. 'Sir, I have lost my sons to those who invade our lands. I am not a fighter but I would like to join you.'

'Sir, as a son who has lost a father, I would be glad of your support,' answered Douglas, who then shouted to the crowd. 'If you don't join me, who will defend you?'

'We will join!' answered a group of eager men. 'And us!' cried another group, as excitement started to fill the air. Many others gladly gave their pledge that day to support the cause of Douglas.

The scene was repeated throughout the Ettrick forest, first Tweeddale, then Teviotdale and then the lands of Peebles and Annandale. There were many who saw in Douglas their only hope for a decent life, a life free from the terrors that they had become accustomed to over these past years. Throughout the borders, Douglas continued to attract the support and trust of these loyal people.

Douglas and his men disappeared as quickly as they arrived. Many wondered about the strategy that Douglas was adopting. They were recruited into his army, and yet, apart from a few individuals, they all stayed at home and went about their normal daily business. They knew that some day they would be called upon. They did not know when.

'We need to take advantage of these times,' declared Douglas as he discussed tactics with his men.

'I agree,' said Robert Hall, a Selkirk man who had joined Douglas to seek revenge on his enemies and who was not content to sit at home while others fought for him. 'Edward II is weak compared to his father Longshanks. There are many English nobles who are not pleased with his leadership in warfare. We should take advantage and strike while the English have their own problems in the south.'

'You are well informed. From where do you get your information?' asked Douglas.

'What I say is common knowledge. However, I have a brother who has given his life to the worship of Christ; he is at Jedburgh and has informed me of this news.'

'This is good to know. Both you and your brother may prove to very useful,' said Douglas thoughtfully.

Over the next few months, something unusual and powerful started to grow within the Ettrick forest. A network was developing, a network of intelligence and communication. With the deadly sensitivity of a spider's web, each strand reached out across the towns and villages of the borderlands. Life would appear dormant, and then the alert would be given indicating the presence of any intruder or prey. The network continued to expand as Douglas developed his invisible army, whose eyes and ears stretched from Douglasdale in the west to Berwick in the east and from Lothian in the north to Nithsdale in the south-west.

Anything that attempted to move in or out of these lands triggered the secret network and immediately resulted in the information arriving at the place where Douglas quietly lay in waiting.

It had rained relentlessly for the last few months; the miserable autumn harvest had been disappointing for many. Those who had managed to reap anything worthwhile did so with great urgency as they gathered their stock and retreated into hiding. With winter approaching those with food were the most vulnerable to any hungry attacking enemy. The castle of Bothwell was no different, with many hungry English bellies waiting inside for the overdue delivery from the south.

Douglas first heard the news when the English wagons, bringing fresh provisions, passed through Berwick and headed on towards Roxburgh. At each stop, wagons were unloaded and much needed provisions delivered to the resident garrisons. 'When shall we do it?' was the question that was put to Douglas. 'Let's follow them. We don't need to rush,' he answered, in a manner that suggested this next course of action might actually be fun.

The enemy wagons rolled north as they transported their goods towards Selkirk. Within the shadows of the forest there were those that followed them on their way. For many miles, invisible eyes and ears watched and listened as provisions were transported to the invading forces. From the steep hillside a sudden rush of water came thundering down from the controlled dam burst and caught the last wagon unawares. The flash flood of water blocked the way ahead and flooded an already sodden trail. The wagons in front continued on, oblivious of the dangers from behind. The small group of soldiers tried in vain to push the stuck wagon on its way, as both they and wheels sank deeper into the black mud.

Without showing face, the invisible attackers from the forest edge suddenly released a deadly hail of arrows. Those with the stranded wagon did not know who was attacking them, as one by one they fell slain upon the flooded trail.

A short time later, a few English soldiers on horseback returned to check the straggling wagon. There was no sign of it, no sign of any wheel tracks, no sign of any men and no sign of any ambush. As they came to a clear stretch of the trail they realised that their return journey had been a waste of time as the wagon had apparently mysteriously disappeared somewhere along this forest trail. 'Douglas!' shouted one of the soldiers, and their minds filled with fear, realising that only one man could have organised such a cunning and daring act.

Douglas and his men continued their silent harassment of the English wagons as they headed north on their journey towards Bothwell. Additional wagons were taken and more English guards were slain by the cunning invisible hunters who stalked their prey each mile along the dangerous route.

Throughout the borders the silent attacks continued. The provisions being sent north to support the many English garrisons were constantly being attacked and looted. The attackers hid in the shadows of the forest, their faces were very rarely seen, and their sudden appearances and surprise attacks were matched only by their equally amazing disappearance into the depths of the dark forest with their prize. Their gains were many, their losses few.

In the town of Selkirk a peaceful morning disguised the pains of hunger and worry that existed there. The look of misery and despair on the faces of the market traders told the story; there was little to trade and very few customers able to offer suitable exchange to purchase. The atmosphere of gloom was immediately lifted by the inspirational sight of the gallant Douglas leading his men into the town square. Crowds gathered, as excitement grew with the presence of this hero in their town.

Douglas sat proud on his horse; his tall, broad-shouldered frame immediately commanding respect amongst the local folks. As he stretched out his arms to remove the stiffness from his aching limbs, many silently stared with a look of admiration. He gently twisted his head from side to side, and then slowly drew the fingers of both hands through his long black hair to reveal his handsome face, a face that was unblemished, and yet had a misleading look of childlike innocence.

The dark eyes of Douglas made contact with those that surrounded him, and he smiled. It was a warm smile which conveyed deep affection for those he cared for. As many had been, they were mesmerised by him. Like a Greek god, he looked every part the ideal hero.

Douglas spoke. 'Good people of Selkirk, I made the promise to you that if you gave me your support you would benefit from anything that I would acquire. I am delighted to return to you your good men, who have supported me. I believe they may have something to share with you.'

The men of Selkirk rushed forward with the wagons of provisions and proceeded to share the much needed plunder amongst the townsfolk. There was great joy in Selkirk that morning. Douglas had honoured his commitment by delivering the plunder to the benefit of those who gave him their support.

Douglas gestured to two of his men; it was time to move on. The ever-loyal Cuthbert along with Robert Hall, who had recently joined the cause, came over to Douglas. 'In case we forget,' said Douglas, 'take note, for what you see in front of you is why we do what we do.'

The sight of plundered goods being distributed in borderland market squares became a common one. For some, starvation caused by the poor harvest was kept at bay for a few more weeks as a result of these daring raids. Many a life had been saved and those who were owed that life to Douglas. The reputation of the 'Good' James Douglas was spreading amongst those who benefited from his deeds. On the other side, the frightful demon image of the evil 'Black' Douglas was also spreading and causing great terror amongst those who were forced to travel into the borderlands.

Word continued to spread and more men offered to support the Douglas cause. They were supplied with the weapons of war taken from the victims of the many raids. Douglas now had at his disposal many hundreds of men; these were men who had seen his good side and put absolute faith and trust in their gallant leader.

The relentless rains had continued to drench every inch of the borderlands. The sodden trails made travelling difficult as hooves and wagon wheels sank deep into the murky mixture of black mud and rotten leaves. The pace of travellers had slowed considerably as the winter depression followed them on their strenuous journey.

A few weeks later, Douglas and his men were once more distributing the takings of another recent plunder. This time the people of Kelso were the ones to share in the surprise gifts that were in reality repayments for previous losses to the invading raiders from the south.

A panic-stricken rider came charging into the busy town centre, his face partially disguised with a mixture of bloodstains, mud and sweat. 'Douglas, I must speak to Douglas,' he shouted in desperation, as the crowd scattered before him. Two of Douglas's men blocked his way, and prevented him reaching the man he sought. 'Let him pass,' Douglas called out.

Barely managing to remain on his exhausted horse, the man called out 'They have attacked Jedburgh, killed many and stolen our cattle.'

'Where are they now?' asked Douglas.

'They are still there, but not for long, they will surely be heading south,' he answered.

'How many?' asked Douglas.

'Sir, about twenty. Please sir, please help us,' pleaded the man, as he fell exhausted from his horse.

There was no shortage of volunteers to ride with Douglas as he headed south-west towards Jedburgh. Almost an hour later, they were about one mile outside the town when Douglas called his men to stop. 'We will split up here. Cuthbert, please take half the men and follow the trail south towards Otterburn. Do not attack until you see me on the other side.' Several asked the same question: 'How on earth are you going to get to the other side of them?'

'Are you going to sprout wings and fly?' asked Robert Hall.

'Not quite, but almost,' answered Douglas who then shouted towards Cuthbert. 'Please go now.'

The group of men who remained with Douglas wondered what he was going to do next. 'Which way Sir,' asked one man who was at a complete loss to what was about to happen.

'Across the fields,' shouted Douglas. 'Courtesy of Agricola, that ancient Roman invader, we will take the old straight trail that heads south over the hill moors. If we make good time we can get in front of them.' The men all looked at each other. The plan was so simple. The forgotten Roman road would enable them to get in front of the fleeing enemy and set an ambush with Cuthbert coming from the other side.

'How do you know we can get in front of them?' asked Robert Hall who was still puzzled by Douglas's plan.

'They can't herd cattle in the night. It would be too dangerous; they would lose too many beasts,' answered Douglas. 'As long as we can get in front of them by morning, we can then lie in wait.'

The lung-bursting pace at which both man and horse progressed over the eerie ancient moor road was a frightening experience for those who had not travelled with Douglas before. Every step forward in the dark night was done so with the confidence that firm ground would always be present underfoot. Many times this was not the case as horses hesitated and stumbled along the way.

Making their way over the Cheviot Hills, they arrived at Rochester several hours before dawn. The few hours of well-earned sleep was suddenly broken by Douglas as he gave his men their next instructions. 'We will now head back towards Jedburgh. Two riders out in front, as far apart as possible, but still within sight. When you see them, stop and wait for us to catch up,' declared Douglas.

'Sir, let me go in front,' requested Robert Hall as he looked around for others to also volunteer. Several came forward to offer to perform what would be a very dangerous and possibly their last task. Douglas raised his hand. 'I am proud of your brave gesture. However, it is not on this occasion required.'

Douglas mounted his horse and invited Robert Hall to follow a short distance behind him. They made their way north along the Jedburgh road and then passed through the Redesdale forest. The pace was slower than the previous night, still with a sense of urgency but this time with greater caution as all eyes scanned the way ahead. The waterfowl remained undisturbed as they fed on the south flowing River Rede that ran alongside the narrow road.

It was almost two hours after they had set out when the first indication of something, or someone, coming in the opposite direction was noticed. They were approaching Ramshope Burn when a loud harsh 'snark' broke the stillness, as an adult grey heron rose from the riverside. Something coming in the opposite direction had disturbed the lone hunter at its breakfast.

Douglas stopped. A short distance behind Andrew Hall also stopped, and signalled to those behind him. Douglas waited. At first he thought it was a wild animal coming towards him. As he stared into the distance he saw another one; it was cattle, being driven from behind. He waited; several more appeared round the bend in the road.

As the first horse rider appeared, Douglas gave the signal, which was repeated by Robert Hall, who then prompted the men behind him to catch up and yet still remain out of sight. Douglas stood his ground as more riders came into view. They had not yet noticed him; their eyes focused on their stolen cattle as they guided the prized beasts along the trail.

Eventually they spotted him, the lone figure on horseback in the middle of the trail and blocking their way ahead. The cattle hesitated. Some tried to turn, others stopped, snorted and stared, as if they knew the man with the long black hair on horseback who stared back at them. The cattle still being driven from behind piled up in front of Douglas. Three abreast and about six deep they provided a barrier between him and the approaching English raiders.

'Get the hell out of the way,' shouted the nearest horseman.

'I was here first,' answered Douglas politely.

'Well you won't be here much longer,' replied one of the other horsemen.

'I would be delighted to let you come past, but not these cattle,' said Douglas.

'Oh! You would, that's very kind of you, and who do you bloody well think you are?' the horseman shouted back.

Douglas smiled, and stroked his long black hair, as he teased and offered up a clue to these men who were shortly about to meet their fate.

'Who would you *not* like me to be?' asked Douglas, as the English horseman became more frustrated with his impertinence. They looked at each other questioningly. 'It can't be. It's impossible. Not on his own!' The answer to the question was given as Robert Hall and the rest of Douglas's men slowly came up behind him.

'I believe that you may have heard of me.' said Douglas. 'My name is Douglas. I will repeat my offer. You may pass, but the cattle don't.'

'It's a trap!' cried one of the English riders as they turned their horses around. 'We must go back or we will be killed.'

Douglas and his men allowed the English riders to head off in the opposite direction before they charged through the herd of stolen cattle, scattering them to the side of the road.

The slaughter was swift and brutal as Douglas and Cuthbert, followed by their men, closed in from either side. With their confidence so abruptly shattered by the sight of Douglas appearing on his own, the English riders were no match for these skilled warriors and their eager followers whose strength was inspired by the reputation of their leader. One rider was spared; he was allowed to live provided he take a message back to his own people. That message was one word – 'Douglas!'

A few hours later, the stolen cattle were herded into a deep low-lying glen on the east side of the road, a few miles south of Jedburgh.

As Douglas and Cuthbert headed on towards Jedburgh they passed through the narrow gorge at Lintalee. 'This place would make an ideal base,' declared Cuthbert as both he and Douglas looked up at the steep red sandstone walls that flanked either side of the gorge that the Jed Water flowed through. 'It's on the main route to the south, it's central, perfect for ambush, and close for us to call on many men,' said Cuthbert.

'I agree,' replied Douglas, adding, 'I feel this place is suitable for us, and I would like to rest here, but first we need to return these cattle to their rightful owners.'

After checking that there were no enemy troops based in Jedburgh, the stolen cattle were brought up from the deep glen. Douglas rode in front of his men as they herded the livestock into the town. The local people started to gather in the main street. The sight of Douglas bringing back their stolen cattle brought combined tears of joy and loud cheers from the crowds.

Douglas called out 'My dear friends, I bring back your stolen cattle, but regretfully I can't bring back your loved ones whose lives have been taken. Those who have committed these terrible deeds against you will never do so again, that I can promise. I regret I was not around to provide you protection and I promise that I will not be far away should you ever need my help.'

Men, women and children, many still grieving from the sad loss of their loved ones, ran towards Douglas. Like a royal prince from a fairy tale, they mobbed him with love and affection. He made them feel safe, he was their saviour, their protector and their hero. They embraced him both physically and in their warm hearts. There was no one in these lands who inspired them with such love and affection.

Cuthbert, Robert Hall and the rest of Douglas's men looked on in amazement. They were witnessing something unique, something that would be recorded in their nation's books of history for all times. They saw in front of them their leader; the good James Douglas, the man most loved by his own people and yet most feared by his enemies. In James Douglas, there was someone who was more than just an ordinary man. His fearful reputation terrified his enemies, his kindness and love they saw for themselves as Douglas embraced his many friends.

A short time later, they retreated to Lintalee. 'There is definitely something about this place that appeals to me,' remarked Douglas as they once more made their way alongside the Jed Water and on through the narrow gorge. As he looked up at the steep sandstone walls Douglas said. 'There is something mysterious here and yet ideal for our needs.'

'Hopefully not so ideal for our enemies from the south,' said Cuthbert.

18

SOUTHERN RAIDS

WITH EDWARD II SHOWING less concern about the affairs of Scotland than his cruel father, and preoccupied with internal strife amongst his own English nobles, the people of Scotland enjoyed several years free from the invasions and cruel persecution of past years. There were, however, many cross-border raids and subsequent counter-attacks that forced Douglas and his men always to be on the alert.

Lintalee had proved to be the ideal location. Many a band of enemy invaders were ambushed as they passed through the dark gorge. Many a wagon was plundered, the rich rewards once again being distributed amongst the local people. Occasionally one of Douglas's men would head north with a purse of money; there were two delivery points, one was Blackhouse Tower and the other was wherever King Robert the Bruce was residing.

Douglas was comfortable at Lintalee; this place had proved to be a good choice of base, central and within easy access for most of the key towns. He had sheltered in the deep cave above the gorge for the first few months but now its strategic position was used to provide a safe lookout point for his men, who watched all comings and goings.

Douglas and his men built a small shelter in the thick forest that flanked the west side of the Jed gorge. This shelter served their needs well and kept out the rain and bitterly cold winter winds that swept across the land. The shelter became the control centre for all of their activities.

A few miles to the north of Douglas's camp was the splendid abbey of Jedburgh, a magnificent place of holy worship that stood tall and proud, proclaiming its message of love and peace across these lands. Lone visitors could regularly be seen quietly coming and going as news and tidings of recent happenings were exchanged between the places of sanctuary.

One such messenger was Brother Michael from Melrose Abbey who wished to meet with one of the Jedburgh monks. A few hours later, under cover of darkness, a monk quietly left the abbey and made his way along the short distance south to Lintalee. Douglas and his men had eaten well and were now resting. 'It's your brother,' declared the guard to Robert Hall. 'Good evening, my dear brother, I have news for Douglas,' announced the monk.

'What news do you bring my good friend?' asked Douglas.

'I have a message from our King. He wishes to meet with you as soon as possible,' answered the monk.

'Do you know why?' asked Douglas.

'I believe that he is immensely pleased with what you and your men have achieved and I suspect that he may have a specific task that he would request of you.'

'Where have I to meet with him?' asked Douglas. The monk leaned over and quietly whispered the name of the secret location in the ear of Douglas.

Several days later Douglas and a small band of his most loyal men arrived at a place somewhere near Dumbarton. Since Douglas had received the message to meet with Bruce, his curiosity was getting the better of him as he constantly wondered what request his King had in store for him.

'Sire, I come here at your request,' announced Douglas, as he greeted his King.

'My dear James, relax, you are too serious. My most trusted friend, I am most pleased to see here today.' Bruce instructed that Douglas's men be given food and a place to rest.

'James, please join me, I am about to eat,' said Bruce. ''Douglas thanked him and sat down to a much-desired meal. Few words were spoken as these two men took their first bites from the mouth-watering roasted game that was placed before them.

'This is delicious,' said Douglas, as he washed down the game with a gulp of wine.

'Do you mean the food or the wine?' asked Bruce.

'Both!' answered Douglas, as he wiped a small dribble from his lower lip.

'James, I am astonished and immensely pleased with what you have achieved in the south. You appear to be gradually extending your control across all areas of the borderlands and have caused great pain and frustration to our invaders,' said Bruce, as he smiled at his good friend. Douglas, unable to answer until he swallowed the large mouthful that he had just bitten into, paused for a moment and then said 'Sire, I am grateful for your appreciation. I have many good people at my disposal who have shown great loyalty towards our cause. They are the true reason for our success.'

Bruce smiled, took another sup of wine, and then gave more praise to this young warrior who was fast developing an amazing reputation. 'James you are a good man and the loyalty that you show towards your own people is much to be admired. However, I have heard from many reliable sources of the daring deeds that you have planned and executed. You may truly have good men at your disposal; however, I have heard of so many tales of your unique cunning and bravery which has caused our enemies to fear you more than any other. You are the true reason for your own success. Your father would have been most proud of you.'

Douglas bowed his head in embarrassment at hearing this lavish praise. 'Sire, why have you called me here?' asked Douglas, trying to change the subject of conversation.

'Edward II, son of Longshanks, is not like his father. He is weak and presently struggling to unite his own nobles in the south of England,' replied Bruce.

'Sire, this I also know. Do you wish something specific of me?' asked Douglas.

'Edward II will, with time, unite his nation again. They will return and commence war against us, of that I have no doubt. You have slowly gained control of the borders, but we need to do more,' declared Bruce.

'What more do you wish?' asked Douglas.

'We must attack the lands in the north of England; we must push their armies further south. In order to protect ourselves we now need to become the invaders,' answered Bruce.

'Sire, I have no wish to invade any other nation, I merely wish to take back what is mine and remove those invaders from our lands and return ownership to its rightful people,' answered Douglas, whose raised tone of voice surprised Bruce.

Bruce laughed loudly. 'James, your moral values are to be applauded. However, I do not wish to invade England, I simply want to discourage them from invading us and I would like your support in doing so.'

Douglas breathed a loud sigh and replied 'Sire, you know that I would not refuse you a request of support. If our purpose is as you say, then my men and I are at your disposal.'

'James, the look on your face suggests that you are still uncomfortable with what I ask of you. What troubles you?' asked Bruce as he leaned over and patted Douglas's arm.

'Sire, I have spent these last years at war with the evil that our enemies have inflicted upon our people. I cannot bring myself to commit similar acts upon the people of England, for to do so will make me as evil as those who have done so to us,' replied the distressed Douglas.

'James, not all armies are evil. We can invade, we can occupy, and we can acquire their goods, we can do all this without inflicting evil. I promise you that our strategy will be only to raise arms against those who offer forceful resistance against us. The barbaric methods that have been used against us will not be used by us, of this you have my solemn word. My intention is simply that we defend ourselves, and that we will do with the longest stick that I have.'

Douglas rose from his seat, and approached his King; with bowed head, he knelt before him and with an apologetic tremble in his gentle voice said 'Sire, forgive me, I should have known better than to question your morality. You have my undivided support.'

Several weeks later the autumn month of September had just arrived. Throughout the country the poor harvest once again suffered due to the constant rain was being quickly collected to minimise any further losses. For many there was barely enough to survive the expected long winter months; for others there was only one option and that was to plunder the harvest of their enemy neighbours.

The border messengers were secretly moving from town to town and abbey to abbey. Word quickly spread. Douglas needed all able-bodied men to join him, and something significant was about to happen. The centre of Kelso was busy; many strangers to the town had arrived, and yet many others knew them. Those who did not know what was happening were puzzled by the sudden commotion of the last few days. There was an air of unusual excitement; someone special was about to arrive.

The first riders to enter the town galloped straight into the market square. The confused and frightened crowd separated, creating a space in the middle. The riders maintained that prized space, as if it were of great value. The mystery was suddenly explained when the large group of riders came charging into the square. At the front was the man they loved the most. Douglas, his long black hair hanging gracefully down upon the shoulders of his family coat of arms, presented a magnificent and welcome sight. Behind him rode someone they had not seen before and yet from the first glimpse they knew who he was. Their King, Robert the Bruce, with his colourful entourage had privileged them by his presence.

For many this day would be a day to remember. Their humble world had suddenly been transformed with the arrival of Bruce and Douglas. The strength of numbers that surrounded them gave them great confidence and for the first time in their unhappy lives, a genuine hope for the future. The colourful garments, bright shields and gleaming swords added to the spectacular scene before them.

Many wanted to hear the voice of their King, they wanted to hear what he had to say, and they wanted to find out what kind of a man he was. Their wish was granted when Bruce spoke.

'My dear loyal people, I have come here today to offer my thanks and appreciation for your continued support. In my good friend, James of Douglas, you have a great leader, one who, with your support, has achieved magnificent success. When I thanked him for his efforts he refused the praise; instead, he gives you all the credit for the success you have won. I say this here today, I am truly grateful to all of you and to Douglas for the loyalty that you give, not just to me, but to our nation which we all love and will if necessary die for.'

The crowd erupted with cheers of joy and appreciation of their King and leader. 'Bruce! Bruce!' the chants continued for several minutes and then switched over to 'Douglas! Douglas!' The crowd were still shouting when a smiling Bruce raised his hand. The deafening noise was replaced with a deadly silence. No one moved, no one even blinked in case they missed what was about to be said.

'My dear people, today brings a new chapter in the history of this nation. For so long now we have been persecuted, murdered, raped and robbed by our enemies, who have tried to take our lands and our nation from us. Today we will commence attacking our enemies. Yes, we will plunder and we will take back what was taken from us over many years. It is not my wish to avenge evil with evil. We will not murder in cold blood. Those who oppose us may be slain, but that will be their choice not ours.'

The cheering recommenced, and was accompanied by many volunteers rushing forward to offer their services. Everyone present had been greatly moved by these words from Bruce, there was no one who did not want to offer their support. Every man, woman and child was with him.

The first target, a few days later, was the land near to Berwick that belonged to the Earl of Dunbar. Douglas, as a child recalled being told by his father, Sir William, that this Scottish Earl was on the side of the English and was a traitor to their nation. Douglas therefore took great delight in participating in this raid. The estate was looted, the plunder shared and sent home. Bruce wanted his men to feel that they were fighting for themselves and not for yet another selfish landowner.

The raids continued south along the English border, across Northumberland and along the southern side of the Cheviot Hills. No town or village was spared. Money, cattle and grain were the prime acquisitions. Bruce was true to his word, and only those few who offered a forceful resistance were slain.

As they entered one of the many towns the sudden shouting and screaming brought great terror to the local inhabitants, many of whom ran for their lives at the mere sight of these fearsome northern warriors. Douglas rode at the front of his men; his reputation was their most effective weapon. The sight of him, with his coat of arms and sword held high above as his long black hair waved in the breeze, caused a tidal wave of terror to sweep through the unsuspecting town.

A local man, on hearing the commotion outside, stumbled and fell at his own door as he struggled to help his wife and two children flee from these invaders. His luck was not with him, as Douglas rode up directly in front of his house and blocked the only escape for this man and his family. The sight of Douglas's sword gleaming in the morning sunshine brought terror to the unfortunate family. The only item that the man could use for a weapon was a thin log of firewood that lay on the ground. Picking it up the man screamed in fear as he made his feeble attempt to defend his family, waving the stick and threatening to crush the skull of anyone who approached.

Douglas looked at this brave man, whose face was a burning crimson red as he attempted to intimidate the strangers with his most frightening look in order to defend his loved ones. The dirty tear-filled faces of his wife and children stared, petrified, at the fearsome Douglas sitting high up on his horse only a few yards in front of them. Douglas lowered his sword and smiled.

'Sir, I am Douglas and I am afraid of no one. All of my enemies fear me more than any other. Yet you stand here in front of me with a stick and you say that you will crush my skull should I approach. I say this, I have never met a braver man than you. Go back inside. I promise you, neither you nor your family will be harmed and I also promise that your possessions will be safe.' Douglas shouted to the two children. 'Tell your friends, tell all of them that your brave father chased off the Black Douglas.' The man smiled; it was a smile not just of relief but also of admiration.

While Bruce provided the political leadership, it was Douglas who provided the cunning and daring in the planning and execution of each attack. Douglas organised the looting and taking of the plunder, which was carefully chosen in order to maximise the return on their efforts.

Bruce would be seen in discussions with the envoys of these estates. Money was offered in exchange for a truce. The plunder was needed to feed his army, but money was much needed to fund his future plans. Across the Northumberland region, many towns offered their submission; their only choice was to pay a ransom that would guarantee their safety and immunity from any future raids. Bruce accepted these offers of truce.

With confidence high, the raids continued. The unexpected nature of the attacks was the now familiar signature of Douglas. The English were unable to predict or to prepare for the next assault on their possessions.

One evening Douglas approached Bruce. 'Sire, I can't understand what's happening. These raids have become too easy, they offer no resistance. It is well known that Edward II has internal strife with his own nobles, but in time of war I would expect them to unite. Why does Edward II not come to the aid of his own people?'

Bruce laughed. 'Douglas, haven't you heard?'

'Heard what, Sire?'

'The Earl of Cornwall,' replied Bruce.

'Who?' asked Douglas.

'Piers Gaveston,' answered Bruce.

'No I haven't, who is he?' asked Douglas.

'You have obviously led a very innocent life, my dear James,' answered Bruce.

'Sire, can you please explain. What is significant about Gaveston?' asked the now confused and frustrated Douglas.

'He is the lover of Edward II,' answered Bruce, as he waited for the response from his young friend. For the first time in his life Douglas was speechless. 'Do you understand now?' asked Bruce. Douglas nodded bemusedly.

Bruce spoke. 'The conflict that Edward II currently has with his own nobles is further complicated by the Gaveston situation. As long as he is around many powerful nobles will not give their support to their King.'

'I suggest that we therefore want to see Edward II and Gaveston living happily ever after,' replied Douglas, as he smiled still in disbelief at the good fortune that this situation had given them. 'Of course!' replied Bruce.

For three whole weeks the raids across the English borders continued. Bruce was well pleased with the results; the plunder had been most welcome, the fearsome reputation of Bruce's army had been enhanced, and above all else, large sums of money were agreed with the nobles of Northumberland in exchange for a truce.

At his base at Corbridge, Bruce approached Douglas. 'James, there is a task that I would request of you, a dangerous task I may add. The town of Durham has many riches; much wealth exists within its walls. If we were to carry out a successful raid on Durham, the returns would be such that we could end our siege of these lands and return home.'

'When do you wish me to do this?' asked Douglas.

'As soon as possible. I would, however, suggest that you move in under cover of darkness,' replied Bruce.

'I would be glad to accompany you,' said Edward Bruce who had been a key player in the raiding activities of the last few weeks. 'We can't have Douglas claiming all of the glory,' he added with a hint of laughter.

'Tomorrow night then?' suggested Douglas. The King and his brother nodded in agreement.

The following evening, Douglas and Edward Bruce led their men towards the town of Durham. A few miles outside the town wall they stopped. Douglas spoke to Edward Bruce. 'Sir, I suggest that we leave a group of men here under your command to act as a reserve should the main force get into difficulty. I would not advise us all going in at the same time.'

'I agree, but should you encounter any dangers please send back word,' replied Edward Bruce.

The bright red rays of early morning were emerging over the horizon as the market traders prepared for another day of profitable business. The moving shadows in the distance that appeared to becoming closer were ignored as the townsfolk went about their business.

They arrived quietly, and from all directions. Many thought that they were traders who had come to sell, or hopefully buy the goods on display.

The normal battle cries and loud screaming that accompanied the recent raids were suspended as the raiders attempted to maximise the element of surprise. Douglas and his men were upon the town before being noticed. When they drew their swords the wave of panic began. Many fled in terror at the sight. Others refused to believe what confronted them and offered up a foolish and, for many, fatal resistance.

Fires were started, buildings were pulled down and destroyed. Fear and panic fuelled the chaos that spread fast throughout out the shocked city. Only those who dared present any resistance were slain. 'Lay down your arms and you may live,' shouted Douglas's men as they continued to ransack all around them.

The raid had been successful; many provisions were taken, along with vast numbers of cattle. Loaded wagons which had been abandoned in the market square were immediately taken away. Every one of Douglas's men had his hands full as they left almost as quickly as they had arrived. The many horses that had been acquired were put to good use to swiftly carry away the seized plunder. Many goods were left behind due to insufficient men to carry them.

The only disappointment of the day was that the nobles and wealthy aristocrats of the town managed to seek protection within the great walls of the castle and cathedral. Their capture would surely have meant a goodly ransom being negotiated.

The highly prized acquisitions were handed over to Edward Bruce who along with his men started to prepare to make the return back to Corbridge.

'Are you not coming back with us?' asked Edward Bruce as he looked to Douglas and his men who appeared uneasy.

'No! There is an opportunity that presents itself that I do not want to pass by.'

'What opportunity is that?' asked Edward Bruce.

'An opportunity to acquire even greater riches,' replied Douglas.

'And where may that be?' asked Edward Bruce.

'Hartlepool,' answered Douglas.

'Hartlepool! What riches could you possibly seek in such a place?' replied Edward Bruce.

'Be patient and you will see,' replied Douglas.

A short time later, Douglas, accompanied by his loyal and trusted companions Cuthbert and Hall and a group of about forty good men, entered the peaceful coastal town of Hartlepool. There was a difference in the way they ransacked this town. No fires were lit and no blood was spilt. The object of their attention was not more plunder but the wealthy merchants who, if captured, could be traded for significant ransom.

Many prisoners were taken along with the wives of important men who thought that they could outsmart Douglas by taking refuge out at sea. Douglas issued the instruction. 'Treat them with care and respect, as if they were your own,' he called out, as the screaming women were taken. Douglas made his way back through Durham where he picked up more prized possessions. He reminded these people that he had taken their goods but had not caused the death of any innocents. 'I may not be so generous the next time,' he called out to those who looked down from the castle walls.

The fear and terror that these raids had caused spread south like wildfire. Many an English noble and common Englishman could not believe that the warriors from the north could so easily invade their native land and cause such devastation. A great uneasiness was felt by the subjects of Edward II, uneasiness which, given time, would have to be put right.

Bruce was delighted to see the safe return of Douglas and his men. He was even more delighted with the bargaining strength of the many prominent hostages presented to him. Much wealth could be acquired in exchange for these individuals. 'These prisoners will surely command many thousands of pounds for their exchange,' declared Bruce as he embraced Douglas and thanked him immensely for his efforts.

'Is there anything that you are not capable of doing?' asked Bruce as he smiled at Douglas and continued to express his appreciation.

'Sire, what you have seen so far is nothing compared to what I now present to you,' declared Douglas as he gestured to Cuthbert to bring someone forward.

'Sire, I have someone who would like to meet with you. He is not a prisoner, and he comes here of his own free will.'

From the assembled throng emerged a tall, elderly, broadly built figure dressed in black, with white hair and a grey beard. 'Lamberton!' shouted Bruce. 'My God, you are alive, how are you?' he asked, as his good friend came closer.

Lamberton, Bishop of St Andrews, loyal and trusted friend of Bruce and guardian of Douglas as a young child, who had been taken prisoner shortly after the battle of Methven, stepped forward. They embraced and then wept. The tears were tears of joy and tears of thanks to God for allowing these two lives to continue through such troubled times.

'Sire, I am fine, and I am proud of what you do. It has taken many years but you are now close to achieving your purpose. God is surely with you,' said Lamberton as he held out his powerful arms and squeezed the hands of Bruce.

The room was silent.

'For a man of the cloth you have some grip on you. God help any man who's on the receiving end of one of your blows,' declared Bruce, and the room rang with laughter.

A short time later Lamberton was alone with Bruce. 'Sire, Edward II has many problems with his own nation. Many of his nobles are displeased with his actions, and they expect of him many things of which he is incapable.'

'Such as?' asked Bruce.

'They expect strong leadership, they expect him to defend and unite his now disjointed nation.'

'Well I hope he takes his time, and a long time at that, in doing so,' replied Bruce, who paused and then asked 'Your Excellency, I sense that there may be a specific reason for the concern that you show towards that English King. Am I correct?'

'Sire, Edward II has many troubles; he does not have the evil mind of his father. If we as a nation were to offer him comfort, we would surely move a step forward in bringing peace to our lands,' declared Lamberton.

Bruce stared at Lamberton, his eyes trying to penetrate into the hidden thoughts in the mind of his good Bishop. 'What of Gaveston?' asked Bruce, who suspected that the lover of Edward II might be the King's only real trouble. Lamberton looked as if his inner thoughts had suddenly been exposed on the ground in front of him.

'Sire, as you have no doubt heard, the story of the King's forbidden love is in fact correct. If we were to offer forgiveness to Edward and sanctuary to Gaveston, Edward would be most pleased and our nation would be in his good favour,' said Lamberton in a gentle voice, as he presented the logical argument for consideration.

'Tell me?' asked Bruce in a most serious tone of voice. 'Has Edward II asked you to plead this case to me?'

Lamberton paused. With head bowed he hesitantly replied in his most humble and compassionate manner. 'Yes, Edward has asked me to present this case; he has asked me to plead with you for protection and asylum for his friend Piers Gaveston. In return we will have his support and lasting peace in our lands.'

'What is the likelihood of the King of England keeping a promise to the King of Scotland when he does not even honour the promises that he makes to his own nobles?' was Bruce's immediate response. 'I cannot put my trust in such a man; his word will not deceive me.'

Bruce placed his hand on the shoulder of his most trusted Bishop. 'Your Excellency, you clearly demonstrate your strength of faith in the Lord when you offer up such compassion and forgiveness to the leader of our cruel enemies. Unfortunately, I don't possess such strength as you. I have faith in the Lord, but not in that man who calls himself King of England.'

With eyes filling with emotion, Bruce embraced his good friend. 'What would you have me do now?' asked Lamberton.

'Come home with me. Our people need their faith more now than at any other time in the history of this nation. I may unite their hearts but they need good men like you to unite their souls,' answered Bruce.

19

ATTACK ON ROXBURGH

AS THE YEAR 1314 approached, life in the borders appeared to be in a period of temporary suspense. For many, survival through these months of hardship could only be achieved by following the example of the wise animals of nature. Evolution has taught these creatures that in order to survive such times they must retreat into their silent suspended world of hibernation in order to cope with the constant cold and shortage of food.

Many lived these months in such a manner, their fires constantly burning in order to keep the bitter cold at bay as they lived off the fats of the rich plunder from the previous autumn harvest. Excessive movement, which quickly consumed valuable energy, was limited to essential tasks only. The attacks on the enemy were few due to the overall reduction in movement of enemy activity.

Douglas's men had a priority more important than any nationalistic cause. Their families came first, and it was with them that they chose to spend these winter months. Douglas was no different; there were loved ones in his life that he had seen very little of during recent times. There was something that caused him concern, something he could not understand; something made him feel uncertain about the future, and this uncertainty worried him. The lack of any activity aggravated these feelings. He needed to be with his own family during these times.

Douglas and his good friend Cuthbert, whom he viewed as being a member of his close family, made their way through the deep snow that covered the trail towards the Blackhouse Tower. A freshly killed young buck straddled his saddle; it would surely make a welcome sight on their arrival.

'James! My son, I am so pleased you have decided to come home. It's been a long time,' declared Lady Eleanor as she greeted her famous son of whom she was most pleased and proud.

'Mother, I am sorry that I have not been home sooner. I have had much to do,' said Douglas.

'Yes, so I have been hearing,' replied Lady Eleanor with a proud smile. 'I hear that you have been getting quite a reputation for yourself.'

Douglas laughed. 'Mother, don't believe all that you hear.'

'My son, if I were to believe only half of what I hear, then you must be the good fearless hero who protects and provides for all of his people and who constantly terrorises our enemies,' declared Lady Eleanor, as she looked at Douglas with her eyes stretched wide open as if to say 'Well is it true?' Douglas replied, with a hunching of his shoulders and an innocent childish look as if to say, 'Who, me?'

As they continued their conversation, loud footsteps could be heard coming towards the doorway. The door abruptly burst open. 'So you have decided to honour us with your presence,' shouted the voice of a tall youth, as he entered the room.

'What have you been eating?' said Douglas, as he admired the height of his brother Archibald. 'Good honest hard-earned food, not the plunder that you have been living off,' answered Archibald cheekily, with the brotherly sarcasm he was accustomed to display.

'Does that mean that you won't be joining us later to savour the taste of fresh venison which I have brought you?' asked Douglas.

'Well, if my eating your fresh venison makes you feel good, and helps with your guilty conscience for ignoring your family, then I would say that I would not refuse my good brother such a request,' replied Archibald with a wide grin.

The duel of words stopped as both brothers hugged each other; they were truly pleased to see each other and were proud of their respective progress in life. A tear appeared in the eyes of Lady Eleanor as she witnessed her two sons show such affection for one another. For a mother there can be few more beautiful sights than that of her children showing love and affection towards each other. Lady Eleanor revelled in these loving moments.

'And what of Hugh? How has he been?' asked Douglas. 'He is fine,' replied Lady Eleanor. 'He comes home frequently for short periods, but his heart and mind are with God. He has many a good word to say of the monks at Melrose. Those holy men have given him a sense of purpose and direction to his life.'

'I am glad,' replied Douglas. 'I must make the time to go and see him soon.'

'Aren't you forgetting someone?' asked Lady Eleanor, frowning at Douglas. 'It may appear so, since I have not asked. But I haven't forgotten. Where is Sophia?' said Douglas.

'She spends a great deal of time on her own. Over these last few years, she has kept much to herself. She only appears to have one thing on her mind,' answered Lady Eleanor.

'And what may that be?' asked Douglas.

'You will have to ask her yourself,' replied Lady Eleanor.

Sophia was in her room, quietly sitting at the side of the burning fire, her gleaming green eyes switching back and forth between the dancing flames and the garment that her skilful and nimble fingers were in the process of creating. Her long reddish hair sparkled as the radiant light reflected off each perfect gleaming strand. With her head bowed and her pale complexion falsely coloured by the warm glow from the burning flames her face was almost expressionless. However, careful observation would show a hint of thoughts of someone in a distant place.

There was loneliness in this sixteen-year-old girl. It was a loneliness caused by something that was missing in her life, and yet a loneliness that contained much happiness and contentment in the life that she led as an adopted child living with the Douglas family.

The quiet scene was interrupted by the voice at the door. 'Sophia, can I come in?' asked Lady Eleanor.

'Yes, of course you can, Mother, you don't need to ask,' replied Sophia.

'My dear, the reason that I ask is because I bring someone with me.' Lady Eleanor moved away from the open doorway to reveal her eldest son. 'James would like to speak with you,' she said, as she left the two for private discussion.

Sophia raised her head and looked up, her hands resting on the unfinished garment on her lap. Her eyes lit up and her face glowed, but not from the warmth from the burning fire, more so from the warmth in her heart towards the person who stood here in front of her.

Douglas slowly walked towards her, and as he did so he gently called out 'Sophia.' The sound of her name spoken softly by the manly voice of this tall figure, who cast long shadows across the length of the room as he moved closer, caused her to tremble. His powerful frame towered over her as she looked up into his smiling face. 'How are you?' asked Douglas.

She could not speak; her throat dried up and the words would not come out. It was as if the image that she had in her mind as she stared at the burning flames had suddenly come to life. Her whole body trembled at the sight of him. She did not understand, nor could she explain what these feeling were.

Douglas saw that he had caused her to feel uneasy. She crouched down in her chair before him, disguising the true beauty of her presence and attempting to hide her embarrassment as she bowed her head. Douglas leaned forward and gently held her small hand. 'My dear Sophia, it has been so long since I have seen you. You grow more beautiful each day. How have you been?' asked Douglas. She raised her head and looked at him with eyes that showed great affection and at the same time great anxiety. With much effort, she managed to quietly whisper. 'All right.' 'Have they been looking after you?' asked Douglas. She nodded. 'You don't appear to have much to say, do you?' She shook her head from side to side.

'Would you like me to tell you all about what I have been doing these last few years?' asked Douglas. She nodded eagerly. 'All right then I will, but only after you have told me what you have been doing these last few years,' replied a smiling Douglas, who eventually forced a giggle out of his young admirer.

The room went silent. 'Your turn to speak,' declared Douglas. The silence continued, for Sophia could still not utter a single word. Douglas looked at her and smiled. He stuck his tongue out and forced his large dark eyes to come together. The sight of her handsome hero making such a ridiculous face caused her to burst out laughing.

'You're mad,' shouted Sophia.

'You're beautiful,' replied Douglas.

'James?' said Sophia

'What?'

'I have missed you; I like it when you are here. You make me feel good; you are the link to my past, and I am grateful for the family that you have given me.'

'What troubles you, my dear?' asked Douglas. Sophia paused as she looked into the flames of the burning fire and then returned her gaze to the dark eyes of Douglas.

'I have no future. Yes, I have a good and kind family, and I am well cared for, but I have no future,' replied Sophia.

'What do you dream of?' asked Douglas, as he sensed discomfort in the mind of this angel of beauty who sat before him.

'There are some things that a gentleman should not ask of a lady,' replied Sophia, with a look that clearly gave the answer to the question.

The winter months closed in with a vengeance, as the bitter cold winds that brought an unpredictable combination of rain, sleet and snow relentlessly savaged these lands into submission. There was one common activity among the inhabitants as they sheltered and waited for winter to pass. Many a mind was impatiently focused on the first signs of spring and everyone looked forward to the ending of this winter nightmare.

The residents of Blackhouse Tower shared in the hardships. However, there was a significant benefit that these folks were privileged to share in. The forest provided the fuel for the constantly burning fires that kept their bodies warm and their spirits high. Food was the other critical need and therefore hunting skills were in great demand for those who had insufficient stocks to last these last few cold months of misery.

In Douglas and Cuthbert they had not just two of the greatest warriors in these lands, but also two of the most efficient hunters. Their experience of hunting and stalking men was easily converted to hunting the beasts of the forest. As they prepared one morning to leave on such an outing, Archibald approached his older brother. 'James, would you like me to come with you and help?' Douglas looked surprised. 'Why? there is no need, we can manage fine and hopefully return with rich game,' replied Douglas. 'I am sure you can, but my question is really more a request to learn, rather than to offer help,' replied Archibald.

'How do you rate yourself as a hunter?' asked Douglas, as he smiled at his younger brother.

'Having not actually seen an expert such as you perform, I have no means of assessing how good or bad I am. However, there is always room to learn more.'

'Be quick if you want to come along,' said Douglas, as he looked to Cuthbert, smiled and shook his head, as if to suggest that today's hunting may not be quite as successful as planned.

The hind was busy scraping away at the surface snow as it attempted to reach the precious lichen underneath, its ears constantly erect and nervously twitching from side to side in order to the sound of approaching danger. With the wind direction in their favour, the three hunters split up and flanked the unsuspecting beast. Douglas signalled to Archibald to crouch down and be prepared as he and Cuthbert set off to make their way to either side of the beast.

Archibald lay motionless, his body frozen with the pain of kneeling in the deep snow, unable to rub or blow into his numb hands for fear of alerting the hind. He nervously checked and rechecked his hunting bow and loaded arrow. 'Only one shot, only one chance,' he thought to himself.

Douglas and Cuthbert finally got into their desired position on opposite sides from where the beast was searching for food. Unable to see the exact spot where Archibald was hiding, they decided to move into action. The small stones that they regularly carried while hunting were brought out and simultaneously thrown. The pebbles landed several yards on the unmanned side of the hind.

The startled beast, alerted by the sudden noise, looked up as more stones landed in front of it. Its head turned as its eyes caught the movement of Douglas and Cuthbert. There was only one safe way for the beast to flee and that was straight towards the hidden Archibald.

As the animal bolted off, Douglas and Cuthbert started to move, their loud whistling acting like a sound funnel that guided the unsuspecting beast towards the hidden Archibald. The ear-piercing whistles alerted the young hunter a split second before the animal appeared almost on top of him.

With frozen fingers that could barely move, his numb hands managed to pull back the stiff bow. The release of the arrow was more of a reaction to the fear of the beast as its terrified eyes looked into his frightened face.

Douglas and Cuthbert finally arrived. The sight that greeted them was of Archibald dancing, as he blew with all his might and rubbed into his hands. 'I'm absolutely frozen,' cried the young hunter, as he pranced up and down trying to generate some form of heat within his perishing body.

'I take it you missed?' asked Douglas.

'Don't know,' answered Archibald, as he continued to rub his hands.

'Where did it go?' asked Cuthbert.

'Over there,' pointed Archibald.

The three hunters walked the few yards through the thick snow-covered bushes. Spots of bright fresh blood marked their way. On the other side lay the dead hind, its flank pierced by a single arrow.

'Well done, young man,' shouted Cuthbert, as he patted Archibald on the back.

'Are you still cold?' asked Douglas, as he smiled at his younger brother. 'Yes,' replied the shivering Archibald. 'OK, let's heat him up,' shouted Douglas, as he and Cuthbert lifted the beast up onto the shoulders of the frozen Archibald. 'Now we don't want to hear any complaints that you are too warm,' said Douglas, and he and Cuthbert laughed aloud.

The sight of young Archibald carrying the prized possession as he returned to Blackhouse Tower brought more loud laughter. He no longer felt the cold; instead, aching limbs and complete exhaustion had replaced one set of misery with another. As they warmed their hands at the burning fire, Douglas and Cuthbert both called out 'Oh! It's bitter cold out there, isn't it?' The exhausted Archibald lay on the floor unable to move. 'I don't feel the cold, in fact I don't feel anything,' he said weakly. 'I hope you have learnt much about hunting today,' said Douglas, as he smiled and looked down at his exhausted young brother.

Later that night the evening meal was served. Everyone praised Archibald for a good day's work. 'Will you be going hunting tomorrow,' asked Lady Eleanor. 'Maybe in a few weeks time,' answered Archibald.

After they had eaten, Douglas and his mother sat on their own. The harshness of this winter had brought them together again and they were happy in each other's company.

'James,' said Lady Eleanor, then paused before completing her question. 'Over the last few months Archibald has been repeatedly saying to me that he would like to join up with you. As he is also the son of your father, Lord William, he feels that, just like you, it is also his duty to fight to reclaim this family's inheritance. What would you say to his request?'

Douglas stared at his mother, and tried to assess from her expression the answer that she was looking for. Her blank look gave nothing away. 'Mother, my success is partially due to my independence. I have been able to overcome many dangers with the knowledge that I have not had to look out for anyone other than myself. If I had a family member with me, I would be constantly looking over my shoulder in order to offer protection and would be distracted from my cause.'

'Anything else?' asked Lady Eleanor.

'Consider the risk of what would happen if he were taken hostage. That is a risk that I would not be prepared to take.'

Lady Eleanor sat silently as Douglas continued to list reason after reason as to why young Archibald should not join up with him.

'I have a question for you to seriously consider,' declared Lady Eleanor. 'If Archibald was your older brother, and led such a life as yourself, would anything prevent you from joining with him?'

'Only the need to stay and provide protection to you my mother,' Douglas immediately answered. 'Mother, let me ask you this question. What do *you* want for him?'

'James, when you were about his age you left home on your own to join up with King Robert. You were young, innocent and inexperienced, but you were proud and had a purpose in your heart that has become your life,' she calmly answered him.

'Why do you tell me what I already know?' asked Douglas.

Lady Eleanor rose from her seat. 'It's time for me to retire for the night.' Looking at Douglas she finally said 'I think you know why', and the door was quietly closed, as Douglas sat on his own and attempted to answer his own question.

The dawn of the New Year arrived. It was 1314, a year that would become the most memorable in the history of this nation. It would be a year that all sons and daughters of Scotland would remember. Douglas spent the first few weeks of the year in the close company of his younger brother.

Hunting skills were taught and passed between loving brothers, survival techniques were shared, knowledge of warfare was discussed, and tales of successful campaigns were told. Archibald was given the privilege of being tutored by the nation's most loved and yet feared warrior. Douglas spent many days with his younger brother; as well as sharing his skills, his knowledge and experience, above all else he shared what was in his heart.

Returning from yet another successful hunt, Archibald walked beside his heroic older brother. 'James, I would like to go with you when the winter is over and you return to your men. I dearly want to be part of your cause. It's all I can think of,' declared Archibald.

'My dear brother, I cannot say yes or no to your request. However, you have a choice; come with me, or stay and protect our beloved mother. The choice is for you to make,' said Douglas.

Young Archibald stopped to pause and think. 'How can I make such a choice. I can't leave my mother unprotected, and yet I want to be with you,' he declared.

'Then you are unable to make your choice,' declared Douglas.

'Perhaps there is an alternative,' suggested Archibald as they followed behind Cuthbert, who was always close by.

Douglas stopped, turned, and stared at his brother in surprise. 'And what may that alternative be?' he asked, as Cuthbert, who had been listening to this conversation also turned round.

'As I see it, there are three of us, and it is necessary that one of us stays here and looks after Mother. I suggest therefore that we all play our part and agree that we each take a turn at looking after her while the other two go about fighting our cause. A simple solution to a simple problem,' replied Archibald, with his usual cheeky confidence. Douglas and Cuthbert stared at each other in total disbelief.

Douglas asked for Cuthbert's opinion of this proposal.

'What do I think? I am honoured that I am considered as one of you. Both of you may have forgotten that I was providing protection to your mother long before either of you ever did for me. Such a suggestion, would not be a problem, I would consider it a privilege.'

Elsewhere the shortage of food had brought great hardship throughout the borderlands; none felt it more than the castles held by English garrisons who had had their supplies cut off by the daring and successful raids executed by Douglas's men. Towards the end of January, a messenger arrived. 'It's Roxburgh; the English garrison have been coming out and raiding Kelso. They have taken all that we had,' cried the tired man as he gasped for breath while explaining his dilemma to Douglas.

The following day Douglas made his preparations to leave Blackhouse Tower. He embraced his mother as she thanked him and wished him well.

'Please take good care of him,' she said.

Douglas smiled and looked to his good friend Cuthbert. 'Looks like an extended winter break for you my friend, take good care.' 'And you,' replied Cuthbert.

'Come on, hurry up, we have got important business to attend to,' shouted young Archibald.

'James,' shouted Lady Eleanor, 'aren't you forgetting someone?' 'Where is she?' he asked. 'Over there,' answered

Lady Eleanor as she pointed towards the large oak tree several yards down the trail.

Sophia's head was bowed as he approached. She appeared to show no interest in him as she stared in the opposite direction, down the glen, but intermittently glanced round at his approaching presence. His horse gently moved nearer. 'Sophia,' Douglas called out. 'I regret that I have not spent more time with you over these last few weeks.' She shook her head. He knew in his heart that the more kindness and love that he expressed towards this girl, the more pain that she would suffer. What she did not know was that he was starting to experience that same pain, a pain that he was unaccustomed to.

Archibald caught up with him. 'Are we going now,' he asked. 'Yes,' said Douglas. As they quickly made their way towards Lintalee, Archibald spoke with his brother. 'James, what's so significant about Roxburgh?'

'It's one of the many great castles that are currently occupied by enemy forces. Stirling, Edinburgh, Berwick and Roxburgh, they are all manned by large garrisons that pose a great threat to our people,' replied Douglas.

'I realise what you say, but is there anything specific about Roxburgh?' Archibald asked.

'It's a perfect strategic location for enemy forces, within easy access of the English border, perhaps too close for comfort. Apart from that, I don't like the idea of an enemy garrison so close by and I am not going to stand idle and watch them plunder the neighbouring towns,' replied Douglas.

They arrived back at Lintalee where they met up with the rest of Douglas's men. Word had spread that he was returning and many had arrived early. Douglas addressed his small army.

'My good men, word has come my way that the enemy garrison at Roxburgh has been attacking the town of Kelso. We must deal with this situation, they must be stopped,' declared Douglas.

'We can't attack a castle, not one as tall and secure as Roxburgh. Have you seen the size of those walls?' shouted one of the men.

'My friend, I share your concerns, but we will find a way to get in, believe me. I don't as yet know how, but we will find a way in,' answered Douglas.'

Archibald stepped forward. 'Can't we just climb the dammed walls and then kill them?' he asked. The rest of the men looked at this stranger and then looked at Douglas.

'Oh, by the way this is my younger brother, who as you can see has many good exciting ideas,' said Douglas, almost apologetically. The rest of the men tried to hold in their laughter.

'It's not such a daft idea,' declared Simon of Ledhouse, a man from the district of Clydesdale who had been a loyal follower of Douglas for some time.

'What do you have in mind?' asked Douglas.

'A ladder. I can make a ladder of rope and narrow strips of wood. It could be as long as you like, depending on the height of the walls,' answered Simon.

'Would it be able to hold a man?' asked Douglas.

'Yes, no problem. I have made many such ladders before,' replied Simon.

'How would a rope ladder be able to stand up against a wall?' asked a puzzled Archibald. The men all looked at each other.' He may talk daft, but he does have a point,' declared one of the men.

'An iron hook. Simply throw it over the wall and then climb up,' said Simon.

'Will we be attacking at night?' asked Archibald.

'Yes, it's the only way without being noticed,' said Douglas.

'Then we will have to do something about the iron hook,' replied Archibald.

'What do you mean?' asked Simon.

'Think about it, you're in the castle, it's a quiet peaceful night and then the iron hook comes over and bounces off the sandstone walls. It will be like midnight church bells suddenly ringing and frightening the life out of everyone,' explained Archibald.

Douglas and his men stared at young Archibald, One of the men whispered as he looked at Archibald 'Someone once said, that there's only a fine gap between madness and genius.' They were not sure which was the most appropriate description, for this unusual young man.

'A brilliant thought. How did we ever manage without you, I wonder?' said Douglas, with a wide grin.

As the month of February ended, Douglas gathered his men and made his way towards the castle of Roxburgh. The castle garrison was constantly on the lookout for approaching danger. The fear that the actions of Douglas had caused amongst his enemies over these last few years had not escaped this secure fortress.

Although they had not yet cast eyes on him, the fearful image of Douglas was constantly in the minds of these enemy soldiers. 'It's him, he comes towards us,' shouted the guard on the battlement as he took his evening watch. 'Where?' called the other guard as he came running towards him in support. 'He's vanished, where the hell did he go,' the guard called out. 'Have you been imagining things again?' called his companion. 'I swear I saw him. A ghostly lone dark horseman, he was coming towards us and then just disappeared in the mist,' explained the confused guard. 'He has been seen by others on other watches, coming towards us and then disappearing,' he added. 'Was it the Black Douglas?' 'I think so,' answered the frightened guard, who was unsure if he had just seen a ghost.

About one mile to the west of Kelso, where the rivers Tweed and Teviot make a failed first attempt to come together, stands the castle of Roxburgh. Douglas, along with young Archibald and Robert Hall, made his way along the stretch of land flanked on either side by the two rivers. Hiding in the forest edge, they watched the patterns of movement and planned the timing of their attack.

The following evening, darkness descended and ended the day of Shrove Tuesday. The late February winter night saw cold mist slowly rising from both rivers and spreading across the land. Like low-lying clouds, the pockets of mist lingered on the open grounds around the castle walls.

On the castle ramparts, the guards looked out on their evening watch, the only movement being the mist that drifted closer along the ground in front of them. One guard thought he saw something, as he focused his eyes through the darkness aided by the battlement torches that glowed bright in the eerie night.

'What's that?' he asked his partner.

'Where?' came the reply.

'Over there.'

'It's an ox, you fool,' laughed the second guard.

'I must be imagining things again. Look there's more of them, the short grass must be the attraction.'

'Their owner is surely chancing his luck by allowing such prized beasts to roam so freely,' said one guard.

'If Douglas comes along, the owner's luck will be over, for they will surely be gone by morning,' laughed the other guard as they both made their way indoors.

On the ground in front of the castle, the movement of large dark objects continued. They appeared to randomly graze on the short grasses. 'My hands and knees are frozen,' whispered Archibald as he crawled along the ground with a dark cloak over his back. 'Quiet!' hissed Douglas, who crawled beside him and in front of the other men, who were also covered in dark cloaks.

As the sound of the guards faded, Douglas quietly called out 'Quick, let's go.' The first few men rushed up against the base of the castle walls. 'Made it so far. Did any of you hear them? They genuinely think that we are oxen,' whispered Archibald. 'My dear brother,' said Douglas in a soft whisper.' 'What?' shouted Archibald. Douglas replied with a warning finger over his mouth.

Simon of Ledhouse stepped forward with his purpose-built rope ladder. Being too heavy to throw up and over the wall, long poles were used to gently push the top of the ladder over the battlement and engage the strong hook in a secure location. 'That should do it, let the poles go,' whispered Simon. As the two men did so, a loud clank was heard from above. As Simon quickly hurried up the ladder, those at the base all stared at Archibald. The look told him that they should have listened closer to what he had to say.

Simon was about half way up when a voice was heard calling out 'What was that noise?' The sound of running footsteps could be heard. Douglas immediately started to climb up the ladder. The observant guard arrived at where the ladder was positioned and attempted to push Simon back over just as he was just about to reach over the ramparts. Simon lunged at the guard, grabbing hold of his clothing, and plunged his long dagger into the guard's neck. Still clutching the guards clothing, Simon, with a twist of his body, pulled the slain man towards him and saw him disappear over the castle wall.

The dull thud of the dead guard hitting the ground was the signal for the others to start to ascend. As Douglas stepped over onto the battlement, he witnessed Simon being attacked by a second guard. Once again, Simon calmly brought the man down as his knife penetrated deep into the vital organs of the guard's body. Douglas was pleased to have this man from Ledhouse as one of his men; he was even more pleased to have him in front of him on this cold dangerous evening.

The folks of the castle were all in the great hall. There was much singing and dancing as they enjoyed their feast before the long fast of the forthcoming Lent. The loud laughter provided the direction for Douglas and his men to follow. The sound of running footsteps echoed along the narrow corridors as Douglas led his men into attack.

The door of the great hall burst open to the terrifying cry of 'A Douglas! A Douglas!' The sound paralysed those within. To hear such fearsome words called out in such a secure place brought terror to the minds of the inhabitants.

Some were brave and bold enough to attempt a feeble challenge, but were quickly slain as the swords of Douglas and his men lashed out at the brave bodies that dared cross their path. No mercy was given to those who resisted. The loud war cries, along with the screams of pain and terror in such a confined space, caused panic amongst the castle residents. Others in the large hall attempted to escape through the doors at the opposite end.

The castle warden, Gilmyn de Fiennes, saw that he could not hold back this attack and retreated with others into the great tower within the castle and barred the door. As the resistance against Douglas's attack dwindled, prisoners were taken and the castle secured. The only activity that remained was the siege of the tower where Fiennes sought refuge. Unable to break down the door, Douglas and his men were at a loss for what to do next. They did not want to stay here too long for reinforcements might come by.

Douglas called to his men. 'Those who are archers, apply your skills to aiming at those openings,' as he pointed to the various narrow windows that were positioned around the high tower. 'If we are lucky, you may hit the right victims and force the opening of the doorway.'

A bombardment of arrows was fired at the tower windows. Inside, the occasional scream of pain could be heard as an unfortunate victim was hit, but still the door did not open.

Douglas, standing at the door, called out 'Listen to me. I am Douglas. Only those who have resisted me today have perished. I am a man of my word. Open this door and surrender and you will come to no harm.' He waited, but there was no response.

The arrows continued to penetrate the tower windows. Inside, the inhabitants sheltered under furniture, tables, chairs, dead bodies, anything that could be used to block a deadly arrow. There was no safe hiding place, as many arrows coming through the windows were deflected off the walls with such force that those who thought they were safe were hit.

The siege continued into the following day. A loud scream echoed within the tower. An arrow had hit the warden in the face, causing him great pain and loss of blood. He called out 'Douglas, are you true to your word?'

'Yes,' replied Douglas. 'What is your request?'

'I ask for the lives of those in here with me and my own life. Grant us safety and we will immediately offer our surrender,' shouted the warden. Douglas agreed to guarantee their safety in exchange for their surrender.

The tower door slowly swung open to reveal the sight of many slain and maimed bodies. 'Come on out,' shouted Douglas, as his men escorted the few remaining survivors. The last one to step forward was Fiennes, blood pouring from his face wound which still contained the embedded arrowhead.

Douglas stepped forward. 'You will be given horses and provisions to enable you to leave our lands and return to your own. Should I ever see you here again I will not be so kind to you.'

Fiennes, covering his bleeding face with his hand, nodded his agreement. The other prisoners thanked Douglas for the mercy he had shown. A group of about ten of Douglas's men agreed to act as escorts for these hostages and to aid their journey south.

Everything that could be salvaged from the castle was taken. Food, stored provisions, livestock and weapons were all collected.

'What are we to do with this plunder?' asked Robert Hall.

'Each man is to be given a fair share that he can carry,' answered Douglas.

'And the rest?' asked Simon.

'To be taken to Kelso,' answered Douglas. 'However, I also have a specific request of you, Simon of Ledhouse.'

'What would that be?' asked Simon.

'You have performed a valuable role in the taking of this important and significant castle. I wish you to take a message from me to our King, Robert the Bruce. Please tell him what we have done here today, and mention yourself and your ladder. Ask him what he wants done with this place. Do we occupy? Or do we destroy? Take some good men with you for your protection.'

A few hours later, almost fifty men made their way into the town of Kelso. Some were on foot, others were on horseback. They all carried something or herded livestock. The people of Kelso had not seen so many men before in one place. Only the English enemy had come there in such numbers. As they grouped in the town square, the locals started to gather around. A small band of horse riders suddenly entered into their midst. They immediately recognised the leader; they had seen him before. Archibald rode behind his brother. He was amazed by the adoration being shown by common people towards the one they called 'the Douglas.'

Douglas addressed the townspeople. 'My good friends, today these men that you see with me have attacked and taken the castle of Roxburgh. The garrison have been defeated, those who opposed us have been slain, those who surrendered, including the warden, are being escorted across the border and back to their own lands.' The crowd cheered, delighted at such good news.

Douglas raised his hand. 'My friends, I believe that over the years you were the victims of many a raid by that castle garrison. My men would like to return some of what was stolen from you.' With great pride and joy, Douglas's men shared their plunder with the grateful people of Kelso.

Word spread throughout the borderlands of the taking of Roxburgh. The knowledge that the English garrison was no longer around to raid and plunder and take revenge against anyone who supported Douglas brought with it a wave of fresh confidence and increased support for Douglas and his men. Many more came to join him. The following day, the men who had escorted the castle prisoners south returned with news that Fiennes had fallen off his horse and died, the cause of his death being the wound to his face, which had been more serious than was at first realised.

Several days later Simon returned from visiting King Robert the Bruce. He was well pleased that Douglas had asked him to carry this message, as he had been generously rewarded.

'How is our King?' asked Douglas.

'He is well,' replied Edward, brother of King Robert. 'Our King has sent me here to assist in pulling down the walls of Roxburgh. He is most pleased with you and thanks you and your men.'

20

FAMILY REUNION

AS THE BRIGHT and cheerful months of springtime arrived, fresh life appeared throughout the lands, oblivious of the significance of events yet to unfold. The newly born of man, beast and plant life projected the image and magnificence of their great creator, as their beauty and innocence demonstrated the purity and splendour of the gift of life.

These new arrivals were to be the last born into the tragic divisions of these times. They would be the final ones to be born into a nation that was in disarray and discontented within itself. Future generations would be born into a nation that was united; a nation that was free, at one with itself, and that stood proud in its own right. These were the thoughts of Bruce as he dreamt of what the future could be for his beloved Scotland.

Douglas and his men had returned to Lintalee. The success of the attack on Roxburgh had greater significance than they could imagine. Of all the remaining strategic castles, only two still remained occupied by English garrisons, Edinburgh and Stirling. The taking of Roxburgh generated an air of excitement about what might happen next.

The border raids continued relentlessly. No English convoy was safe from attack by Douglas as he and his men gradually choked the supply chain to the enemy garrisons in the north. With each success, confidence continued to grow and more men agreed to join up with Douglas. Their strength in numbers was now greater than their needs demanded. The cunning ambushes, the midnight attacks, such strategies did not require many men. Many were therefore requested to be patient; the day that they would be called was not far away.

Cuthbert had returned from Blackhouse Tower and had rejoined Douglas. 'I would like to stay a while longer. After all, I don't believe that our mother is in any danger,' declared Archibald, who had begun to make a name for himself as the cheeky young brother of Douglas.

'Our mother will be safe. There are other good men that I know and trust to care for her. However, one of us will need to go back soon,' replied Douglas.

The sound of someone approaching alerted those on guard. 'It's a message for you,' called Cuthbert, as he directed the familiar monk towards Douglas.

'My good man, how are you?' asked Douglas, welcoming Brother Michael from Melrose Abbey into his company. 'Please eat with us.' Douglas gestured to his friend to help himself to the plentiful repast that was laid out before them.

'Thank you, I don't mind if I do,' replied the hungry monk, who appeared to be more interested in filling his belly than passing on his message.

'What of that brother of mine. Have you any news?' asked Douglas.

'Brother Hugh is well and happy. He has found peace and purpose in his life,' answered Brother Michael, with his mouth full.

'Is he still as daft?' asked the grinning young Archibald, who was sitting nearby listening to the conversation.

'Who are you?' asked Brother Michael, as he paused before answering the impertinent question.

'This is Archibald, my youngest brother,' said Douglas.

'Define daft,' said Brother Michael.

'He's no richt in the heid,' replied Archibald, as he sniggered with a cocky look.

'Well young man, let me tell you what he says about you. He is constantly praising both you and all of your family. He is immensely proud to have you as a brother. He is in constant prayer for your safety and well-being. He has chosen a humble life of holy sanctuary where he can devote every day to the worship of God and to the welfare of others. No day goes by where your brother does not perform good deeds to help others.'

Archibald was silenced. His face showed his regret at words he had wrongly chosen when speaking of his brother.

'If he is daft, as you say, then I too and many others must also be daft. It is a choice we make and we are proud to do so,' declared Brother Michael. All eyes, including Douglas's, stared at young Archibald.

The youngest of the Douglas family blushed. His ability to balance his desire to impress alongside his innocent ignorance was self-evident. With head bowed he quietly said, 'Sorry.'

'Pardon?' said Douglas, 'We didn't quite hear you.'

'I said I am sorry,' replied Archibald, louder this time, remorse written all over his face.

'What news do you bring me,' Douglas asked of Brother Michael, to break the embarrassing silence. 'The castle of Edinburgh has been taken, the garrison have been slain. A magnificent victory if ever there was,' answered Brother Michael with a proud smile.

'That place is impregnable,' said Cuthbert. 'How did they do it?'

'They climbed up the steep cliffs, in the darkness of night they say,' replied Brother Michael.

'Impossible! I have seen those cliffs. No man could perform such a daring act,' declared the disbelieving Cuthbert.

'There is always a way,' said Douglas, as he asked Brother Michael. 'What more can you tell us?'

'A secret route was discovered. That's how they got over the wall. The say that a man, William Francis, I believe, who as a youth had lived in the castle and had cause to visit his lover in the town, one night he found this secret path and had kept it to himself ever since.'

'Whoever led such a brilliant attack must be a man of great courage and daring. Do you know who it was?' asked Douglas.

'Sir, it was the Earl of Moray,' replied Brother Michael.

'Who? I know of no such man,' said Douglas, puzzled.

'Sir, I think you do know him. It's Thomas Randolph,' replied Brother Michael.

The stunned silence lasted for several moments. Cuthbert was the first to speak. 'How did a traitor who fought against us become an Earl?' spat out the confused Cuthbert.

'They say that he has found great favour with King Robert. He has pledged his loyalty to our King and country and has been rewarded with many lands and the title of Earl of Moray,' declared Brother Michael.

'Tell that to Fullerton,' shouted Cuthbert, as he openly expressed his disgust with the actions of Bruce.

'Who's Fullerton?' asked Brother Michael.

'Stop!' shouted Douglas. 'We must have faith in our good King. If he has chosen to reward Thomas Randolph then we must respect that decision.

Cuthbert, still fuming at this news replied 'Sir, I accept what you say. However, compare what you have achieved against what Randolph has done. There is no comparison, and yet you have been granted nothing.'

'It's nothing to do with what one has achieved. It's all to do with birth,' replied Douglas.

'What do you mean birth?' asked young Archibald.

Douglas shook his head and was unable to hold back a sigh of frustration. 'He is the King's nephew, no matter what I or anyone else achieves, blood relations will always come first. We must accept this situation.'

'So what happens now?' asked young Archibald. 'It seems that Stirling is the only strategic castle that's left in enemy hands, so where do we go from here?'

The others looked on in disbelief at the advance in maturity that this young man had just demonstrated in such a short period of time.

Douglas sat quietly for a few minutes and then spoke. 'I sense that there is a major turning point about to unfold in our lives.'

'Sir, what do you mean,' asked Simon of Ledhouse, who very rarely strayed from the side of his good friend Douglas. Douglas sat quietly and pondered over this question before answering.

'I have heard news of the recent murder of Piers Gaveston, King Edward's close companion. I have heard that many powerful and influential English nobles have overcome their disgust at that relationship and have shown compassion and tolerance by renewing their allegiance to their King.'

'What do you think will happen next?' asked Cuthbert.

'If we look at recent events, the English are starting to reunite under Edward II,' replied Douglas. 'We have taken all but one of the major strategic castles, and we ourselves have inflicted terror and great pain upon anyone who attempted to cross these borderlands. There can only be one outcome'.

'James, what do you believe that to be,' asked a polite young Archibald.

'A great army will come north, an army too large to ambush, probably the largest enemy army ever to enter our country,' declared Douglas.

'What do you suggest we do?' asked a concerned Cuthbert who feared the worst.

'We must prepare to do battle, army against army,' replied Douglas.

'But that is not our way,' one of the others called out.

'Yes, I hear you. Our way has always been to ambush, and to hit and run; we are masters in such warfare. But we will be forced to meet the army of our enemy on the battlefield, of that I have no doubt.'

'We don't possess the tactics or the knowledge of such fighting,' shouted one of the others.

'You are *almost* correct, my man.'

'What do you mean almost?' asked Archibald.

'Some of us have the experience,' replied Douglas as he looked around at several of the elderly battled-scarred warriors who had fought with his father. 'We need to talk and share the methods of open warfare and if possible apply the skills that we are good at,' answered Douglas, as he smiled at the venerable warriors who knew what he was talking about.

Several weeks passed by. Each day was spent discussing and sharing the many tactics of open warfare. The experiences of the elderly warriors, some of whom had survived Falkirk, were listened to with great interest and admiration.

'The archers and the charging cavalry, that's what defeated us in the past,' declared one elderly man who proudly bore scars from wounds received when he fought with Wallace. 'We could not stop them, no matter how hard we fought.'

Cuthbert spoke. 'Let's think about it. We have defeated many a charging cavalry when we have had time to prepare and agree our strategy. When we come to know the time and place we will do the same.' The men agreed. 'There is nothing we can't do if we have the time to plan,' stated Cuthbert.

'What about the archers, how do we stop them?' called one young man.

'With great difficulty,' Cuthbert answered, knowing how deadly such weapons could be. 'One of two things needs to happen. Either we stop them firing their arrows or we seek shelter once they are released.' Archibald joined the discussion. 'If we seek shelter we cannot fight and if we can't fight then they will win.'

'An excellent observation, my dear brother. We therefore only have one choice and that is to put maximum effort into destroying the capability of any archers as soon as possible,' declared Douglas, who up until now had been sitting quietly listening to this discussion.

Several days later, a stranger appeared at the perimeter of the camp. 'What business do you have here?' asked the guard. 'I must meet with Douglas,' replied the stranger. 'Your name Sir?' asked the guard, as the well-armed man dismounted from his tired horse. 'Davidson,' replied the stranger. 'Tell Douglas that I am here,' replied Davidson, with great urgency in his voice.

The conversations on the tactics of warfare were still going on when the guard approached Douglas. 'He said his name was Davidson,' said the guard. 'Shall I send him away?' Douglas jumped up, and smiled. 'No, in time we will send him away, but I am sure we will all be going with him. Please bring him over to meet with us.'

There was not much to separate their ages, nor the lives that they had led which had been totally devoted to the fight for freedom. When the two good friends first caught sight of each other, their hearts were filled with emotion. Douglas was first to call out. 'My dear David, this is indeed a day of great joy.' Davidson did not reply. Overcome with sentiment, he embraced his most dear friend. Only a few recognised this young man, who bore a close resemblance to Douglas.

'Who is he?' asked one of the men. 'A very good loyal friend of Douglas and Bruce,' replied Cuthbert.

'How are you my good friend? It's been a few years since we last met,' said Douglas, who was delighted to meet his companion of days gone by.

'Yes, and a busy few years at that. I am fine and well. Some of those tricks, which you taught me with a sword have come in very useful. You appear to have made quite a reputation for yourself over these years,' answered Davidson.

'Well maybe, but reputations alone won't win our lands back,' said Douglas. 'What news do you bring?'

'Could we talk alone?' asked Davidson.

'We can. Come with me,' said Douglas, as he put his arm around his good friend.

'James, I bring a message from Bruce, a message which he says only I can deliver to you,' declared Davidson.

'What message do you bring that can only be entrusted to you?' asked Douglas.

'James, you know me, you know what I stand for. I ask this, do you truly trust me?' asked Davidson as he prepared Douglas to hear his message.

'Of course I do, like no other,' replied a puzzled Douglas.

'The English are heading north. They will shortly be coming to do battle with us,' answered Davidson.

'Where?' asked Douglas.

'We believe somewhere near Stirling,' replied Davidson.

'Well that comes as no surprise,' declared Douglas, who then asked 'Does he want me to intercept their armies as they cross the border?'

'No, you will not be able to,' answered Davidson.

'Why not?' inquired Douglas.

'There will be far too many of them. It will be one of the largest armies ever to invade our nation,' said Davidson.

'Would it not make sense that I at least try to capture their nobles?' suggested Douglas.

'Word has arrived that along with the army on foot, many galleons are being prepared to sail north. Even the great Black Douglas cannot stop such a force,' replied Davidson.

'What are Bruce's plans and what does he want of me?' asked Douglas.

'Bruce has said that the hide and seek has to stop; the days of ambush, hit and run tactics which have so far been successful have come to an end. In order for our nation to be truly united he wants us to meet the great might of the English army on the open battle field,' explained Davidson.

'Such an act on its own would be suicidal. What other plans does Bruce have?'

'Edward Bruce is at this moment laying siege upon the castle of Stirling. The commander has been forced to declare that unless he is relieved by an English force by midsummer's day, he will give up and surrender. The good work that you and your men have performed in limiting the flow of supplies has made this situation possible,' announced Davidson.

'What role does he want my men and me to perform?' asked Douglas.

Davidson put his hand on Douglas's shoulder. 'Sir, I am a mere common man, like many who follow you. I fight for the same cause. This nation which we call our own is ours as much as the rich nobles who have fought amongst themselves and betrayed us for so long. They may have the titles of ownership, but we have the ownership of being the race that occupies this land. It is our battle as much as theirs. Bruce shares this vision and he asks this of you. Every able man at your disposal, every resource that you can muster, he asks that you make available and through your leadership bring your forces to his aid.'

'You have presented our king's request with touching words and a clear purpose that I also share. My answer you already know. It can only be yes. However, the price that is asked of my men can only be committed with their approval,' declared Douglas.

'I would expect no less of you,' replied Davidson, who then added 'What I have shared with you is confidential, for your ears only. Edward II must not hear of Bruce's plans.'

'If Bruce's plans were betrayed, it would not be by any of my men,' replied Douglas. 'Let us eat first.'

'I was wondering when you were going to offer. I'm starving,' said Davidson.

'You have changed in many ways, my good friend, but I am glad to see that some things have not changed,' answered Douglas as they laughingly joined the others.

After they had eaten, Douglas gathered his men together. As they sat around him, he addressed his loyal followers; they sat silently and gave him their full attention.

'We have been having discussions over these last few weeks about meeting our enemy in open battle. We now need to make a decision. I ask this of you, are we ready?'

An almighty roar went up that echoed through the dark evening and frightened the many beasts that lived in the forest around Lintalee. Every man rose to his feet. 'Yes! A Douglas! A Douglas!' the men repeatedly called out their loud war cry, determination in every syllable.

Douglas nodded his approval and without saying anything further sat down. Davidson, eyes wide open in total disbelief, smiled at Douglas, and said 'I should have known. Is there anything you don't know?'

A few days' later two men on horseback approached Melrose Abbey in the early morning sunshine. They dismounted and walked the last few yards towards the arched doorway. Brother Michael answered the loud knocking. 'I was not expecting you so soon,' he said as he gestured for his visitors to enter. 'Wait here and I will have him called,' declared Brother Michael, as he left his visitors waiting. No words were spoken as the two men sat and stared at the bare stone walls. The only sound was that of men chanting in common prayer somewhere along the dark corridor.

Several minutes' later footsteps could be heard approaching. The door gently opened to reveal Hugh Douglas, the second son of the late Lord William of Douglas. The strong emotions at this meeting of loved ones who have not seen each other for many years caused words to be temporarily suspended. The need to touch and embrace overcame the need for any discussion as the three Douglas brothers hugged one another and wept in the happiness and joy of each other's company.

The feelings of love and affection were so strong that it took several minutes for the brothers' composure to be regained.

'Hugh, I am so sorry that I have not been to see you before now,' said Douglas, as he held his brother's hands.

'I knew you would come some day, I prayed for you to come,' replied Hugh.

'We have been busy, but we need to talk to you,' declared Archibald. 'Later,' said Douglas, who then asked his brother

'Hugh, how have you been? Are you in good health? Is there anything that you need?'

'In here I have everything that I need, and that I may add is not very much. Your presence today was all that I ever desired,' replied Hugh.

Douglas sat down. 'Hugh, a great battle is about to take place. Many men will surely die. We Douglases may be good fighters, but we are not immortal. I would like us all to come together as a family for what may be our last time together. Will you come with us to be with our mother?' Hugh looked at his two brothers. There could only be one greater experience than this, and that was to have also the pleasure of their mother's company. 'Yes, I will,' he answered.

Darkness was starting to descend in the glen where the Blackhouse Tower provided the shelter and protection to the mother of the Douglas family. The three approaching riders were startled when two archers suddenly jumped out in front of them accompanied by two others with swords drawn. Frightened and yet delighted that these guards had demonstrated such alertness, the three riders were pleased at being so confronted. The guards, on recognising who they had just surprised, stepped back to allow access. 'Thank you, you are doing a fine job,' declared Douglas.

'Is anyone at home,' shouted Douglas as he entered.

'Who is it?' cried Sophia as she called from along the narrow hallway.

'Three lost souls looking for comfort,' shouted Hugh, as he, along with Archibald and Douglas, entered the main room, which was unoccupied.

'Where is she?' asked Archibald.

The sound of footsteps running along the hallway could be heard approaching. 'Here she comes, I can't wait to see her face when she sees the three of us together,' said an excited Douglas. The running stopped as Sophia appeared at the doorway. 'Oh heavens! It's you, the three of you all together at once,' shouted Sophia. The look on her face told a story, not one of happiness at seeing her adopted brothers in front of her, but one of worry and concern.

'What is it, Sophia?' asked Douglas. 'Is our mother all right?'

'Come with me,' requested Sophia as she made her way back along the corridor.

The door of their mother's bedroom was opened as they urgently approached. Inside several candles flickered in the cold draughts that circulated throughout the house. The air was contaminated with a damp musty smell that they were not accustomed to. Lady Eleanor lay motionless on her bed, an occasional cough being the only signal of life still present. A small table contained items that indicated she had been receiving attention.

Douglas had faced many a terrifying moment in his life, he was afraid of no man, and yet as he approached the bed of his mother he felt real fear. It was a feeling that he was unaccustomed to. His stomach was in knots, his throat suddenly became dry and burned inside, and his head was pounding. The difference this time was that he had no control over the situation. He tried to compose himself for the benefit of his younger brothers.

'Mother,' said Douglas gently. Her head gave a gentle hint of movement. 'It's us, your three sons; we are all here with you.' He looked at Sophia as if to seek permission to go closer. She gestured him to approach. Leaning over, each of the three sons gently kissed their dear mother. Her head lay still, a single tear appeared in her left eye and slowly trickled down her cheek. With all her energy, she summoned a soft smile, indicating that she knew that they were there.

'What's wrong with her?' asked Archibald.

'She's been like this for several days,' answered Sophia, with a distressed look on her face.

'Please, let me help,' said Hugh, in a surprisingly confident voice that indicated he might be able to offer assistance.

'She's been burning inside,' whispered Sophia, who looked exhausted after several days of constant bedside vigilance.

Hugh moved over towards his mother's bed and touched her burning forehead; his gentle caring hands stroked the side of her face and neck and then took hold of both of her small tender hands. He finished his silent examination by gently touching and softly squeezing her outstretched limbs.

'Can you help?' asked Douglas.

'I have seen this before,' said Hugh.

'What's wrong with her?' asked Sophia. 'She has a fever caused by a hot burning inside her,' answered Hugh.

'Can anything be done to help her?' asked Douglas.

'I'm not sure. It may be too early,' said Hugh, as he shook his head.

'Too early for what?' asked Douglas.

'There is a cure that I have seen being given to others. It involves crushing and mixing the flowers of two not so common water plants,' replied Hugh.

'What are these cures? Where can they be found?' asked Douglas impatiently, indicating that finding this remedy was of a greater priority than anything else in his adventurous life.

'Bogbean and yellow water lily. We need to search the nearest upland marshes and streams, for that is were we will find them. But it may be too early,' replied Hugh.

'At first light we will all go searching,' declared Douglas.

'If we try to keep her warm and comfortable we may still have a few days,' replied Hugh as the others bowed to his valued knowledge.

The hills above Blackhouse Tower were searched; the water edges of many small lochs and clear streams were thoroughly scoured for the early signs of these two precious plants. At the end of each day the exhausted plant hunters arrived home weary and distressed that their day had been unsuccessful. For five whole days they searched with no success.

'What do these plants actually look like,' asked Sophia, who had been staying at home nursing Lady Eleanor. Hugh looked at Sophia; he was exhausted and starting to give up hope of ever finding the elusive plants. 'The leaves of the bogbean consist of three rounded leaflets on each stalk; the small beautiful fringed flowers are both pink and white. The yellow water lily has floating oval leaves, the flower is bright yellow, cup-shaped, and rises clear of the water; its flowers smell like wine,' answered Hugh.

Sophia turned to Douglas. 'I have seen these flowers. I know where they can be found. We must go now.'

'It's too dark to go back up those hills,' answered Douglas.

'Listen to me please,' shouted the frustrated Sophia. 'I have seen them along the waters edge of St Mary's Loch, a short distance from here; your mother and I have spent many hours admiring the beauty that grows there. If we light a torch we can search for a few hours.'

About a week later, the bright early morning sun shone through the narrow window of Lady Eleanor's sickroom. The colourful rays of sparkling light injected life into the otherwise dreary atmosphere that had lingered here these past days. Lady Eleanor finally awoke. Her fever had gone and the burning sensation in her lower back had all but disappeared. Confused, and without memory of these past weeks, she looked around her. As her eyes adjusted to the brightness she saw the outline of several figures who appeared to be sleeping nearby. 'Who's there?' she called out.

They awoke with a startle. 'It's us mother,' called Hugh who was first to waken. 'How are you?'

'I'm fine. How long have I been here?' she asked as she tried to unravel the confusion in her mind. 'You have been very ill,' answered Hugh as Archibald and Douglas also woke to see their mother recover to good health. They both approached her bed and stood beside Hugh. The three Douglas brothers each kissed her in turn and in turn embraced their dear mother.

Archibald was the next to speak. 'Mother, it was Hugh, he knew of a secret remedy to cure you; we owe your life to him.' Lady Eleanor smiled at Hugh, but it was a smile that was to be shared by all three of her sons.

'Where's Sophia,' asked Lady Eleanor as the room door burst open.

'What's happening?' shouted Sophia as she rushed into the bright sunlit room.

'She has recovered,' answered Douglas.

'This is the one we should all be grateful to,' said Hugh.

'I agree. Her love and admiration of God's beautiful creations was the reason for your recovery,' declared Douglas, as he held out his hand to thank Sophia. As she came closer, Douglas embraced the lovely Sophia and escorted her over to the bedside of his smiling mother. The sight of these two together was something very special that gave Lady Eleanor a great feeling of joy and happiness.

The next few days were spent nursing Lady Eleanor and supporting her return to good health, for she was still very weak.

After a few days Douglas approached his mother. 'What troubles you my son,' she asked as she recognised that familiar look that suggested he had to go away.

'Mother, I only intended to stay a short time. There is something very important that I need to be involved in. Edward II is at this moment coming into our country with a great army. I need to go and join with our King Robert and meet the might of England in battle.'

'Then you must go my son,' replied Lady Eleanor.

'Every able-bodied man will be needed,' declared Douglas. 'However, one of us has to stay here to care and protect you.'

'Are you asking me to choose?' asked Lady Eleanor.

'Yes, your decision will be final,' replied Douglas.

'Give the others a call,' requested Lady Eleanor.

As they all gathered round, Lady Eleanor addressed her family. 'My dear sons, my dear daughter, you have all been very loving and kind to me over the years and have come together to save my life. But more important than saving my life, you must save your own. The strength of the approaching English army is not to be underestimated; they have vast resources, as I for one surely know. You have a choice to make: go with James to fight with our King Robert, for he needs every man, or stay here and care for me.'

Sophia answered first. 'I don't think I would be much use at fighting, therefore I will stay.' The others were amused at her reaction and laughed aloud. Douglas looked at his mother and then glanced in the direction of Sophia and said 'I don't think I would be much use at nursing, therefore I will go fight with Bruce.'

'Now there's a surprise if ever there was one,' said Archibald, who walked over towards his mother and embraced her. 'Mother, you know how much I love you and that I don't want to leave you. However, that elder brother of mine needs to have someone look out for him, and who better than I to watch his back. I will go with James to fight with Bruce.' Douglas shook his head. 'Who's going to watch his back?' he thought to himself, as he chuckled out loud.

Hugh stepped forward. 'Mother, I have never killed anything in my life and I don't intend to start now. I will stay here and protect you. Should your illness return, Sophia and I can help you.'

The three brothers, young Sophia and Lady Eleanor all embraced, aware that this could be their last time together. Concern for each other replaced the laughter of a few moments ago. 'You will take care, won't you?' said Sophia, as she hugged James and at the same time held the hand of Archibald. The tears in her gentle eyes were recognised by Douglas as being tears of love generated by the special feelings she had for him. He responded, and when he kissed her it was a kiss that showed his feelings of affection and love towards this beautiful girl, and it was also a kiss that said 'I love you but I can't stay with you.'

21

BANNOCKBURN

IT WAS THE BEGINNING of June. The town of Lanark had not seen such activity since the uprising started by Wallace many years earlier. The arrival of many men, some on foot, some on horseback, generated an air of excitement and optimism throughout the town. The men of the borders arrived in great numbers. They brought stories of a vast English army that was following behind and close to the border at Coldstream.

The border warriors, led by Cuthbert, Simon of Ledhouse and Davidson, set up camp on the outskirts of the town and waited. Some had brought their whole families. There was no one left to care for or protect them, and so their only option was to go with their men. The many families carried provisions and cared for their men as they travelled into battle.

They waited, patiently at first and then the doubts started to creep in. Some had not seen him and wondered if the stories about Douglas were exaggerated. 'Is he coming?' asked one man who stood with his young daughter. 'I hope this is not going to be a waste of my time,' he added.

'He will be here, I can guarantee that,' replied Cuthbert, who was also growing concerned about the delay in the arrival of his good friend.

'We did agree to meet here, didn't we?' asked Simon of Ledhouse, who was also starting to doubt if his leader would arrive.

Many hundreds of men from the borders, wives and children continued to wait. 'If he doesn't get here soon the English will be upon us,' shouted one impatient young man. Others had arrived at Lanark to join with Douglas; they also were becoming impatient as their confidence started to dwindle.

The afternoon sun brought great comfort; the cold wet miserable weather of recent years was forgotten in the warm sunshine that made their lives more pleasant and bearable. A loud rumbling could be heard in the distance. Like an approaching thunderstorm, the sound grew louder. 'They're coming,' shouted a lookout, who stood high up on the thick branch of a nearby beech tree.

They suddenly came into view. Douglas rode at the front, his coat of arms gleaming bright in the afternoon sun. His shield and armour sparkled and singled him out from the many men of Douglasdale that followed behind him. With heads held high, they felt proud to be following the true Lord of Douglasdale into battle against the invading English army.

'What kept you?' shouted Davidson.

'We were searching for water lilies,' replied Archibald, who rode immediately behind his elder brother.

'Oh, really, did you find any?' asked Cuthbert.

'Yes, we did,' replied Archibald.

'I'm so glad to hear that,' answered Davidson sarcastically, as he and Cuthbert looked at each other in disbelief.

Douglas dismounted and greeted his loyal men. 'Are you all ready?' he asked.

'Ready long before you,' replied Davidson, with a hint of laughter in his voice.

'Any news of the English army?' asked Douglas.

'They have been organising themselves at Berwick, but reports say that their troops are ready to cross at Coldstream. I would have preferred to meet them on the other side of the Tweed,' said Cuthbert.

'Yes, there could be advantages in meeting them there, however, they would be fresh and have unlimited resources. When we meet them at Stirling, they will be tired and weary from their long march. Much easier to defeat a tired army,' said Douglas.

'When do we leave for Stirling?' asked an impatient Davidson. Douglas remounted his horse and grinned. 'We do want to get there before them, don't we?' he replied, and then turned to address his men.

'I don't believe that it is necessary for me to speak words of comfort to you, nor shall I insult you by making false promises of the certainty of victory in these next days. You all surely know that what lies ahead of us is the greatest challenge ever to our nation. I only ask one thing of you good men, and that is to give to our King Robert the same effort and loyalty that you have given me on many occasions. Do this and we will be victorious in battle against that enemy who comes here to take our lands.'

They looked at Douglas. There was an unaccustomed silence in their midst. They looked at each other, knowing that, unlike the many ambushes and secret attacks that they had become familiar with while following Douglas, this forthcoming battle would be entirely different. It would be a battle out in the open against the mighty English army. There was uncertainty, but there was trust in their leader.

Douglas shouted his last instruction to his men. 'We must make speedy progress to meet with our King at Stirling; much preparation will be needed before we engage our enemy. Have faith, and may God bless us.'

They headed north towards Falkirk; their eagerness gave them the extra energy to cover more miles than expected in the remaining long daylight hours. They crossed the River Avon and passed close to where Wallace had been defeated sixteen years earlier. Someone who recognised the area called out that they should stop.

Douglas assented. 'Many of our fathers met their final day of rest on this sacred ground. We will honour their lives by resting here for the night. We will pray for their souls, and perhaps their spirits will guide us on our day of battle.'

As they tried to sleep that night, many were restless, for they knew that what lay before them was going to be the most difficult and challenging event of their lives. Some were afraid and could not sleep. Most did not want to show their fear and lay still during the hours of darkness. Douglas lay beside his younger brother. He was proud to have him with him and yet he feared for his safety. The cockiness of young Archibald had been a valuable attribute in the past but somehow Douglas would have to find a way of controlling the eagerness of this young man in order to prevent him getting into difficulty.

The following day Douglas and his men crossed the River Carron and arrived at the forest of Torwood, a few miles south of Stirling Castle. 'It's here that we have been requested to meet,' announced David Davidson, who rode beside his good friend Douglas. As they approached the forest edge, some armed men came out from the shadows and asked 'What is your business?' Douglas, recognising that they were not the enemy, immediately replied 'I am Douglas of Douglasdale. These good men and I have come to join with our King Robert. If you know where he is take us to him.'

A short time later Douglas and his close companions were led into Bruce's camp. 'Sire, as you have requested, I come here with my men to offer our support and fight for your cause,' declared Douglas, as he approached his King and bowed before him. 'My dear Douglas, I am truly grateful for your presence, there are few, if any that I would chose to have here before you,' replied Bruce. 'Sire, it is an honour for us all to be here,' answered Douglas.

As he looked round the tent, he glanced at the faces of the many knights and nobles. Some he recognised, others he was not sure of. They all stared at him as if he were some sort of freak show who had come to visit. The tall, handsome, dark-haired young man who stood before them was the one whom the English were becoming more afraid of than any other Scotsman. This was the man who controlled the borders, the man that they had heard about, whose father, because he fought with Wallace, had been killed by Longshanks and his lands confiscated. Some of them had previously fought with him in battle and knew the stories were true. Others thought he was just a myth, exaggerated during the many tales from battles fought in the past.

There was one amongst them who knew the stories were indeed true. It was someone who had been on the receiving end of a revengeful Black Douglas attack. 'I'm delighted to see you again,' shouted the voice from behind Douglas. In the split second that it took Douglas to turn around, he recognised that voice; it was the voice of someone that he wanted to kill more than any other.

Douglas and Thomas Randolph, now Earl of Moray, eyed each other. The shorter, slightly stocky Randolph smiled at the taller Douglas. The look on the face of Douglas was very different, as he looked angrily at Randolph and Bruce in turn. He did not speak, but his displeasure at the presence of this traitor, who had been party to the death of Fullerton, his friend and family guardian, was evident for all to see.

Instinctively Douglas put his hand on his sword and stared into the face of Randolph. 'James!' Bruce called out. 'We must let the past go, and together build a better future.' Approaching Douglas and Randolph, Bruce put a hand on the shoulder of each of them and gently said 'Over these last years we have seen many good men fight both with us and also against us. Whatever their reasons, they made their choice as you have both made yours. Without both of you, we would not be here today. James, you achieved a great victory when you took Roxburgh. Thomas, you also, when you took Edinburgh. Think what we as a nation can achieve if you and all other Scotsman unite and stand together to defend our freedom.'

Randolph, unsure of the response that he would get, presented his hand to Douglas who in turn hesitantly presented his. A truce had been established, albeit for the pleasure of those present, but friendship was still far off.

'I regret allowing the situation to happen when your man was beaten,' declared Randolph, who then quietly asked 'How is he?'

'He died. The beating that your men administered caused his death,' replied Douglas sharply.

'I am deeply sorry. We only wanted him to talk and tell us your whereabouts,' answered a remorseful Randolph.

'He was my family's loyal guardian and my very good friend. He would never have talked,' said Douglas curtly.

Randolph looked at Douglas. He knew that no words could ever bring back the loyal man Douglas thought so highly of. 'Sometimes we lose good friends and sometimes we gain others. I may not be worthy, but I would like some day to be your good friend,' declared Randolph. Douglas, sensing that these words were indeed genuine, gave a gentle grin and replied 'My lord, true friendship has to be earned.' Randolph responded by saying 'Yes indeed, but perhaps these next few days will present us with many opportunities to earn the friendship of many.'

'Soon we must discuss our battle strategies,' instructed Bruce, but first I want to meet with your men. One by one, Bruce's brother Edward, Thomas Randolph, and the young Walter the Steward, cousin of James Douglas and heir to the name of Stewart, and James Douglas himself all presented their men to their King.

Bruce went round the vast number of men that had been assembled. They all looked physically capable of carrying out the task ahead of them. As he stopped to talk to them, he saw that their hearts were also ready and willing; he saw that there was determination and absence of fear. He saw that their leaders, who would be his division commanders, had prepared them well and that their purpose here was clear and would be carried out with unquestionable commitment to his cause.

Bruce called his council together. 'My lords, the English are fast approaching with great strength of numbers and are well prepared to fight for the control of Stirling. But don't be deceived. Stirling is simply the final doorway they seek to enter in order to conquer our nation.'

'They will not succeed,' shouted Edward Bruce.

'Aye, but only if we prepare well,' replied Bruce.

'What do you have in mind, Sire?' asked Douglas.

'There are many thousands who have come here to join us. Let us arrange ourselves into four divisions and position our men so that when our enemy approaches we move back toward the New Park area of land,' said Bruce.

'Sire, why should we go there?' asked Randolph.

'We are unfortunate that there are no mountain passes or narrow gorges where we can entice and trap our enemy. However, one thing this nation possesses in rich abundance is water. Look around you; there are many wide rivers, twisting burns, soggy marshes and deep bogs in this area. We will use these to our advantage,' answered Bruce. 'We will force them to go beneath us and pass over the marsh.'

'Sire, your idea to take advantage of the land is exceptional. However, we will be unable to fight on horseback in such conditions,' said Douglas.

'Neither will they!' shouted Bruce. 'And that is the purpose of my plan. The cavalry is the English army's most lethal weapon of war, whereas, we only have a few hundred light horsemen. If we can force them to dismount and fight on foot we may be able to take control of the situation.'

The others looked at Bruce; they applauded his tactics and gave their approval.

Bruce spoke to each of his closest nobles in turn. 'Thomas, Earl of Moray, I ask that you take the vanguard. These last few years you have regained my favour and I have seen in you fine qualities of noble conduct and chivalry. I ask that your loyal nobles and their good men be assigned to your division.'

'Sire, I'm honoured to be chosen by you to lead our army into battle. I will not fail you,' answered Randolph.

Bruce approached his brother Edward. 'My dear loyal brother, you have served me well. I request that you take command of the centre division. I am sure that you will display the same conduct that you are accustomed to and give our enemies plenty of cause for complaint.' Edward Bruce smiled, and bowed his head in acceptance.

'Sir Robert!' Bruce called out, inviting Sir Robert Keith, the Marischal, to step forward. 'I would like you to lead your horsemen. Although we will be mainly fighting on foot, there will be a need to move swiftly to strengthen any weakness that may develop.' 'My pleasure, Sire,' replied Keith.

'And what of you, Sire?' asked Edward Bruce.

'I will play my part; I will take a division and lead the men of Carrick, Argyll, and Kintyre and of the Isles.

Bruce moved closer to Walter Stewart. 'My young lord, you have inherited a great title as Steward of Scotland. Your men need to see you out there in front of them. They need to be united in determination of purpose. I ask that you take a division and serve me and your men well.' 'Sire, I too am honoured and I will not fail you,' answered Stewart.

'We must prepare now,' declared Bruce. His close commanders looked at each other in surprise, and then back again at their King. There had been no mention of Douglas. What was to be his role? No one was prepared to ask the question, as Douglas stood silently in the background. Douglas, deep in thought, recalled the discussion with his own men when they heard of Randolph being made Earl. 'It's all to do with birth, it doesn't matter what you achieve, it's birth that counts,' he had said to them.

Douglas cast aside these depressing thoughts, albeit there appeared to be some element of truth in them, and started to make his way back to his men. Bruce shouted towards him.

'Douglas, please stop. I have not omitted you. Your reputation has spread throughout this nation; no man has achieved more for me than you have.'

'Sire, what do you ask of me?' replied Douglas, who was clearly disappointed in not being asked to take a division.

Bruce approached Douglas and embraced him. 'My dear James, there is a task that I ask of you. It is not to take command of a division, it's much more important than that,' declared Bruce. A smile appeared on the face of Douglas, but it was a forced smile that contained an element of confusion. 'Sire, what exactly would that be?' asked Douglas.

'The English are cunning. They need to be watched. We need to monitor their approach, and we also need to monitor our progress in battle and be ready to make any changes should the fighting go against us. This is what I ask of you,' declared Bruce.

'What, you want me to be a look out?' said Douglas, with a clear tone of disapproval.

'I don't want to tie you down to a division.'

'What then?' interrupted Douglas.

'Please let me finish. I want you to accompany young Walter, for he is inexperienced in warfare.'

Douglas immediately interrupted again. 'So you want me to be a look out and a nursemaid!'

Bruce saw that his loyal friend did not approve of what he had planned for him. 'I also want to keep you in reserve, good or bad. Whatever the result we will either be escaping with our own lives or chasing our enemies from our land. I want you to be ready for whatever happens. I want you to be free to do as you see fit, for there are none who possess such sharpness of mind and sword in battle.'

Douglas looked embarrassed. At twenty-eight years old, he was still a relatively young man compared with the others in his company and was prone to the odd bout of impatience. 'Sire, please accept my apologies for daring to doubt your wisdom,' he said.

'Assuming that my plans for you are to your liking, is there anything that you had in mind for yourself?' asked a smiling Bruce.

'Only that I be allowed, if the opportunity presents itself, to meet Lord Clifford face to face in battle, for he has taken the life and freedom of my people of Douglasdale.'

The others, who had been listening to this most unusual conversation, were again taken aback by the reply from the daring Douglas.

'My dear James, I am sure that you of all people would not let a personal vendetta get in the way of our cause.'

'No Sire, I certainly would not,' replied Douglas.

Bruce spoke again. 'However, should the opportunity come your way, you certainly have my approval.'

Douglas nodded his acceptance

As the English army continued to march north, Bruce and his men prepared their defensive strategy. On hearing that the invading force was now in Edinburgh, Bruce quickly ordered his men to vacate the Torwood and move north towards the ancient royal hunting grounds of Stirling known as the New Park. They crossed the twisting burn known as the Bannock and stopped. Bruce stood up on his stirrups and scanned the area. He called to his commanders. 'Sirs, we will start to prepare here, the ground is soft. Dig small holes, holes that a horse's leg would fall into, dig many like a honeycomb, hammer into them sharpened sticks, and cover them with moss and grass. Work through the night if needed, for we must be ready by tomorrow.'

The following morning was a Sunday. It was 23rd of June 1314, midsummer, and the day before the feast of John the Baptist. The heat from the bright sun produced an eerie mist along the Bannock burn as the water evaporated into a vapour that hung suspended in the still air. Bruce and his commanders quietly entered the small church of St Ninian's. Many of their men followed behind them. They prayed to God for the forgiveness of their sins and for their right to be free men in their own land. The service was short, simple and intense as each man made his own peace with his creator and asked for his protection.

Bruce, along with his chosen commanders and close nobles, inspected the surrounding area. He looked into the faces of his men. These were men he did not know but dearly loved. They looked back with hope and determination as they stared in admiration at their King. These men were prepared and ready for what lay ahead. Bruce, sitting proud on his horse, circled the area for a few minutes.

'You men of Scotland, the time has come for you to raise your arms against he who comes to invade us. I say this, if there is anyone among you whose heart is not brave enough to stand firm and be prepared to win or die with honour, then I ask that you depart now. I ask that those who remain are prepared to stand with me to the end and take the fortune that God has sent.'

An almighty roar was the reply from his men. Not one left the field.

The men of Scotland who had come here today represented their nation. They were here for their families, for their mothers and fathers, for their sons and daughters. They were the proud ambassadors of their communities. For many their only possessions were the clothes that they stood in. Some had to borrow to come here today, such was their commitment to this cause that they were prepared to die fighting for.

Bruce requested that the camp followers, the many wives, children and family members who had come to give support to their loved ones as they prepared for battle, leave now and find a place of safety. A few riders helped direct and escort these folks away as they openly wept and called out their last words of encouragement to their fathers, brothers and sons.

A messenger arrived with word of the advancing English army. 'Sire, they rested last night at Falkirk. They are approaching fast. A few hours away I would say.' Bruce thanked his good man and turned to his commanders.

'We must begin. My Lord Randolph, I want you and your men to protect the road leading to the kirk and prevent any attempt to make way north to the castle.'

'Aye, Sire, I will do as you wish,' replied Thomas Randolph.

'Douglas!' Bruce called out. 'I want you to take some horsemen and go watch the son of Longshanks approaching with his army; find out what you can.'

Bruce then turned to Sir Robert Keith. 'Sir Robert, please go with him,'

'Aye, Sire,' came the immediate answer from Douglas and Keith.

After riding for a few miles in the hot sunshine, Douglas and Keith ascended a small hilltop that overlooked the road south to Falkirk. Their horses eagerly obliged by effortlessly taking them up the last few steep feet to the summit. They both arrived at the top together and looked down in the direction towards Falkirk.

They simultaneously rubbed their eyes in disbelief at the awesome sight that lay before them. They stared. There was a temptation to curse, but they certainly did not want to offend God, not now, not when they saw what was before them. Their faces paled with shock.

The English army was a short distance below them and stretched for as far as their eyes could see. Their numbers were greater than Douglas or Keith could ever imagine. What was before them looked more like an invading nation than an invading army. Like a vast river sparkling with a multitude of bright colours, the sunlight reflecting the many thousands of glittering pieces of armoury, it slowly flowed forward towards them.

Douglas scanned the brightly coloured banners that flowed in his direction. There were many that he was unable to match to the names of their owners. However, there was one banner in particular that he was looking for and it stuck out from the others, not by its bright colours, but by the unusual blue and yellow checked pattern at the top and bottom. Douglas focused his attention on the man who was associated with this banner. It was Sir Robert Clifford, the man to whom Longshanks had given his father's lands, and who now claimed ownership of Douglasdale.

There was a frightening look in the eyes of Douglas, the same that had sometimes been seen in his face before. It was the look of a cold and determined desire for revenge, and it was aimed at only that one man who rode close to the front of this army of many thousands.

Douglas spoke first. 'I could easily express fear for what I see in front of me, for that is surely the largest army that I have ever seen, larger than all others that I have ever encountered put together. However, I say this, size does not matter in warfare; we have proved this before and will do so again. It is with cunning and commitment to our cause that we will win this battle. Our victory will be all the more significant when we defeat an enemy many times our own size and strength.'

Suddenly shouting could be heard coming from down below. 'Look,' said Keith. 'Their scouts have spotted us, we must return now.' Keith and the rest of the men turned and made their way down from the hilltop.

'I will hold them off,' shouted Douglas. As he waited, he had something in mind. As the first English scout came within range, Douglas untied his small hunting bow and released a single arrow that penetrated the left thigh of the unsuspecting scout. The shocked victim screamed out in agony and alerted his comrades who came rushing to his aid. Douglas smiled. He did not want to kill in cold blood, but he did want to hear the sound of his enemy cry out in pain, and he also wanted the leaders of that army to hear the cries of pain from their own kind.

Keith, along with the rest of the men, had stopped and waited as they heard the loud cry of pain as Douglas's victim lay in agony on the ground.

'What happened?' asked Keith.

'I wanted to make sure that they knew that we were here,' answered Douglas, as they all looked at him.

'Don't you think that was a bit dangerous?' asked Keith. 'No,' replied Douglas. 'I have drawn the first blood of this battle, and if God is with me I will draw the last.'

Douglas and Keith quickly returned to Bruce. 'Sire, we must speak with you alone,' declared Douglas. Bruce gestured for the others to leave. Douglas moved closer towards Bruce. 'Sire, they are many, much more than we have ever seen, they are well armed and prepared. Their army stretched as far as we could see, we will need every man to produce his best and much more if we are to achieve victory,' declared Douglas.

Bruce listened carefully to these words, for he knew that they were true. 'You must not talk about this to the others, for it will surely weaken their spirit,' declared Bruce.

'Sire, what would you have us say?' asked Keith.

'Tell them that you saw disorder and that Edwards's army is ill prepared. I ask this of you, for many a defeat can come from the wrong word, and many a victory has come from belief in oneself,' replied Bruce

The words of Bruce were passed amongst his men; they were encouraged and comforted by what they heard. They believed in themselves and anticipated a great victory.

The English army was now only two miles away and soon within sight. As they slowly emerged from the Torwood, Bruce's scouts gave out the call 'They are coming!'

The English force emerged in two groups; the main one, led by Edward II, made its way towards the New Park where Bruce's men were stationed. The other group, much smaller and led by Sir Robert Clifford, took the easterly route and made their way towards Stirling and therefore avoided Bruce's prepared defensive zone.

The afternoon was passing fast as Edward II and his men questioned whether the timing to attack was in their favour. They had travelled a long distance and had marched that very morning from Falkirk in the hot midsummer sun. 'Should we fight this day or rest and be better for it tomorrow?' Edward asked his close nobles. 'Sire, we need to rest. Our men and our horses are tired. Tomorrow we would be better prepared,' replied one of his knights.

Edward's vanguard, led by the Earls of Gloucester and Hereford, was out in front and unaware of the decision to rest for the night. Crossing the waters of the Bannock burn, they carefully rode towards Bruce's position. Henry de Bohun, the impatient young nephew of Hereford, rode out in front of the others. 'Where are these Sots hiding?' he called out. A lone horseman appeared in front of him, followed by Scots pikemen.

De Bohun could not believe his eyes as he slowly moved a few yards closer. Here in front of him, and out on his own, was the leader of these rebellious Scots. Bruce stopped and stared back. De Bohun, realising that this opportunity must not be allowed to go by without his taking advantage of the situation, immediately dug his spurs into his horse and charged at maximum speed towards the ill-prepared Bruce. The large charging beast presented a fearsome sight as it moved in full flight carrying its heavily armoured rider with lance lowered and pointed in the direction of the prized target.

Bruce braced himself; he knew that he should not have got himself into this situation. However, he had no time to retreat. His only option was to face his opponent no matter how ill prepared he was. Not wearing any heavy armour and sitting on a much smaller and lighter horse, Bruce waited for his moment. He faced De Bohun head on as the English knight came thundering towards him. Bruce pulled his reins gently to the left and then to the right alerting his horse to the fact that it would soon be required to move one way or the other very soon.

De Bohun's lance was only a few yards away when Bruce pulled to the left; his quick-footed pony immediately responded as the deadly pointed weapon brushed past. Instinctively Bruce stood up in his stirrups and immediately brought the full force of his battle-axe down on the head of this fearsome English knight. De Bohun, his head split in two, was dead before he hit the ground. His charging horse continued on without its dead master.

With the shaft of his broken battle-axe still in his hand, Bruce was immediately joined by his cheering pikemen, who had witnessed this amazing feat. They immediately presented themselves between their brave King and the approaching English vanguard. As others tried to succeed where De Bohun had failed, they were immediately repelled by the advancing pikemen who began to move forward in a tightly packed formation. Many an English horseman was brought down and slain. No mercy was given. Hereford, distressed at his nephew's death, gave the order to retreat. As they ran, some stumbled and fell and were ruthlessly slain by the attacking Scots.

When Bruce's commanders heard of these events they rebuked him for the foolish act of risking his life in such a way. 'You could have lost all of us our lives,' shouted an angry Edward Bruce. 'What on earth were you trying to prove?'

'Look at my axe,' said Bruce. 'It's been broken by the head of an English knight.'

Some continued to pour scorn on Bruce's actions, while others laughed and cheered at what must have been an amazing sight.

Meanwhile, Sir Robert Clifford and Sir Henry Beaumont along with their division were making their way towards the castle of Stirling. Their purpose was to bypass Bruce's men and arrive at the castle without engaging the Scots. They headed along the route known as the Way and passed unseen through the marshy land, a low flood plain known as the Carse, as they attempted to bypass the New Park area completely.

Thomas Randolph's division lay in wait in the area where the Way passed by St Ninian's Kirk. Randolph himself had left his division and had been with Bruce when one of Douglas's lookouts rode into their midst. Douglas called his man over to him to obtain the news. 'Sir, it's Clifford. He has many men. They ride unopposed towards the castle. They will soon pass by the kirk,' declared Douglas's man. Bruce, who was standing beside Douglas, heard these words and immediately ordered Randolph to go join his men. As Randolph departed, Bruce angrily declared 'A rose of that man's chaplet has just fallen, for I expected him to keep the Way and prevent them passing.'

Randolph quickly rejoined his men and immediately ordered them out into the open to face the advancing Clifford. As the English division came into sight, Randolph shouted 'Don't be afraid; set your spears before you and form back to back, with all spears pointing out, so no matter which way they attack we will still be able to defend ourselves.'

With Randolph's men assembled as instructed, the English attacked. The first, Sir William Daincourt, galloped straight into the protruding Scottish spears and, falling from his horse, was immediately slain by a swordsman who leapt out from the tightly packed schiltron of pikemen. Other English horsemen changed at Randolph's men, but none as daring as Daincourt.

With no way to penetrate, the English horsemen surrounded Randolph's schiltron and began lunging at them with their weapons. The response from Randolph was to lunge back with the long pikes and force the enemy from their horses. As they did so, the same pattern was repeated whereby swordsmen would rush out from the schiltron and slay the thrown riders. In frustration, the English horsemen began throwing their weapons into the tightly packed schiltron. As they did so they became the object of attack by small groups of Randolph's men who were now able to single out unarmed horsemen.

As more English fell, still more arrived to take their place. Randolph's men were becoming exhausted; the long day, the hot sun, and now the relentless charging English cavalry were all beginning to take their toll.

A short distance way, Douglas and his small band of cavalry nervously watched the events unfold. 'Enough!' shouted Douglas as he rode back to Bruce. Galloping up to where Bruce was stationed, Douglas pleaded 'Sire, Randolph is in danger, he is in the open field and surrounded on all sides. Unless he is helped soon his foes will overcome him. With your leave, I request that I go help him.'

'You shall not take one step towards him. If he does well let him take the credit,' replied Bruce, who was still clearly angry at the earlier actions of Randolph. 'Whatever happens to him, win or lose, I will not for him change my purpose,' declared Bruce.

'Indeed, Sire. However, if he is defeated Clifford's men will get to the castle of Stirling of that I have no doubt. With your leave I will prevent this happening,' pleaded Douglas. Bruce stared at Douglas. He knew that look and he trusted it with his life. 'Do so then, and hurry back,' answered Bruce.

Meanwhile Randolph and his men continued to hold back the attacking English cavalry. Their pace had slowed down considerably, as they fought with their very last ounce of energy. Douglas and his horsemen appeared on the horizon and started to close in on them, moving slowly and deliberately. Clifford, on seeing Douglas, recognised the colours of the Lord of Douglasdale; this was one man he did not want to meet in any battle.

The sight of Douglas and his men slowly coming towards them caused great fear amongst the English riders. Some started to fall back, and as they did so Randolph's men managed to find a fresh surge of energy and went into attack. Douglas knew by the retreat of the English that they were defeated and that Randolph had finally won the day.

'Stop!' Douglas called to his men. 'Those who you see fighting before you are of such determination and valour that their foes will surely be beaten. They do not need our help, for to do so would take away the well-earned credit that they have magnificently achieved.'

With the bodies of many dead horses and their riders starting to pile up all around, the sight of which caused great concern and discontent amongst the invading force, Clifford and Beaumont grew worried at what looked like defeat from a smaller force. Randolph ordered his men to continue to attack. The turning point happened as a few started to run and then many others followed. Clifford finally gave the order to retreat as his men had had enough. He led his men back to the safety of numbers with the rest of Edward's forces.

Randolph and his men stopped, exhausted. Some removed their armour and outer clothing. Like clouds of steam, the vapour from their burning hot bodies rose up in the warm summer afternoon. As they looked around, they were amazed that only one of their own men had been slain. Looking over at Douglas in the distance, Randolph gave a friendly gentleman's wave, for he knew that his presence had helped. He also knew that Douglas had helped restore his good name by not coming to his aid this day.

As the evening sun began to settle, the atmosphere in both camps was in complete contrast. The English were in disarray, tired from their long journey and now humiliated. The slaying of Henry de Bohun occupied much conversation, likewise the suicidal charge of Sir William Daincourt and the failure by Clifford's men to get to the castle of Stirling caused much anger and discontent. 'That marshy ground is full of holes and deep trenches. We need to move,' declared King Edward.

Meanwhile Bruce and his men were well pleased with the events of the day. They had presented themselves well and gave their King great pride in their actions. Bruce addressed his nobles. 'My Lords, we ought to express our love to the almighty God that sits above us. He has sent us a fair beginning this day and has caused great discomfort to our foes. Many a heart will still be wavering, and if the heart is discomforted, the body will not be worth a mite; therefore, I know that a good ending shall follow our beginning. Nevertheless, I say this to you, if you think that it is right to fight, we shall fight, if you say that we should depart now, then so be it. As your King I shall consent to your desire. Speak your mind now.'

There was no delay with the answer from Bruce's men. 'We shall fight, we will not fail you for fear of death, nor will we be lacking in any effort till we have made our country free,' one man called out. Every other man present voiced his agreement with these brave words.

As the hot summer sun finally disappeared, the arrival of the cool hours of darkness presented the opportunity for peace and rest within the Scottish camp. The New Park was quiet as Bruce's men took advantage of these short hours. All rested, apart from the few who were chosen for guarding duties and taking the watch of the English camp close by.

The early morning sun of Monday the 24th June 1314 majestically raised its sleepy crimson face, and brought with it the magnificent dawn chorus. This was a day of celebration, not for man but for nature. As the great wave of heat and light slowly and gently swept across the country, nature responded by wakening from its night of rest. The flowers of midsummer opened up to present their many colours, the birds sang in harmony with the tune of nature's happiness at yet another precious day of life. The dark silence of the night before was gently replaced by the noise of daily activity.

Word had arrived from lookouts that the English had moved during the night. 'Sire, they have crossed the Bannock and are grouping on the other side of Balquhiderock Wood,' announced the guard to Bruce. Amazed at what he had just heard, Edward Bruce spoke. 'Sire, you predicted that they would move to that area, how did you know?' 'It's one of the few places where they would have room to manoeuvre,' replied Bruce. 'Is that not to our disadvantage?' asked Randolph, who had joined the conversation. 'The advantage that we have is that they are now surrounded on three sides by rivers, streams and marshes. There is only one way for them to come, and that is towards us,' replied Bruce, who then ordered his nobles to meet with him.

Bruce called his men around him. A short Mass was held out in the open to seek God's forgiveness for the many lives that were about to be taken, and for the safe return and success of the people of this nation who were about to fight for the freedom that God alone gave them. The many Scottish nobles, their brightly coloured coats of arms worn with great pride, held their colourful banners in front of them as their loyal men stood proudly behind.

Douglas stood with his men. Head bowed, his mind was concentrating on the words of each prayer. He knew that, more than most, he would be taking the lives of many men today, and he prayed for God's forgiveness for what he was about to do. His father's coat of arms, white with a blue horizontal band along the top containing three white stars, was worn with the greatest of pride. To his right, his younger brother Archibald impatiently stood beside him. Fidgeting and constantly shuffling his feet he repeatedly waved the Douglas flag that he held in his right hand.

To the left of Douglas stood his closest friend, Cuthbert, a man he had known all his life, his most loyal servant and one who had also fought with his father, Lord William. Cuthbert, frustrated at the constant fidgeting of young Archibald, leaned forward and caught the eye of the excited young man. No words were spoken, just the menacing look that said 'Be still, or else.' Archibald immediately stood to attention with his eyes focused on the priest who delivered the Latin Mass.

When Mass was nearly done Sir Robert Keith stepped forward accompanied by Bruce. Keith called out 'My Lords, and you good men who have gathered here today, as is the custom before battle, our King Robert the Bruce, the true King of Scotland, who today unites our nation, would like to bestow the honour of knighthood on his most worthy servants.'

Bruce stood in the centre, his sword drawn and held by his side. 'Walter Stewart,' Keith called out, as the first name was announced. The young man stepped forward. Excited at being the first, his face showed his great pride at receiving this grand honour. He knelt before his King. The sword of Bruce touched each shoulder in turn, as Bruce called out the words 'Arise, Sir Walter.' Sir Robert Keith then presented a small ring, one of several, which was taken from a silver plate and handed to Sir Walter as a token of this event. A loud yet dignified applause arose from the large congregation.

Other names were called out, each man expressing the same pride and joy at being given this great honour by their King, the applause from the onlookers being the same each time. Young Archibald started to fidget again. 'What about you?' he whispered to his elder brother. 'Haud your wheesht man,' replied an angry Douglas, who was starting to regret bringing his younger brother with him.

As the sound of the applause for the latest recipient diminished, one lonely ring was left on the silver plate. Douglas's mind had drifted; he was not interested in such official affairs. He thought of his mother. 'I hope and pray that she is well,' he said to himself. He thought of young Sophia, the most beautiful Sophia. He had brought her into his house for his family to care for her and yet it was she who was caring for them. 'Will I ever see them again?' he asked himself.

A sharp pain suddenly penetrated his right side and caused him to awaken from his trance. The elbow of young Archibald was about to repeat the gesture when he heard his brother speak. 'It's you,' shouted Archibald, as he pointed forward. The heads of others started to turn round. 'James Douglas of Douglasdale,' shouted Sir Robert Keith as he announced the final name for a second time.

Douglas started to walk forward towards the temporary altar. As he did so his men behind him cheered. He turned to thank them with a smile, but the look on their faces caught him by surprise. As well as the smiles of delight on every single one of them there were also many tears of joy and expressions of great pride in their brave gallant leader.

Douglas knelt before Bruce and looked up into the face of his king; the official ceremony prohibited any informal conversation. However, the look on Bruce's face told the real story. A gentle nod of this King's head accompanied by a sincere smile conveyed the message to Douglas that he occupied a very special place in the loving heart of his dear King.

As Bruce raised his sword, Douglas bowed his head. Placing the blade on each of Douglas's shoulders in turn, Bruce called out 'Arise Sir James, Lord of Douglasdale.' The crowd broke out in loud applause. The service was now over. Free to call out what they wanted, the men of Douglasdale started to chant 'A Douglas! A Douglas!'

Surrounded by his men, Douglas was embraced and congratulated on achieving this honour. Cuthbert came over and embraced his good friend. 'Well done, and well deserved.' Young Archibald, standing back in admiration, smiled at his older brother. Douglas smiled back and tossed his prized ring towards him. Archibald jumped, immediately caught it and replied 'Thank you, Sir James!'

Bruce called for his men to assemble. 'For now is the hour,' he declared. The men cheered loudly. There was something unique that these men felt; it was an experience that only exists when men come together united in battle. It was a feeling of purpose, and a sense of belonging. When men bond together in such circumstances they experience the comradeship that comes from a united people. They had their families, whom they loved; they had their friends and the communities that their lives were built round. However, being here today with Bruce gave them something else. All differences were cast aside, and their background and wealth were of no significance.

Under the leadership of Bruce they were all equal in that they stood tall and proud in spite of their variations in rank and nobility. They were also unique; no army in the history of this nation had ever contained such unity. They were vastly outnumbered, but they were brave and determined. In Bruce they had a king who brought them together in a united Scotland. These men were not rich in terms of money or estates. However, they possessed a wealth of privilege, the privilege of being here on this day, and to be a Scot and about to fight for the freedom of your nation was a privilege reserved for these men only.

A short time later Bruce's army moved into position on the open ground in front of the New Park forest. At the same time the English were also in the process of agreeing their final strategy as they formed a straight line of cavalry ready to attack. Bruce noticed that there were still many of his camp followers who appeared in disarray and unsure of what to do or where to go. 'Let them take refuge on Coxet Hill. From there they can watch and be ready for whatever happens,' he ordered.

Suddenly the vast numbers of fighting men who were present this morning appeared to slot into perfect order as the two sides finally positioned themselves. The straight line of brightly coloured powerful English cavalry on one side faced the curved arch of the three Scottish divisions of schiltrons.

'Surely they are not going to dare fight us this day?' said an astonished Edward, King of England, as he watched his enemy's final preparations.

'Yes, Sire, indeed it looks that way. Our brave knights on open ground against that rabble on foot, we will easily beat them, of that I have no doubt,' replied Sir Ingram Umfraville.

'All this way for such an easy victory,' declared Edward, as his knights laughed at the weak army that lay before them.

'A final prayer!' shouted Bruce, and every one of his men dropped to their knees to recite the Lord's prayer.

Edward II, King of England, on seeing the Scots on bended knee, called out 'Look yonder, they now pray for mercy.'

'Yes, Sire, they do ask for mercy, but not of you, but from God alone for their sins. I say this, that those men will win or die today, for none will flee,' declared Sir Ingram.

'So be it. Sound the call,' shouted Edward.

The English cavalry made the first move as they began the slow trot forward to the sound of blaring trumpets. Bruce and his brother Edward, along with Randolph, called out to their men and gave the final words of encouragement as the three divisions of schiltrons braced themselves for the first charge.

The archers on both sides became the first to engage, as deadly arrows were exchanged over the short distance that separated the two armies. Like dark synchronised swarms of autumn starlings, the lethal clouds passed by each other, their purpose to permanently roost in the flesh and bodies of their respective targets.

The power of the English longbow showed its worth, as many Scots became victims of the deadly penetrating arrows. The Scottish short bow, not as lethal but more accurate, caused more of an inconvenience to the English forces as the two armies continued to draw closer.

The Scottish schiltrons continued to surge forward in the face of the deadly longbow arrows, in spite of many who fell victim. The impatience of the Earl of Gloucester got the better of him as he called out to his vanguard to 'charge.' As they did so, they made contact with the Scottish division led by Randolph, who called out to his men, 'Hold tight.'

The small cavalry division jointly led by Walter Stewart and Douglas had dismounted and were ready to assist where needed. Seeing the charge of the English vanguard, they quickly joined up in support of Randolph's division. Gloucester, unable to break through, charged into the deadly array of Scottish pikemen. The horse of the brave but reckless Earl rose up in absolute terror only to be speared on its underside by several pikemen who then brutally ended the life of the English commander.

The English vanguard, shocked at the sudden loss of their leader and at the unusual sight of a Scottish schiltron daring to attack charging English cavalry, became confused and started to break up as they persistently tried to come in direct contact with the Scots. The English archers continued to aim their lethal array of arrows over the heads of their own vanguard and claimed more Scottish lives. A few breaks in the Scottish ranks allowed the English to penetrate. The English arrows, unable to distinguish between friend and foe, also claimed many an English life.

Douglas, accompanied by Cuthbert and his own over-eager young brother Archibald, finally worked his way into the thick of the fighting. Cuthbert struck first as he plunged his sword into a fallen horseman. Douglas, constantly looking out for his young brother, also claimed his first victim as he swung his axe at a charging English knight whom he killed without any thought for noble mercy or ransom.

Archibald rushed forward, his sword blindly waving in all directions as he loudly screamed at the attacking enemy. Several Scottish warriors were forced to take avoiding action at the wild antics of Archibald. Douglas shouted to his brother 'Come by my side. Don't wave so erratically,' and then added 'Stay beside me and be my second sword.' Archibald, desperately in need of advice in the bedlam that surrounded him, immediately obliged.

Bruce called to Sir Robert Keith 'Sir, you have an immediate task. Those English longbows need to be dealt with.'

'I will go immediately, Sire,' answered Keith. Along with five hundred horsemen he immediately mounted a charge against the English archers. The charging horses, the plunging spears and waving swords quickly brought terror and disarray to the English archers who fled in panic.

Douglas, with Archibald close by his side, continued to cut his way through many attacking bodies. 'Now!' shouted Douglas, as he gave instructions to his brother on when to plunge forward with his sword. As confidence in their partnership grew, the two Douglas brothers fought as one.

The mind of Douglas controlling both sword and axe suddenly became an effective execution machine as they pushed and cut their way forward. Their weapons were able to cope with the variations of armour worn by those who charged towards them.

All sense of time was lost during this violent and bloodthirsty morning. As yet another victim fell before him, Douglas was able to take a momentary break from his concentration. 'Where's Cuthbert?' he shouted to Archibald, as they both looked round. 'I don't know,' replied Archibald. They both looked round again; there was no sign of Cuthbert. 'Did he fall?' asked Douglas, who was starting to feel a sense of sudden panic. 'I don't know, I was with you,' shouted Archibald who felt that blame was being aimed at him.

'Let's go back,' shouted Douglas, who now put the welfare of his good friend above all else.

'We can't, what about the English?' said Archibald.

'Were going back. Now!' screamed Douglas, who appeared to have become possessed by some sort of demon.

As they slowly made their way back over the carnage of slain bodies, they checked those who lay face down to see if their friend Cuthbert had fallen. Douglas grew more impatient. 'No sign of him, where is he?' shouted Douglas as he looked towards his young brother.

'I don't bloody well know,' replied Archibald, who had now lost patience with the constant hints that he was to blame.

Suddenly, a fallen horse, fighting for its last breath as it lay dying on the ground, gave a snort. They both turned. Its dead rider, with a sword plunged into his side, lay beside it. They could see the shape of someone else on the other side of the horse. They both rushed over. It was Cuthbert, and he too was dead. An arrow had penetrated his light armour and remained embedded in his chest. His left leg was trapped under the weight of the dying English horse.

Douglas said nothing. He knelt down beside his friend and lifted the hand that had given him much protection over the years. Clutching Cuthbert's still warm hand close to his chest, he bowed and gently kissed the back of it. Tears of sorrow burst from him in his grief. He paused for a few moments. Archibald said nothing, but placed a hand on the shoulder of his brother.

'That arrow, he would not have felt any pain, he must have died quickly,' whispered Archibald as he tried to comfort his brother.

'Look at the sword still in that enemy body. It's Cuthbert's. He did not die before taking his last revenge,' said a weeping Douglas.

'James, I am sorry, is there anything that I can do for you?' asked Archibald.

'Thanks,' answered Douglas, pausing and attempting to regain his composure. 'But I have lost my father, our dear friend Fullerton, and now the man who was practically an older brother to me. I don't want to lose any more of you.'

'What can I do to help?' asked Archibald.

'Go home now and take the body of our dear Cuthbert with you. Have him laid to rest beside Fullerton. Please do this for me,' pleaded Douglas.

Archibald embraced his brother. 'So be it. Anyhow, I am not of much use at warfare,' replied Archibald.

'You do have your uses, albeit they are few,' replied a weeping yet smiling Douglas.

'What of you James? What will you do?' asked Archibald.

Douglas looked back over at the fighting that was still raging between both sides. 'I have a mission in life, the purpose of which I am not sure, but I say this, I will not rest until that army are beaten and forced back over their own border. The English will be more afraid of me than any other Scotsman, that I promise.'

Douglas slowly walked towards the battlefront. Archibald stayed behind to attend to Cuthbert and honour his brother's request. As he came within a few yards from where the heavy fighting was taking place, Douglas drew his battle-axe, and said a silent prayer, not for forgiveness for what he was about to unleash but for the soul of his dearly departed friend Cuthbert.

As he finally came to stand beside Randolph, Douglas turned round to face his men. Raising his axe, he loudly shouted 'Let's take it to them.' He turned and walked out of the schiltron. A charging knight recognised the Douglas coat of arms and sped towards him. Douglas waited, feinted to his right at the last second and then hammered his axe into the left-hand side of the knight. The men within the schiltron stayed together, but inspired by this act charged at the oncoming cavalry.

The relentless fighting continued. Bruce, Edward Bruce, Thomas Randolph, Douglas and all the other nobles inspired their men with their bravery and courage. As the schiltrons pushed forward, the enemy started to break up and move back in retreat.

There was one man that Douglas had in his mind, one set of colours that he was searching for. He spotted him a few yards to his right. Sir Robert Clifford had led his English division effectively, and was balancing caution with bravery and courage. Douglas fought his way forward. Both of these men would represent sizeable ransom if captured by opposing sides. However, capture and ransom was not what Douglas intended.

With close fighting going on all around, Douglas finally arrived to confront the man to whom Edward I had given the lands of Douglasdale following the death of his father. The blood-stained tunic of Douglas was unrecognisable from a distance; however, as he approached Clifford, the English lord recognised those colours of days gone by, days when he fought with the father of the man who was now approaching him. As their eyes met, the faces of both men showed their true purpose. Each would benefit from the death of the other.

Douglas gestured Clifford to come forward. The English lord duly obliged by digging into his stirrups and forcing his horse to charge. Douglas stood his ground. The powerful horse forced a gap through the fighting, as men separated and moved out of its way. Clifford raised his sword and stood high on his stirrups. Douglas stood tall and still. As the horse thundered towards him he braced himself. As the moment of impact fast approached, Douglas suddenly dropped to his knees and with both hands pulled back his axe and unleashed the most powerful blow that he could summon. Clifford's horse, its lower left leg completely severed, immediately dropped in agony.

Clifford was thrown over and landed on his back, his sword being lost in the process. Stunned for a split second he struggled to get to his knees only to be confronted by the sight of the avenging Douglas looking down on him. 'For my Father,' screamed Douglas, as he pulled out his long dagger. He grabbed hold of Clifford and finally ended the life of the English Earl.

Douglas paused for a moment. His dagger had been given to him by his brother Hugh with the request 'only to be used against evil.' He thought to himself 'I hope Hugh would agree that the evil act of taking my father's land and then inflicting such cruelty on Douglasdale would justify my using this dagger against the perpetrator.'

Seeing one of their key commanders slain without mercy caused many of the English cavalry to become disheartened.

The fighting continued as the Scottish schiltrons continued to push forward against an enemy who was beginning to falter.

Bruce shouted to his close nobles. 'Our men are fighting so well that they have caused our enemy such confusion and disarray that if we push harder they will soon be defeated.'

Over on Coxet Hill, the camp followers were watching the events of mid-morning unfold. 'What's happening?' shouted an elderly man to a young boy who had climbed a tree to get a better view.

'I think we're winning. We're pushing them back, we need more men.'

'Let's go help them,' shouted a barefooted young girl who was worried about her father and older brother who were in the thick of the fighting.

A short time later one of Bruce's closest companions called out. 'Sire, look over there.' Bruce turned round; the sight in front of him brought tears of pride and joy to his eyes. They came running down in their thousands. The camp followers, women and children, the young and old, some who were sick and lame, came swarming down from Coxet Hill to help their menfolk. Some had weapons, some had made their own, and others carried sticks and stones. Many had made their own flags and banners, which they waved with great pride.

The advancing camp followers appeared to outnumber the entire Scottish army. The English force, seeing what looked like a fresh army coming towards them, lost their confidence and started to run. A few broke at first and then others followed. The English nobles Sir Aymer de Valence and Sir Giles d'Argentan saw what was happening. Concerned for the welfare of their King, they organised his immediate departure, which signalled the final break-up of the English army.

As the English army retreated, the forces of nature came to the aid of Bruce. The deep waters of the River Forth and the Bannock burn presented great obstacles for the fleeing English army to cross. Many fell, many were drowned, and many got caught on the steep muddy banks and were confronted by the choice 'between death by water or death by a Scottish spear. Whatever the choice, death came to those who found themselves trapped.

Bruce had won the day from the moment that Edward sneaked away, his army defeated not just by the Scots but also by the poor preparation and commitment of the English leader.

The carnage over, Bruce's men gathered around their proud King. His men cheered and experienced the rare taste of victory, but the taste that was the sweetest of all was the taste of freedom. This victory, achieved by a truly united Scottish nation, was their proudest moment.

Only a few of the many names there on that day would be remembered in the years to come. However, the significance of what they had achieved would make each and every one immortal. This day would be one that all true Scotsmen of future generations would recall with great pride, and would recognise as the most significant in the history of their nation.

Douglas approached his victorious King. 'Sire, the lord God himself has surely been with you this day. A truly great victory won by a great man,' he declared.

'Thank you, Sir James, for without you and your men we might not be enjoying this moment. Please take pleasure in you and your men's share of the many riches of provisions and wealth that Edward brought with him,' said a proud and smiling Bruce.

For Douglas the battle was not yet over. The look on his face showed there was more to come. 'Sire, I request your leave to ensure that Edward's army leaves our lands. They are still of greater number than we. They could regroup and may also take revenge on our people as they depart.'

'My dear Sir James, you are the most loyal of all. Take as many men as you require and do what you believe is right,' said Bruce.

'Three score on horseback will be all that I need. We will move fast and pursue them,' said Douglas.

Douglas and his men mounted their horses and swiftly made their way through the Torwood. There was an unusual determination in him as he rode out in front of his men. The self-confidence resulting from such a magnificent victory, the loss of a dearly loved friend, the constant need for revenge and the continued search for his own destiny all spiralled around in his mind as he led his men in chase of the defeated enemy.

A short time after coming out of the Torwood, Douglas and his men were met by reinforcements coming to join the English army. A leading figure, whom Douglas recognised, led a band of around eighty men who confronted Douglas on the narrow road.

'Ah! Sir Laurence Abernethy, good day to you sir, or should I say, good late day to you and your men,' called Douglas as he confronted yet another Scotsman who came to fight for the English cause.

Abernethy and his men stared in disbelief. 'What do you mean sir by good late day?' asked Abernethy, who had come here today only to do what was required in order to protect his borderlands in Roxburghshire and Berwickshire.

'Sir, today Edward II has been defeated, Bruce has been victorious. I now go to ensure that the English go back home without causing our people any more harm. You Sir, and your men, have a choice. You may leave now and join the fleeing English army, or you can redeem yourself by joining me as I rid this nation of those who came to invade us,' answered Douglas.

'My good Douglas,' replied Abernethy, in a most courteous manner. 'Like you I lead my men into battle in order to defend our lands from invasion, whether from friend or foe.' Abernethy then turned to his men, and with a serious look asked them 'Well men, do you wish us to join with this man otherwise known to his enemies as the Black Douglas and chase the English from our lands?' To a man, they gave the reply 'Aye! We do!'

With his numbers now more than doubled, Douglas and Abernethy gave chase in pursuit of Edward's forces. Passing by Falkirk, they overtook many lonely individual English solders who were desperate to retreat from the failure and embarrassment of this day. They presented no threat to anyone. The look of defeat and the despair on their faces showed Abernethy that these men had no wish to be here.

'Why do we pursue a defeated army?' asked Abernethy, as they approached the outskirts of Linlithgow.

'They may be defeated today, but their numbers are so great that they could come back tomorrow and be victorious,' replied Douglas with a determination in his voice that many had not witnessed before.

Their first sight of the massive fleeing English army was as they came closer to Linlithgow. The backs of the rearguard riders, about six in total, could be seen lagging behind Edward's retreating force. Instantly Douglas forced his horse into a wild charge as with sword drawn he focused his revenge on those unsuspecting souls who felt safe in their great numbers. His companions instinctively followed without question. The English rearguards were caught by surprise as they became the first victims of the vengeance that Douglas was about to unleash on the nation that had caused his so much pain and grief.

Like a pack of wolves, Douglas and his men continued to stalk and attack the remnants of Edward's fleeing army. Any who dared to fall behind or stray off the main route or stop to rest, eat or attend to their personal needs were dealt the same fate. Panic spread along the long line of the fleeing army as the loud screams from the latest victims could be regularly heard from behind.

'Can no one stop them?' a concerned King Edward asked his close companions.

'Sire, it's you they are after. We must not stop or they will surely be upon us,' advised Sir Hugh Despenser as they approached Winchburgh, a small village about ten miles outside Edinburgh.

'We must rest or we will be slain,' shouted Edward. 'Call our men together. We will rest for a short time and then complete the final part of our journey.'

'But Sire, it's well over fifty miles to the border. We will not make it, your safety is at great risk,' declared a deeply worried Sir Henry Beaumont.

'Trust me, I have a plan,' replied King Edward. His companions looked at him with great suspicion.

'Let us rest,' shouted Douglas, as he too called a temporary stop to the relentless pursuit which had been going on for many hours.

Meanwhile, King Edward was being questioned by his close nobles on what plans he had been referring to.

'My lords, I appreciate your concern for my safety, but please don't fret. There is a trusted man, the Earl Patrick of Dunbar, who has been in my favour and has arranged transport by sea for me. If we can get to Dunbar I will be safe,' declared Edward.

'What of us, Sire?' asked a concerned and suspicious Sir Hugh Despenser.

'Those Scots and that dammed Douglas are only interested in me. When I escape they will cease their relentless pursuit. You will be safe if you stay together and ride south to Berwick where I will meet with you,' replied the confident King Edward.

There was great frustration and murmuring amongst the Edward's nobles. 'If only he had put the same efforts into planning his battle tactics as he has in planning his retreat. Perhaps we would not be in this mess,' whispered someone, expressing what others were thinking.

A short time later the retreat by Edward and the pursuit by Douglas continued. The same pattern was followed as the stragglers were picked off one by one. As they approached Dunbar, Edward's men were grouped tighter than before. The pursuing Douglas was presented with fewer and fewer opportunities to cause damage.

A short distance from Dunbar Castle, Douglas and his men were suddenly confronted by a double line of Edward's English cavalry almost four times their number. They were spread out in a manner that prevented any access to the coastal castle. Douglas ordered his men to stop and called out 'They are too great in number to meet in open battle, we must wait.'

'My lord,' shouted one of Douglas's men. 'Look, a ship sails from below the castle.' Douglas, acknowledging that his prey had escaped, addressed his men. 'Edward, King of England, sails home. We have failed to capture him, but I do believe we have caused him to think again before coming back. Let us also return home, for there are many who worry for us.'

22

OVER THE BORDER

'Hush ye , hush ye, little pet ye,
Hush ye, hush ye, do not fret ye,
The Black Douglas shall not get ye.'
(Traditional lullaby)

THE MIGHTY ARMIES had dispersed from the Bannockburn battlefield. All that remained were the slain and mutilated bodies of those who fell. Bruce walked amongst the fields of motionless bodies. 'This battle is now over,' he announced, 'and by good fortune and the grace of God we have won. Let us demonstrate our faith by showing care and compassion towards our dead and injured enemy.' The digging of graves to accommodate the mass burials was immediately ordered.

'What of the prisoners?' asked Sir Robert Keith.

'Those who would command a ransom, have them seized, those who don't, let them go home,' replied Bruce.

'What of the many wagons of provisions and riches that they brought with them?' asked Sir Robert Keith.

'We must first reward those who made today possible. Have the wagons seized and distribute the food and provisions to our men,' replied Bruce.

'What of any valuables?' asked Edward Bruce.

'Have them seized and guarded. We will decide in time who gets what,' replied Bruce, glancing in suspicion at his brother and wondering why he needed to ask that question?

Douglas and his men returned to Bruce. Abernethy followed behind. 'Sire, I have failed you, he has escaped. He had a ship waiting at Dunbar. Earl Patrick was in his favour,' declared the disappointed Douglas.

Bruce smiled. 'My ever trusted and loyal Douglas, if only those closer to me had some of your fine qualities,' replied Bruce, glancing at his brother. King Robert put his hand on the shoulder of Douglas and said to his good friend 'You for one have certainly not failed me. Today has been our nation's greatest victory. Your contribution has been immense. I am sure Edward II will not be coming back.'

'Sire, what would you now require of me?' asked Douglas.

'Go home and rest, for since the hour that we first met, you have looked forward to this great day,' replied Bruce. He appreciated the undivided loyalty from this young man who had given everything and taken nothing.

'Sire, I will go home, but only for a short time, said Douglas. 'There is much still to be done. A fool may lead the English, but as a nation they are not fools. They will not take too kindly to defeat this day.'

'What do you plan to do?' asked Bruce.

'Sire with your approval, I will build a wall, but unlike the Romans, not a wall of stone but a wall of men. I will build a war wall that will protect the good Scots blood of our nation and we will attack our enemies in their own northern counties,' replied Douglas, who still had revenge on his young face. 'Perhaps if our enemies suffer some of the indignity of being invaded, they may think twice about invading others,' added Douglas.

'You have my full support,' declared Bruce.

A few days later Douglas returned to his family at Blackhouse Tower. The house occupants were in mourning as they gathered round the body of Cuthbert before putting him to his final place of rest. Young Archibald was first to great Douglas as he entered. 'I have done exactly as you have asked,' he said, as he welcomed the return of his older brother.

'Thank you. I appreciate you bringing his remains here,' replied Douglas.

Lady Eleanor, on seeing her victorious son return from battle, could not hold back her joy. 'James...' she softly called out. Douglas said nothing; the only reaction he could summon was a nod of his head, for once again he was overcome by grief at the loss of his most dearly loved friend. As he looked round the candle-lit room, the faces of the mourners all turned in his direction. His brother Hugh, doing what he did best as he led the prayers of comfort and forgiveness, nodded in his direction. Sophia, radiant and beautiful as ever, looked in his direction. Her soft pale face was expressionless, there was no smile, no emotion, but like a marble statue she simply stared towards him.

Several others were present, but Douglas did not recognise them. They continued with their prayers of mourning. 'James,' Lady Eleanor called again. 'There are some here that I would like you to meet with.'

Douglas asked for a few moments to say his private words of farewell. Kneeling before the body of his departed friend, he bowed his head and said a short silent prayer. A few moments later, he rose again and approached his mother.

Lady Eleanor grasped the right hand of her newly knighted son; she knew what Cuthbert meant to him, she knew that in Cuthbert, James had followed in his father's footsteps. The guidance, wisdom and advice of this family friend and ever-loyal guard had been immensely influential in the development of her James. 'James there are people here that you must meet with,' she quietly whispered. Douglas requested that those who wanted to talk should leave the room and not disturb the remaining mourners.

A small elderly woman, her back hunched from the many years of hard work and strenuous toil of coping with these difficult times, slowly stepped forward. As she came nearer

Douglas saw a look in her worn out and tear-stained face. It was a look he recognised. Lady Eleanor spoke. 'This is Margaret.' As Douglas tried to force a friendly greeting, he noticed that there was something familiar about this woman. He had never seen her before, yet there was something about her that he immediately recognised. 'Margaret Cuthbert, the mother of Stuart,' continued Lady Eleanor.

Douglas stood motionless; he did not know what to say. Cuthbert had never discussed his private life with him, but of more concern to Douglas was the fact that he himself had never asked about his friend's family. He realised that throughout all these years he had taken Cuthbert for granted. The guilt of such selfishness was more painful than anything Douglas had ever experienced. 'And this is Morag and William, his dear sister and nephew,' announced Lady Eleanor. Douglas stared at the middle-aged woman and the tall, well-built young man who strongly resembled his uncle and who looked only a few years younger than Douglas himself.

Morag spoke first. 'My family and I would like to thank you for what you have done for our Stuart over the years; you have been very kind and helped him to provide well for us during difficult times.'

Douglas, still shocked at finding out that Cuthbert, whom he had known all his life, had such a family answered 'My dear lady, I am the one to be grateful, I am the one to express thanks and appreciation. Stuart devoted his entire life to the safety and welfare of the Douglas family; he has saved my own life on many an occasion. I will forever be in your debt.'

William, nephew of Cuthbert, spoke next. 'Sir, my family have been honoured that my uncle was allowed to serve with you. I would be honoured if you were to allow me to take his place.'

Douglas wiped the remaining tears from his eyes with the back of his hands and replied 'I greatly admire and appreciate your offer, but I cannot ask any more of your family. Your uncle devoted his life to protecting the Douglas household. I ask only one thing of you, and that is for you to look after and protect your own family.'

William stepped towards Douglas and embraced him.

'Should you ever need me for anything, you know where to come,' declared Douglas.

The following day the remains of Cuthbert were finally laid to rest. Afterwards Douglas approached his youngest brother, Archibald, and said 'I have to leave now, but first I have a request that I must make of you. Please ensure that the family of Cuthbert are always provided for. We will forever be in his debt.' Douglas handed his young brother a large purse of silver. 'This should provide for their needs for some time,' he said.

One by one, Douglas embraced Cuthbert's family and bid them goodbye. Turning to his own mother and family, he spoke. 'Archibald, I need you to stay here and look after them,' and then, turning to Hugh, 'My good gentle brother, there is a place for you, but it is not here. It is with those who devote their lives to the worship of God. I will call on you from time to time.'

Douglas put his arms round his mother. Weeping, she asked him 'Why do you need to leave? You and your Bruce have won your battle.'

'Mother, yes, we have won a battle, and we have beaten our enemy, but we now have a war to fight and win. I must go and continue with our cause,' he replied.

As he looked over to Sophia, she turned and walked away. The number of times that he had broken her heart had finally reached its limit. She walked over towards young William as he prepared to leave. He was only a few years older than her. The two of them started talking; they looked unusually interested in each other. Lady Eleanor glanced at them and then looked back at Douglas. 'Are my dreams of James and Sophia about to be shattered?' she thought to herself.

Several days later Douglas and his men reassembled at their Lintalee camp a short distance south of Jedburgh. Their hearts were bursting with pride as a result of the victory over their more powerful enemy. Their confidence was high, and they were willing and ready to yet again follow their leader, who was now recognised as Sir James, Lord of Douglasdale.

Douglas addressed his men. 'My good and loyal men, you may all feel proud and content with your achievements. Your families and all those who possess even the slightest trace of Scots blood will always remember you with great admiration. You have given them one of life's greatest privileges; you have given them their nation, a nation whose sons and daughters will always hold their heads high. With time, your names will be forgotten, but your actions will be immortal. I say this to you; our fight does not end with one battle, our fight goes on. The son of Longshanks is not like his father; he is weak in character and not skilled in warfare. We have a choice. We can rest and enjoy our victory and wait for our enemies to overcome their disgraced leader and then return for their revenge, or we can do to them what they have done to us.'

'Do what?' shouted one of the men.

'We can invade England!' answered Douglas, as his men, to a man, raised their swords and cheered.

And so it began. By way of Berwick, accompanied by many others including Edward Bruce, Laurence Abernethy and numerous other knights, Douglas and his men crossed the border into Northumberland. The roles were reversed as the terrified villagers fled for their lives hunted by the Scottish raiding parties. Many took to the hills or hid in the forests as their cattle were seized and their homes and crops destroyed by fire.

Those who were fortunate enough to possess any wealth were forced into negotiating a ransom for the safety of their prized possessions. Many places were plundered: Appleby, Brough, Kirkoswald along with many other northern towns and villages. The burning fires raged in all directions; like a great ocean wave, fear and terror flowed towards the safety of the south as word spread of the one called Douglas who led his men on this hell-bent unstoppable vengeance.

They frequently returned home with their acquired plunder. For many months, the cycle was repeated as they invaded further south on each occasion. King Robert Bruce was pleased not just with the fruits of these raids, but the unity that they brought to his cause. More Scots who had been in the favour of the English switched sides each day. A meeting of the Scottish nobles was called.

'You have done well. England under the young Edward is in disarray. We must take advantage,' declared Bruce.

'Sire, you are my dear brother, but I have to ask of you, is this cause of yours for yourself or for your nation?' asked Edward Bruce.

Taken aback by this outburst from his younger brother, King Robert asked the others to leave. As they retreated Edward Bruce called out 'Douglas! Please remain.'

'What troubles you my dear brother?' asked King Robert.

'Sire, you have asked, and I will give you my answer. This united Scottish nation that you have created has one weakness,' replied Edward Bruce.

'And what is that?' asked King Robert.

'It is too small to accommodate the ambitions of two Bruces,' answered Edward, as his brother looked at him in disbelief. Douglas stared at Edward Bruce; it was a suspicious and slightly hostile look. There were many Scots, too numerous to mention, who changed sides as frequently as the unpredictable Scottish weather. 'Surely Edward, the brother of King Robert Bruce, was not one of them?' Douglas thought to himself. 'Or could treason, perhaps a ransom, be the motive for such a daring statement?' Douglas considered the possibilities.

'What do you have in mind?' asked King Robert.

'Ireland,' replied Edward.

'What?' asked a shocked and surprised King Robert.

'The English have been attempting to defeat and control all Ireland. The Irish currently lack the strength of leadership to defend themselves,' answered Edward.

'And what would you expect to get out of supporting them may I ask?' asked King Robert.

'In return for ridding their nation of the English, just as you have done here, I have negotiated that the crown of Ireland be placed on my head,' answered a smiling Edward Bruce.

Bruce, stunned by this revelation, paused for a few seconds. 'But you are not of pure Irish blood,' declared King Robert.

'Are you of pure Scottish blood?' asked Edward.

The king did not answer; there was an embarrassing silence.

'Sire, my Lord Edward, may I speak with you?' asked Douglas, breaking into the silence. 'If my Lord Edward were to go to Ireland, the English forces under Edward II would be depleted. Such a situation would be to our advantage and would aid our cause here.' The two Bruces looked at each other. There was truth in what Douglas had said.

'I would be in favour of you undertaking such a campaign,' declared King Robert.

'I am glad of your support, my good King and brother. However, there is one request that I would like to make of you, Sire,' declared Edward.

'Next to me, you are the heir to the crown of Scotland. You have my blessing and I will grant you whatever you desire to ensure your success and hopefully your safe return,' replied the smiling King Robert.

Edward paused and looked into the face of his brother and his loyal companion. 'Douglas,' said Edward. 'Give me Douglas, for he and I have fought side by side, and there is none more deadly with the sword or more skilled in the art of cunning warfare.'

The Bruce looked at his first lieutenant, his most loyal and trusted servant. 'How could I ever let him go, but for the safe protection of my brother there is none better,' he thought to himself.

'What do you say?' asked King Robert as he looked directly at Douglas.

'What precisely do you ask of me?' replied Douglas, as he attempted to avoid giving an answer.

'Go with him to Ireland, give to him the loyalty you have given me, that is what I ask,' answered Bruce.

Douglas bowed his head. No answer was given, and he closed his eyes.

'Douglas!' prompted King Robert. 'Your answer please!'

The silence continued for several moments. Douglas slowly raised his head and looked deep into the eyes of his beloved King.

'Sire, my life has been devoted to your cause, but that cause has been a common cause to us both, to rid our nation of our invading enemies. My purpose in life is to avenge my father's name and reclaim that which was taken from my family and me. By giving you my support, I have achieved much. However, I say this; I have no desire to set foot on any foreign soil. I have suffered much from being invaded by our enemies and I only seek to stop them. Please, I beg you, do not ask this of me for I must refuse.'

Bruce, secretly delighted that his first lieutenant had shown good favour towards his own people, replied 'Go then and guard our borders. Our nation may be vulnerable if we send many with Edward to Ireland. Our nation puts its trust in you for its protection.'

Bruce turned to his brother. 'Edward, there are others who will gladly go with you. Douglas is my protector and the protector of the borders of Scotland.' Bruce turned back to face Douglas and gently smiled. He recalled the time when the English lords Percy and Clifford took Douglas's father prisoner at Irvine. He remembered those blood-curdling screams as Lord William Douglas cursed and swore vengeance against those who were about to betray their people. He remembered Lord Douglas calling out 'I will be avenged,' as he was taken to his death.

Bruce approached Douglas. 'James, I say this to you. Your father can now rest in peace, for you have truly avenged his death, for that I am sure he would be proud.'

'Sire, my mission now is to avenge and protect our nation, for as long as I live, I will not allow our enemies to repeat their past deeds of evil upon our people,' replied Douglas.

Douglas returned to his camp in the heart of the Ettrick forest. Many had still to arrive; they were taking advantage of the well-earned rest from battle and enjoying the peace and absence of enemy invaders who had constantly harassed their lives over these years.

It was mid-afternoon, the rain had returned. It was the typical light forest rain that fell without the assistance of any wind, silent and penetrating everything underneath. Douglas had directed his men to build a more permanent residence. He stood thinking, his back to one of the many fires. The damp wood which had been thrown onto it intermittently sparked and spluttered as it struggled to ignite, finally producing great pillars of white smoke that shot straight up in the windless forest. 'Perhaps one day my family will live with me,' he thought to himself. 'But for that to happen I need more than a humble wooden shelter in this forest. I will build a lodge where we can live in more comfort and safety.'

Douglas's men were still working when a small band of familiar faces from Melrose arrived at Lintalee, led by Sir Adam Gordon. They looked exhausted and harassed. 'My Lord Douglas, I come to seek your help.'

'What can we do for you?' asked Douglas.

'They have attacked us again, this time at Melrose. They took our cattle and raided our stores. We could not stop them. Some of our people were killed, many more will die of starvation unless we do something. Can you help us?' said the distressed Gordon.

Douglas did not reply. Instead he turned and shouted for his men to join him as he immediately mounted his horse. 'Who was their leader? Which way do they head?' roared Douglas.

'It was Edmund de Cailow, a knight of great fame, a Gascon. He is in charge of Berwick. They must be running low on food. He and his men will right now be heading back to the castle with their plunder,' answered Gordon. 'He has many well armed men at his disposal, we need to be quick,' added Gordon.

'The more the merrier,' shouted one of Douglas's men.

'We must be careful,' said Gordon.

'Best say a prayer for Cailow,' said another of Douglas's men as they rode off followed by Sir Adam Gordon and his men.

They rode hard and fast. No words were spoken, no instructions were given, for none were needed. 'Follow Douglas,' was all that was said when anyone asked 'where they were going'. Several hours later and several miles outside Berwick, the raiders were confronted. Without discussion or careful appraisal of the situation, Douglas and his men found themselves suddenly upon them. Young boys and servants were herding the cattle as they came towards Douglas and his men. The mass of armed raiders rode behind and suddenly moved in closer to protect their leader, Edmund de Cailow.

'My Lord there are twice as many of them as us, is this wise?' asked Sir Adam Gordon.

'Yes, they are greater in number, but I say this, they once again take what is ours, and they must be stopped. I ask that each of you think of a loved one, a mother, a sweetheart or a son or daughter. We fight to save and protect them. The size of our enemy shall not deter us,' answered Douglas, as his face filled with the now familiar expression of controlled burning revenge.

Douglas ordered his men to group beside a nearby ford. The enemy raiders came towards them. Douglas unfolded his banner and gave it to one of the younger members of his group to hold aloft. Cailow's men, on seeing the Douglas banner, knew that they were in for a hard fight. 'We are greater in numbers than they, have no fear,' shouted Cailow as he ordered the attack.

Douglas's men immediately responded with a counter-attack. Led by their forever-inspirational leader they fearlessly lunged in at the attacking enemy. The determination and blind faith in achieving victory caused every one of Douglas's men to lift himself above his own expectations as steel was met with steel. The blood poured. Many screamed as they fell slain. The battle continued at a hectic pace, and every ounce of strength was maximised in those few moments. Douglas had only one aim, and nothing would prevent him, as he cut through limb after limb to get within reach of Cailow.

With many men maimed and slain on both sides, Douglas finally confronted Cailow. Calling upon his remaining reserves of energy Douglas lunged at his prey; the skilful English knight deflected his first challenge as he drew his sword to protect himself. Several more strikes and thrusts were deflected in a similar fashion until Douglas, with superior skill and agility, final caught his target unawares. As the sword of Douglas was pulled from its dying victim, others panicked and fled. They had been beaten once again not just by an inferior force, but one that was led by the fearless demon Black Douglas.

Douglas and his men recovered what was theirs, and returned to Melrose. As before, the sight of the brave good Sir James, returning with their stolen livestock and provisions, delighted everyone who was witness to this magnificent deed. 'Sir James, I thank you most dearly,' declared Sir Adam Gordon, as he looked at the smiling people of Melrose who were once again protected by their hero. Douglas blushed. He had returned to his quiet, humble, almost shy self. Those who did not know him, and who had not seen the earlier transformation into an avenging knight, would not believe what this man had achieved. Douglas once more had enhanced his reputation as the most feared Scotsman as word continued to spread south amongst his English enemies.

Douglas and his men continued with the building of the forest lodge at Lintalee. They enjoyed the satisfaction of the creative work as a pleasurable alternative to the continuing warfare of these times. The men felt pleased that they were able to repay their Lord Douglas for what he had given them. They maintained their skills by hunting the rich prey that the forest provided.

An appetising smell, strong enough to cause the taste buds of any passer-by to water, lingered throughout the damp forest as the men feasted on the delicious roasted meat from the wild boar carcass that was still being turned above the flames of the smouldering fire. Each night they sat round the great burning log fires, eating, drinking and telling stories of past events and proudly fought battles.

Simon of Ledhouse, forever now in the company of Douglas, told of a story that he had heard. 'They say that there is an English knight, Sir Robert Neville by name, who is camped south of Berwick. They say that he disbelieves the tales of our Lord Douglas's great feats of warfare. They say, that he claims that it's all old wives scary stories for their weans. He claims, that if all that is said about Douglas were to be true, then it means that there can be nobody of any merit other than Douglas, he says that the tales of Douglas are absurd and an insult to all good noble men.'

Many laughed at what this English knight Neville had been reported as saying. 'Has he ever met you, my lord?' asked one of the men. 'Not to my knowledge,' replied the uninterested Douglas.

'He claims that should he ever meet you in battle, the banner of Douglas will be destroyed along with your life and the old wives tales of the Black Douglas will come to a sudden end.'

Douglas looked at his men; they all laughed loudly as they continued eating their food and drinking ale.

'Help me here. Are you saying that he has challenged me?' asked Douglas, directing his question towards his friend Simon. 'Yes, he is, and he makes it well known,' replied Simon of Ledhouse. Douglas gestured to his men. 'What do you think? Should I oblige?' he asked, with a hint of sarcasm. 'We could be doing with some entertainment,' declared Sir Laurence Abernethy, who found the whole topic very amusing. 'Then I will oblige and help this English knight have his wish,' replied Douglas, as he yawned out loud. 'Time for my bed, I need my sleep if I am to take up such a mighty challenge,' he laughingly declared.

A few days later, the early morning sun cast a warm glow across the east coast of the borderlands. The residents of Berwick awoke to the smell of burning; it was a smell that they had grown accustomed to over these years. It was one of the prices to be paid for living in such an industrial town that also happened to be the centre of constant warfare between the rival nations. Several early risers had noticed the dark clouds of smoke rising a few miles to the south.

'Sir, look' called the English guard as he pointed out something unusual to Robert Neville. 'The southern villages are on fire,' he added. 'Call the men,' shouted Neville, his voice echoing throughout his camp.

Within the hour, Neville and his men were riding south towards the burning villages when a terrifying sight suddenly confronted them. 'Douglas,' shouted one of the riders. 'It's the banner of Douglas!' They all froze and looked in the direction of the nearby hilltop. A lone rider slowly appeared over the horizon, casting a long shadow across the hillside in the low-lying early morning sun as he made his way gradually towards them. 'It's him, It's Douglas,' called the guard closest to Neville.

Neville stared at the approaching rider. 'What bloody arrogance!' he shouted. 'He comes here alone, apparently fearing no one. Well perhaps this will be his final day of judgement. This morning, for sure, I will put an end to the damage that yon savage rascal has caused us. Let's go meet with him.' 'Sir, be careful it could be a trap,' called one of the suspicious guards.

As they moved closer together, Douglas dropped down into a narrow wooded gorge. Neville and his men waited. A few moments later the tension was getting the better of some of them when one guard whispered 'Where did he go? He's disappeared; he should be up by now.' 'Be patient!' shouted a nervous Neville. 'He's not a dammed ghost!'

The stomach churning sound of a deadly arrow whistling towards them and penetrating deep into soft human flesh broke the eerie silence, as the guard on the left side of Neville screamed out in great pain and dropped to the ground. Panic broke out as the riders tried to control their startled horses. Douglas's men came out from both ends of the small wooded gorge and positioned themselves on the road either side of Neville and his men.

Several more of Neville's men became victims to Douglas's archery skills as yet more arrows plunged into their defenceless bodies. From both sides Douglas's men attacked. Neville shouted to his men. 'Before us we have the flower of this country, but we have more men than they. Let's attack, and end their savage reign of terror on our northern lands.'

Both sides became engaged in deadly battle. The clashing of spears and swords could be heard loudly ringing. The severed limbs and open wounds caused much blood to flow as each side plunged and swung at each other. As Douglas cut his way past each slain victim, he grew concerned for the casualties that were being encountered amongst his men.

The battle continued relentlessly as both sides struggled to gain the advantage. Douglas was entirely focused on his almost suicidal mission to get within reach of Neville. Slaying the leader of his enemies was becoming the predictable tactic of the avenging Douglas. Finally, the two leaders met. There was no time for words or exchange of inappropriate greetings as Neville swung his sword at Douglas, narrowly missing his opponent's left shoulder. Douglas responded with a thrust towards the unprotected stomach of the knight who immediately drew back in temporary retreat. Many blows, plunges and swipes with the cold deadly steel blades were viciously aimed and deflected by each other until the sheer strength of Douglas finally forced his victim to fall. A split second was all that Douglas required as his blade cut across the neck and shoulder of the one who dared to challenge him.

Standing over his victim, Douglas raised his blood-covered sword and shouted 'A Douglas! A Douglas!' The deadly bloodcurdling war cry was heard by all, as they looked and saw the victorious Douglas stand tall over the slain body of Neville. The fighting stopped. Neville's men ran in all directions. They had seen Douglas do exactly what others had said of this mighty warrior. He had once again defeated a much larger force; he had also defeated their hearts and injected further fear and terror as the one known as the Black Douglas.

Like many victorious warriors, Douglas and his men claimed the fruits of their victory as they ravaged the land and seized all that they could find. The burning continued and the terror spread as the avenging Douglas delivered yet another blow in the name of his cause.

As calmness returned, the humble, gallant Douglas took no profit from the seized plunder. Encouraging his men to keep to themselves that which they had earned, they repaid his kindness with deep love and affection. He openly wept over his own men who had fallen and praised even those who had no heart or great skill for fighting. Even the coward, for there were some, became brave and fearsome under Douglas's leadership. They respected and followed their Lord Douglas with great commitment and loving passion.

With the death of Neville and Cailow by the sword of Douglas, word spread further south, into the heart of England, of this fearsome Scottish knight, the one who frequently defied the code of conduct of taking knights and noble prisoners as ransom but instead slayed the leaders of his opposition. Tales of terror and unimaginable horror swiftly spread throughout the English nation. Misbehaving children were threatened by the mention of his mere name. Those who he loved dearly loved him back but those he considered his enemies feared him like the devil out of hell.

Douglas and his men returned to Lintalee. The enemy had been dealt yet another costly blow. Many thought that they would be safe for a short time to come. Douglas knew that in these times it was never safe, as he prepared in his mind his next campaign.

23

SOUTHERN CAMPAIGNS

THE LOW-LYING CLOUDS of damp white mist slowly swept westwards along the Jedburgh forest floor. Like suspended rain that refused to fall to ground, the ghostly packs of moisture continued to weave their way round all that stood in their path. Akin to an invasion by nature come to attack this forest, the ominous clouds rode past. One by one they drifted silently and inexorably. The occasional break in the ranks was quickly taken advantage of as the morning sun sent its rays of light bursting through the precious gaps, reassuring those below that they would not be forgotten.

The first deaths that morning were perpetuated by the flocks of rooks who marched along the forest floor eagerly devouring their early morning meal; all other life appeared to be suspended in the damp dreary atmosphere of this early morning.

The newly completed forest lodge stood in the clearing high above the Jed Water. Using the resources that the forest and rocky hillsides had offered, along with the many talented skills of his own men, Douglas had done well in planning and creating such a safe and comfortable sanctuary for those to whom this place had now become their second home. The elements of nature would be kept at bay, as the regular attacks by ravaging winds and relentless rains would, by the skilful construction, be inhibited from invading this homely place.

The only weakness of this forest lodge was the absence of large castle-like stone walls to prevent and repel any attacking invader. However, this fortress had other means of defence, the main one being the lethal sword of Douglas, which few would dare to challenge.

Only a few men remained. Their task was to prepare the feast for the return of Douglas who had decided that this was the time to invite his family to his own home. The remainder of his men had taken his advice, and had also gone home to be with their loved ones. They, like Douglas, were due to return in a few days time.

Edward II, King of England, on hearing of the Bruce's forays in Ireland, called the Earl of Arundel, Warden of Northumbria, to his council. 'With the Bruces having apparently abandoned the nation that they claim to protect, and preferring instead to seek their fortune in Ireland, now is the time for us to go back to that cursed Scotland and finish what we should have done earlier,' declared Edward.

'Sire, your timing could not be better, for Douglas is the only one who stands in our way as protector of Scotland. Many say that if we take Douglas, then Scotland is ours,' declared Arundel, who was excited about the possibility of being the one Englishman to finally put and end to the terror inflicted by the Black Douglas.

'Do you have knowledge of where he can be located?' asked King Edward.

'Yes, a short distance over the border, about a mile south of Jedburgh, he has built his own forest lodge,' answered Arundel, who was pleased that he was able to answer with such precision.

'So, he's just over the border in an easy to get at location. If you knew that, why haven't you attempted to take him before now?' shouted the angry Edward. Arundel blushed with embarrassment, and bowed his head in shame. 'Sire, if you allow me to lead this raid, I promise I will not fail you.'

'He's only one man for God's sake; he doesn't even have a large number of men. Why has one man caused us so much pain and embarrassment? You'd better not fail me,' declared the still angry King, as he gestured to be left alone.

A few days later Douglas and his men made their way back to Lintalee. There was an unusual nervousness as they headed towards Jedburgh and to the safety of his newly built forest lodge. They were more careful than ever before as they scanned every corner and constantly watched for even the slightest hint of danger. There were members of this party who were more precious to Douglas than even his trusted and beloved King.

Lady Eleanor, looking remarkably healthy for her age, controlled her horse with surprising skill and anticipation, as the group forded the many streams and obstacles that cut across their pathway. Riding abreast with her adopted daughter, Sophia, she followed immediately behind her James, her famous son in whom she was most pleased.

Several riders rode far out in front of the main group in order to identify any dangers and ensure safe passage for the family of their leader. Douglas glanced and smiled at the rider who rode alongside him. Archibald, his youngest brother, had matured to a fine young man over these past few years. He was no longer the erratic juvenile whose head was filled with the constant desire to impress his elders. There was an air of calmness about this young man, and combined with a sense of purpose, there was now fulfilment in his life. The events of Bannockburn had transformed this confused youth into manhood.

Douglas turned round. 'Are you two all right?' he asked of the two riders behind him. 'Of course we are,' replied Sophia, who had developed a habit of abruptly answering each of

Douglas questions with a hint of sarcasm. 'Do you think your mother and I can't ride a horse as well as you?'

'No, I didn't mean that,' said Douglas. 'Well don't ask, if you don't know what you mean,' replied Sophia, as Lady Eleanor smiled at the exchange of romantic hostilities between these two.

The group of riders continued on their way for the next hour until they finally arrived at Jedburgh. Some of Douglas's leading men had stopped up ahead and were deep in conversation.

'Stop!' shouted Douglas. 'Wait here. Archibald you stay with them,' called Douglas, as he nervously looked first at his confused and alarmed mother and then at Sophia.

Douglas dug in his spurs and galloped on ahead.

'What's up?' asked Douglas when he reached his men. 'It's the bloody English again. They have killed all of the men that we left behind at the lodge,' replied Sir Laurence Abernethy, who had been riding out in front.

'What of our lodge? Are the English still there?' asked the now raging Douglas.

'Yes, my lord. It's the Earl of Arundel's men. He has left a small garrison at the lodge while he and many men search the forest for you,' replied one of Douglas's men.

'What shall we do?' they asked of Douglas. With his normally pale complexion now converted to a burning crimson rage, he gave his reply. 'There is a safe house in Jedburgh that my family can be taken to. Sir Laurence, I would be grateful if you could attend to this matter most urgently. You know the place I refer to. The rest of you follow me,' said Douglas as he quickly headed south towards Lintalee.

At Lintalee, the new occupants of the forest lodge enjoyed their rich findings as they attempted to devour the large feast that was meant for others, washed down with the wines and ales that had been brought to celebrate the completion. As the afternoon wore on the intruders slowly became intoxicated by their own greed.

Douglas and his men abandoned their horses and approached on foot. 'How many do you think there are?' he asked one of his men who been here earlier.

'Possibly thirty, many more searching in the forest,' the man replied.

'What shall we do, Sir?' asked Simon of Ledhouse.

As he looked through the forest camouflage and observed the goings on, Douglas gave his answer. 'We will wait for a short time and then walk in and join in the banquet. Give them about another hour and they will be drunk and unfit to offer any resistance,' declared Douglas.

'He's right, there's more to be drunk in that lodge that in the Jed Water,' replied Abernethy, who had returned after ensuring the safety of Douglas's family. 'They are safe my lord, no need to worry,' he added.

About an hour later Douglas rose to his feet. Drawing out his sword and wiping it clean he called out 'Let's go,' and calmly walked forward out in to the open clearing that surrounded his lodge. Several English soldiers were sitting slouched at the front of the lodge. 'No quarter!' shouted Douglas as one of them tried to waken from his state of drunkenness. With the ease of a slaughter of domestic animals, each invader who had remained outside was silently approached and calmly slain.

Inside voices could be heard shouting and laughing as the fruits of their efforts were enjoyed by these invaders. Douglas gestured for several of his men to go round the back; others were directed to guard the few windows. The main body stood behind Douglas as he fearlessly opened the main door.

'Who the hell are you?' shouted one of the guards.

'Who's the leader of this bunch of drunks?' asked Douglas.

'I am,' replied the intoxicated Elias, a clerk who had been left in charge while Arundel searched for Douglas. 'And who, sir, are you?'

'The one that none of you really wants to meet,' answered Douglas. He rushed at Elias. 'I pray that my actions will be seen as justified and not just cold-blooded revenge,' thought

Douglas as he lifted his sword and decapitated the drunken clerk.

The shock of this savage attack caused the others to become temporarily sober as they rose to their feet to defend themselves. Douglas, more sympathetic towards the others, halted their recent hours of pleasure by humanely ending their lives.

Douglas's men quickly completed their task and began the removal of the bodies. All but one, another drunk, who remained alive. 'What shall we do with him, sir?' they asked Douglas.

'Put him on his horse, along with the body of Elias and send it towards the border,' replied Douglas.

'What of his head?' asked Abernethy. 'What do you think we should do with it?'

'Use your imagination, man,' shouted the angry Douglas.

A short time later, Arundel and his men, who had unsuccessfully searched the forest for any sign of Douglas, were making their way along the main road that runs from Jedburgh to the English border. As they headed through the steep narrow gorge they first heard and then saw an approaching rider who appeared to be carrying a large and awkward load. 'It's one of our men,' shouted Sir Thomas de Richmond.

'The bloody savages,' shouted Richmond, as the horse came nearer. 'Look what they have done.' The rider, still drunk and unaware of what had been going on, had been strapped onto the horse to prevent him falling off. Also strapped and straddled across the same horse was the decapitated body of Elias, whose head, facing inwards, had been tightly tied to his own bare backside.

The many tales of the evil Douglas now abruptly seized the minds of these men and filled them with fear for their own lives. They had suddenly lost all heart and confidence in attempting to capture the Black Douglas. As they spoke amongst themselves, their leadership, now confused and in complete disarray, only wanted one thing, and that was to go home.

The conversations were continuing when a bombardment of arrows and rocks suddenly showered down on them from the shelter of the trees that rose high above the narrow red sandstone gorge. Many fell; many horses bolted, some in the wrong direction, some to the north, others into the depths of the Jed Water. The bulk of them panicked and rushed to make their way south.

In contrast to the panic amongst Arundel's men, Douglas calmly and deliberately led his main band south in pursuit of the now terrified fleeing force. Just as he and Abernethy had done at Bannockburn, Douglas increased the pace of his deadly pursuit of a much larger force. One by one, the stragglers were overcome and slaughtered, injecting more fear and panic upon those who fled further ahead.

'Richmond!' shouted the panic-stricken Arundel. 'We run from someone smaller than us. We are in disgrace. I command you to take your pick of men and hold them off until our main band has time to flee.' 'But, my Lord ...' replied a terrified Richmond. 'Don't talk back. Do it!' screamed the panicking cowardly Arundel.

Richmond, having forced himself to regain some of his lost composure, prepared his men for the anticipated attack by Douglas. They waited at the point where the gorge opens out into open countryside. The wait seemed like an eternity as they constantly imagined that they could hear and see him coming towards them.

Suddenly a group of riders came out through the narrow gorge. Douglas was not one of them. 'Where is he?' shouted the confused Richmond as Douglas's men came slowly nearer. 'Would you be looking for me by any chance?' shouted a loud voice a short distance to the west of the main road. Richmond turned, there he was, his full coat of arms on display for all to see. 'Douglas, you heathen, you coward, you murderer,' shouted Richmond. 'I take it there is something about me of which you disapprove?' said Douglas.

'There is no need for senseless killings. This fight only need be between you and me,' shouted Richmond. 'As you wish,' replied Douglas. 'On two conditions,' added the smiling Douglas.

'What conditions?' said Richmond.

'If you kill me, my men go free. If I kill you, your men go free, winners therefore on both sides,' declared Douglas.

'So be it,' replied Richmond.

Douglas was the first to make a move as both sets of followers gradually moved back and gave them the space they needed. He slowly moved towards the confident Richmond. 'I have prayed for this situation for some time,' shouted Richmond. 'What, to meet your maker?' asked Douglas. 'No, to meet with you alone in battle,' replied Richmond. 'Sounds like the same thing to me,' answered a laughing Douglas.

Richmond suddenly pulled on his reins and forced his horse in the direction of Douglas. A few short strides and the required speed had been achieved. Sword drawn, he focused his many battle fought years of skill and experience towards the oncoming rider. Douglas, calm as ever, slowly trotted towards his speeding attacker.

As he closed in, Richmond raised his sword above his head. Douglas, his sword still sheathed, stopped and waited. Richmond, now approaching at galloping pace, had clearly shown his intended actions. Douglas withdrew his sword and firmly grasped the razor sharp blade about three-quarters along its length in his gloved hand and held it close to his chest.

'What is he doing?' Abernethy loudly called out.

'Wait and see. You will be impressed,' answered one of Douglas's long-term serving men.

As he covered the last few yards, Richmond stood up on his stirrups in order to bring maximum force down upon his targeted victim. The full body of Richmond, unprotected with his sword held high, and offering the perfect target, would only be presented for a split second. That was all that Douglas needed, as his own sword suddenly became a lethal spear, and was thrown directly at the chest of the oncoming speeding English knight.

Richmond's sword did come down upon the planned target area, but not upon Douglas, who had cunningly thrown himself off his horse immediately after he had lunged his own sword like a spear in the direction of his attacker. Richmond's horse continued for a short distance before its rider fell face first to the ground. His men ran towards him and were confronted by the horrific sight of the point of Douglas's sword sticking out of the back of their brave but now slain knight.

Douglas, fearless as ever, walked over to the remainder of Richmond's men. 'You, sirs, as promised, can go home now. No harm will come to you. But I say this. I have seen your faces, I know where you live, and should you ever come back to harm my people, I will do to you and your mothers, and your wives, and your children what I have done to your man Elias.'

Darkness was starting to descend when Douglas returned to Lintalee. Several lights could be seen burning brightly as he and his men approached. A pillar of smoke rose above indicating activity inside. 'I hope the ones who stayed behind have removed and dealt with the dead bodies,' said Douglas.

As he walked through the main doorway, the picture that greeted him brought him tears of long overdue joy. His mother, Sophia and Archibald had been brought from safety and were now enjoying themselves and relaxing in the comfort of what he had created.

'James!' Lady Eleanor called out. 'Where have you been? We have been waiting for you.'

'I had one or two things to attend to,' answered Douglas, with an embarrassed grin. 'What do you think of this place, then?' asked Douglas, as he proudly showed off his new residence. 'Brilliant!' answered the highly impressed Archibald, as he looked around the newly built lodge, and glanced at the debris left over from some sort of wild celebration. 'Looks like good times have been had here,' added Archibald.

'Mother?' asked Douglas. Lady Eleanor looked round the room, the movement of her eyes indicating disapproval, not of the lodge, but of the lifestyle. 'It appears to be quite comfortable, for your needs anyway,' she replied. 'I'm glad,' replied Douglas.

'Aren't you going to ask me?' said Sophia, in her now familiar sarcastic manner. 'OK then, Sophia, what do you think of my New Forest Lodge?' asked Douglas with a loud deliberate voice which forced everyone to stop and prepare for what was sure to be a very interesting expression of opinion. 'It's a pig sty, and it stinks to high heaven of stale ale. You live like an animal, in fact animals are cleaner than you,' she replied, as everyone else joined in an outburst of loud laughter at hearing the tongue of this young woman putting the fearsome mighty Douglas in his place.

Douglas shook his head and sat down for a well-earned rest. He looked back at Sophia, and smiled with a wide grin that reflected his feelings of admiration for this young lady. A similar look was returned from Sophia. It was a look that conveyed a hidden conversation between these two; it was a conversation not of words, but of looks, of smiles, and feelings of affection. Above all else, it was a conversation of growing love, and a conversation that neither of them knew how to fully express.

24

THE REVENGE OF BERWICK

FOR SEVERAL WEEKS the Douglas family lived the quiet serene life that was meant for them, together, happy and enjoying the pleasure of each other's company. The forest lodge, although newly built, had now acquired the warmth and comforting look of a family home as the feminine touch of the two women, Lady Eleanor and Sophia, injected the loving calmness that men enjoy but often take for granted.

Douglas took advantage of this restful period. It was a time for reflection, a time to think about the future, a time to get to know his family as they grew older each day. It was a time to decide. 'Why should I, one man, while others enjoy the riches and wealth acquired through greed and selfishness, have to give up my whole life, my family, and my future to protect this nation? Why me?' he painfully thought to himself as he sat in the warm mid-morning spring sunshine.

Sophia came outside. It took a few moments for her eyes to adjust to the brightness. Walking from side to side in order not to appear too eager, she slowly made her way towards the object of her attention and then paused before asking her question. 'May I sit with you?' 'Of course,' answered Douglas, as he broke from his deep thoughts, and moved over on the wooden bench that was positioned several yards to the side of his new home.

'James, you look troubled, what bothers you?' 'Nothing,' replied Douglas. 'Doesn't look like nothing to me, not with that miserable look on your face,' declared Sophia. 'Have you had enough of all this fighting and constant warfare?' she asked innocently, as she shuffled up closer beside him.

Douglas looked at her, her face a picture of perfection, her pale clear silky skin, her ever sparkling and smiling eyes, her long, soft, reddish tinted hair illuminated with the reflection of the distant sun that glowed brightly behind her. He paused before answering; he wanted to say something, something to explain his feelings towards her. Her beauty, her loveliness, what it was doing to him. He hadn't been in her company for as long as this before; in the past it had only been for short periods. He knew well before now that he felt something very special towards her, but he was never around long enough to allow those feelings to grow or to be expressed.

She stroked the back of his right hand with her small fingers; he looked down at his own large battle-scarred hand, a hand that had slain many an enemy, a hand that was now slowly melting into submission. Her soft touch sent shivers though his body as she slowly and gently drew the tips of her figures across the many dark hairs that acted like sensors picking up every movement of affection. Embarrassed and uncomfortable with such soft and intimate touching, Douglas grasped the gentle hand and embraced it in his own. She felt his powerful hand imprison hers. The two sets of contrasting interwoven fingers, touching and comforting, provided a gateway, as the expressions of affectionate feelings passed through their bodies. The image of the gentle and powerful hand of Douglas grasping the small soft hand of Sophia conveyed a simple yet innocent message of truth; it was a message of suppressed mutual love and deeply felt affection.

'You haven't answered my question,' said Sophia, as she blushed with embarrassment at her hand still being firmly held by Douglas. 'The answer is yes, I have had enough of this constant fighting, but the end is still a long way off,' replied Douglas, who now, feeling uneasy, pulled his hand away. 'There is much more to be done,' he added. 'Like what?' asked Sophia.

'They still come to invade our lands. In fact there are lands which belong to us which are still in their possession,' declared Douglas, with the same determination that he had shown during previous conversations. 'Are you not doing the same to them, by invading their lands? Surely that can't be right?' asked Sophia, as she presented Douglas with the awkward question to answer.

Douglas paused; there was truth in what Sophia was suggesting. 'Yes, I invade their lands, but only as an act of revenge and retaliation for the brutality that they have brought to our nation. If they stop, I will stop.'

'James, do you hate the English?' Sophia asked in a most serious and direct manner, as she gently wiped her long hair away from her face.

'If I were to say yes, then it would mean that I hate my own mother,' replied Douglas, who quickly regretted letting a family secret slip out.

'What do you mean, hate your own mother! What kind of thing is that to say?' asked Sophia.

'I have been taught not to hate because of who a person is, or what race they belong to. If I have any hatred it is directed only at those who perpetrate acts of cruelty towards others,' replied Douglas, in the hope that this conversation would now end.

'I understand now,' replied a smiling Sophia, slowly leaning over and softly kissing the cheek of her dear James.

Over at the lodge, the main doorway was slightly ajar. Lady Eleanor secretly stood inside in the shadows, observing the scene outside that was a delight to her eyes. 'If only these days could last forever,' she said to Archibald, as he struggled to rise from another one of his many extended morning sleeps.

'Am I right in thinking that you want to stay here?' inquired Archibald. 'That would be nice, but not possible,' replied Lady Eleanor. 'Why?' asked Archibald, as he let out a loud yawn and then rubbed the remaining sleep from his eyes.

'I sense that he will want us to go back home in order for him to resume with his business.'

'Business, what business is that?' asked the confused Archibald.

'That wretched obsession of his, his cause, his vendetta, call it what you like, it's ruining his and all of our lives,' replied Lady Eleanor, as her frustration at the many years of suppressed and restricted family life finally boiled over into anger.

'Why don't you talk to him?' said Archibald.

'Oh, I intend to, and this time he will listen,' she promptly answered.

A short time later Sophia came back into the lodge. Her gentle smile of contentment was evident for all to see. 'Good morning everyone,' she loudly called out, with each word projected with the sound of sublime happiness.

'Someone appears to be in a good mood,' said Archibald.

'And why shouldn't I be? It's a very nice morning, in fact it's a nice morning for everyone to enjoy,' answered the ecstatic Sophia.

'Is he still out there?' asked Lady Eleanor.

'Yes,' answered Sophia, sensing an unusual abruptness in her adopted mother's voice.

'Don't let anyone disturb us,' Lady Eleanor ordered, as she walked out.

Douglas sat staring at the ground in front of him. Only one thought occupied his mind, that tender kiss from Sophia. He replayed those few precious moments over and over again. He put his hand up to his face and slowly touched his cheek, which was still tingling from that simple but powerful expression of

369

love and affection. Two words entered his mind, one of which he knew he would have to choose. 'War or love,' he thought to himself as his mind battled with the natural desires of his body against the cause that had become his obsession.

Lady Eleanor approached and sat beside him. 'James, tell me, how do you feel right now? I want your honest answer.'

'What do you mean?' asked Douglas.

'I have just spoken to Sophia. At this precise moment that girl is in heaven, a picture of perfect happiness if ever I saw one,' declared Lady Eleanor, as she looked directly at her son and then asked the same question again.

'Mother, you can obviously read my thoughts. I too am happy,' answered Douglas with a forced smile.

'But not as happy as Sophia,' said Lady Eleanor. 'What's going on in that mind of yours?'

'I keep thinking of Berwick,' answered Douglas. Lady Eleanor looked at him in surprise.

'What? Why Berwick?' she asked.

'Mother, you of all people know why. It was at Berwick that for me it all started,' said Douglas, with sadness and anger combined in his expression.

'That was many years ago, you were just a wee boy, what do you remember of Berwick?' asked Lady Eleanor as she comforted her son. Douglas hesitated, there were some things better forgotten, some things best kept in the past, but he had to answer this question. It was a question directly relating to when it all began for him.

'I remember crying, I could not stop, I was afraid. Longshanks's army unleashed hell on that town. I remember the screams. I remember the panic and confusion. I remember we had to hide. I remember crying with fear as I sat in the boat and looked back at you and my dear father, who waved his last goodbye to me. I remember seeing him standing on the shore. And I remember the look on his face as he waved goodbye. It was a look that I will never forget, and it was a look that made me feel that he was depending on me. I never saw him again.' Douglas had to stop, he was out of breath, there was something inside him that burned fiercely, something that was the source of his relentless determination. Regaining his composure, he continued. 'When you were both out of sight I remember saying to Bishop Lamberton that one day I would avenge Berwick.'

'What did Lamberton say when you mentioned revenge?' asked Lady Eleanor.

'He was not pleased. He said that the gates of heaven would be closed to those who choose vengeance rather than forgiveness,' answered Douglas.

'Why did you not take his advice?' asked Lady Eleanor.

'I told him I would rather be victorious in entering the gates of Berwick than the gates of heaven,' replied Douglas.

'What did he say to that?'

'He said that I should not allow bitterness to poison my mind. Other than that he did not say anything; he simply bowed his head and said a silent prayer. He knew I meant what I said.'

'So what happens now?' asked Lady Eleanor.

'Berwick. The time has come for me to fulfil the promise I made when I last saw my father,' declared Douglas.

'And what of the rest of us?' asked Lady Eleanor.

'Go back to Blackhouse Tower, for that is our true home. It is safe there,' said Douglas.

'And what of Sophia? She is no longer a child. If you don't take her hand someone else will.'

Douglas glanced over at the lodge and then looked back at his mother. There was a slight hint of redness in his eyes, as the conflicting emotions fought within his mind.

'You know how I feel about Sophia, you know how she feels about me, but I can't give up on what I have set out to achieve. Some day, hopefully not too far away, I will stop and give my time to her and the rest of our family. I ask for your patience and understanding.'

Lady Eleanor pondered over the words that her son had spoken, words that merely confirmed what she already knew; she had to give it one more try. 'James, you say that Berwick is next, I ask you this, what's after Berwick? Whatever your answer is, I ask again, what's next? When will it ever end? Will there ever be an end? Will there ever be an end to this fighting and constant warfare?'

Douglas put his arms round his mother. She was tiny compared to him, but her strength of character and sheer determination for the things that mattered in her life vastly outweighed her physical presence. As he gently and tenderly hugged her he quietly sobbed. He did not want her to see his tears; he paused and wiped his eyes. 'Mother, you ask when it will end. I cannot answer. I can say this, when you and my father put me on that boat, that's when it all began. The ending I do not know. I can only say that nothing, and I mean nothing, will stand in my way. There are those who love me and those who fear me. As I do the things that I have to do there are many who will come to love me even more and there are many who will fear me even more. However, because of their own actions, that is their choice.'

'But why? Why do you drive yourself in pursuit of an endless dream?' asked Lady Eleanor.

'It is not a dream, though it could be endless,' said Douglas. He raised his voice. 'Our good departed friend Robert Fullerton, whom I dearly loved, once told me that when my father was taken prisoner at Irvine by the English Lords Percy and Clifford, as my father was forced to surrender at the point of an English sword he called out that he would be avenged. Those words constantly ring in my ears. Those words were meant for me to hear, and I have heard them. But I have not yet completed my task. I don't know when it will be completed. Perhaps at my death? Or perhaps when our enemy invaders stop taking that which is not theirs.'

Douglas finally looked into his mother face; he had to have the last word. 'Mother you must go now. I will visit, please take care of yourself and our family. Do not worry about me, but direct your prayers to the souls of those unfortunates who stand in my way. I admit there are many that I have killed, and there will be many more to follow. However, they, like us, are the victims of these cursed and violent times.'

Lady Eleanor pulled Douglas towards her, and hugged her beloved son. 'No mother could be more proud of her son than I am of you,' she confessed.

Lady Eleanor rose to her feet. Douglas held on to her hand. She searched for the final words that would force him to change his mind and abandon his obsession. 'She may not wait for you,' she said.

'What?' asked a confused Douglas.

'It's William. He called in at Blackhouse Tower a few times, they talked, but I know that she wanted to wait for your return. I think she may be attracted to him.'

'Do you mean William Cuthbert?' asked Douglas.

'Yes,' answered Lady Eleanor, who then corrected herself. 'I mean no, his name by birth is not Cuthbert, it's Keith. Anyhow, William appears to have developed a strong attraction towards Sophia, she is after all no longer a child but a very beautiful and highly desirable woman.' Lady Eleanor now realised that she had entrapped her son in this conversation.

'Could he support her?' asked Douglas. His face took on a sad and imprisoned look, caused by his own life's obsession which had made him now unable to enjoy the pleasures of the freedom that he fought so determinedly for.

'Yes,' answered his mother. 'He has inherited the estate at Galston; he is also related to Sir Robert Keith, his cousin I believe. I am sure therefore that he would have no difficulty in providing for her.'

'Who is this William of Galston? I have not heard of him, in battle or otherwise,' asked Douglas in a surprisingly calm manner.

'Not much is known of him. He is a quiet young man, some say a bit like you, apart from the fact that he stays at home caring for his mother and grandmother and does not go away fighting. The last I heard Sir Robert was arranging his knighthood,' answered Lady Eleanor.

'Sounds like a good man and a good choice for Sophia, if she were to choose him,' said Douglas, letting go of his mother's hand. His look indicated that his determination to pursue his cause was unmoveable.

Around this time, King Robert Bruce had returned from Ireland, leaving his brother Edward behind to continue with his ambition to seek the crown of all Ireland. All were glad to see their King return to his homeland. Many came to greet him and express their gratitude for his leadership and protection. Bruce sat in deep conversation with his Marischal, Sir Robert Keith.

'They have you in their hearts, they worship you, and yet you still appear discontent,' said Keith.

'Yes I am,' answered Bruce, 'and I will continue so until every inch of Scottish soil has been cleansed of the enemy who still occupies our lands.'

'But Sire, there is only one town where that is the case,' answered Keith, as he tried to console and offer comfort.

'One town too many,' replied Bruce. 'If only we could get past those walls, we could recover it, that I am sure.'

'Sire, there may be a way. I have a cousin who resides in that town. I am sure that if offered payment he would come to our aid,' disclosed Keith.

'Is he a Scot?' asked Bruce.

'Yes, Sire, and he can be trusted,' replied Keith.

'Oh I am sure he can, provided we pay him enough,' answered Bruce, as he shook his head in an expression of disgust at someone wanting payment for helping to recover his own land.

'He would be taking a great risk, both to himself and his family,' said Keith as he raised his hands and gestured for a decision to be made.

'So be it. Who do you want to assist you?' responded Bruce, to a shocked Sir Robert.

'But Sire, I did not intend to do this myself, merely a suggestion on my part,' replied Keith with a now distinctively worried look on his face.

'My dear Sir Robert, you have presented a suggestion, a good one at that and one to which I give my support. Now I ask you to follow it through. Tell me, who do you want to go with you? And what will it take to recover that stolen town? You can ask Douglas or Randolph to lead the attack. The choice is yours. Please arrange it,' ordered Bruce.

Still shocked and stunned at finding himself in this difficult position, Keith cunningly replied 'Sire, those two whom you mention are great leaders and highly skilled in battle. If I were to choose one, the other would surely become annoyed at not being asked. I therefore propose that we ask both of them to lead the attack. I will devote my time to drawing up the plans and coordinating the strategy for what could prove to be a long drawn out affair.'

Bruce smiled at Sir Robert. 'My good man, there are many who are skilled in battle while others may possess less violent skills. You have my full support, but please don't take too long with your plans and strategy details, and please call me at once when your men enter the castle walls, for I want to be there when all of Scotland finally belongs to us once more.'

Several weeks later, Douglas and his men arrived at the park of Duns in Berwickshire where Lord Randolph was in the process of putting the finishing touches to a grand and magnificent castle. The success and popularity of both of these ever-faithful lieutenants to King Robert had spread throughout the land. As individuals in battle they were invincible; together; along with their loyal men, they presented the most effective fighting force in all of Scotland.

'Keith should soon be here,' said Randolph, as he entertained his friend and guest prior to embarking on yet another joint battle.

'Do you think he will bring many men?' asked Douglas, as he took a large gulp of wine to quench his thirst.

'You know what that one is like; he will not only bring many men, he will probably also bring his mother, grandmother and every distant cousin that he can contact. In fact, the more he brings the less the chance of seeing him in action,' answered a sarcastic Randolph.

Douglas laughed, and then devoured yet another mouthful of wine. 'He's not a fighter, more of a planner and coordinator, and I suppose we need someone to do that work and free us up to do what we do best,' Douglas conceded, wiping the spillage from his mouth.

'Aye, provided the plans meet with our agreement,' said Randolph.

The following day Sir Robert Keith finally arrived. 'I have brought a request from our King Robert. He wishes us to perform a dangerous task. I must consult with you about the plans in private,' said Keith, in a quiet almost apologetic manner. 'Do you mean his plans or yours?' asked a loud-voiced Randolph. Keith looked at Douglas, who gestured for him to answer. 'Both, it's basically his request with myself planning the detail,' answered the almost frightened Keith, who felt intimidate by being in the presence of these two fearsome individuals.

For the next few hours, the detailed plans were presented. As the discussions went on, loud shouting could be heard from inside the closed room. 'Eight hundred bloody pounds, is that what he will get for helping us save him, his family and townsfolk?' shouted Randolph on hearing about the deal set up with the Berwick man known as Spalding.

'Can he be trusted?' asked Douglas.

'Oh yes, definitely,' answered Keith.

'You say that he is a cousin of yours?' asked Randolph.

'It's his wife who is my cousin,' replied Keith.

'And you have set up the deal for payment?' asked Randolph suspiciously.

'If money is the problem then I will gladly pay the bribe,' Douglas called out, in an outburst of frustration.

'No need. Bruce has provided the funds for this payment,' said the exhausted Keith.

'When do we leave?' asked Randolph.

'In a few days, maybe next week, when more of my men will have arrived,' answered Keith.

'How many are coming?' asked Randolph.

'Many from Lothian,' replied Keith.

'Exactly how many?' Randolph asked, as he started to become more irritated by the apparent delay.

'I don't know, possibly five hundred, but it could be more,' answered Keith.

Douglas sat quietly and listened to the conversation. The targeted destination had been in his mind since he was ten years old. Nothing was going to stand in his way and prevent him from retaking that town, the place where he last saw his own father alive. He stood up and slammed his partially filled goblet of wine on the nearest table, causing it to fall over and roll along the stone floor. Like the violently spilt blood of those who had lost their lives in the town of Berwick many years ago, the dregs of red wine spluttered over the dark stone slabs, penetrating into the many deep cracks, and finally disappearing before their eyes. Randolph and Keith, taken aback by Douglas's sudden outburst, stared down at the fallen goblet as if it were trying to tell its own story.

'We leave tonight, so whatever men you have, get them ready,' Douglas calmly called out.

'What! That's impossible,' replied Keith.

Randolph, for once speechless, looked on in amazement as Douglas explained.

'Sir I respect the wish of our good King Robert, and I appreciate your efforts in planning these events, but I am not going to sit here for weeks and wait for our enemies to hear of our plans, for they surely will. We leave tonight under cover of darkness. If I and my own men have to go alone, then so be it.'

It was a Saturday night, the second day of the month of April, as Douglas and Randolph made their way on horseback and led their men through the darkness towards the east coast. Guided by the illuminated glow in the eastern sky from the many torches and fires that burned and signalled the location of the far off coastal town of Berwick, they carefully made their way unobserved towards their destination.

'How many do you think will be there?' asked Sir Thomas Randolph, who along with his men had joined Douglas in the quest to take back this strategic location.

'A lot more than us,' answered Douglas. 'It all depends not on how many, but on how well prepared they are. Surprise could turn out to be our deadliest weapon,' he declared.

'Aye, maybe a good fright in the night from the Black Douglas and they will all run away,' shouted Randolph, and he and his men laughed.

'You could be right,' replied Douglas, who had developed a close partnership with Randolph as he had got to know more about him since Bannockburn.

'Sir Robert mentioned the name of the local man residing in the town, the one he said would help us,' said Douglas.

'Aye, that's right,' answered Randolph.

'What was his name again?' asked Douglas.

'His name is Spalding. He will be on guard duty on the wall tonight,' replied Randolph.

'Spalding. I remember now, I had forgotten, my mind was elsewhere. Anyhow, another cousin of Keith. They are everywhere.'

'What do you mean?' asked Randolph.

'Oh, it doesn't matter, it's just that I have knowledge of another cousin of Sir Robert, someone that he wants to have knighted, probably irrelevant,' replied Douglas.

The clear night sky was still. There was no wind or rain, and the only noise was that of the horses' hooves pounding the hard ground. As they approached within a few miles of the town boundary, Douglas called out the order to stop. 'We will make our way from here on foot. We must approach in silence.'

His men immediately followed his instructions without question and began their own silent synchronised trot as they followed his dark shadow along the trail that headed towards the glowing lights.

Randolph matched the pace of Douglas and encouraged his men to blend in with those of the commander who had become his good friend. 'A few minutes and we should be there,' declared Randolph. Obedience and determination showed in their every move as the combined forces of these two men represented not just a strength in numbers, but also a strength in confidence, bravery and cunning that was unmatched by any other Scottish force.

The first solo of the dawn chorus had begun, a solitary blackbird, standing proud on the south-facing town wall which showed off its gifted vocal skills and filled the air with the music. After a short time, others started to join in, a few trying to take over the lead but not having the same power as the leader of this serenade. Soon the angelic sound of chirps, chants, and warbling echoed throughout the sleeping town creating a rich harmonious welcome that celebrated the beginning of a new day of precious life.

Douglas and Randolph had arrived at their destination. They and their men hid in the many gorse bushes and low-lying shrubs that surrounded the west side of the town walls. There was only one instruction issued to the men: 'Be silent and patient.'

At the same time, Sir Robert Keith and his men arrived at the north side of the town, the area inhabited mainly by Scots who were imprisoned within their own homes. A single torchlight flickered in the early morning breeze from high above on the thick stone town wall. Every once in a while a dark figure would walk past and temporarily block the light from the torch. Unlike a patrolling guard whose movements would be predictable, there was a hesitancy in the movements of this figure.

'Sir, is that him? Is that Spalding?' whispered one of Keith's men. 'We will soon find out,' answered Keith, who then ordered 'Light a torch!' As the figure on the wall above came close, a torch was lit and then waved. Up above Spalding immediately acknowledged the signal by waving his torch in reply.

Sir Robert Keith ordered his men to the wall, and rope ladders with iron hooks were thrown up towards Spalding who secured them and signalled to Keith to come on up. Within a few minutes, most of Keith's men were inside and taking cover under the early morning darkness. Spalding, accompanied by several of Keith's men, made his way towards the west wall to arrange entry for Douglas and Randolph.

'Who goes there?' shouted one of the sentries on duty, alerted by the sound of Spalding's footsteps. 'Nothing to concern you,' shouted Spalding, as he and his men slipped past and headed towards where Douglas and Randolph waited patiently. The unsuspecting sentry accepted the answer and replied 'Make less noise then. Some folk are trying to sleep.'

A lighted torch was thrown over the top of the wall and landed close to where Douglas and Randolph were positioned. Within seconds they were at the foot of the town wall, their rope ladders opened out and hurled overhead for Spalding to secure. Douglas was first over and immediately scanned all around for any guards on duty. Spalding, having secured the iron hooks, headed back towards Keith and his men. Douglas signalled the all clear, as Randolph and the rest of their men then climbed over and hid within the dark shadows of the town of Berwick.

'What do we do now?' asked one of Douglas's men. 'We wait till dawn,' answered Douglas. 'What then?' inquired Sir Laurence Abernethy, who, although a close companion tended not to be taken into confidence when the detail of such events was being discussed. 'Revenge, sir, revenge which is long overdue,' answered the serious looking Douglas, who felt an unexpected emotion at setting foot back in the town that had haunted him for so many years.

'Do you want us to kill them?' asked one of Douglas's younger followers, who was inexperienced and unsure of what to do next. Douglas looked at the young man, who looked slightly fearful at the uncertainty facing him. That frightened yet innocent look reminded him of how he felt many years ago, when his family was residing in the town during the brutal attack, on Good Friday of all days, by Longshanks's army. Everyone stared back at Douglas, waiting for his answer.

'I seek not to harm the innocent,' answered Douglas. 'However, those who resist with force will be met by force.' The young man smiled, nodded his head in approval, and along with the rest of the men acknowledged these words from their brave yet compassionate leader.

'You look uneasy, my Lord Douglas,' said Simon of Ledhouse, who was never far from Douglas's side and had become a very close and trusted friend over these past years. Douglas gestured for his men to come closer. 'Listen, all of you. We will be vastly outnumbered, even with the many men that Lord Randolph and Keith bring with them, it will still be a difficult task.'

'You know that you can rely on us,' whispered one of the many loyal and long-time followers of Douglas.

'Yes, I know that I can trust you. You have proved yourself many times over. I say this, our enemy, who have taken siege of this town of ours, are many. We will only be victorious if we fight as a united body of men with a clear purpose. We must stay together and have confidence that we can achieve yet another victory. For I say this, no battle that I have fought in the past means more to me that that which we are about to engage. I ask you once again to put your trust and faith in me.'

Douglas's men responded, not by sound but by individually approaching him and embracing the leader in whom they were most proud.

They continued to wait. For some this was the worst part, as impatience became unbearable. A lighted arrow suddenly flew over their heads, illuminated the last hour of darkness and indicating that the time had arrived. Douglas was first to rise to his feet. His garments were cold and damp from the early morning dew. Raising his voice, he called out 'Remember this, when we raise our swords against the evil that invades our nation, we have the almighty Lord God himself on our side. Do what is right by him and we will be victorious.' The men gave a final bow of their heads and then followed the gesture from Douglas to attack.

They did not run, nor did they call out the familiar and frightening battle cries. They merely proceeded to walk into the town. As they approached the first inhabited building, torches were lit and thrown onto the thatched roofs, which immediately burst into flames. Doors were kicked in, causing the residents to panic and run for their lives. A few brave residents raised their arms in counter-attack only to be confronted by Douglas's heavily armed men blocking their way and offering them the choice to fight or flee. For most, the latter was the preferred option.

Randolph and his men headed north through the town to meet up with Keith and his men. His men showed less discipline than those of Douglas. Randolph's men plundered and looted their way forward. Likewise, Sir Robert Keith and his men had started their attack and were adopting the same tactics as the residents fled in panic and fear for their lives.

Overcome with the hysteria that surrounded them, many of Keith's and Randolph's men lost control of their prime purpose and became, as others had in the past, the victims of the demon forces that overcome good men and drove them to commit evil acts of greed and cruelty upon this unfortunate town. Their pathways became one of bloodthirsty carnage and plunder as they ran amok amongst the townspeople.

Douglas and his men had a specific plan, and that was to allow all those who wished to escape to do so. They continued to awaken the sleeping inhabitants, who came running out in terror. They forced them out onto the main roadway that headed towards the south gates. The plan was working, as the road became busy with escaping men, women and children who chose to quickly flee rather than wait for the carnage that was about to unfold.

It didn't take long, only a few minutes, and then the first English guards arrived on the scene. Vastly outnumbering the early morning invaders, these men would not be running away so easily. Keith and Randolph's men were first to be confronted as the English soldiers counter-attacked. The war cries from both sides were roared at maximum volume accompanied by the predictable venom and aversion reserved for these occasions. 'Bastards! Scum! Savages! Your wives are whores! We're going to kill you all and then eat your weans!' The barrage of antagonising and intimidating chants of hatred and anger were exchanged between both sides as the intensity finally reached boiling point.

One of Keith's men was first to make contact as he bravely lunged in with his sword, only to be brutally slain as several trained English swords immediately cut into his unprotected body. The others paused, but only for a split second, and then it began as the men on both sides met one another in a battle to the death.

Randolph shouted to his men. 'Let's regain this last part of our Scotland, for our King and our nation,' he yelled as he drove hard into the wall of English troops. His deadly skill with a sword was evident as he penetrated many a body and severed many a limb. His men followed him and bravely fought against the much larger force.

Douglas and his men continued to encourage the inhabitants to leave via the south gates and then started to work their way towards Keith and Randolph. About an hour after it had begun, Douglas and his men finally joined up with Keith and Randolph.

'What kept you,' shouted the angry Randolph, who had regrets about taking on such a larger force.

Douglas, seeing his good friend and many loyal men engaged in battle against the much larger enemy, immediately replied 'Pull back, this is hopeless.'

'What?' shouted Randolph.

'Trust me!. You must trust me,' screamed Douglas at the top of his voice.

Immediately the fighting stopped as Randolph and Keith called their men to cease fighting and step back. Douglas raised his hand and held it above his head for several seconds.

Everyone looked at him. 'What the hell's going on?' asked Keith. 'Trust him, wait and see,' replied Randolph.

Douglas stood with his men, who appeared to be much fewer in number. 'Where are his men?' asked Keith. 'Be patient,' shouted Randolph.

The English troops looked on and questioned their own leaders on what to do next. 'Looks like they have bitten off more than they can chew,' replied one of the commanders. 'We can't let them just go,' shouted one of the English soldiers. 'Let's go after them,' shouted another.

Douglas, his hand still raised, turned round, and looked up to the rooftops of the surrounding buildings. He saw what he wanted and immediately dropped his hand to his side. The first flight of deadly arrows, carefully aimed with the precision of the many skilled hunters who followed Douglas easily hit their targets as many an English soldier dropped to the ground maimed or slain.

The cunning move by Douglas caused the English force to panic and break up as they ran for cover. Douglas shouted 'Attack!' as the three Scottish leaders led their men once more into the bloody fighting. 'They have broken up. We can take them in much smaller numbers,' shouted Douglas. Randolph smiled and shouted back. 'Well done, my friend.'

The English force did not run, but had broken up and made the task easier for the avenging Scots. The morning hours quickly passed by, as the savage fighting relentlessly continued with both sides suffering many casualties.

The majority of the inhabitants had escaped, and only those engaged in battle remained in the town. Slowly the fighting moved northwards towards the castle. Some, mainly those unskilled in warfare, had retreated inside the castle walls. With both sides heavily engaged in hand-to-hand combat, Douglas's archers had to abandon their strategy and join in the fighting on the ground.

Still outnumbered, and becoming weaker by the hour, Douglas and Randolph started to lose confidence that this day would be won. They had fought many a battle over the years, and whether it was the superior numbers, the long trip on foot during the night or simply age starting to creep up on them, they no longer anticipated victory. Defeat was the more likely outcome. Their men were exhausted and many of the survivors had received battle wounds. They sensed a loss of faith in victory as their leaders started to lose confidence.

The English soldiers, still greater in number, knew that, given time, this attacking force would tire and lose their aggression. 'Victory will be ours if we hold on,' shouted the English commander.

As they became weaker with each blow, both delivered and received, their energy all but gone, the Scots continued to slacken off. Many men were now falling down slain or maimed. 'We can't continue like this,' shouted Douglas. 'Agreed,' replied Randolph.

Suddenly a group of fresh arrivals, men whom Sir Robert Keith had called to arms, burst through from behind the Scots ranks and took the initiative in leading the fighting. These men, fresh and eager to give their support, quickly engaged in battle with the enemy forces. 'Thank God,' shouted Keith. 'Thank you,' shouted Randolph and Douglas who were glad of the additional support.

As the screams of men filled the air one man, a tall stranger who had just arrived with the recent reinforcements, forced his way through to the front line. While many others tiredly swung blindly with their now almost ineffective weapons, this stranger attacked with a deadly precision and skill that was not common. Energy was not wasted with ineffective blows or strikes; each cut and thrust of his deadly sword drew blood. The enemy recognised a skilled knight, someone who was a trained killing machine coming towards them.

'Who is that?' asked Douglas, as he looked over at the right hand side of this deadly warrior, whose face he was unable to see.

'I don't know,' answered Randolph. 'Never seen him before.'

As Douglas tried to see through the mass of bodies restricting his view, he caught a glance of this stranger blocking an attack and then plunging his sword into the side of one the enemy soldiers.

Douglas's face went white. He still could not see the face of this stranger. However, he did recognise that move; it was a technique that he had once tried to learn from a very close friend of years gone by, but was unable to master with the precision that he had just witnessed.

'I must go over to him!' shouted Douglas, as he diagonally cut across to be by the side of this mysterious swordsman. The tall stranger continued to push forward with enemy soldiers to his left and right as well as in front of him. Three English swords would plunge at him simultaneously; all three would fail as he twisted and turned and deflected each blow before delivering his own style of execution, first to the one on the left and then to the one in front. A split-second delay and the one on the right lunged his sword at the face of the stranger only to have the sword of Douglas penetrate his unguarded side.

He was still unable to see the stranger's face due to the metal head guard. 'Who are you, sir, what is your name?' asked Douglas.

'I am Keith of Galston. Sir Robert is my uncle,' came the reply 'Why do you ask?'

'You fight like someone that I once knew,' said Douglas. A short break in the fighting allowed both men a few seconds of discussion. 'That could be my other uncle, a very good friend of yours, Stuart Cuthbert,' said William, as he removed his head guard and exposed his young face to the startled Douglas.

Other than a smile from Douglas, no more was spoken between these two men. Side by side they fought. The synchronised use of their swords, the cunning feints and deadly precision as each blow and strike easily achieved its target and brought down yet another enemy soldier became the unspoken conversation. The deadly pairing of a Douglas and a Cuthbert had been resurrected as both skilled swordsmen inspired their men to victory.

The English garrison lost confidence as the Scots acquired their second wind and came at them with a deadly viciousness that was even greater than before. Randolph saw Douglas and the stranger in action and moved to join them. The sight of these three swordsmen cutting through the English ranks caused panic and terror to their victims and revived confidence and inspiration in their own men. Finally, the English started to run, a few at first, and then many followed all heading to the sanctuary and protection inside the great castle walls.

It had taken until mid-afternoon. It was one of the most difficult battles that Douglas and Randolph had fought. They had recovered Berwick; first they had taken the town; the castle would be next, and would take much longer. Douglas had looked to this day almost all of his life. Nothing else had mattered to him, and nothing that he could imagine would be more precious to him than achieving victory this day. Yet there was something else which he felt was far more precious. Seeing Sir William fight like his Uncle Stuart had done in the past, alongside his own sword, greatly pleased him. Douglas embraced the nephew of his dearly loved friend.

'Your uncle would have been most proud of you today,' declared Douglas.

'I thank you for such kind words, sir. I suspect that you two were quite a formidable force in your day,' replied a smiling Sir William.

'You make that sound like my day is almost over,' answered a laughing Douglas.

'Well, based on what I have just witnessed, I would say that there are a few years in you yet.'

'Oh, thank you very much,' said a smiling Douglas, as he put his arm on the shoulder of his knew friend. His mood abruptly changed. 'By the way what's the story regarding you and Sophia?' he said gruffly.

Sir William, slightly shocked and embarrassed at the sudden change in conversation, replied 'My lord, there is only one man in her heart, and that is you. She worships you.'

'Not bad then for someone who is ageing fast!' laughed Douglas.

'What do we do now?' asked Sir Laurence Abernethy. Randolph and Keith, on hearing this question, simultaneously turned and looked towards Douglas; he had taken the lead so far and appeared to have a clearer sense of purpose than the others. 'Wait,' answered Douglas.

'What do you mean wait?' asked Sir Robert Keith.

'Wait for what?' asked Randolph.

'Wait for them to surrender and come out,' replied Douglas.

'That could take days, weeks, months even,' said Keith.

'I have waited almost all of my life to see the day when this place was returned to its rightful people. A few more days will not cause us any pain,' said Douglas.

Douglas climbed up onto a cart that lay nearby. Even before speaking, he had their attention as all eyes looked to him for inspiration and direction. 'It may not be so apparent to you, but today we have returned this town to the ownership of our beloved nation. Those who take refuge in the castle will be dealt with in due course. But first there is one man who needs to join us and celebrate this great occasion.'

'What man?' asked Sir Robert Keith.

Douglas looked to him and smiled. 'The man who has led us to freedom, the man whose love for his nation and determination to remove our enemy is the reason many of you are here today.'

'Bruce!' shouted several men loudly. Douglas nodded.

'I will send men to tell him of our success and ask that he joins us,' declared Sir Robert Keith. Douglas again nodded his head.

'What do we do in the meantime?' asked Randolph, as they all looked to Douglas.

'You have risked your lives, you have given your support and loyalty, and it's now time to take your rewards, for you have earned them. This town is rich in provisions and many pleasures that we have been denied. The killing is over; let no more blood be shed, let no harm come to those who remain here. I invite you all to take your share of the pleasures and comforts you have earned.' The men cheered and began to pick their rewards from the rich town.

Standing alone now, Douglas slowly dropped his sword at his feet and then, with his arms hanging loosely by his side, raised his head to the heavens. Filling his lungs with the smell of the fresh Berwick sea air, he savoured this moment. It had been a long night and a difficult morning, but even more it had been a long time since that night many years ago when as a child he was forced to leave his own family. He had achieved what had been his lifelong ambition. He thought of his father. 'What would he say if he could see this day?' he asked himself, as tears filled his eyes.

The sudden exhaustion which sometimes strikes when one finally achieves a demanding objective abruptly took hold of him and he collapsed to the ground. He lay there, helpless and unconscious as the unexpected fatigue took hold and forced a self-protective shutting down of his exhausted mind and body.

Others were too busy occupying themselves with the spoils of war. However, one man was not far away and came to the aid of Douglas. Clutching Douglas in his arms, he sensed what was happening.

'Is he all right?' asked Simon of Ledhouse, who was also close by 'He will be in a moment' was the reply 'What's wrong with him?' asked Simon. 'Bloody exhausted,' was the answer.

It took several minutes before Douglas's body slowly started to recover. A sudden kick of his legs and then a twitch from his arms were the first signs that he was returning to consciousness. His head moved slightly, and his eyes opened, the whites showing as the precious senses fought to regain their control and composure. His breathing returned to normal as he finally looked up at the face of the kind man who held him in his arms.

'Are you all right, sir?' asked Sir William Keith, as he stared into the face of the man to whom his Uncle Stuart had given a lifetime of support. Confused and puzzled at what had happened Douglas looked up. 'Aye,' he answered as he breathed deeply. 'Take your time, sir,' whispered Sir William, as he continued to hold and protect his uncle's friend. 'What happened?' asked Douglas. 'Sir, you fainted,' answered Sir William. 'Sir, if I may be allowed to say, you are exhausted and need to rest, not just for a few minutes but for several days.'

Over the next week, the siege of the castle continued without the assistance of the exhausted Douglas. The challenge was a test of patience and belief in the words of Douglas, as both sides waited. A reversal of fortunes had taken place. The townsfolk were now free and enjoying the rich resources that surrounded them while the castle inhabitants huddled in fear as the pains of hunger and thirst started to attack their bodies.

As each day passed, many of the townspeople, who had fled in terror of their lives, started to return. Large numbers of them had been born into these cruel and brutal years of enemy occupation. This was their home; they knew of nowhere else, they knew of no other life. Like Douglas, many of the older inhabitants had prayed for this day, and they rejoiced in their liberation. They remembered the horrors of that Good Friday twenty-three years ago when Longshanks put their town to the sword. They sang and danced in the pleasure of having their town and homes given back to them. Special celebration was reserved for the return of their freedom, a freedom that was now enjoyed in a united and truly free Scotland.

The waiting continued into the following week. Eventually, with provisions running low and no sign of any help from King Edward II, the garrison announced their intention to surrender. Randolph discussed the terms and agreed to let them return to their own lands. 'It's just as he said,' declared Sir Laurence Abernethy. 'What do you mean?' asked Randolph. 'Douglas, he said all that we would need to do was wait, and he was right,' replied Abernethy.

As the English soldiers started to leave the town, Douglas rose from the bed that he had slept in constantly over the last week. 'Sir, it's too early, you are not ready,' advised Sir William

Keith. 'Too early or not, this is one sight that I must witness,' answered Douglas, as he splashed a handful of water over his face and then walked out to observe the departing garrison coming towards him. Their heads were bowed in shame. Defeated and having been conquered by a much smaller force, the prospect of the humiliating return to their own land was not being welcomed.

Douglas, unarmed and on his own, walked out in front of the departing English troops. They looked at him; a few recognised him as his name was fearfully uttered amongst their ranks. 'That's him, that's the Black Douglas,' they whispered. He stood in their way, as they stopped and stared. 'By the grace of God alone your lives have been spared,' shouted Douglas. Those at the front began shaking. How one man could stand in front of so many and cause so much fear they could not understand, but they were still terrified of his reputation. They had heard of his many victorious battles against the best that England could offer, they had heard countless tales of terror, and knew that he would do as he said.

'I say this to you,' continued Douglas, 'if any of you ever return to these lands which are not yours, then God will not be so generous to you, and I will enforce his revenge upon you. Go home and tell your King what I have said.'

Many of Douglas's men stood by, and watched and listened in amazement as their leader injected yet more fear into the minds of their defeated enemy. Sir William of Galston, enjoying this rare occasion, shouted 'And tell your King Edward that the Black Douglas is coming to get him.' The defeated troops began to move on and picked up speed as they desperately rushed towards the border.

Douglas walked over to Sir William. 'Tell Edward that the Black Douglas is coming to get him. Aye, maybe after a wee rest,' laughed the smiling Douglas, as Sir William grinned back at him.

A crowd of local people started to follow and gather around Douglas. They had heard of his reputation, they had heard the many tales; some exaggerated, but mostly true. They looked at him as if he were a godly mythical figure who was born to avenge them. His enemies feared him more than any other; these people now loved him more than any other. Some were still unsure and afraid as the young children scattered in his path. 'He's coming to get us, the Black Douglas is here,' they shouted as they ran bare-footed in front of him.

One young boy, not looking in front of him and holding the tiny hand of his little sister, stumbled in front of Douglas. Both children fell to the ground at the feet of the fearsome warrior. His bare dirty knee bleeding from the cut from the stony ground, the young boy knelt over his sister and offered her protection. Douglas stopped and looked, as other children shouted in fear 'He's going to get those two.' Douglas hesitated when he heard these calls, and then bent down and picked up a child in each arm. Their faces were paralysed with terror as they both stared at him with wide eyes.

Clutching each of them, he raised them up to face him. 'Are you going to kill us?' asked the frail looking little girl. Douglas smiled. 'Are you both good children and do you do as you mother tells you?' he asked. Still paralysed with fear they both nodded their innocent dirty little faces in reply. Douglas kissed both of them on their foreheads before placing them back on the ground. Wiping the young boy's bleeding knee, Douglas then handed a silver coin to each of them. 'This is for you, for being good.'

The children's expression changed to delight as they ran clutching their new found wealth. A few yards further on they were joined by other children. They all turned back to look at him, smiled, and then loudly called out 'Black Douglas is going to get us; Black Douglas is going to get us.' Douglas smiled and shook his head in disbelief as those around him burst into loud laughter.

It was around noon of the following day when the peaceful silence was broken by the sound of a horn. It was a sound that many recognised, announcing the arrival of Bruce. As his vast army of followers entered into the town, every man woman and child came out to welcome their beloved King of all Scotland. Suddenly they felt important; their town had been liberated, the enemy had left, and now they were privileged with a visit from their own true King. They applauded, they cheered, they danced, and they wept tears of joy and happiness as they savoured these precious moments.

Lord Randolph and Sir Robert Keith finally greeted Bruce and his accompanying nobles. 'Sire, I give you Berwick,' declared Keith.

'You have done well, sirs, I am indebted to you for your bravery and courage,' answered Bruce, as he looked at those present.

'You have performed magnificently,' called out Sir Walter Stewart who stood slightly behind Bruce.

'Sire, please join us, we have food and good wine aplenty,' said Sir Robert Keith.

'So how was the battle? Did your man Spalding earn his money?' asked Bruce as they headed towards the great hall, which was prepared with a feast for this special occasion.

'It was hard fought and many have perished; they were all brave men,' answered Randolph, as Bruce continued to look around and search for a special face amongst the crowd of knights and nobles.

'Spalding was true to his word. He has still to be paid,' said Keith as he hinted that payment should be made soon.

Bruce was first to sit down; the others followed as they all took their place to feast in the company of their King. They waited for Bruce to begin to eat first. He hesitated, as he scanned the large hall for the face that he was looking for. Uneasiness developed as the hesitation continued.

'Sire, is anything wrong?' asked Sir Robert Keith.

'No!' came the abrupt reply from Bruce, as he continued to stare at each face in front of him.

Finally, the tension was broken when Sir William Keith of Galston asked to speak. 'Sire, if I may, without causing offence, inform you that the Good Sir James of Douglas is at this moment resting from exhaustion. He is well and should be back to good health in a few days time.'

There was a silence. 'Who was this impertinent young knight, who dare speak directly to our King,' many of the elderly nobles thought to themselves.

'Sir, what is your name?' asked Bruce.

'Sire, he is one of my kin, William of Galston,' replied Sir Robert Keith. Bruce rose to his feet and looked directly at Sir William. 'Young man, you possess awareness and perception that no other in this room appears to have, you have read my thoughts well, and I thank you for what you have just told me. Now, let us eat.'

The following day Bruce sat in conference with his nobles. 'Sire, it's Douglas, he has come to meet with you,' the King's servant informed him. Bruce immediately rose to his feet and asked the others to leave.

Douglas, still tired and looking as weary as he felt, entered and was greeted with a loving and welcoming embrace from his dear King. 'My dear Sir James, I am glad that you are well. I was concerned for your health. How are you now?'

'Sire, I am fine and glad that you have come here to reclaim that which is yours,' replied Douglas.

'I have heard the many stories of your bravery and courage in the recovery of this town, and yet you hide in the background and avoid the recognition that you have justly earned,' declared Bruce.

Douglas sat down. 'Sire, there are many good men, some of whom have perished, who have proved their loyalty to both you and our good country. It is they who deserve the recognition not me.'

Bruce smiled in admiration at these humble words of his lifelong friend who always put others first. 'James, I have a request of you, or perhaps better still an offer that I would like you to consider,' declared Bruce.

'Sire, I will do what ever you ask of me,' replied Douglas.

'James, the last Scotsman to have commanded this town many years ago was your own father. Today I would be delighted to announce that a Douglas was restored as commander of Berwick.'

Douglas sat silent and stunned; he did not expect this offer of the command of such a prestigious place. 'Sire, what you offer, humbles me and would have truly pleased my father. Since I was of age, I have devoted my life to the hope that this day would arrive. I am truly appreciative of what you offer me. However, I am not one to sit in one place for too long. If it is your wish I will accept your offer.'

'Tell me then, what would be your wish?' asked Bruce.

Douglas responded without hesitation. 'Sire, let me continue as I have done before. I cannot change my life now; it's all that I know.'

Bruce pondered over the reply from Douglas. 'What exactly do you have in mind?' asked Bruce.

'Sire, I will defend and protect Berwick, but not from within its own walls. Edward's men will be back, that I know for sure. They are greater in number than us. If all that we do is stay here and defend the town then it will only be a matter of time before it is taken from us again. I request your permission to invade the northern English counties. If I can push them further south I will divert their armies and resources to defending their own nation rather than attacking ours.'

Bruce grinned at his most loyal lieutenant. 'You my dear James are a very remarkable man; you never fail to impress me with your unselfish determination and devoted loyalty. I will offer Berwick to Walter Stewart, and I am most grateful of the offer which you now present to me.'

'I will not fail you, Sire,' declared Douglas.

'My dear James, you will never fail me,' answered the smiling Bruce. 'Take Randolph with you, for he is much like you.'

'Thank you Sire, a very good choice if I may say,' said Douglas.

'There is one other who may be worthwhile asking to join you,' said Bruce.

'Who would that be?' asked Douglas.

'A young knight, and someone who cares very deeply for you,' replied Bruce.

'Do you have his name, Sire?' asked Douglas.

'I believe his name to be William of Galston,' answered Bruce.

Douglas chuckled to himself, shook his head, and then replied 'Another good choice, Sire.'

25

THE MYTON CAMPAIGN

'WHERE ARE WE GOING?' the men asked. The answer from Douglas and Randolph was the same as before. 'To protect our people and safeguard our nation.' A continuous string of questions and answers were exchanged, as the two leaders, with an army of fifteen thousand men, much larger than what they were normally accustomed to leading, slipped over the English border one dark cold night.

Back at Berwick, Bruce and his nobles continued to bring in additional men to strengthen the castle garrison and prepare for the expected revenge of Edward II's army. Unlike previous occupations, where castle walls were pulled down, the walls of Berwick were strengthened in many areas. Additional resources, committed to the protection of this town, continued to arrive each day to the delight of the local people.

'Sire, John Crab, the Fleming whom you requested, has arrived,' announced one of Bruce's servants. A stranger was brought before Bruce. 'Thank you, sir, for responding to my request so promptly,' declared Bruce as John Crab approached him.

'Sire, why do you request me? What do you want of me?' asked Crab.

'I have good information that you are an expert of a certain kind, is that not correct?' asked Bruce.

'And what kind of expert did you have in mind?' asked Crab.

Bruce invited his guest to sit down and summoned for refreshments to be brought.

'Sir, I have a great need for your skills in building weapons of warfare. I have knowledge that you are a master craftsman in such matters.'

Crab, not surprised by the request, immediately answered 'Sire, I would be delighted to present my skills to be at your disposal.'

'I thank you, sir, you will be well rewarded,' replied Bruce.

'Sire, I need to know one thing before I can help.'

Bruce, suspecting the worse, awaited the next comment.

'Sire, would you be requiring weapons of defence or attack?' asked Crab. Smiling with relief, Bruce answered 'My purpose is to defend this castle, which the English King and his army will surely try to retake. Can you build for me the weapons that will aid our defence?' Crab bowed his head and replied that he would be honoured.

'Let me know what you need in the way of men and materials. All involved, including yourself will be well rewarded,' repeated Bruce.

As Douglas and Randolph crossed the border, they split up and briefed their men with the clear instructions that they were long waiting to hear. 'Our task is simple,' said Douglas. 'Our prime aim is to cause distraction and force Edward to return south and remain there. One by one, each village we come to, we will raid, pillage, and burn.'

'How will this cause King Edward to be distracted?' asked Sir William of Galston, who had agreed to join Douglas's party of raiders. Douglas called those closest to him to hear what he had to say. 'There is nothing surer; when he hears that Berwick has been taken from under his nose, he will seek his revenge and attempt to recover what he believes is his. His wealthy nobles in the south, whose patience is about to snap, have had enough of their incompetent King. When he hears that we are heading south and ransacking everything in our way he will be forced by his own nobles to retreat to protect his own nation or they will simply replace him.'

As dawn broke the first of yet more revengeful raids on the northern English counties began. Small villages were singled out and chosen as the starting point. As the torches were thrown onto the thatched rooftops, the pillars of dense smoke signalled the start of the campaign. The locals grabbed hold of their loved ones and fled in panic as they ran for their lives from the plundering Scots.

Cattle and livestock were seized first; stores of grain along with precious provisions were then looted and taken by the dawn raiders. Like a colony of giant ants, they formed a steady stream of carriers heading back home with their plunder as others forged their way onwards and continued the attack on other unsuspecting villages.

The relentless waves of surprise attacks continued to spread across Northumberland and penetrated deep into areas of northern England previously untouched during these times of war. Douglas and Randolph drove their men with a harshness and determination that many were unaccustomed to. Messengers were constantly arriving and departing. Word had arrived that Edward II and the Earl of Lancaster were leading a large army towards Berwick, intent on achieving its recovery.

Stopping at Boroughbridge after yet another successful raid, discussion on the safety of Berwick was uppermost in many minds. Randolph and his men had rejoined Douglas's party. Both leaders were surrounded by their closest of companions. 'Do we go back and protect our King and the town of Berwick?' asked Simon of Ledhouse. 'No!' answered Douglas. 'We will force Edward to come after us.'

'Exactly how do you plan to do that?' asked Sir William of Galston, who although highly skilled in the use of a sword, was naive in many matters concerning the strategy of warfare.

'We will attack York!' answered Douglas to the sound of silence and bemused looks from all.

'That's bloody daft!' shouted one of Randolph's men, who then apologised for the sudden discourteous interruption. Randolph gave his man a look of scorn, and then said 'There is a certain prize awaiting the one who takes York.'

'And what may that prize be?' asked Douglas.

'The prize that awaits our capture is none other than Queen Isabella, wife of Edward. She currently resides at York.'

'Lord Randolph, you are well informed, sir. However, based on what I hear of Edward's personal preferences, his good Lady Queen Isabella may not be such a prize. Her safety will, however, be a concern to many of the most senior English nobles and her capture would be of great value to us,' replied Douglas.

Later that day, as dusk arrived, the invading Scots took a few hours of precious rest before yet another night raid. A few were moving around and preparing themselves prior to settling down. No one noticed the shadow disappearing into the forest and heading south. It was common for individuals to be seen coming and going. All were considered as good loyal men, for they had after all proved themselves many times over. However, there was someone who had only recently joined up with Randolph's men.

A few days later Douglas and Randolph had set up camp near the town of Myton situated almost twelve miles north of York. It was around midday, and the Scots had just finished eating a well-earned meal. No one noticed or sensed the many eyes that were watching from a short distance away. The success of the Scots had bred complacency as their sentries failed in their duties.

Several hundred yards away, an unusual army had slowly and quietly sneaked up within striking distance of the invading Scots.

'Your Excellency, we are not fighting men, is this wise?' asked the Bishop of Ely as he addressed Archbishop William de Meltoun.

'We fight for God and the safety of our good Lady Isabella,' replied Meltoun, as he turned to address the many men he had urgently gathered to repel the barbarous Scots. They were not experienced fighting men, but priests, laymen, and many other God fearing religious men who had no choice but to defend themselves and the people of their parish.

Meltoun turned to the solitary figure who had guided him here. 'Spalding, I would advise that you now depart. Should they find out that you have betrayed them, God only knows what will become of you.' Taking this good advice, Spalding, his pouch full with the payment for the information he had given them, left their company and disappeared into the forest.

'Shall we announce our attack?' asked Bishop Ely.

'And give away the element of surprise! No, we will attack without warning,' answered Meltoun, as he signalled to his army. The first ones started to move, a slow trot at first and then, gathering speed, they charged.

The Scottish lookouts heard the sound of many footsteps rushing towards them. A few managed to give the signal before the attacking clergy cut them down. Their weapons never far from reach, the Scots grabbed their swords and spears and immediately presented their now customary schiltron of deadly pointed blades at the oncoming attackers.

Douglas and Randolph were immediately alerted. 'What's happening?' shouted Randolph. 'We're being attacked by an army of priests,' replied Sir William of Galston.

Douglas was the first to mount his panic-stricken horse. Some, who did not know him or did not believe the many tales of bravery, shouted out 'Yet another leader abandons us in our hour of need!' Douglas pulled on his reins, turned his beast towards the attackers, and led the counter-charge.

The sight of Douglas wearing his coat of colours, holding his sword high above his head and singly charging at the oncoming attackers inspired his men to do likewise. The secret weapon that had won them many previous battles was brought to good use as they screamed and shouted at their enemy. The ear-splitting battle cries were called out as the Scots charged. The army of clergy, unaccustomed to such venom and vocal hostility, immediately lost their confidence and panicked by turning and running away.

The pursuing Scots showed no mercy for the men and their followers of the church; after all, these same men belonged to the very clergy who had forced the excommunication of their nation. One by one they were slain. Rank, age or holy status had no bearing as the slaughter continued. Many who had escaped the lethal Scottish weapons perished as they tried to escape across the deep waters of the Swale River. Those who survived that day did so by the grace of God and by the arrival of the hours of darkness.

Douglas and Randolph summoned their closest companions. Douglas spoke. 'We have won a victory, but not one that we should be too proud to tell. We have been betrayed, for they knew of our whereabouts and lay in wait. We will send riders to Berwick and ensure that King Edward hears of this day.'

'What of tomorrow? What do you plan?' asked Sir Laurence Abernethy.

'We will continue as we have done over these last few weeks. We will continue to raid their towns and villages,' answered Douglas.

'When does it stop?' asked William of Galston.

'Only the son of Longshanks can answer that question,' replied Douglas.

Back at Berwick the siege was still in place as King Edward failed to recognise that success was not to be his. His determination to retake this town was losing him many followers as each day passed without success. A close loyal noble approached Edward with the news from Myton. 'How many did you say?' asked Edward. 'Sire, they say about four thousand were slain; many priests and men of the church formed the main body. They even killed the mayor of the town. They say that about another thousand drowned as they tried to escape across the Swale. Many have been taken prisoner for ransom,' replied the noble.

'We must send some men to their aid, at once I say,' said Edward.

'Sire, we cannot aid men who are dead,' said one of the other nobles.

The Earl of Lancaster spoke. 'Sire, my advice would be that we leave here and go protect our own lands. The Scots know that as long as we are occupied trying to retake this worthless castle then they are free to raid and plunder our beloved England. Our priority is to protect our own lands and our own people.'

King Edward stood motionless and realised that he had lost yet another battle against these savage Scots, who had once again caused him to feel shame. 'Lancaster, your words are wise and well spoken, we will do as you have advised. We can return here some other time and continue with this frustrating task,' declared the defeated English King.

A few days later Douglas received word from his network of contacts spread across the Scottish borders that Edward's army was heading his way. 'Time for us to go home,' shouted Douglas. 'Great!' came the reply from his men. 'Don't be getting too comfortable. We may be forced to come back sooner than expected,' he added jokingly.

Over the next few days they headed for home by means of westerly routes that passed by the northern regions of Carlisle and approached the borders of Dumfries and Galloway.

On arriving at York, Edward was outraged that the Scots had outwitted him once more and that they had been able to return home without being engaged by his forces. Tired and further disheartened he disbanded his army and allowed them to return to their homes.

On arrival home, Douglas and Randolph informed their King of their achievements and briefed him on the morale and status of their enemy. Bruce greeted their return with a lavish feast for them and their men. They ate and drunk their fill, enjoying the unaccustomed luxury and freedom, for they had not experienced many days like this in their lives. They were free men; their nation had been cleansed from invading armies. All towns and castles were back under Scottish ownership. England was demoralised and dejected under the poor leadership of Edward II.

Sitting in the great hall, they started to talk. 'What now?' asked Walter Stewart, who had also achieved great success as commander of Berwick during the many weeks of hostile siege. They all looked at Bruce and allowed him the first reply.

'We will enjoy this rest and be grateful for what God has given us.'

'Aye, we are in need of a long rest,' declared Sir Thomas Randolph.

'We need to discuss land ownership, the question of who gets what,' said Sir Robert Keith, as other nobles nodded in approval, desperate to get their hands on the many disputed estates and acres of land now recovered.

'Sire, when do you intend that we discuss these important matters?' asked Sir William Soules, a noble who was developing a reputation for the devious tactics he employed to enrich his own purse.

Bruce drank slowly from his cup, his eyes peering over it at the nobles who appeared to be more interested in what wealth they might be able to acquire. Douglas, who had also been enjoying the feast, looked up. He caught the eye of Bruce and asked to be allowed to speak. 'My Lord Douglas, what do you have to say about such matters?' said the King.

Douglas looked around the table. There were many here that he did not trust, but they were present and had to be considered. 'The question of land ownership is important to every man here, including myself, for I have lost much and gained very little. But if we sit here today and can only think and talk of what lands we may personally acquire then I say that we are misguided,' replied Douglas.

Above the disapproving murmuring of those present, Bruce spoke to Douglas. 'What guidance would you offer this council?'

Douglas glanced at Randolph, the only other man apart from Bruce that he truly trusted. 'I say that we continue to attack the northern English counties.'

'Rubbish,' 'For what purpose?' 'They are already beaten, do we need to do it again?' came the responses from various nobles.

Douglas stood up and gave them a look that clearly said 'Cross my path at your own peril.' Some of those present feared him more than any other man, and their reasons were known only to themselves. However, he could sense treachery as easily as he could sense the whereabouts of his enemies. They sat quietly and waited for him to speak.

'Edwards's army is not defeated, it merely lacks effective leadership' declared Douglas. 'Yes, we have won a few battles, but we have not won the war. They will come back, that I say for sure.

''Why do you wish to attack them again?' asked Bruce, as the others sat motionless and stared at him.

'We have the good fortune of having the best ever opportunity on our side. There is a deadly plague that sweeps their lands in the south, killing their cattle and livestock. Their rivers are full of dead fish that are diseased and decaying. The same species of wildfowl that we are fortunate to feed upon here today are lying dead in the southern counties from the same plague,' declared Douglas, as he glanced at Randolph. 'If we attack now, I don't expect them to surrender, but we could force a truce which if negotiated by our King Robert could lead to many years of peace between our nations.' Douglas sat down and continued to eat without making any further eye contact.

Bruce sat back in his chair and stared at Douglas. 'How many times has that man surprised and impressed me?' he thought to himself. He then called out 'My lords, enjoy your feast today.'

He turned to Douglas. 'My dear James, you have my full support. Let me know what you need.' Douglas looked up and smiled at Bruce, a quick glance across at Randolph and a nod of his head was all that was needed to indicate what he wanted.

They waited until the approach of November. The crops had been collected and stored for the oncoming winter. Douglas and Randolph recommenced their relentless raids on the northern English counties and led their men on many more attacks on their unsuspecting enemy neighbours. The precious crops were seized, the healthy cattle and livestock taken, houses and barns, many of which were recently rebuilt, were destroyed and burned to the ground. At the same time, the plague that was attacking the south began to head north. As Douglas and Randolph retreated, they set the fields behind them on fire and prevented the deadly plague from spreading north.

As the month of December ended, the most senior nobles of Edward II requested a meeting of council. He was presented with an ultimatum. A meeting between the senior ambassadors to both kings was then arranged. On the 1st January 1320 a truce between the two nations was finally agreed. It would last for two years. The relentless efforts of many, none more so than the Good Sir James Douglas, had finally achieved freedom and peace for Scotland.

For many the much long overdue need for rest from constant warfare was not fully appreciated until the next few months of normal life had been experienced. They lived as their God expected neighbouring nations should live. However, there was one battle that had not been won, a battle fought not with swords and spears and large armies, but a battle of wits, a battle where the minds and souls of good men would be stretched to their limits. Bruce called his nobles to engage in such a battle.

26

THE DECLARATION

'WHY HAS OUR KING called us here?' asked a concerned Lord James Douglas, as he quietly entered through the main archway of the grounds of the ancient holy abbey of Arbroath. Thomas Randolph, his good friend and now regular companion, guided his horse as he walked by his side. 'I know as much as you, and that is not very much,' replied Randolph.

'Who else do you think will be called here today?' asked Randolph.

'I was going to say only us two, but look over at those men attending to the horses, look at their colours. Looks like there are many others, nobles, I presume, whom he has called,' replied Douglas.

'As they entered the cloister and joined the company of the earlier arrivals, many old friendships and acquaintances were being renewed as the good noble friends, and some former enemies, who had become separated during these war torn years finally came together again.

'It would appear that everyone who has been close to our King has come here for this meeting,' said Randolph. 'But why, I wonder?'

Douglas paid no attention, and appeared to be looking for someone particularly special as he walked amongst the many nobles who acknowledged him with a nod and a smile and then whispered to each other as he gently brushed past. 'How can one man, such as he, cause the English so much fear and terror?' said some. He ignored the voices, some in praise, some sleekit, that muttered behind as he moved on in search of someone from his past.

'My Lord Douglas, I have been asked to fetch you,' declared the elderly monk who pushed through the crowd to get to Douglas. 'Who wants to see me?' asked Douglas. 'A friend I believe,' answered the monk in a soft whisper. Douglas looked over to Randolph who glanced back. 'Only you, my lord, if you please,' said the monk as he led the way into the warming house where the heat from the constantly burning fire would remove the many pains and discomforts caused by the bitter cold winds that savaged the east coast.

The damp, musty smelling room was in partial darkness, apart from the gentle glow of the flickering flames that reflected off the dark stone ceiling. A tall figure stood in front of the open fire, warming his outstretched hands and meditating as he stared into the mesmerising dancing flames.

The sound of Douglas's footsteps, clattering along the stone floor, announced his dramatic arrival. Without saying a single word, the elderly monk pointed inside, bowed his head and then retreated. Douglas scrutinised the back of the tall figure whose head was bowed down and staring into the burning log fire. The flickering shadows, like demons from hell, continued to dance.

'Why don't you join me for a heat,' called the tall figure, his powerful voice suddenly overcoming the emptiness of the large room as he continued to stare down at the fire.

Douglas walked forward, slowly and deliberately, finally standing beside the dark figure and looking into the fire;

he stretched out his hands and enjoyed the pleasure of the comforting warmth. 'It's been a long time since we both enjoyed something together,' said the tall figure, continuing to stare down at the fire.

'Yes, it certainly has,' replied Douglas. 'How are you my good friend?'

'I am fine,' replied Bishop Lamberton. 'And you?'

'I am as well as can be expected,' answered Douglas.

'What of your mother, the good Lady Eleanor, and your two brothers?'

'They are in good health, for the moment anyway,' answered Douglas, as he gave this question deep thought.

'You are very fortunate in having such a loving family. Many have been less fortunate and have lost their loved ones during these tragic times,' declared Lamberton.

'I too have lost good friends; Fullerton and Cuthbert, they were good loyal men to my father, to my family and to me also,' replied Douglas, with a sincere regret and continued grief at the loss of those dedicated men.

'I will pray for them,' replied Lamberton, as Douglas bowed his head in thanks.

A short time later, the quiet meeting between these two long time friends was interrupted. 'Your Excellency, my lord, King Robert requires your attendance,' the monk called out from the doorway. 'Why are we here? Why has he called us? What's going on?' asked Douglas. 'Impatient as ever! Have you not learned anything?' asked a laughing Lamberton. 'No,' answered Douglas, with a cheeky childish look as he grinned at his former guardian for whom he had the greatest admiration and respect.

They gathered in the abbey chapter house, the place normally reserved for business discussion. The hum caused by the vast number of discrete conversations filled the air. Many were seated; some stood as space was restricted. King Robert Bruce finally entered, and they all rose to their feet. 'God save our King!' they called out and bowed their heads as he walked to his reserved and decorated seat.

409

Along with the others, Bruce sat down; Lamberton sat by his left side. It took a few moments before total silence was achieved. Finally Bruce spoke. 'My lords, good nobles, your Excellency, and clergy, thank you for coming here today. I have called you together in the past to raise arms with me and fight in battle, you have done so, and with your loyal support we have been victorious. We have achieved much, but the unity of our nation is the one achievement that we should be immensely proud of, this I truly believe.' 'Here, here,' came the reply from those present, as they clapped and stamped in approval.

'We have won the fight on the battlefield; we must now win a much greater fight, one that does not involve the spilling of blood. As a nation, we have put our faith in the grace of God whom we worship and love. However, we are in the unfortunate situation where the leader of our church, the very Holy Father Pope John XXII, is not in our favour, for I, and many of you here, have caused him to reject us from the bosom of his church.'

Bishop Lamberton stood up and gestured to speak. 'Your Excellency,' acknowledged Bruce.

'Sire, what exactly do you ask of those present here today?'

Bruce paused before answering. He looked at those around him; they stared back at him, the puzzled look on their faces indicating to him that there was something missing. There was a prolonged silence before Bruce finally called out 'I would like to give you something, something more important than a victory over a larger enemy nation, something even more significant than having a good King to lead you. I would like to give you something that would truly belong to you, something that would give you pride in who you are and what you stand for.' He paused again, as he searched for the right words to express what he was seeking to tell them.

The suspense was finally broken when he declared 'To those here today, I ask for your thoughts. Who we are? What was our past? What is our present, and what will be our future?

What is our purpose? What is it that makes us proud of our good nation? Who is our true leader: Is it me? Is it you? Is it the Holy Father? Is it God himself? We say we are Scots, but who are we? These questions I ask you to seriously consider. The consensus of your answers will be documented, and once sealed by you will then be presented to our Holy Father requesting that he give recognition to this nation of Scotland.'

No one spoke; they all looked at each other. 'What did he mean by all those questions? Where is this leading?' they started to murmur amongst themselves.

Roger Mowbray was first to call out. 'We are a nation of murderers.' The others looked at him; some shook their heads in disagreement.

'We are being punished for the shameful sins of our own King,' declared William Soules.

'Rubbish man,' came the immediate reply from one of the others.

'We would be better making peace with our enemies and uniting with them as one nation,' David, Lord of Brechin, called out.

'Aye, that will be right,' shouted an angry sarcastic voice.

'We will always live in the shadow of the English,' declared Patrick Graham.

'You mean as their slaves,' replied Thomas Randolph to shouts of agreement.

The others looked suspiciously upon the clique who had uttered these words of betrayal against their nation. Those with outspoken views sat grouped together; they suddenly felt trapped and isolated. 'Was it by accident, or did they deliberately conspire to share the same beliefs of disloyalty?' was the common concern from those with opposing views.

Finally, Walter Stewart of Scotland raised his hand to speak. 'We are free men who belong to a free nation.' Immediate applause was heard.

'Our great and noble forefathers came from the corners of the earth,' shouted the earl of Lennox.

'Over one hundred kings of our own blood have reigned over us,' shouted Gilbert Hay, Constable of Scotland.

'Aye, and many a hundred more will follow,' shouted Donald Campbell.

Bruce smiled; these were the words that he was looking for. He looked towards Lamberton. Not wanting to ask him out loud, he smiled for him to speak. The loyal Bishop responded. 'No man is above God, as a nation we are answerable to God first and all else second.' The uncontrolled shouts of support suddenly calmed down. Others began to express their views without the barrage from the hecklers.

'Our King is the principal servant of our nation,' declared Robert Keith, Marischal of Scotland.

'We fight for glory and the riches of success,' declared Eustace Maxwell to a silent response.

Bruce looked around at all the faces that were staring in his direction. There was one man who had not spoken. He had not even commented on what was previously said. Bruce caught his eye; the dark eyes looked back in reply. Douglas knew he was being asked to speak.

'We fight for one thing. It is a precious thing, more precious than any wealth or riches. It is called freedom. For as long as I am alive, I will never yield to English domination,' declared Douglas, his voice low but determined. Those around him applauded his choice of words and the sentiment behind them.

Bruce turned to his scribes, led by Abbot Bernard Linton. They signalled that they had captured what had been said and that they would retreat to complete the finished document. 'We will meet again tomorrow,' said Bruce, concluding the meeting.

For the remainder of the day and well into the late hours of darkness, Bruce, along with Lamberton, worked with Linton on composing the final document. Others were called one by one to expand on their words of faith, hope and inspiration. It was late afternoon of the following day when they reassembled.

The knights, nobles and clergy were seated as before. Bruce joined them. They talked amongst themselves. 'Is this all necessary?' uttered one voice. 'Will it make any difference?' asked another. 'Probably not,' came the reply, from one of the elder nobles. Bruce sat silent and listened. 'Faith, that's what's been missing, faith in ourselves as a nation,' he thought to himself. The others continued to express discomfort and frustration at being here. The long wait continued. 'This is a waste of time, we could be doing something more useful,' whispered William Soules to those close to him.

The silence was finally broken when Abbot Linton, led by two monks carrying candles, entered. Instinctively all rose to their feet, not knowing why, but feeling that what was happening had suddenly taken on a serious purpose. Linton, carrying a large scroll, gestured for them to be seated. Bruce acknowledged his arrival and requested that he continue.

Standing in front of them, Linton opened the embellished document upon which all eyes were focused. In his usual quiet, well-spoken, articulate voice he called out 'Sire, my lords, your Excellency, I will read out this letter, which, subject to your approval, will be sent to the very Holy Father.' Some bowed their heads, as if to prepare for prayer, others stared at Linton.

'*To our Lord and Very Holy Father in Christ, Lord John, the Supreme Pontiff, by God's Providence, of the Most Holy Roman and Catholic Church, his humble and devoted sons ...*' Linton read out the opening words, and then proceeded to call out the names of those present. As each name was called, the individuals responded with a deliberate bow of the head.

Linton continued. '*Among other noble nations our own, the Scottish, grows famous for many men of wide renown.*' They sat mesmerised as Linton continued his reading. Taken from the writings of the ancient books, he described the source and history of the Scots nation, their journey from Scythia by the Tyrrhenian Sea, the wars against the barbarians, the repelled invasions by the Norwegians, Danes, and English. '*In this kingdom have reigned a hundred and thirteen kings of our*

413

own royal blood, and no foreign man has been among them. Our Lord Jesus Christ, who is King of Kings, called us among the first to his most firm faith, after his passion and resurrection, the apostle Andrew who is our protective patron.'

Lamberton looked up. 'These words were indeed a true record of this nation, its history, its religion, its faith,' he thought to himself and he continued to listen to every word spoken.

Linton continued. '*Our nation has lived in freedom and peace under their protection until that time when Edward, the father of the English King who reigns today, came in disguise and took advantage when we had no head. No man, woman, child or holy clergy was safe from the slaughter, massacres and horrors inflicted by that king, whom you held in great favour.'*

Linton paused for a second and then continued. '*We have at last been freed from these innumerable evils by our most valiant sovereign King, who, with our consent has been passed the right of succession.* Bruce looked up. His heart was filling with emotion, and he felt proud and privileged in being able to liberate his nation from these horrors of recent times. He smiled at Linton to go on. '*Yet our King Robert, if he should ever make us, or our kingdom, subject to the King of England and their nation, we would cast him out and put in his place another King of royal Scots blood to lead and protect our nation.'* As these words were heard and their meaning understood, reactions of horror were being uttered by those loyal to their King. They all looked at Bruce.' What would be his reaction to that verse?' Bruce gently nodded his head and smiled indicating his approval of what had just been read.

Douglas sat still, his head bowed and trying hard to pay attention to every single word, words which he felt uninspired by. 'Meaningless words, spoken by those, who always say the right thing, but who would be more likely to sit on their backsides and do nothing,' he thought to himself. He breathed a loud sigh of frustration as Linton continued to read on. '*For as long as a hundred of us remain alive, we will never be subjected to English domination.'* Douglas looked up in surprise; these were words that he associated with.

Linton continued. *'We fight not for glory, nor for riches nor honours, but for freedom alone, which no good man gives up except with his life.'* Douglas immediately rose to his feet, and ignoring the unofficial protocol he loudly applauded the words that had just been spoken, words that conveyed how he truly felt, and words that meant so much to him.

Linton stopped reading. Thomas Randolph was the next to rise, and looking over to Douglas; he repeated the same approving gesture of loud applause. Others also, a few at first until all, apart from one, their King, stood and applauded. Hands were violently clapped until they hurt, feet loudly stamped until legs felt numb; they cheered like never before, indicating that there was something special, something unique in these inspirational and immortal words.

Bruce remained seated. He was also proud of these inspiring words, words which he had a hand in writing the night before, but he was more proud at the response from his nobles and in particular his first lieutenant the ever loyal James, Lord of Douglas.

Linton, having taken advantage of the break from reading continued. *'We pray that you admonish that King of England who should be content with what he has since it was once shared by seven before him. We ask that he leaves us Scots to live in peace, for we wish to live content in our poor little Scotland, beyond which there is only the great treacherous seas where no man can dwell.'*

Those present were now firmly holding on to every spoken word, every meaning. Each new verse created an association with the hardship and horrors of recent times which were ringing true in their minds.

'Most Holy Father, it is your choice to do this or to offer your support to the heathen who rages savagery against the fellow Christians who occupy our land. You must see how it will blacken the name of your holiness and lead to the anger of

the almighty god himself if the church were to abandon us and suffer discredit during your time.'

With his voice slowly rising as he approached the final sentences, Linton continued to read. *'We ask that you admonish the acts of the deceitful Christian princes, who for false reasons, driven by their greed and determination to overcome their smaller and weaker neighbours, refuse to go to your aid in the Holy Land. Our Noble King Robert and many good men of Scotland would gladly go to defend our beloved Christian faith if he, the King of England, would leave our nation in peace.'* At these words a shout of 'Here, here!' was heard from Bruce.

Linton's voice continued to rise. *'But if, through being told lies or receiving bad council, Your Holiness was to continue to put faith in what the English have declared. Then the blame for the slaughter and persecution of our nation, that would follow, would, we firmly believe, be charged against you by the most High God almighty himself.'*

Linton stopped reading for a short moment. Those present were impressed by the eloquent and yet assertive manner of the well-chosen words that dared to challenge the most powerful body on earth. Amongst themselves they quietly whispered their approval and delight at what had so far been stated in this declaration.

Linton took a final deep breath. *'We are bound and ready to obey you and in this letter we submit our cause to you our most high King and judge, in you we place our care and trust. We give you our faith and pray that you put your trust in ours and recognise our enemies for what they are.'*

Linton paused for a second, and then proceeded to finish his reading. *'May the Most High preserve you and our Holy Church in holiness and in health for many days to come. Given at the Monastery of Arbroath in the Kingdom of Scotland, on the sixth of April in the year of our Lord one thousand three hundred and twenty and in the fifteenth year of the reign of our good King Robert Bruce.'*

Linton placed the now precious scroll, along with a duplicate copy, on the small table at his right hand side and gestured for the two monks to prepare the partially melted wax for sealing. Bruce, along with Bishop Lamberton, sat still and content, and watched as each of the nobles took their turn at registering their seals on what was to become the most articulate and inspirational political statement ever produced by any nation.

When the business was completed, Bruce quickly arranged the letter to be dispatched to His Holiness. He quietly spoke to Lamberton and several other close nobles. 'Even if he agrees to our request, it will take some time for any noticeable change to occur. We must therefore continue with our struggle, but we must do so as a nation who respects our faith and only defends what is ours. We do not want to be accused of that of which we accuse our enemies.'

Lamberton approached Bruce. 'Sire, what you have created here this day will forever be remembered. It is a credit to you and those around you.' Douglas came towards them; the delight on his face clearly indicated his acceptance. He hesitated as he was about to speak. 'I am proud of what has been written, and I am proud to be a humble servant to the main author,' declared Douglas, as he then knelt before his King.

27

THE END OF THE TRUCE

MANY CREATURES OF THE Selkirk forest did not benefit from the two-year truce, as Douglas and those who resided with him at Lintalee regularly practised their stalking and hunting skills on the abundance of game that the forest offered to them.

The lodge at Lintalee had long been completed and could now accommodate all of Douglas's needs. Welcomed visits from his two brothers, sometimes on their own, sometimes together, were greeted with great joy as the three Douglas brothers enjoyed yet again each other's company. They began to catch up on the many pleasures of brotherhood that had been denied to them for so many years.

Short irregular visits to Blackhouse Tower, some only lasting a few hours, was all that Douglas could offer to his mother. 'Why don't you stay for a few days?' asked the now ageing and frail Lady Eleanor as she once again attempted to get her son to spend more time at his family home during such a recent short visit. Douglas shook his head. He could not answer, and yet he did want to be here. 'Yes this is my home,' he thought to himself, but each time he came here the uneasiness returned and he had to depart sooner than others wanted him to.

'Why?' asked Lady Eleanor. 'Please tell me why you can't stay longer? I want to know' she demanded.

'I don't know,' mumbled Douglas. 'I just can't stay here for any length of time. I have got to go.'

'Are we not good enough for you? Is that it?' she asked.

'Of course not,' replied Douglas, who still could not find the right words to explain his strange behaviour.

Lady Eleanor finally grabbed hold of her son, the most feared knight in all of these isles, and the tears ran down her face. Shaking with anger and distress, she shouted at him 'Is it because I am English? Answer me now!'

The brave Douglas, the Black Douglas to his enemies, the knight who had slain countless enemy warriors, stood towering above his much smaller mother as she continued to shake him with all her strength. The tears started to flow down his weather-beaten face and his lip trembled. 'Mother, I love you and all of my family very dearly. I fear for your safety more when I am here than when I am away,' he declared, as he put his arms around her.

'But that's silly, how can we be more at risk when you are here to protect us?' she asked as she wiped away the tears.

'There are many who would give vast sums of money to hear that we, the Douglas family, are all here in once place at the one time. The King of England to name but one, and many others that would surprise you,' said Douglas, as he slowly regained his composure.

'But why would we be safer when you are not here?' she asked.

'Mother, my success, and all of my achievements, I regret to say, have now become my liability. If our enemies came here and found you alone, you would be taken ransom in exchange for me, that I can guarantee. Your life would probably be safe. If we were found all together by our enemies in one place, our lives would end at that precise moment, and that is why I cannot stay,' answered Douglas.

Suddenly the door burst open and Sophia entered the room. Douglas and his mother were now wrapped in each other's arms. 'Oh! I see you're still here,' she sarcastically commented, as she looked over at Douglas who immediately wiped his eyes. 'I would have thought that you would have left before now,' she added, as she deliberately left the door wide open. Lady Eleanor looked into the dark eyes of her handsome son James. She saw deep genuine affection, not just for herself, but the single tear that still lingered in Douglas's eye told her again what she always wanted to know, and it was his love for Sophia. She hoped that some day, when peace was permanent, her lifelong dream for these two would come true.

The tired and battle-weary people of both nations, rich and poor alike, benefited from the safety and tranquillity of two years of heavenly peace. Life had returned to normal, presenting for some the opportunity to appreciate the many comforting pleasures of life. However, there were many who were not born into such a life and were unaccustomed to such pleasures and who waited impatiently for the return of hostilities.

Word spread up the east coast between the two nations that King Edward was once again leading his army to finish off a task that had evaded him for so long. Having learnt many lessons from failure and having personally observed the cunning practices of a much smaller and effective enemy, his strategy this time was different. Unlike the invading armies of the past, which were accompanied by an excess of baggage, his army moved swiftly as it headed north. They travelled light, and like the Scots, only carried sufficient supplies to last a few days. A fleet of ships loaded with ample food and the logistics to support his men set sail a few days behind. This time there was confidence within the ranks and a firm belief that victory would be theirs.

As they crossed the border, they did not notice anything unusual as their surprising speed led them into a false sense of security. The only resistance that this stubborn hostile land offered was the howling winds and relentless driving rain that pulverised anyone who dared challenge nature's authority.

Behind them the supply ships were temporarily grounded as the gale force winds held back their progress. Exhausted by the unaccustomed speed of their journey and now caught without food, Edward's hungry army reached the outskirts of Edinburgh. Bruce, who had been alerted to Edward's approaching army, waited patiently at Culross on the north side of the Forth. His plan was now about to take effect.

Having been caught without sufficient food, Edward ordered his men to search the neighbouring fields and farms for cattle to feed his army. For three whole days they searched unsuccessfully, until, as dusk was setting on the third day, a group of men returned with one lame miserable looking frail cow. The pathetic look of depression and expression of hopelessness on the poor beast as it was dragged towards him mirrored the look of failure on the face of a King.

Once more, they slept with empty stomachs. The following morning they mounted and headed south towards the border. 'Have faith my men!' shouted Edward. 'We will take our revenge on their many wealthy and traitorous abbeys. They slaughtered our clergy at Myton, we have the right to do likewise to theirs.' No one cheered; no one acknowledged his words; there was a deathly silence as they continued to follow him.

Douglas had returned to Lintalee. His brother Hugh had recently paid him a surprise visit and had brought him a gift of some delicious smoked fish from the abbey at Melrose. Hugh, once again carrying a generous purse given by his brother to contribute to good causes, had returned to the abbey that same morning.

The peaceful autumn midday stillness was shattered as a desperate lone rider came charging into the grounds of Douglas's forest residence. His horse, foaming at the mouth and dripping with sweat, was near to collapsing as the rider dismounted and ran to Douglas. Unable to make sense or

speak more than one word, the rider tried to shout. 'My lord…
it's…it's… the son of… Longshanks, he's about to…attack…
the abbey…at… Melrose,' the rider finally called out, as he
dropped with exhaustion into the arms of Douglas.

The following day, about one hour after dawn had broken
through the early morning haze, the high towering sandstone
arches of Melrose Abbey started to gleam as the first rays
of sunshine gently arrived. A tall well-built monk, his face
completely hidden by the dark hood which hung over his
bowed head, slowly swept the leaves from the pathway that led
from the open gateway and into the abbey grounds. There was
no sense of urgency present as his broom was gently swung
from side to side, exposing the well-worn stone pathway once
again.

The sound of thundering hooves rudely interrupted
the peaceful morning as a small band of riders wearing the
fearsome colours of the enemy nation suddenly arrived
outside the abbey grounds. A short distance behind them,
others, about three hundred in total, waited for their signal.

The first one to dismount shouted 'You there!' as he rushed
into the abbey grounds with the others following behind. The
monk remained silent as he continued with his humble early
morning duties. 'I'm talking to you!' shouted the soldier as he
approached nearer. With head still bowed, the monk turned
round, shook his head, and put his finger up to his mouth as if
to indicate 'Sorry, I'm not allowed to speak.'

'Perhaps this will help you find your tongue,' shouted the
soldier, as he drew out his sword.

The sudden shock of the broom handle breaking his jaw
as it shattered across his face caused the stunned soldier to
collapse in agony. 'You bastard!' shouted one of the others
as they collectively rushed at the lone monk. 'You're dead
meat!' screamed another of them as he also drew his sword.
In a single move, consisting of a slight twist and bending of his
body, the monk removed his robe and threw it over the face of
the first of the oncoming attackers.

Daylight was not seen again by that individual as Douglas's sword plunged straight into the attacker's throat and ended his life. The others stopped in their tracks, as they recognised the colours and description of the tall dark-haired figure who now blocked their way. Two more came rushing at Douglas. They erratically waved their weapons to disguise their fear for their own lives, and were immediately slain with a lightning cut and thrust from the deadliest sword in all of these islands.

Other English riders had arrived outside the grounds and immediately witnessed Douglas putting an end to the agony of the first soldier, who was still on his knees, spitting blood and teeth from his smashed mouth. Douglas now stood alone in the grounds of Melrose Abbey. The English riders, unsure of their next move, paused and stared at him. Douglas raised his sword above his head and shouted 'A Douglas! A Douglas!'

The spine-chilling call from their leader was the signal that Douglas's men were waiting for as they rushed out from hiding and attacked the unsuspecting enemy who now turned and retreated. Douglas ran to the side of the abbey and mounted his horse, but as he pulled to turn his brother Hugh blocked his path. 'Was that really necessary?' Hugh asked angrily. 'Maybe not. Best say some prayers for them and one for me,' replied Douglas as he joined his men in yet another pursuit of a fleeing English army.

Douglas's men, incensed by the attempted attack on such a place of holy worship, especially after a period of agreed truce, could not control their anger as they took their revenge on Edward's men. One by one, the fleeing soldiers were cut down leaving only a handful who were able to escape and make their way back to the main body of Edward's army, which was now encamped on the northern banks of the Tweed at Dryburgh.

Although tired, starving and demoralised, Edward's army was still too great in numbers for Douglas and his men to attack. Unable to do anything they waited and watched in horror and frustration as the abbey of Dryburgh was looted of its few provisions, several inhabitants tortured and killed, and then the abbey itself burnt to the ground. Word had been sent north to Bruce who was now on his way with a large force of men to deal with this situation.

Douglas, burning inside with rage, could wait no longer. He had to attack. Archers were sent in to pick off and harass the outer sections of Edward's men who one by one were deserting and returning home. Eventually, through hopelessness, King Edward ordered his men back over the border and home to the safety of his own land. Or so he thought.

The combined forces of Bruce and Douglas, who were now joined by Randolph, continued to pursue the disgraced King Edward. Once again the counties of northern England were raided, plundered and burnt by the avenging Scots desperate to protect their own lands.

Bruce, with age catching up on him, and ill health crippling his weary body, had returned home to Cardross where he took much needed rest. Douglas spent many days with him in council listening to the views and opinions of his beloved King. A message arrived one morning, delivered by a monk who was not from these lands. Bruce read the short letter. 'Is it more bad news, Sire?' asked Douglas, who was becoming more concerned about the welfare and state of mind of his King.

Bruce raised his head and looked straight at Douglas. He had never before seen his King cry, but here in front of him sat the once mighty Bruce with tears in his eyes.

'Sire, what news do you have that causes you such pain?' asked Douglas.

'It is a message from His Holiness, Pope John XXII, and sealed by himself,' replied Bruce.

'If he has rejected you once more, I say that you ignore his words and continue to give your loyalty to He who has no superior,' declared Douglas.

Bruce violently coughed and then spoke. 'Our Holy Father does not reject me; in fact I am humbled to say that he has finally recognised me as King of Scots.'

'But Sire, why do you appear displeased with this message, surely this is great news for our nation?' asked Douglas.

'There is no condition attached to this long awaited recognition; however, there is an expectation that the Holy Father mentions,' said Bruce.

'What expectation?' asked Douglas.

'We would be expected to take sides in the event of a war between Edward's England and Charles IV of France,' declared Bruce, as he gently shook his head in disgust.

'Surely he would not expect us to take sides with Edward?' asked Douglas.

Bruce, with sadness and disappointment written all over his face, replied 'I have been recognised as King of Scots with the expectation that I would put my armies at the disposal of Charles IV.'

Douglas cursed; it was not something which he was accustomed to doing, but on this occasion he felt it was justified. 'Sire it would be easy to lose faith and put blame on our church as a result of such a misguided request. I suggest we wait and if we do anything it would be to discourage such a war.'

Bruce bowed his head and still looking at Douglas quietly said 'My dear James, you have not been born of royal blood, but the support you have given me, even at this sensitive moment, has been greater than that from any other, for which I thank you most sincerely.'

Bruce, his head tilted towards the floor as his eyes stared into emptiness, took several minutes to reflect on his thoughts. He turned and looked at Douglas. 'The future of our nation can no longer be achieved through continued warfare and the spilling of more blood. Our own lives will some day end; our country's future therefore must rest on the shoulders of our sons and daughters. It is in them that we must invest in order to ensure that what we have so far achieved will become the foundation for the future of this nation. That future has to be earned by agreeing peace with our neighbours, who some day may be part of our own dearly loved families.'

As Douglas headed back to Lintalee, the words of Bruce were still ringing in his ears. 'What did he mean, as part of our families?' But there was another thought that continued to haunt Douglas. 'Our sons and daughters ... I have none. What happens when my death comes? Who will follow me?'

The next few years saw normality return, as families, separated and destroyed by constant warfare, became reunited and rebuilt, as love and compassion returned to occupy the hearts and souls of many. Douglas spent several days at Melrose Abbey. The thought of how close his own brother came to being killed by Edward's men still terrified him and caused him great uneasiness.

Sitting together one evening, as they shared supper, Hugh spoke to his elder brother. 'James, you are the one who everyone talks about, your achievements, your battles; your bravery will be remembered for future generations to look back in amazement. You have become immortal. Without you, our King Robert the Bruce would not have achieved his great success and united our proud nation.'

Douglas smiled at his younger brother; the words were complimentary and appreciated. However, there was a tone present, a tone that had a slight hint of disapproval, and had been expressed many times by Hugh. 'I thank you for those kind comments,' replied Douglas. 'I sense, however, that, although your well spoken words recognise my efforts, there is a hint of disapproval in your voice. I sense that there is something else that you would like to say. Am I correct?' asked Douglas, as he urged his brother to speak his mind.

Hugh could not look him directly in the eye; instead, he stood up and walked towards the small window. As he stared out into the evening sunset, he paused and then gave his answer. 'James, you have asked and I will now tell you. Compare the reputation of the two of us. You are Sir James, the Good Douglas, the hero, the famous warrior and will be remembered as such. I am known as Hugh the Dull. Some, perhaps many, will remember me as the foolish, even stupid brother of the Lord Douglas.'

Douglas listened as Hugh continued, struggling to maintain control. 'Consider the different lives that we live.

You have killed many men, perhaps hundreds, your armies, thousands. I have never killed a single thing in my life. You have travelled many miles to seek your revenge. I have only travelled a few miles to this abbey in search of peace, which I have found in God.

Hugh paused and took a deep breath. 'You are the hero, the brave knight who avenges our nation against the terrible enemy invaders, while I kneel on cold stone and pray for the souls of those that you slaughter. You openly practise revenge, retribution, and inflict death on your enemies, while I pray for their forgiveness and offer compassion and tolerance to those who seek to harm us. Yet you are seen as the hero and I the idiot.'

Douglas had been attentively listening to his brother's expression of his inner thoughts. 'Hugh, you are not the fool, your ways are not wrong. I respect and admire the path in life that you have taken. There is much that I could learn from you, your kindness and compassion towards others no matter their actions, is truly remarkable, and shows that there is true holiness in your heart. We have chosen different ways and have devoted our lives accordingly. Perhaps we can learn much from each other.'

Douglas put both his hands on his brother's shoulders. 'My dear Hugh, as my brother whom I have ignored for many years, I say this, if there is ever anything that I can do for you, you must let me know.'

Hugh embraced his brother. 'James, there is a very simple and easy to perform task which I would ask of you.'

Douglas waited for the request. There was a moment's silence, and then he asked 'What?'

'Stop hating the English!' declared Hugh. Douglas was taken aback by this appeal.

'What do you mean?' asked Douglas.

'You still think that I am the fool, don't you?' said Hugh.

'Of course not!' replied Douglas.

'That evening, when our mother told you that she was English, after you had left, she also told Archibald and me that we were your half brothers and that we have English blood running through our veins. She is proud of who she is and we are proud of who we are, even if that means being half English and half Scots.'

Douglas, physically shaken by this sudden reaction from his brother, held his breath in disbelief. He had to answer, but first he would have to choose the right words.

'Hugh, our mother put the same question to me,' said Douglas.

'And what was your excuse for an answer?' asked Hugh.

'I stated that my revenge is against the evil actions of others and not dependant on who they are or to whom or where they have been born, or what race they belong to. We are all the sons of God. My chosen destiny has only been to take revenge against those who have murdered and stolen from us. If they leave us in peace, I will leave them in peace.'

Douglas gently grabbed hold of his brother with both hands. 'Hugh, perhaps some day all men will be like you and live in a world without war, a world where nations respect each other's differences and live in peace. A world where invasion of another nation's land is avoided at all cost, a world where the kings and leaders share your values, a world where life is sacrosanct.'

The two brothers stared at each other. Words had stopped. Their eyes showed feelings of regret and yet also openly expressed deep love as they finally embraced.

28

THE WEARDALE CAMPAIGN

THE SUBJECTS OF EDWARD II had finally had enough. It was one thing having a King who disgraced and brought shame on his position, it was something else having a King who was incapable of protecting his people, especially from the invading Scots. Something sinister was being discussed amongst the English nobles.

Throughout the Scottish borders the restlessness was becoming contagious as many who were unaccustomed to long periods of peaceful times found difficulty in changing the habits of a lifetime and struggled to acclimatise to what for some were considered times of boredom.

Hugh had decided to spend the next few months in the company of his frail mother. Archibald seized the opportunity for a break from nursing his mother and joined his brother James at Lintalee. 'I've come to help you fight the English,' said Archibald, as he barged in with a wide cheeky grin on his face. Douglas, who had been sitting talking to his companions

Sir William Sinclair and Sir William of Galston, looked up in amazement.

'How many men have you brought with you?' chuckled William of Galston. 'It's just me, on my own. I thought you might need my help. I've been practising with my sword, morning and night,' replied Archibald, who felt proud of himself.

Douglas looked at him and with an expressionless face calmly commented 'My dear brother, what can I say? You have arrived just in time; your help is urgently needed for an important task.'

'I'm only here to help; I knew that you would be needing me. What do you want me to do?' said the eager Archibald.

'Is your knife sharp?' asked Douglas.

'Yes! Look it can cut a hair in two,' Archibald replied, as he performed a demonstration on a freshly plucked hair from his own head.

Douglas, William Sinclair, and William of Galston all looked at each other, and then nodded their heads in agreement. Douglas, with a most serious look on his face then spoke. 'My dear brother, the task that I have in mind involves great skill with a knife; it involves the spilling of much blood, cutting deep into raw flesh and the severing of many limbs. Do you have the stomach for such an important task which needs to be urgently carried out this very evening?' Archibald nodded his head in acceptance. Douglas then pointed to the young stag carcass spread across the table on the other side of the room. 'Please prepare our dinner,' ordered Douglas, as the others struggled to hold in their laughter.

Without saying a word, Archibald proceeded to go about butchering the beast. As he did so, Douglas and his companions continued with their conversation. Several hours had passed; Archibald had made frequent visits outside the large forest lodge. They did not notice what he was doing, nor did they happen to notice the appetising smell that had gradually crept up on them, as they continued to engage in serious conversation.

'OK, it's ready,' shouted Archibald. The three of them, silenced by the sudden shout, turned round and looked on in amazement. On the table was a large plate, overflowing with delicious looking thin tender cuts of braised venison, garnished with wild herbs and accompanied by roasted mushrooms. Four tankards of freshly poured ale sat at each corner of the table. 'Who would like the honour of saying grace?' asked the grinning Archibald.

Their bellies filled with the excellent meal, their minds numbed with the excessive ale, they slept soundly and at peace with themselves. The following morning the guard had to shout several times to attract any attention. 'A message for Lord Douglas.' There was still no reply. 'A message for Lord Douglas,' shouted the guard again. The sore heads were rubbed in sequence as they grunted and slowly rose from their beds.

'What does it say?' asked Archibald, as Douglas carefully studied the letter. 'James! Tell us, what does it say?'

Douglas crushed the letter tightly in his hand and looked at those around him. 'It's Edward II, King of England. His own nation have had enough and they have imprisoned him,' said Douglas. Sir William Sinclair and Sir William of Galston both cheered. Archibald followed them by shouting 'Thank you, God! I have only spent one night with you and look what's happened, their King has been imprisoned!'

Douglas said nothing; he quietly sat down on his own and stared at the floor. 'My Lord, is there more that you don't tell us?' asked Sir William of Galston, who sensed that something was not right. Douglas looked up. 'Yes, there is. There is another one, another Edward. The grandson of Longshanks. He is only fifteen years old and yet he gathers an army of over fifty thousand men at York. They have made him their new King,' said Douglas.

Archibald immediately started packing his things. 'Shouldn't you be getting ready?' he asked, as he looked to the others.

'Ready for what?' asked Sir William Sinclair.

431

'Well I don't expect you lot to sit here and wait for Edward III to arrive,' answered Archibald.

Douglas stood up, stretched his arms, sighed, and said, 'He's right, we best tell our men to get ready.'

A few weeks later they crossed the border. Douglas along with Randolph and other nobles, led their men, who were almost ten thousand in number, deep into the unsuspecting counties of northern England. A few highly trusted men were sent ahead to identify the exact whereabouts of the young King's army.

'This could take weeks,' declared Archibald, as he rode alongside his brother. Douglas looked at his men. They had been on the move for several days, always travelling with minimum equipment and very little food. He knew they would have to stop and restock. 'My dear brother,' said Douglas. 'The time has come for you to truly assist us. Take sufficient men and go bring whatever you may find that will sustain our men on this campaign.' Douglas turned to Simon of Ledhouse and gestured for his trusted friend to accompany his younger brother.

As they headed on past Hexham and through a steep pass south of Blanchland Moor, two of their scouts returned with news. 'My lords, we have seen the young King's army, they are heading into the Weardale valley, close to the town of Stanhope. They are many in number.'

Randolph, because of his royal bloodline, had once again been assigned overall command. Looking to Douglas, he asked 'Lord Douglas, do you agree with open battle, the way that true gentlemen should conduct themselves in times of warfare?' Douglas, raising his voice for everyone to hear answered 'My lord, I believe that true gentlemen should not participate in warfare. Open battle is fine when all things are equal, but they are not on this occasion. We are outnumbered by five times. Open battle may be gallant and noble, but would, on this occasion, be unwise and surely lead to our deaths.'

'Look!' interrupted one of the men, nervously pointing to the high ridge on their west side. 'It's them, they have been watching us all this time,' he called out. On the hillside, high above, English flags and banners could be seen flapping in the wind. Douglas turned to Randolph. 'So much for the gentleman's approach to warfare. As you can see, our enemy seeks to surround us and cut off our retreat to the north.'

'Let's head to Stanhope. If they want a battle we will give them a battle,' shouted Douglas, as he looked to Randolph to give the command. Randolph, although senior in rank and now one of Douglas's closest friends, had not forgotten the incident when he himself, at that time in the favour of the enemy, was captured by the daring Douglas at the Water of Lyne. Randolph raised his hand. The Scottish army then headed on towards Stanhope.

A few miles further on, Archibald Douglas, along with his men, who were heavily loaded with much needed provisions after successfully raiding the county of Durham, rejoined the main body. 'You have done well,' said the proud Douglas.

Simon of Ledhouse interrupted. 'We came across many men from the east counties; they were on their way to join the army of the boy King.' The blood on their garments told the story of the outcome. Archibald, showing he had much improved in maturity, said nothing. Only his smile hinted how proud he was to be able to perform such a task.

The recent heavy rains that had drenched the surrounding hillside had resulted in the River Wear being in full spate. Like two large groups of children playing hide and seek, both armies attempted to outmanoeuvre and outwit each other, as they teased and taunted from both sides of the treacherous fast-flowing river.

'We need to pull them towards us,' declared Douglas. 'Otherwise we could be in grave danger.' Randolph and Donald, Earl of Mar, who along with Douglas represented the command of the Scots army, both asked 'why'. 'Remember Bannockburn?' answered Douglas. They both nodded. 'The deep flowing waters of that burn claimed as many lives as all of the Scottish swords put together. I do not want the Wear to become our Bannockburn.'

That night the Scots retreated from the banks of the Wear and into the Stanhope Park where they set up camp. To the north lay a large mile-wide bog, which no man, let alone any army, could cross.

'Is this wise?' asked several, who were starting to doubt the wisdom of their commanders. 'Trust the Douglas, he will not fail you,' declared Archibald, who was also growing concerned, but did not want anyone else to question the wisdom of his brother.

Over the next few days the cat and mouse tactics continued as bands of men from both sides attempted seek advantage over one another. The English suffered many losses on each occasion. Thomas Randolph, frustration getting the better of him, once again presented his case for open battle. 'When the time is right, that's when we fight in the open,' declared Douglas. 'When will the time be right?' asked the Earl of Mar. 'When they have been beaten by their own minds,' replied Douglas, to a look of puzzlement from those around him.

Few fires were lit that night in order not to disclose their whereabouts. Many covered themselves with spare clothing and extra blankets, as the cold evening wind showed no mercy and relentlessly penetrated deep into the bones of their shivering bodies.

Douglas, along with many hand-picked men, their armour cast aside to enable them to move silently, swiftly made their way towards the perimeter of the English camp. Like a silent pack of creatures hunting in the darkness of night, they approached the tents of their enemy. 'Remember, silence is our main weapon, they must not be allowed to call out. When you hear my horn you retreat,' whispered Douglas, as he pulled the hood of his long dark cloak over his head.

Death came to many, as they lay sleeping, some restless, others in deep dreams of comfort. The sleeping inhabitants within the enemy tents had no time for fear, and they felt no pain, as one by one many they were put to the sword. The guards, who were sparingly dispersed throughout the camp, heard nothing, saw nothing, and suspected nothing as the slaughter continued around them.

The triple Lion rampant flag, gently fluttering in the night wind, and partially illuminated by a single torch held by the guard on duty, caught the attention of Douglas. The large tent in the centre circle could not be easily approached without being noticed, and yet that was one tent that Douglas had to get to. Waving to his men, Douglas whispered 'I need to go alone, stay out of sight and wait for me.' The men took cover and waited for his signal. Oblivious to the cold wet ground, and crawling on hands and knees, Douglas crept up from behind. The guard on duty, his head and ears covered with a thick woollen blanket, did not hear anything as the deadly assassin silently approached. The only sound was the dull thud as the guard's body slumped to the ground. The burning torch was immediately extinguished by Douglas.

'Who's out there?' shouted a frightened child-like voice from within the large tent. 'A most loyal servant Sire, nothing to cause concern,' came the reply, in a most eloquent English accent. 'What are you doing?' asked the nervous innocent voice from within. 'Answering the call of nature Sire. I am unable to leave my post,' was the reply from outside the tent.

There was silence. A few moments later the flap of the tent was opened and a young boy emerged tightly grasping a lighted torch. Douglas stood by the side of the tent and resumed the sentry position of the slain guard, his head and upper body covered by his dark cloak. The young King held the torch up to the face of Douglas; their eyes met. Douglas projected an image of calmness in his expressionless face. The young King Edward, shivering more from fear than from the cold, spoke first, as he hesitantly looked around him. 'Do you think he is close to our camp?' he asked with a trembling voice. 'Who do you speak of, Sire?' asked Douglas. 'That cursed Black Douglas; do you think he is near us?'

Douglas studied the face of this young boy who reminded him of how he himself felt when he first met Longshanks, the grandfather of this young King, at Stirling Castle. Here was a young child, terrorised with fear, his father imprisoned and, according to latest gossip, brutally killed by English executioners, just like Douglas's own father had been many years ago. He felt for this young boy, innocent and harmless and yet expected to lead an army to crush the rebellious Scots. Douglas remembered the conversation he recently had with his brother Hugh. 'Stop hating the English!' 'Perhaps this is the time to stop that hatred,' he thought to himself.

'Sire, if I may be allowed to speak, I have heard it said that Douglas only wants to keep that which is rightfully his. He only attacks these lands in order to protect his own in Scotland,' replied Douglas, in the same disguised English accent.

The young King looked up at Douglas. 'You, sir, appear to be a kind and sincere man. I am fortunate to have you as my guard, but I greatly fear that Black Douglas. They say that he can defeat great armies on his very own, and that he has no equal in battle.' Douglas could not hold back his smile. In front of him was this young man, who was blameless of any wrongdoing. He was pure in the eyes of God, and yet, if allowed, could be influenced by the greed and selfishness of others, and if encouraged could easily inherit the evilness of his grandfather.

The sound of guards arguing as they came towards the King's tent could be heard in the distance. Douglas, sensing the danger, said 'Sire, I must leave now, but before I go let me say this to you. Provided you do not invade Scotland, you will have nothing to fear from the Black Douglas. You would become a great King of England, much greater than both your father and grandfather, if you were to seek peace instead of war between our two nations.'

One of the guards spotted the tall stranger standing beside the young King. 'You! Over there! Stop!' The young King turned his head. Holding his torch up he saw the guards run towards him. Turning back round he saw the rear of Douglas's head. The hood of the cloak had fallen down, the long black hair was waving in the evening air as Douglas blew his horn and disappeared into the darkness. 'That's him!' shouted one of the guards as he ran up beside his King.

'Sire, did he harm you?' asked the guard.

'Who?' asked Edward.

'That man, that was him, that was the Black Douglas,' answered the guard; tonight he has sneaked into our camp and killed many of our men in cold blood.

The young King Edward, shocked and terrified that the Black Douglas had stared straight into his face, and could have killed him with the ease of a flick of an eyelid, nervously shook his head in reply as he recalled the parting words of the dark stranger. 'Seek peace instead of war between our two nations.'

The young King stood trembling, tears of fear running down his childish face. The words spoken by Douglas echoed through his mind. They were words that he would not forget. The guards assisted the terrified and shaken young Edward back into his tent. 'Best you stay inside, Sire,' suggested one of them. 'Say nothing of this... to anyone,' ordered the young Edward, in a quivering voice. 'Our lips are sealed, Sire,' replied both guards.

With sword drawn, Douglas headed back towards his own men. Cutting at the many ropes, he caused panic and confusion as one by one tents collapsed in on their inhabitants. Other guards, alerted to the disturbance, came running towards Douglas, who was now unable to reach his own men.

A short time later, and without Douglas, the night-time raiders returned to their own camp. 'Where is he? Is he all right?' asked Archibald. 'We don't know,' replied several men. 'What happened?' asked Randolph. 'We killed many who lay sleeping in their tents,' replied one of the men. 'What of Douglas?' asked Simon of Ledhouse, who felt he should have been picked for this raid, in spite of his age. 'We saw him approach the centre tent, the one with the triple Lion rampant,' replied one of the exhausted men. 'Holy Mother of Christ!' declared Archibald. With a wide grin he shouted

'He's going to kill their King!' The others stared at Archibald in disbelief.

Stunned, and without Douglas, they were at a loss.

'What do we do now?' asked the Earl of Mar.

'They will be bloody raging if he has done their King in,' replied the shocked Archibald.

'Patience, my good men,' shouted Simon of Ledhouse. 'Been here before, I have seen it many times. Have faith. It will take a lot more than an army of fifty thousand Englishmen to stop our good Lord Douglas.'

The waited and watched. Several hours passed, but there was still no sign of Douglas. 'They must have got him, it's been too long,' one of the men said as they all stood patiently looking in the direction of the English camp. 'Who's watching your backs?' shouted the voice from behind. They turned round to see Douglas. Drenched and covered in black mud, he stood before them, having approached from the inhospitable moor. 'It's been easier to sneak up on you lot than yon English army,' shouted the smiling Douglas.

They embraced him and smothered him in expressions of praise and gratitude. Archibald approached. 'Tell us then, did you kill him?' he asked. 'Kill who?' replied Douglas, knowing fine well who they were taking about. 'That King of theirs,' replied Archibald.

'That King of theirs is a young innocent child, a scared and loveable young boy, whose failure of a father has been imprisoned and is probably dead by now. He is petrified of us, and of the fearful reputation of the Black Douglas,' replied Douglas.

'What happens now?' asked Randolph, who was at a complete loss in trying to predict the next move from the cunning mind of Douglas.

'I say we go home,' answered Douglas.

'He's lost it,' replied Archibald. 'Maybe last night he got a wee bump on the heid.'

The elderly Simon of Ledhouse quickly turned to face Archibald. 'Listen, son, you'll be getting a big bump on the heid if you don't keep quiet.'

Douglas gestured for them to come closer towards him. 'We have beaten them again, and this time without great loss to ourselves. They are demoralised and led by a frightened boy King, who, I guarantee, come dawn, will order them to go home. But first, there is something that we must do.'

'What would that be?' asked Randolph.

'Light our fires, make them burn bright, when this is done, I tell you, this night we will disappear before their very eyes,' answered Douglas.

Fresh wood, along with many thin branches and shrubs, was collected, only a small portion of which was used for the large burning fires. The rest was made into light, easy to carry, raft-like platforms that would be placed underfoot and enable man and horse to cross the treacherous moor. Douglas led the way across the narrow route which he had discovered during the night and which avoided the deep-water filled holes that could easily cause many a leg of both man and beast to break.

The English army watched throughout the night and observed the burning fires. In the morning, no sign of movement could be seen in the Scottish camp. A band of reluctant riders were sent over. It was deserted, with no sign of life other than the smouldering cinders that had also given up their fight. 'Sire, they have gone,' reported the commander to the not surprised King Edward, who in his mind could still hear the haunting words spoken by the Black Douglas. 'Sire, what do you wish us to do,' asked the commander. Edward hesitated. He looked at his men. They were brave, but they were also dejected. 'We also will go home, the fighting is over. I must now try for peace,' answered Edward.

As both armies headed home in opposite directions, there was no great cheer of victory, no great celebration, only relief, and the beginning of a realisation that peace, on a permanent basis, might have finally arrived between these two nations.

It was about noon of the next day. The solitary riders, who always rode out in front and on either side, spotted them first. 'There's a large army heading towards us,' announced the rider who had immediately returned to inform the main army as they headed north. Douglas and Randolph instantly rode forward to meet the oncoming force. 'It's our own King Robert,' shouted Randolph on recognising the many banners. The two groups of men came together near the town of Hexham. Bruce was told of what had happened, and then openly expressed his delight that so many of his fellow countrymen had returned safely. There was much cheering and praise for their safe return. Douglas stayed in the background. Randolph and the Earl of Mar briefed Bruce on the events of the last few weeks.

As they were just about to head back home, Bruce called Douglas aside. 'Lord Douglas, may I speak with you alone?' The two friends dismounted and walked away from the rest of the men.

'Did you speak to him?' asked Bruce.

'Yes, Sire, I did exactly as you requested in your letter to me,' replied Douglas.

'Will he agree if we put the question to him?' asked Bruce.

'Sire, Edward III is a terrified and immature young boy. I am sure your good intention, to offer your own son David in marriage to Edward's younger sister, would remove that fear, and make him feel that at the age of fifteen he would achieve more than either his father or grandfather by uniting our two nations. He will agree, of that, I have no doubt. I would advise that the time is right for you to send your messenger,' answered Douglas.

Bruce embraced his beloved knight, the one that he trusted more than any other. 'My dear James, I thank you. Only I know what you have done for me and for our nation. Your have carved the pathway for the future safety and prosperity of our children and our children's children. My illness constantly tires me and I may not have long to enjoy what we have fought for. I will always be in your debt.'

Douglas, his head bowed and humbled by these kind words, replied 'Sire, it has been my pleasure and I am deeply honoured to have been of service to you.'

The others looked on and wondered what was being discussed. Bruce and Douglas looked at each other. They both realised that their conversation suggested that their life of constant warfare was now over. There was a numbness of their minds; they had not expected the wars between the Scots and English to end so unexpectedly and abruptly.

As they headed home to their much-loved Scotland, an unnoticed messenger left their company and headed south in the direction of Edward's army. The message had already been written and sealed by the hand of Bruce. It was a request for peace, a peace that would be finally sealed with the marriage between a child son and a child sister of each of the two Kings.

29

FAMILY AFFAIRS

A STOAT, ITS BLACK tail waving as it bobbed up and down, was homing in on its prey. Leaping over several tufts of grass before stopping and standing up on its hind legs, it paused and stared. Another deadly predator, one whose speciality was human prey, was also staring, and admiring such instinctive hunting artistry, as the small mammal moved in for the kill. With its eyes locked in on its prey it pounced and disappeared into the long grass. It reappeared a few seconds later with its victim, a field vole, still wriggling as it hung from the mouth of the deadly hunter like a prize being displayed for all to see. Douglas marvelled at the ability of the small predator. 'Well done, my friend,' shouted Douglas, as he applauded such natural hunting skills.

He dismounted and led the weary animal over to the burn that gently flowed down the peaceful glen a short distance south of the Blackhouse Tower. As his horse quenched its thirst, force of habit caused Douglas to look back along the trail that he had just taken. He looked around, his eyes scanning for any sign of being followed. He knew that this time there was no need. However, it was best to be sure.

Deciding to walk the rest of the way up the glen towards the home of his family, Douglas took the opportunity to reflect on what direction his life was now about to take. The wars appeared to be over. His obsession with defending his nation with a ruthlessness that was unmatched by any other had caused him to see the world through distorted eyes. This peacetime world was a world that he was unaccustomed to, a world that he had not taken the time to notice, but most of all a world of which he was afraid.

He waved at the farm worker who was busy tending to the cattle. He did not know the man's name. He was just a face that Douglas had recognised and had taken for granted for many years, one of many who had given a great deal to the care and welfare of the Douglas family.

As he opened the front door, he was immediately struck by the smell of recently cooked fish which lingered in the air. 'Smells good,' he thought to himself as he popped his head into the empty kitchen. The main rest room was also empty. 'Anyone home?' he called. No answer could be heard. Panic started to creep in as he searched each room and still found no one at home.

'Where are they?' he shouted towards the man who was attending to a young calf. The family servant said nothing, but pointed towards the rear of the tower house. Douglas rushed round the side of the building. Her back was to him, she was bending over the neatly cultivated herb garden and picking fresh garnish to go with the recently cooked meal. 'Mother!' he shouted. She slowly stood up and turned round, her back stiff from bending for so long. The sudden shock caused her to pause for a second. 'Do you really think that I have aged that much that I now look like your mother?' asked Sophia as she smiled at Douglas.

He studied her. She did look different, older, and no longer the innocent young girl. Instead he saw a mature woman, a woman who generated emotions in him that caused confusion and nervousness as well as the most exciting and pleasurable feelings that he had ever experienced.

'James! Is everything all right?' she asked, as she stroked her hair and tried to tidy her appearance.

'Sorry, I did not recognise you for a moment. Where is mother?' said Douglas.

'Oh, she has gone to visit a friend who is ill, she should be back tomorrow,' answered Sophia.

'Did anyone go with her?'

'Of course. Do you honestly think that we would let her go alone?' replied Sophia, with her usual hint of sarcasm.

'Where's Archibald? Was he not supposed to be with you?' asked Sophia, as she walked towards the tower-house.

'He's protecting our nation,' replied Douglas, as he tried to respond with his own brand of sarcasm.

'What!' exclaimed a stunned Sophia before she noticed Douglas's attempt to hide his laughter. 'Oh good, I suppose we can all sleep peacefully tonight knowing that such a great fearsome warrior guards our nation.'

Douglas, unable to maintain his pretence any longer, smiled and said 'The war with England is over; no more fighting, no more killing, peace has been achieved. Archibald wanted to stay at Lintalee at the lodge. He will be safe.'

'And what of you? What do you intend to do?' she asked. He gazed at her until she felt uncomfortable.

'Well, come to think of it, there is something that I would like to do with you,' he replied, as he continued to mesmerise her with his large dark eyes. She felt a hot blush sweep across her face, her throat went dry and she struggled to swallow.

'And what would that be?' she nervously asked, as they both collided in trying to enter the narrow doorway at the same time.

Douglas stopped and turned to her. 'I would like us both to eat together, just the two of us. What do you say?' Sophia, too embarrassed to look him in the eye, replied 'That would be nice, there's plenty for both of us.'

Just as they finished their meal, and with perfect timing, the sun slowly disappeared over the Tweedsmuir Hills. The glow from the log fire radiated throughout the room and enhanced the peaceful atmosphere. Sophia lit another candle.

'So what are your plans?' asked Sophia, as she gradually made herself comfortable and shuffled up close to the fire.

'Too early to say,' replied Douglas.

'So are you going to stay or what?' she asked.

'At this precise moment, I don't know,' he answered, and shrugged his shoulders.

'Well then, if you are not sure, why not just stay a few days at least and wait for your mother's return. She will be delighted to see you and to hear that the fighting is over.'

'What about you?' asked Douglas, as Sophia looked over at him. 'What plans do you have?' She was not sure how to answer this awkward question. Her plans were crystal clear in her own mind, but could not be openly expressed at this moment. 'I can't answer that question.' 'Can't or won't?' he asked. 'What are you suggesting?' she asked, as he leaned over beside her to reposition a fallen log on the burning fire.

He turned towards her. Her beautiful face, so perfect and so pure, looked back at him. They looked deep into each other's eyes. Sophia held her breath as his eyes held her.

'Sounds like we both have plans that we can't or won't share,' she replied. 'Perhaps they may be the same plans,' he suggested, causing shivers of excitement to pass through her whole body. 'You could be right,' she nervously answered.

Douglas leaned closer towards her and paused close to her face. She smiled as she unfolded her arms. He could feel his heart pounding faster than it ever had. Her heavy breathing became louder and she closed her eyes as their lips met for the first time, feeling such pleasure, such love. Both shared the excitement of their first loving embrace.

Their lips parted and she kissed him again, on the side of his lean and rugged face. He kissed her on her soft and slender neck. They both wished that this moment would never end. 'Oh, James,' she softly called out, as tears of joy ran down her blushing red cheeks. 'I love you,' she whispered in his ear. His dark eyes pierced into her heart as he gently wiped away her tears and whispered 'Please, don't cry. You know that I love you too. Perhaps our innermost thoughts are the same, perhaps it's time for us to be together at last ... that is, if you want to?' In the past she had often, been unable to stare him out; however, this time their eyes could not part company as she gave her reply. 'Yes, I do,' answered Sophia without hesitation.

About an hour later Douglas stood on the bank of the small burn that was only a short distance away from the house. The dark water reflected the sparkling moonlight and produced the only sound of the night as it splashed, twisted and turned over the rocky bed beneath.

He heard the sound of her approaching, but could not turn to face her. She stood beside him and stared down at the burn below.

'What's wrong? Is it me?' she asked.

'Of course not,' he answered. 'What then?' she demanded.

'I can't,' he replied.

'You said that you loved me,' said Sophia miserably. 'Were you just saying that to be nice to me?'

'I do love you, but I'm sorry, I can't take advantage of you.'

'But you're not taking advantage of me,' she said.

'I want us to be married first,' he replied firmly.

Sophia put her arms around him. 'That's what I also want,' she said, with a look of delight on her face. As they both stood above the gentle flowing burn, they kissed again, but with even greater passion than before.

Over the next few months their romance blossomed as Sophia and her beloved James were never out of each other's company. Lady Eleanor's wish was about to come true as she looked forward to the marriage that would put the final seal on this long awaited event in the lives of her two beloved children.

As they discussed plans for the marriage, the typical family arguments came to the surface, as mother, bride and groom disagreed on the where, when and who detail of this significant event.

'What do you want?' asked Lady Eleanor as she questioned Sophia.

'I only want to be his bride, nothing more,' replied Sophia.

'James, what about you?' asked his mother.

'God's blessing, that's all that matters,' answered Douglas, who was starting to get frustrated with all the fuss. 'Oh, God's blessing you say. Don't you think she's worth a bit more than just a blessing?' asked the angry Lady Eleanor.

As the conversation continued, so did the disagreements. 'We will do what is right,' said Douglas, as he held Sophia's hand and brought the conversation to an end.

One mid-afternoon a messenger came through the glen. 'I must speak with Lord Douglas,' he urgently demanded. Douglas approached the man, took him aside, and engaged in a long conversation. Lady Eleanor and Sophia watched from a distance. 'He'd better not be going away again,' declared Lady Eleanor. 'You know what he's like. If it's a request from Bruce, a snap of our King's fingers and James will drop everything and go running to serve him,' replied Sophia. 'He should get his priorities right,' said the angry Lady Eleanor. 'Priorities? I would say that he has absolutely clear priorities, his King Robert the Bruce comes first, and everything else second,' answered Sophia. 'Does that not bother you, now that you are to be wed?' 'No, that's just James. He will never change,' said Sophia, with a look of hopelessness on her face that she was trying to hide.

The messenger eventually left and Douglas came over to them. 'What's the news? Are you leaving again?' asked Lady Eleanor. Sophia stood watching and listening and expected the worse.

'Yes, but hopefully only for a short time,' he answered with a concerned look on his face.

'Why, has the fighting started again?' asked Lady Eleanor. Douglas looked shocked as he tried to answer. 'No, it's not that, it's our King Robert. He is dying. He has perhaps months, or maybe just weeks to go.'

'James, what does he want of you?' asked Sophia.

'He has asked that I join him in pilgrimage at the holy shrine of Saint Ninian at Whithorn.'

Lady Eleanor put her hand on the shoulder of her son. 'James, that is a request that you should feel honoured to be asked of you. You must go.' Sophia, her voice trembling gave her support. 'I agree, you should go. Our marriage can wait.'

A few days later, Douglas arrived at Whithorn in the south-west corner of Scotland. With no sign of Bruce, he waited outside the small chapel to which many, recognising their precious days of remaining life were coming to an end, came to pay homage to God and seek his forgiveness for their sins.

The soft steady drizzle of rain that had been falling all day gradually changed to a relentless downpour that soaked and pulverised everything outside. Dark raging storm clouds swept in from the great ocean skies like an expression of anger issued directly from heaven. Douglas, though not wanting to enter the holy sanctuary before Bruce, was forced to go inside.

The smell of recently burned incense lingered in the still musty air of the empty chapel. He immediately felt the holy, almost ghostly, atmosphere as he stood and felt the power of God's presence embrace him. Kneeling at the back of the chapel, he stared at the two flickering candles that appeared to stand guard on the large crucifix that commanded the centre position high above the altar stone. Douglas bowed his head and prayed in silence.

He thought of those he had killed. There were many. 'If killing is a sin, then I must be doomed forever to burn in hell,' he thought to himself. 'But how many lives of my own people have I saved? If I kill one and save another, then maybe in God's eyes, I am even. Yes, I have killed many, but I have saved even many more from being tortured and murdered by our enemies, therefore perhaps I have been a saviour of lives.' He looked up at the magnificent crucifix that hung above the altar. The image of Christ, with head bowed and blood flowing from hands and feet, gave him his answer. A tear appeared in Douglas's eye and slowly rolled down his face as he prayed to his Lord for forgiveness. 'I know that saving many and killing even one is wrong. My Lord, my God, I have sinned. Forgive me.'

Time appeared to stand still as Douglas continued in deep prayer. His meditation was finally disturbed by a noise from outside the chapel doors. He rose to his feet, turned and was immediately confronted by the shocking sight of four attendants carrying the stretcher-bound Bruce, King of Scotland, into the holy sanctuary of this small chapel.

The attendants, who recognised Douglas, said nothing and continued to walk past as they carried their King in solemn procession. Bruce, looking tired and having lost a great deal of weight, was awake and aware of what was happening. He saw Douglas, raised his arm, and gestured for his most loyal friend to proceed with him towards the front of the chapel. Douglas clasped Bruce's hand and without a word being spoken they all walked down the aisle.

The resident priest eventually appeared and, along with two elderly abbots, greeted King Robert, and then proceeded to say a holy Mass dedicated specifically to Bruce. Douglas knelt by the side of his King, and offered comfort, as prayers, intermixed with readings from the ancient scriptures, were said.

After the private service was over, Bruce spoke with Douglas. 'My Dear James, there is not much that I can say to thank you that has not already been said. I appreciate you being here, especially when others, some my own blood and kin, chose not to be.'

'Sire, I will always be by your side,' said Douglas, as he looked at Bruce and saw with his own eyes the dramatic deterioration in his good King's health.

Bruce, struggling to make himself comfortable from the many sores that covered his infected body, looked up at Douglas. 'James, I must go home. It won't be long now before my time to depart this life finally arrives. I would like you to be with me at that moment.'

'Sire, I will be with you, but I am concerned about your return back to Cardross. You don't look like you could make such a tiring journey,' said Douglas.

'If I can get back to Ayr safely, I will be fine, as my ship, which awaits me in that harbour, will take me directly to Cardross,' replied Bruce.

Douglas clasped the hand of Bruce and held it tightly, close to his body. 'Sire, I will be with you until the very end, and hopefully, with God's will, into the next life where you truly belong. However, I have a personal matter, involving someone else that I dearly love in a different way, that I beg your leave to go and attend to.' Bruce, ignoring his constant pain for a second, smiled and gave his assent.

A few days later, Douglas watched as Bruce's ship sailed out of Ayr harbour and made its way up the Clyde coast, carrying its precious and dying passenger home to Cardross. He turned his horse and headed eastwards along a route that he had not travelled for many years. It was the road that led to the place of his birth, a place where someone special resided, someone to whom he wished to make an unusual request.

Back at Blackhouse Tower, the Douglas family, without the ever-absent James, were together again, as Hugh and Archibald had both returned to visit their mother. 'So you say that you are to be wed to that brother of mine, and yet he disappears once again, to be with his precious King,' declared Archibald. 'Perhaps he should become the husband of Bruce,' he added, to the sounds of laughter. 'He will be back soon, and we will be married. He promised,' said Sophia, who was annoyed at this unnecessary ridicule.

The evening meal had been prepared, grace said, and then the Douglas family enjoyed the pleasure of eating together. As they sat talking and entertaining themselves to pass away the last hours of this day, their peace was suddenly interrupted by the loud sound of dogs barking outside. 'Someone's coming,' Archibald called out, as he stood and looked out the doorway. 'Who could that be at this time of night?' asked Lady Eleanor. 'It's James, there's someone with him,' shouted Archibald. They all stood up and eagerly waited for the elusive son. It had been a long time since this whole family was together as one. Sophia's face lit up. Archibald looked at her and said 'Perhaps he's come home to get married.'

The door opened. James entered and stood facing them. Seeing all of his family together he smiled, but could not speak for happiness at the sight in front of him. 'Welcome home again. James,' said Lady Eleanor. 'Who's with you?' asked Hugh.

Douglas did not answer. Instead, he looked directly at Sophia. 'My dear Sophia, do you still agree for us to be married?' She blushed and covered her face with her hands. 'Of course she does,' shouted the delighted Lady Eleanor. 'Aye, but when? That's the question,' asked Archibald.

Douglas turned round and gestured to the person behind him to come in. Father Michael, former abbot at Melrose and now parish priest of Douglasdale, stepped forward. Douglas walked over to Sophia and grasped her hand. 'May I suggest now?' said Douglas.

Douglas stayed for several days. His brothers Hugh and Archibald went back to Melrose and Lintalee. Father Michael returned to Douglasdale after informing Douglas that both he and Sophia, although married in the eyes of God, would have to appear at St Brides Kirk and sign the church records for their wedding bond to be legally binding.

Lady Eleanor deliberately kept out of their way, as Douglas and Sophia enjoyed the recently discovered pleasures of newlyweds. For three whole days they were side by side and never out of each other's company. They spoke to no one apart from each other.

At the end of the seventh day, Douglas announced that he would have to go to be by the side of his dying King.

'What! You have just got married! Your young wife needs you, you must stay, I demand it of you,' shouted Lady Eleanor, as she stormed into a rage at hearing this dreadful news.

'Sophia, I am sorry, truly sorry, but I gave him my promise,' said Douglas, as he stood before his wife and begged her understanding. Sophia breathed a deep sigh of frustration and then said 'James, I want you to promise me something.' He nodded his assent before she had even asked. 'I want you to promise me, that when the life of our King Robert is over, that you will spend the rest of your life with me. Do you promise?' Douglas glanced at his mother, a glance that sought her final approval. Lady Eleanor nodded her head. Douglas turned back to his beloved Sophia. 'Yes, I do, Sophia my love. I will never leave you again,' answered Douglas, who was torn between two separate loyalties and two important people whom he dearly loved.

30

AND THAIR BURY MY HART

THE STRONG SMELL of the sea air was only noticeable to those who had recently arrived. Some stayed for only a few hours. Others had taken up almost permanent residence at Cardross. They came to offer their support and comfort to the dying Bruce, who refused to give in, as he fought his final battle against the deadly disease that had constantly attacked and now attempted to consume his remaining fragile body.

A short distance from the shore, a flock of gulls could be seen constantly chasing and harassing the lone fishing boat which sailed past on its way back up the Clyde coast. Taking advantage of the opportunity for rich pickings, the flying scavengers, their ear-splitting screams shattering the peace of late afternoon, swooped down on each highly desirable morsel that was discarded overboard.

Many came to show their love and appreciation to their worthy King who had united their nation, a King who now lay waiting for his creator to call him. Others, whose intentions were more akin to the scavenging gulls, hovered in anticipation, as they also attempted to grab up the rich pickings that were on offer. Each day, for a few hours only, the awakened Bruce would announce rewards of land ownership and noble titles allocated to those who had served him well. Just like the gulls, many an ungrateful noble fought, screamed and scavenged as they selfishly challenged the generous rewards given to others.

Douglas, his mind constantly switching between thoughts of concern for his dying King and thoughts of love for his Sophia, whom he had not seen for many long months, showed no concern for the rewards of loyalty that were being lavishly handed out by the dying Bruce. He sat silent amongst them, and watched and listened, as greed took hold of their minds. 'How many have come because of their love? How many to satisfy their own self-seeking needs?' Douglas thought to himself, as he slowly walked amongst them and listened to them squabble with each other.

As he approached and stared at them, they recognized that look. They knew that he had a nose that could smell treason a mile away. Admiring him and yet fearing him, they ceased their arguments. The huddles broke up. In Douglas's company no one dared even think, let alone say, a wrong word towards the dying King.

'Sire, how are you today?' asked Douglas, who appeared to be experiencing the same painful suffering as his dying King. Bruce, pleased to see his gallant knight, whose presence always seemed to lift his spirits, softly smiled and answered 'Ah, James, my ever loyal good James, I am fine. I have lasted this long; there's still a wee bit of life left in this old dog yet.' Douglas, each day holding back the tears, gently touched the hand of Bruce. 'Sire is there anything that I can do for you? Is there anything that you need done? Is there anything that I can get you?' Bruce's eyes lit up with joy. 'Others come here to ask for titles, estates, and to tell me what lands they believe they should be granted. You, James, are different. I have never heard you ask for anything. All that occupies your mind is my welfare, and for that I am truly grateful.'

There was a short period of silence, as Douglas savoured the kind words his King had just spoken. Bruce, struggling to make himself comfortable, spoke again. 'James, there is something that I need, something that I would like you to do.'

'Yes, Sire?' inquired Douglas as he awaited his instructions.

'James, during my life I have gained much glory and achieved many victories. I would trade it all for the return of those loved ones that I have lost. My dear family, my brother Edward, who was killed in Ireland, and more recently our mutual lifelong friend Bishop Lamberton, who has now departed from this earth.'

Douglas was stunned by the unexpected news of Lamberton's death. 'His Excellency? Now gone? Sire, I did not know,' he said.

'James, I want you to take care of yourself and of your family, for they are your most precious possessions. Do that and you will please me,' declared Bruce. Douglas immediately answered. 'Sire, I will. The time has now come for me to spend my remaining life with my own family. I thank you for your consideration.'

'I have one final request to make. Please send messengers and arrange for the others to come here,' requested Bruce with a serious tone to his voice.

It took almost a full week for the main influential nobles to arrive. Some came by land, others by sea from the western isles. When the last few arrived Bruce finally called them to council. Propped up, and carried with great care by his close attendants, he was brought into their company. Those who had not seen him for some time gasped at the obvious deterioration in his health. His face was covered in open sores, his eyes were heavily bloodshot, but most significant was the frailness of the frame of a man who had once led this nation to great victory.

Bruce coughed and spat a mouthful of bloodstained saliva into a small hand-held bowl. He struggled for breath. When he finally started to speak, his weakened voice trembled with the strain of each word. 'It is time... to give final payments...'

he paused, and violently coughed again, as those around him stared in anticipation of good news. ' ... to those who have remained loyal to the protection of our nation's soul and spiritual guidance.'

'What does he mean?' whispered Randolph, who stood next to Douglas. 'Allow him to finish,' said Douglas.

Bruce continued to struggle as he called out the names of various holy religious establishments who had been supportive and comforting to him during these years of war. As each name was called out, a sum of money was declared as being granted in appreciation. Someone who sat at the back whispered 'He's giving our hard fought wealth to the bloody church that excommunicated him.' A second voice spoke in agreement. 'Aye, the same dammed church that disowned our nation.'

Douglas, who had been sitting with head bowed and listening to every single word, turned and stared directly at the two disgruntled nobles. He did not need to speak; the stare was as deadly as any blow ever delivered by the fearsome warrior. The two outspoken nobles were immediately silenced.

Bruce finally called out 'To Melrose Abbey...'. Douglas looked up for the first time. He nodded in humble approval as the sum of money being granted to this most holy place was announced. A few nobles started to applaud; the others followed as they expressed their support for this kind act of generosity towards the holy places of religious worship.

Bruce stopped for a few minutes. His breathing became heavier as he fought to continue with his final request. Taking a deep breath, he spoke again. 'My lords, and all gentlemen here present today; I have but one final request of you. I have led a life of selfishness, driven by my blind determination to defeat our neighbouring enemies, and I am responsible for the tragic deaths of many good men. As I reflect and repent for my sins, and there are many, I regret that I have not stood firm against the enemies of our Lord God almighty.' Those who were present and listened carefully to the true meaning behind these spoken words also felt remorse. 'Why were we always at war? We have all sinned in the eyes of God,' they thought to themselves.

Bruce stopped again. This time it was a deliberate pause. They all sat, watched, and waited for his next words to be spoken. 'My body can no longer attain that which my heart desires,' declared Bruce. Douglas asked to speak. 'Sire, forgive my interruption. If I may enquire, what precisely does your heart desire?' Bruce appeared to be uplifted by this question. 'My heart desires that I go and fight against the enemies of Christ; the Saracens who attack the holy lands are the enemies of our God. It is there that my heart wants to be, and to fight in battle on the side of the Almighty.'

Bruce paused briefly; he took a drink of water mixed with wine. There was a gasp as he attempted to stand up. Slipping at first, he pushed down on his chair with his arms and raised his tall frame up onto his weary legs. 'When my final day comes, I ask that my heart be removed from this frail and withered body and taken into battle against those of whom I spoke. I ask that you choose one amongst you, one you consider the most worthy and noble, to carry out my final request of you. Do this for me and I will rest in peace.'

They sat stunned with sorrow. Some covered their faces, others turned to face the dark stone walls of the large room; grown men, many fearless, many having fought in countless battles, and now every one of them wept tears of grief in front of their noble King. Bruce sat down; he gave them time to recover their composure, but the weeping continued. 'Do not cry for me, for tears will not ease my pain, nor delay my final breath by one single moment. I ask that you immediately meet in council and consider my request.'

All except one left the company of Bruce. Douglas sat alone; tormented by his thoughts. 'My dear James, please, I ask again, go with the others and assist them to make their choice.' Douglas, unable to look straight at Bruce, turned and joined the others.

Bruce, comforted by his servants, felt the strain and fatigue of what he had put himself through suddenly catch up on him.

He could hear the muffled sound of discussions taking place next door; they were quiet sounds, no shouting, as if agreement had been reached very quickly.

They returned and sat down. Bruce gestured for their decision to be announced. Thomas Randolph rose to his feet. Bruce looked surprised. 'Surely not?' he thought to himself.

'Sire, we have given careful consideration to your last request of this council. We have decided on who best can fulfil what your heart so much desires.'

'Who have you chosen?' asked the impatient Bruce.

'Sire, there was no need to hold council, there was no need for discussion. The one chosen by his own loyalty, and numerous noble acts, all in your good name, is James, Lord of Douglasdale.'

As if his heart had suddenly entered through the gates of heaven, Bruce was immediately overcome with delight at the final decision of his council. 'I asked you to choose, and you have chosen wisely. You have chosen one I hold in the highest regard. Ever since he was a young man, or should I say young boy? And stopped me at Tweed's Well many years ago, and claimed that he wished to offer himself in support of my cause. From that moment until this day, he has achieved more than any other. I am glad that you have chosen him, for it is he that I most selfishly desire to fulfil my final request.'

Douglas remained silent. 'James, you are silent, what do you say of this request placed upon you?' asked Bruce. Douglas rose from his seat and walked towards his King. Kneeling in front of him, he quietly spoke. 'Sire, I am humbled, and I am greatly honoured to have been chosen; no man past or present could ever have been asked to perform a more privileged task. Under your leadership, we are now one united and free nation. You have given us our pride, restored our dignity and made every single one us proud to be Scottish. Sire, I will make this journey not just with your heart, but your very soul, which will, I am sure, be also with me.'

Bruce could not speak, nor could he hold back the tears of affection that now coursed down his face. Others, including the cynics and those who once conspired against their own King, were overcome with such a touching display of loyalty and kindness, so openly and honestly expressed in their very presence. The compassion and sensitivity that was locked away in many of their hearts came to the surface. They felt the grief for a King who was soon to leave them. They felt humbled by the young man who, inspired by the cruel death of his own father, had risen through absolute determination to become the most loyal servant of Bruce and the most loved and feared man north and south of the border. They joined Bruce in sharing his combined tears of joy and sorrow.

Bruce spoke to many of them for the last time. 'My good and trusted friends and loyal men, it is now time for me to be on my own with my dearest and beloved family. I ask that you leave me now. You will be informed when my final judgement day arrives.'

Douglas stood before him; they spoke their final and private words of respect for each other. 'Go home, James, it is time for you also to be with your own family.'

It had been many months since Douglas had left his own family to be with the dying Bruce. His mind had been distraught at the sight of his good King, sadly and painfully deteriorating before his eyes. As he prepared to leave, he realised that another few months and he would have been away from home for a whole year. He thought of his dear mother. She too had fought against illness and could not be expected to live much longer. He thought of Sophia. At long last he would be with her. No more wars, no more risk to their lives should he permanently stay at Blackhouse Tower. As he left the home of a dying man he did not realise that he was heading to a home where life was about to begin.

There was an air of excitement and great expectation at Blackhouse Tower. Sophia, heavily pregnant with the child of her darling James, could not wait for the day of his return. She knew that nothing on this earth would give him greater pride and pleasure than holding his own son in his arms. Hoping that he would return before the imminent birth, she took great care of herself and followed the welcomed advice from Lady Eleanor.

It was early evening; the pains experienced over the last few days suddenly became more regular and more severe. She called Lady Eleanor to her aid. 'Mother, it's coming and he's not here,' she cried out in frustration, as she tried to disguise her extreme discomfort. 'Do not fret child, I will send for him immediately,' replied Lady Eleanor, as she wiped the perspiration from the forehead of the young mother-to-be. Sophia could not disguise her pain any longer, as she screamed out in agony.

Archibald rode through the remaining hours of darkness. There was no time to ask anyone else. He was the only one in the house who knew the way to Cardross and who could fetch his brother James that night. The following day, as noon approached, the brothers met south of Lanark. The exhausted Archibald could hardly speak.

'You're about to become a father,' he announced.

'What, I only...' replied the disbelieving Douglas, shock making him unable to complete his response.

'You only what?' answered Archibald, grinning. 'Yes, you only spent a few days with her, well amazing as it may seem she is about to have your child. That I can guarantee.'

'You go on, I will catch up, my horse is done in,' declared Archibald. Douglas shouted 'Aye, you'd slow me down,' and then dug his heels into the flanks of his horse, which was about to be ridden harder than ever before.

The screams of pain had stopped. A child had been born, a son, a new young Douglas, who would some future day resume his father's cause. Lady Eleanor sat white faced; she had shared in the suffering that had been experienced that night, a suffering that she could not ease and had tried with all her strength to comfort. She held the child close to her bosom. They both cried.

Sophia lay on her bed, the one where she had spent many an hour dreaming of her gallant knight, her James, the Good Douglas. The pleasure of the sound of her newly born child crying had been denied her. She no longer felt any pain or discomfort. The suffering had ended, but so too had the pleasures that she had waited all her life to enjoy. The bleeding had stopped, but not before the very life had drained out of one of God's most beautiful creations.

The newly born child, his tiny face wrinkled and screwed up, but perfect and pure, just like his mother, looked up at Lady Eleanor with eyes that as yet were unable to focus. She comforted him as she tried desperately to contain her grief. 'You poor little angel from heaven, born without your dear mother.' She could not contain her anguish any longer as she uncontrollably wept. Her tears fell on the cheeks of the innocent child whose own tears mixed with hers as if to join in the grief of this tragedy.

Darkness was slowly descending. After a long day of mixed emotions, Douglas finally approached Blackhouse Tower. He paused at the door. He had been away for nine months. He felt more excited than at any other time in his life. The image of his dear beautiful and graceful Sophia holding his own child was the most perfect picture of happiness that he could ever imagine. 'Will it be as I have imagined in my own mind?' he thought to himself, as he nervously opened the door.

The main room was crowded; several people that he did not recognise stared at him. 'Is that him?' someone whispered. 'It's a bloody shame, so it is,' whispered someone else.

'Lady Eleanor, can I get you anything?' a voice called out from near the fireplace. 'No, I'm all right now.'

Douglas sensed something was wrong and made his way towards the voice of his mother.

She sat staring deep into the dancing flames of the burning log fire. It was as if they were trying to tell her a story, or perhaps trying to give an explanation as to the reasons why. 'Mother!' shouted Douglas, as he put his hand on her shoulder and then moved in front of her. His newly born son lay on her lap, sleeping and content. Douglas gasped. 'Oh my God! It's true. Is this really my child?' Lady Eleanor looked at him and answered in a quiet, almost apologetic voice, 'Yes, this is your own son.'

He stared at this newly born and perfect child. He had no thought for anything else but was immediately drawn into the magnificent and mesmerising first sight of his own offspring.

'James …?' She had to repeat his name for him to notice. 'James…?' repeated Lady Eleanor. He looked up at his mother. Her face did not express joy and delight at what she held in her arms. Instead, it showed distress, a grief that was too painful to share with the father of the child that she now held in her lap.

He said nothing as he walked towards her room. The look on his mother's face had told him more than a thousand words. He entered and closed the door behind him. At first he could not look, only staring at the floor. Eventually he raised his head and looked towards her bed. His whole body violently shook as he focused on her outline. Sophia, even in death, looked perfect. Her pale face and perfect features resembled those dreams that he used to have, dreams about the mother he did not even know. He could not move, the tears did not flow, and the grief was so strong that his senses were suspended.

Eventually he walked towards her. Her arms lay neatly by her side, her long reddish hair was neatly combed and gently positioned over her shoulders. Her white gown resembled the wedding dress that she never wore. He touched her hand and gently squeezed it as if to pass the final message of love to this most beautiful creature, then bent down and kissed it. She wore a ring; there was something familiar about it. It was the ring presented at Bannockburn by Bruce to Sir James of Douglasdale, a ring that he remembered giving to Archibald. The tears finally came, tears of sadness, of love, and of regret. They were uncontrolled tears that flowed in the privacy of this room as he stood over the one he had grown to love, Sophia, the beautiful, the elegant, and the graceful niece of Thomas Dickson of Douglasdale.

He returned to the main room, he could not speak but tried to comfort his mother. They both grieved, but he had to ask the question. 'What happened?' Her eyes, red from the painful crying, looked up at him. 'James I'm so sorry, I forced this upon you. I always wanted you to be together. If I hadn't encouraged you, she would still be here.'

'Mother, stop, you are not to blame,' said Douglas, as he held her tighter in his arms.

'The bleeding would not stop; there was nothing that I or anyone else could do. Only God could save her, and it was his will that she depart from us. Why is he so cruel?' sobbed Lady Eleanor.

Douglas bent down and gently lifted his son from the lap of his grandmother. The little infant gazed up at his father. 'God has taken a dearly loved one from us and given us one we will love just as dearly,' said Douglas, as he admired the perfection of the miracle of nature that he now held in his arms. Saying no more, he carried the child back into Sophia's room and closed the door behind him. The three of them were together for the first and last time. These were private moments, as father and son were alone in the company of the one that united them with her precious love.

The winter months passed by quickly. Douglas stayed at home and spent every waking hour with his son. He knew that some day a messenger would arrive with news of the death of King Robert. Until then, every day, every hour and every second would be spent in the company of young Archie. 'That child's well named,' called Lady Eleanor, in response to yet another outburst of crying.

'What do you mean?' asked Archibald.

'Greetin faced and always wanting fed,' answered Lady Eleanor, as she started to prepare yet another feed for the hungry youngster. Douglas immediately burst out laughing and said 'Aye, a well chosen name, two of a kind.'

Archibald smiled, and then shouted 'Mother!'

'What?' asked, the slightly harassed Lady Eleanor.

'Anything for eating?' replied Archibald.

The summer of 1329 had arrived. The month of June brought with it warm sunshine that encouraged a rich lushness across the Tweedsmuir hills and glens. This was a time to relax, and to enjoy the many riches that nature had so kindly provided to these parts. The midday sun forced many to take shelter in the shade. Some were less fortunate in that they had important business to attend to. One such person was the rider who came into the glen one afternoon.

'I have a message for Lord Douglas,' he announced. The servant to the Douglas family pointed to the burn that flowed down the glen towards the Yarrow Water. In the middle of the burn stood a tall broad-shouldered man, bare footed and with the water just a few inches above his ankles. He held a child in his left arm and scooped up handfuls of water with his right. 'Look, another one,' he called out, as he caught a small fish, the sight of which delighted his young son Archie.

'My Lord Douglas,' the messenger called out. Douglas, who had noticed him from the moment he had first entered the glen, but had pretended to ignore his arrival, was now forced to look up. 'Is it about Bruce?' asked Douglas. The messenger nodded in reply. 'Has he gone?' asked Douglas. 'Yes, my lord, he has gone for ever. You are now requested to perform the task you were chosen for.' 'Aye, that I will,' answered Douglas and kissed his young son.

It took Douglas a few days to prepare for his long departure to a distant land. It was early evening; the whole Douglas family was together. Hugh had been called from Melrose and now sat with his mother, brother, and nephew as they patiently waited to hear why they were requested to be together.

'Tomorrow, I must leave to show my respects and attend the funeral and final resting of our good King Robert,' declared Douglas.

'How long will you be, James?' asked Lady Eleanor, who sensed that there was more than just a funeral to attend. 'It should only take him a couple of days,' commented Archibald, as they looked at Douglas and waited for him to answer.

Douglas was holding a rolled up scroll that had been prepared some time before. 'I do not know how long I will be, I could be gone for many years.'

'Why?' asked Hugh.

Douglas explained the request of the dying King. They sat stunned and amazed at what had been asked of him. 'So now you all know. I have been asked to carry the heart of King Robert into battle against the enemies of God.'

'What do you get in payment for such a noble and dangerous deed?' asked Archibald. Douglas shook his head. 'I will receive payment in the form of great pride and privilege. I am deeply honoured to have been chosen from all other men to do this for our good King Robert.'

Douglas unrolled the beautifully written scroll, which he had held throughout this conversation. 'In this document I have listed the many kind gifts and awards of appreciation given to me by our King.'

They sat and waited to hear what he had to say. This family did not live the life of a traditional aristocratic noble family. Theirs was a humble existence with an appreciation of the simpler things in life. It was because of this that Douglas was well loved and greatly appreciated by the common people of this nation.

He started to read from the scroll. 'The forests of Selkirk and of Jedburgh, the lands of Stablegordon and Westerkirk in Eskdale and of Buittle in Galloway.' They gasped in amazement; they did not realise that their James was now the owner of these affluent estates. He read out the names of many others places, lands that were rich sources of income and had once been forcibly held by English nobles.

Finally, he read out the last place name on the official looking document. 'And of the lands of Douglasdale I grant to Lord James of Douglas ... signed this day by Robert Bruce, King of Scots.' They sat stunned, remembering when, as a hot headed youth, he went off to join with Bruce. His ambition had been to avenge his father and to regain his inheritance, but until this moment they had not fully realised what he had achieved.

Archibald, for once behaving more akin to his age, asked a question. 'James, why do you read this out to us, and why now?' Douglas handed the scroll to his brother along with a more recently written document. 'I give it all to you all. It is for our family and for future generations who come to share the proud name of Douglas. I have written my deed of covenant.'

'What of you, what do you get my dear brother?' asked Hugh who was holding young Archie. Douglas smiled at his brother, and then looked at his young son. 'I have all that I desire; I have no wish for anything more.' They were immensely proud of him; he had proved himself worthy of the title of the Good Sir James of Douglas.

When morning arrived, he had gone. No one had heard him leave, but they all knew why. They also knew that they might never see him again.

31

A DOUGLAS! A DOUGLAS!

THEY CAME IN THEIR thousands to show their respect and gratitude to their great King, who had united and then freed their nation. They cried as they cast flowers in front of the procession, young and old called out in anguish, mothers and daughters could be heard wailing long after the procession had passed by. The remains of Bruce were finally laid to rest at the holy and ancient abbey at Dunfermline.

After it was over, Thomas Randolph, along with Sir Robert Keith and several other nobles, met with Douglas. 'Letters of safe passage have been requested from Edward III, and of other Kings of foreign lands, who are all of our faith and will give their support to your cause. They may take many months to arrive. However, the wait will provide you with time to prepare,' declared Sir Robert Keith.

'We have asked for good and trusted noble knights to volunteer to accompany you,' declared Randolph, who was now sole warden of all Scotland. 'They are all good men who will serve you well. Some are here today to seek your approval,' added Randolph.

'Please bring them forth,' requested Douglas. First to enter was Sir William Sinclair, who had long been a trusted companion of Douglas. 'Sir William, I am glad to see you,' declared Douglas. 'My lord, if you will allow me, I would be honoured to be by your side and accompany you on this dangerous journey,' said Sinclair. 'I am most grateful for your kind support,' replied Douglas. Two men of Lanarkshire, the home county of Douglas then entered. 'My lord, Sir Walter and Sir Robert Logan,' announced Sir Robert Keith. 'Two men from my own homelands, who better to join me?' said Douglas.

'My lord, there is one who has come here today. He says that he has fought alongside you in the past. He is not of noble rank but requests to be considered,' said Randolph. 'Can he fight?' asked Douglas. The yet unnamed man, who had been standing waiting outside the doorway, suddenly stepped into the company of these nobles. 'Better than most men who have fought alongside you, my Lord Douglas,' replied David Davidson.

Douglas rose to his feet and ran towards his old friend 'David!' he shouted. 'I can't believe it's you. I have not seen or heard of you since Bannockburn. I thought you had been slain that very day.'

'I was badly injured, and when I recovered, which was many months later, I went to Ireland with Lord Edward Bruce. There are a few tales that I can tell about that place,' replied Davidson.

'David, will you come with me to fulfil the last request of our late King Robert?' asked Douglas, who had suddenly regained some happiness in his life.

'My lord, I would be greatly honoured to play a part in such a worthy event. I would also welcome the opportunity to fight by your side once again.'

The two men embraced like long lost brothers.

'These past years I have lost many good friends and loved ones who were very precious to me. Today I have been rewarded with the return of a very dear friend, one who shares many of my past adventures. I could not ask for a better man to join me.'

Sir Robert Keith called out, 'My lord, there are some important matters that we now need to attend to.' Douglas nodded. 'Lord Randolph! The sword please!' Keith called out. Randolph stepped forward with a large gleaming and well-crafted broadsword. 'My Lord James, it is my privilege to complete our late King's request and present this sword to you which has been forged and etched to commemorate your journey with the heart of our King.'

Douglas knelt before Lord Randolph, who then gently touched the head of Douglas with the sword and called out the words spoken by the late Bruce. 'I will thee charge after I depart, to holy grave and there bury my heart.' The sword bearing the etched inscription was then handed to Douglas who slowly read out loud the immortal words.

'So mony gvid as of the Douglas beine,
Of ane surname was never in Scotland seine,
I wil ye charge efter that I depart,
To holy gravfe and thair bury my hart.
Let it remain ever, both tyme and hour,
To the last day I sie my saviour,
So I protest in tyme of al my ringe,
Ye lyk subjectis had never ony keing.'

Douglas paused as he was reading; he felt a cold shiver run through his whole body as he examined the blade of the sword that had also been etched with the initials of Robert Bruce and Lord Douglas. Between these two sets of initials was etched the outline of a single heart with a pair of hands on either side pointing inwards.

Randolph gestured for all those present to stand. They did so, and waited in silence with heads bowed, as those outside were now requested to enter. The Bishop, carrying a wrapped object, about the size of a clenched fist, on a silver tray, slowly entered, followed by two priests carrying candles.

They stopped immediately in front of Lord Randolph. The two priests stood on either side of Randolph as the Bishop handed him the embalmed heart of Bruce. Randolph gestured to Douglas to come towards him. 'My Lord Douglas, I present you this day with the heart of our noble King, Robert the Bruce, and for you to do as he so requested of you. May our Lord God almighty admit you into his following as a loyal trusted soldier of Christ. May Charity, Chivalry, and Christianity always guide your heart, your soul, and your sword.'

Douglas stepped forward; an assistant handed him a silver casket that had previously been crafted at his request. Douglas opened the casket and allowed Randolph the opportunity to be the last man to touch a part of the body of Bruce. The casket was then sealed. Douglas took it in both hands and gently kissed the outer casing before finally placing the attached chain around his neck. A final prayer was said for a safe journey for he who was about to carry the late King's heart into battle.

It took many months to make the arrangements for the long seaward journey. Douglas had moved to Berwick, it would be from here that he would depart. The letters of safe passage had been received; the final preparations were well in hand as the early summer of 1330 arrived and presented the ideal opportunity for the journey to commence.

'When do you think we will be ready to leave?' asked David Davidson, as he sat patiently waiting by the side of Douglas.

'In a few days time, possibly next week,' answered Douglas as he continued to write letters of a private nature.

'Will you be going back one last time to see them?' asked Davidson.

'I have thought about it more than anything, but it will only cause them more grief, particularly my mother. I don't think they fully understand why I have to do this,' replied Douglas.

'As we don't leave for another week, and if it would please you, I could go and say a last farewell on your behalf. After all, I have met them, albeit many years ago,' said Davidson.

Douglas nodded. 'David, I would greatly appreciate that.'

Davidson immediately prepared to leave for Blackhouse Tower. 'Is there any specific message that you want me to give them?' asked Davidson.

'No words could explain, or convince them of the importance of the journey that I am about to make. I have only one request. Take this sword and give it to my son,' said Douglas, as he handed Davidson the commemorative gift presented to him at the request of Bruce. 'Perhaps they will then understand. Tell them that I love them, and that I hope to see them again soon.'

Several days later all was ready as Douglas patiently waited for the return of Davidson. Although it was early summer, dark clouds had descended over the east coast skies.

'My lord, the weather appears to be closing in. I would not advise us to wait any longer or we will miss another tide and another day,' said Sir William Sinclair, who spoke while looking up at the dark and stormy heavens above. Douglas looked concerned. 'What's keeping Davidson? He should be back by now,' he thought to himself, as he finally called his noble knights together for a departing prayer. Sir William Sinclair, Sir Alan Cathcart, Sir Seymour Loccard and Sir Walter and Sir Robert Logan gathered round, along with two dozen squires and helpers who had been recruited to serve their needs.

The mighty ship stood proud in Berwick harbour. The many colourful flags and banners of the Scottish lords, flapping violently in the strong wind, let everyone know that this was no ordinary ship. Above them all, waving proudly, was the Lion rampant, the banner of Bruce. A few feet below it the Scottish Saltire danced in the strong breeze in a final act of recognition for the King whose heart this ship was about to carry.

They stood on the harbour side and said their final farewells; many who did not even know these gallant knights openly wept as they waved goodbye to the protectors of the heart of Bruce. Douglas waited, but there was still no sign of Davidson. 'My lord,' shouted Sinclair. Douglas gave one last look before boarding and then gave the signal to set sail. The delivery of a few last minute provisions was all that was now holding them up.

A horn being loudly blown by someone a short distance away was heard. It was no ordinary horn; it was the horn of Douglas, a horn that he had given to his good friend Davidson many years ago in a remote Scottish glen, a horn that when last heard by him was also used to attract a ship.

Three riders came into view. As they approached, Douglas first recognised Davidson; following him was Douglas's brother Archibald, and someone that he could not quite make out until they came closer.

'Don't panic,' shouted Archibald. 'I'm not coming with you. I am only here to say farewell to my dear brother.'

'Oh! So you're not coming with us, I'm so sorry to hear that,' replied Douglas, with a humorous tone to his voice.

'Do you really mean that? I could always change my mind,' replied Archibald, with a wide devilish grin. Douglas laughed, and replied, 'No it's all right, I accept your first decision.'

Archibald dismounted. 'There is someone, however, who not only wishes to join you on your journey, but also has our mother's full support. She says he will protect you and ensure your safe return home.'

The third rider, whose face was hidden as he dismounted, came into view. 'My Lord James of Douglas, I beg you to allow me to accompany you and to offer my protection,' declared Sir William Keith of Galston.

Douglas was overcome by such a gesture of support. 'My good Sir William, there is no other knight in this entire kingdom that I would rather have by my side. You are most welcome to join with me.'

The final embrace between two brothers took place. 'James, I promise you one thing, I will look after your young son while you are away. He will be safe with me,' declared

Archibald. Douglas, putting his hands on each of Archibald shoulders replied 'My dear loving brother, all I can say is thanks. I appreciate what you have done for me today, it means a lot to me.'

As the ship finally departed from the harbour of Berwick, those on board made themselves comfortable in preparation for the long journey ahead of them. Douglas stood on deck with both hands grasping the wooden railing in front of him. He stared out at the outline of this ancient town. His thoughts drifted back to when he was a child, and to the night when, because of the brutality of Edward I, he was forced to leave his homeland. He remembered the fear that he felt as he last saw his own father standing waving goodbye to him. It was a fear that he had only ever experienced once. Nothing, even the many battles and dangerous situations that he had encountered during the wars with England, were as frightening as the sailing that night many years ago. He froze then, and he froze now, as that same fear once again gripped his body.

For several days, the threatening storms lingered over the North Sea, and allowed them to make their first landing at Sluys on the coast of Flanders. For over a week they stayed here, and recruited more good men who welcomed the opportunity to fight for this holy cause.

They continued their journey along the coast of France and then out onto the great ocean where they headed south down the coast of Portugal. The air became warmer; it was a comforting warmth that they enjoyed, but it was a warmth that also brought with it strong winds and raging seas. As they headed towards the southern tip of Portugal, the relentless winds forced them to take shelter in the Gulf of Cadiz off the coast of Spain.

In the safety of shallow waters, they anchored and waited for the storm to ease. Douglas was in deep thought when approached by Davidson and Sir William Keith who were both concerned that he appeared to be looking more withdrawn as each day passed.

'My lord, what troubles you?' asked Davidson.

'Do I look troubled?' shouted Douglas, the sharp tone of his reply immediately proving that the question was justified.

'Yes, my lord, you certainly do. Can we help?' asked Sir William Keith.

Douglas paused before answering; he knew that he could not hide his inner thoughts from these two good friends. 'All my life I have fought to remove the cruel enemies who invaded our homelands and took from us all that which was ours by birth. I have always considered it evil for any man to invade another's land. Yet here we are, albeit at the request of our late King Robert, about to do just that. I can see no way to justify the actions that we plan to carry out.'

Sir William spoke. 'My lord, we sent some men ashore, they have returned with news that not far from here, Alfonso XI of Castile, who is based at Seville, is recruiting an army to defend his lands from being attacked by the Moors. They are the Muslims from North Africa. They are they very ones that our King wanted his heart to be taken into battle against.'

Douglas's face brightened. 'Are you saying that instead of attacking, we could offer our services to defend a nation that is as this moment being attacked?'

'Indeed I am,' replied Sir William. A smile appeared on the face of Douglas.

The sail up the River Guadalquiver into the port of Seville was a much more pleasant one after their experience of the stormy ocean seas. Alfonso, who had been informed of their coming, came out to welcome them. He expressed his thanks and great admiration for these good men who had travelled far to help him defend his lands and his faith. He embraced Douglas. 'So you my friend, are the famous warrior, the Black Douglas. Your name has spread to these lands and far beyond the seas. Many a tale I have heard of how you tricked and defeated your much larger enemies. I am honoured and privileged by your presence,' declared Alfonso.

As they continued to exchange greetings, a group of knights appeared nearby. 'Look!' shouted Davidson. 'English knights.' The white garments that they wore displayed the blood red cross associated with the Knights Templar, the gallant and ancient order devoted to the upholding of Christianity, Charity and Chivalry. Sir William Sinclair of Rosslyn immediately stepped forward. 'I will speak with them,' he called out, as he then walked over to meet them.

'Shall I go with him?' Davidson asked Douglas.

'No, please stay here. Sir William knows what he is doing. They are here for the same reason as ourselves. They will soon join us,' replied Douglas. Sinclair could be seen shaking hands and exchanging friendly greetings with the English knights. A few minutes later, they all came over to meet with Douglas. Sir William introduced each knight to Douglas. Each one of them was honoured to meet the brave and gallant warrior, the one who had terrorised their own nation, and who now came here to join them in such a worthy cause. The elder of them spoke. 'My lord, our nations have had their many differences, and I am sure many still to come. Today we are greatly honoured to unite with you as soldiers of Christ in the battle to protect our faith.'

Douglas spoke. 'My lords, I too am honoured, and greatly privileged to be in your company. The good men of each of our nations, and there are many, have come here to unite in the fight against our common enemy. It would be a truly wonderful thing if the beliefs of Christianity could be reconciled with those of Judaism and Islam, but regretfully, today it is not to be. Perhaps if Scots and English can reconcile and be as one, perhaps we can set an example for others to follow.'

The elderly English knight knelt before Douglas. 'My lord, I kneel before you in respect and in admiration of your vision, your kindness, and your compassion.'

Over the next few weeks, others came to give their support to Alfonso. Some came from afar just to see and meet the famous Black Douglas. They had heard many tales of his adventures; many had been exaggerated, but the tales were so numerous that even if only half were true he would still be the most amazing warrior of their times.

One evening, as the gallant knights from different nations dined together, a fearsome foreign warrior, who had overindulged in the consumption of the plentiful supply of Spanish wine, shouted in the direction of Douglas 'I say this to you all, look at me now, look at my face, is it not scarred with the true trade marks of a great warrior? Answer me!' He pointed to his battle-scarred face. He staggered over towards Douglas, who continued eating. 'You sir, they say that you are a great warrior, greater even than I am, and yet look at you; you have the prettiest face that I have ever seen on any man.'

'Prettier than many a woman,' shouted a nearby knight, as they all looked at Douglas in anticipation of what he would do in response to this ridicule.

Douglas finished eating and wiped his mouth with the back of his hand. He then stretched out his arms and said. 'It is only the opinion of others. It is they, not I, who say that I am a mighty warrior. As for my pretty face, well what can I say,' he smiled, fluttered his eyelids and then flexed his fingers. 'I suppose I should be grateful to the good Lord for providing me with such a skilful pair of hands to protect my beauty.' The sudden outburst of laughter immediately eased the tension that had been developing. The foreign warrior shook his head, laughed and then sat down.

A few days later, word arrived that an army of Moors had captured the Castillo della Estrella, the Castle of the Stars, near to the village of Teba. Alfonso approached Douglas. 'My good Lord of Douglas, I would request of you that you take command of the foreign knights and lead your men into battle in the good name of Our Lord.' Douglas replied that he would be honoured.

That evening Douglas called David Davidson into private and secret conversation. 'David, I have a request that I must make of you in preparation for us going into battle tomorrow,' said Douglas.

'My lord, you know that I will be by your side and that I will not fail you,' replied Davidson.

Douglas laughed. 'Of course, I know fine well of your loyalty.' He paused. 'The request that I make of you may appear strange, but please trust me,' said Douglas. 'I cannot allow Sir William Keith of Galston to fight in battle.'

'Why? I hear that apart from you he has no equal with a sword,' said the puzzled Davidson.'

Douglas thought for a few moments. 'He is a close family member, his mother is the sister of my late dear friend Cuthbert. Sir William is her only child,' he said.

'But why did he come here with us? Why did you allow it?' asked Davidson.

'You should remember, he is here at the request of my own mother, Lady Eleanor, she specifically asked that he come with us to provide personal protection to me,' answered Douglas.

'My lord, what would you have me do?' asked Davidson.

'David, I don't know exactly what to ask of you, I only ask that somehow you prevent him from coming with us tomorrow.'

'I'm sure that I can think of something,' answered Davidson.

The blistering and suffocating heat of the Spanish sun finally eased off as darkness descended. However, those who came from the lands of the north struggled with yet another sleepless night as the perspiration poured from their already weakened bodies. The change in climate combined with the unaccustomed eating and drinking habits took its toll, as many a knight twisted and turned in discomfort throughout the hours of darkness.

As dawn came up, they began their preparations for their first day of battle. They mounted and made their way from their camp. Douglas, as requested, led the way, and the foreign knights followed behind. Sir William Keith followed a short distance behind Douglas and was then followed himself by David Davidson. They had ridden for about an hour and were now travelling over hard, dry, rocky ground.

protect the dying Sinclair. They closed in on him, as Douglas came rushing to his aid. The sight of Douglas attempting to rescue him was the last action that brave knight ever saw. The eyes of the dying man met those of Douglas and in his final moment of existence he saw the Black Douglas frantically trying to save his brave English life.

The Saracens turned on Douglas; those closest felt the deadly taste of Black Douglas steel, as he matched them blow by blow. Cut off from his men, he was now on his own. The heart of Bruce lay at his feet. This would be his final stand, as they closed in all around him. The ones in front were easily slain; those to the left and right occasionally managed to reach their target and saw the rare sight of Douglas blood. Those who took the coward's route and attacked from behind finally brought the brave Douglas down, as the swarm of deadly swords brutally plunged into his savagely hacked and now defeated body.

The following morning, the overhanging clouds brought a welcome relief from the blistering heat. The vultures were already circling, and ready to feast on the bodies below. Sir William Keith, his arm wrapped in a supporting sling, and accompanied by Davidson and a group of squires, had come to the battle site; their purpose was to recover the remains of those who had fallen. As they searched each inch of the blood-stained area, one of the squires shouted 'My lord, over here!'

Keith and Davidson looked over; they dreaded the sight that awaited them. Amongst the many slain bodies of the Saracen army, they found the body of Sir William Logan and his brother Sir Robert; close by, the body of Sir William Sinclair lay slain.

Another squire, who stood frozen several yards away, shouted 'Oh my God!' Keith and Davidson rushed over. In the middle of the remains of the bloody carnage was the dead body of Douglas. Lying face down, in his right hand he still held his sword that had taken many a life that day. His left hand still held tight the chain of the casket holding the heart of Bruce. Both men dropped to their knees and wept as the nervous squire turned Douglas over to reveal the silver casket that had been covered by the body and stained by the blood of Douglas. For the next hour they neither moved nor spoke, but knelt and prayed by the side of the body of the Good Sir James of Douglas.

It was the following springtime. The valley of Douglasdale was as beautiful as ever as the early morning sunshine brought warmth and colour to mix with the many riches that Mother Nature had provided. A few gentle clouds lingered in the skies above, and caused the rays of sunshine to split like illuminated streaks of light from heaven, and shine on the fortunate lands below. There was something unusual about this place, something strange. Normally many would be outside and going about their daily business. No human life, no movement could be seen, none apart from those inside the Kirk of St Brides.

Father Michael stood silent. His hands held together in preparation for prayer, he bowed his head, looked down, and stared at the cold stone floor that lay before him. The packed congregation wept, as they waited for the immediate family to enter. Space had been left at the very front for them; they would be here soon.

All heads turned, as the rear side door finally opened. Sir William Keith stood in the doorway and nodded to Father Michael, who silently nodded back. A few moments later, they entered. At the front, and carrying the oak coffin containing the remains of their brother, were Hugh and Archibald Douglas. At the rear were Sir William Keith and David Davidson. Behind them walked Lady Eleanor, holding tight the small hand of three-year-old Archie, the son of James and Sophia.

The coffin containing the remains of the Good Sir James of Douglas was carefully placed immediately in front of the altar. Several close family friends, who had followed behind, carried various objects. Hugh took the newly woven mantle bearing the Douglas coat of arms and carefully placed it over the coffin. Archibald then stepped forward and placed the etched sword, given by Bruce, and laid it down on the centre of the coffin.

Sir William Keith of Galston, who had brought this famous son of Douglasdale home, stepped forward. He carried a small object in his hands. It was the embalmed heart of Douglas, mounted in a protective silver casket. As he took the final steps towards the altar, the congregation recognised what was in his hands. There were loud cries of anguish from those present. Sir William placed the heart of Douglas directly on the centre of the coat of arms that lay across the coffin, gently bowed his head, and then stepped back.

No one could remember what was said during the service; their grief was too strong. All that they remembered was the bonnie wee boy, who repeatedly called for his father. As the family left the kirk and allowed the remains of Douglas to be entombed in the family catacombs below, Archibald relieved his mother of the fidgeting affection of the son of the Good Sir James Douglas, and lifted the youngster up into his arms. Archibald stood at the doorway and allowed his mother to make her exit. The young Archie looked over his uncle's shoulder and stared into the faces of the mourning congregation, their eyes filled with the burning tears of love and grief. In a final gesture of farewell to the father that he hardly knew, yet had heard so much about, the young Douglas raised his arm, and with clenched fist loudly shouted 'A Douglas! A Douglas!'

THE END

EPILOGUE

THE HEART OF KING ROBERT the Bruce was brought back to his beloved Scotland and laid to rest in the grounds of Melrose Abbey. The remains of Sir William Sinclair were also returned and finally laid to rest in Rosslyn chapel, the ancient place of worship, near Edinburgh, associated with the Knights Templar and according to legend the resting place of the Holy Grail.

Seven hundred years later, and I am standing inside the ancient Kirk of St Brides and staring at the tomb in front of me. The message on the small plaque attached to the wall above attracts my attention. I slowly read the words. *'The Good Sir James of Douglas. Killed in battle with the Moors in Spain while on his way to the Holy Land with the heart of King Robert the Bruce. 25th August 1330.*

I step back, turn, and look around inside this holy and historical place of ancient worship. The magnificent stained-glass windows, that tell many a tale, illuminate this otherwise darkened place of sanctuary, as the brilliant rays of sunlight enter and inject today's life into this hallowed place. Standing a few feet in front of the altar, I look down at the object on the floor. I am now completely lost for words. The bronze plate attached to the floor-mounted encased and embalmed heart reads *'The Good Sir **James** of **Douglas** Died 1330.*

Over the last few years, my life has become an obsession as my search for information on this truly great man has constantly occupied my everyday mind. As I marvelled at the amazing feats of bravery and the many gallant acts that have been recorded by various chroniclers of the times, I ask myself two questions. The first is 'Was there ever a more gallant and loyal son of Scotland?' And the second 'Would there still be a Scotland if it were not for this man?'

I now have one final question to ask. 'Why has his own nation, the one that he devoted his whole life to protecting, failed to recognise the life of this brave, gallant, and noble son?'

PATRICK M KANE

ISBN 141202412-9

9 781412 024129